W9-BOF-722

THE
HOLY BULLET

Luis M. Rocha

Translation by Robin McAllister

G. P. PUTNAM'S SONS
New York

PUTNAM

G. P. PUTNAM'S SONS
Publishers Since 1838
Published by the Penguin Group
Penguin Group (USA) Inc., 375 Hudson Street, New York, New York 10014,
USA • Penguin Group (Canada), 90 Eglinton Avenue East, Suite 700, Toronto,
Ontario M4P 2Y3, Canada (a division of Pearson Canada Inc.) • Penguin
Books Ltd, 80 Strand, London WC2R 0RL, England • Penguin Ireland,
25 St Stephen's Green, Dublin 2, Ireland (a division of Penguin Books Ltd) •
Penguin Group (Australia), 250 Camberwell Road, Camberwell, Victoria 3124,
Australia (a division of Pearson Australia Group Pty Ltd) • Penguin Books
India Pvt Ltd, 11 Community Centre, Panchsheel Park, New Delhi–110 017,
India • Penguin Group (NZ), 67 Apollo Drive, Rosedale, North Shore 0632,
New Zealand (a division of Pearson New Zealand Ltd) • Penguin Books
(South Africa) (Pty) Ltd, 24 Sturdee Avenue, Rosebank,
Johannesburg 2196, South Africa

Penguin Books Ltd, Registered Offices: 80 Strand, London WC2R 0RL, England

Copyright © 2007 by Luis Miguel Rocha
Originally published in Portuguese by Paralelo 40, 2007
Translation © 2009 by Robin McAllister
All rights reserved. No part of this book may be reproduced, scanned, or distributed in any printed or electronic form without permission. Please do not partici-
pate in or encourage piracy of copyrighted materials in violation of the author's
rights. Purchase only authorized editions. Published simultaneously in Canada

Library of Congress Cataloging-in-Publication Data

Rocha, Luís Miguel, 1976–
[Bala santa. English]
The holy bullet / Luis Miguel Rocha ; translation by Robin McAllister.
p.   cm.
Originally published as: Bala santa. Madrid : Suma de Letras, 2008.
ISBN 978-0-399-15600-7
1. John Paul II, Pope, 1920-2005—Assassination attempts—
Fiction.   I. McAllister, Robin.   II. Title.
PQ9318.O34B3513   2009   2009023791
869.3'5—dc22

Printed in the United States of America
1   3   5   7   9   10   8   6   4   2

BOOK DESIGN BY AMANDA DEWEY

This is a work of fiction. Names, characters, places, and incidents either are the
product of the author's imagination or are used fictitiously, and any resemblance
to actual persons, living or dead, businesses, companies, events, or locales is
entirely coincidental.

While the author has made every effort to provide accurate telephone numbers
and Internet addresses at the time of publication, neither the publisher nor the
author assumes any responsibility for errors, or for changes that occur after
publication. Further, the publisher does not have any control over and does not
assume any responsibility for author or third-party websites or their content.

THIS BOOK IS DEDICATED TO
IOANNES PAULUS PP. II
KAROL JÓZEF WOJTYLA
May 18, 1920–April 2, 2005

To all men of faith.

—JC, February 26, 2007

No bullet can kill unless it is His will.

—SISTER LÚCIA, *letter to Karol Wojtyla*, April 1981

Hitler couldn't have been as bad as they say. He couldn't have killed six million. It couldn't have been more than four.

—SAN JOSÉ MARÍA ESCRIVÁ DE BALAGUER,

letter to the members of Opus Dei

THE
HOLY BULLET

1

___

I am writing a book in which I will tell the whole truth. Until now I've told fifty different stories, all of which are false.

—MEHMET ALI AĞCA, *the Turk who shot Pope John Paul II,*

Anno Domini MMVII

E verything has a beginning.
      The start, the departure point, the zero, Sunday, the starting gun, the sprouting seed pushing through the earth for light, the splash into water, the earliest heartbeat, the first word, the first stone of a village, villa, city, wall, house, palace, church, building. Of this building in an unnamed city. A luxury restaurant occupies the ground floor and basement, as indicated by the menu displayed at the side of the door. Its status is not openly announced to the world at large, but suggested by the tinted-glass doors, always closed, and by the haughtiness of the doorman, impeccably dressed in a burgundy uniform. The absence of prices on the menu and the many phrases in French are also a sign of its exclusiveness, even if the city is located on French soil, which is neither confirmed nor denied. What is certain is that this restaurant does not need to advertise any of its services, which, in itself, presupposes an exclusive clientele.

      Any diner who wishes to enjoy the favors of this establishment must first seek approval; without such authorization he will never pass through the tinted-glass doors. Usually this can be obtained through the recommendation of a frequent client, a member of sorts, who has influence with management, or by a formal request that involves a long process of investigation into the private life of the applicant. A large bank account is useful, but not enough, since some pretentious newly rich are frequently rejected, although many members of old families are turned down also. Such rejection, and bear in mind the word "rejection" is never used, is communicated by a letter in a white envelope with no return address. Once this decision is made, it can never be revoked. In the case of acceptance there will be a long list of rules. There is, for example, a provision in the statutes for the expulsion of a member in the case of serious offenses, even if such expulsion has never happened.

Acceptance happens differently: a telephone call at home inviting him to dinner. Upon arrival, the uniformed doorman compliments him and opens the tinted-glass doors. Inside, he is treated with a deference that is never excessive. Another employee relieves him of his coat. Immediately he is led to a table that, from that day on, will be his alone, no matter the hour or day of the week. He can bring any guests he desires, as long as he informs the manager of their names five days in advance. The morality of the guests is not important. This is the privilege of the selected clients, who can share whatever with whomever they desire—favors, business negotiations, intrigues, blackmail, purchases, the destiny of others, their own—without anyone pointing a recriminating finger, accompanied by food for the refined palate, breast of chicken stuffed with pâté of bacon and mushroom sauce, wine, and brandy. No financial transactions take place here, except those discussed at the table, which are many. Members pay a monthly fee by bank transfer of 12,000 euros that covers the privileges of having the kitchen available twenty-four hours a day, seven days a week. Thus this restaurant functions in every city of major political and economic influence in the world, as it does in this unnamed city.

Today, at noon, the restaurant is half empty. The clients of the empty tables are occupied with their personal or professional lives. The table that matters to us is the thirteenth; the two men seated there aren't superstitious. In their opinion the table is as acceptable as any other. What matters is the here and now. Everything else is useless, unproved theory. Above all, these men adapt to time and circumstances. Each case is unique. In a world driven by money, this philosophy has advantages, and the two of them know how to make use of it.

Reasons of security and privacy prevent mentioning the name of the city with this restaurant, its table thirteen, and two men, seated face-to-face. The one with his back to the dining room is the member; he could be the father or even grandfather of the man sitting in front of him. No family ties connect them, except Adam and Eve, who unite us all. They aren't even friends. The younger is an aide to the older, if not a servant, a term no longer used these days. Let's not call what he's receiving "orders," but instructions or suggestions. They're dressed conservatively like any executive or businessman seated at the other tables. They're eating delicious halibut with spinach, mascarpone, and slices of Parma ham, an exception to the rule that one eats little and poorly in exclusive restaurants. They're drinking a Pinot Noir, Kaimira, 1998, chosen by the member without consulting his guest. They're courteous, since they aren't given to excess or speculation. The word "exception" is not part of their vocabulary. Everything is what it is, here and now, always.

"I haven't had the opportunity to ask you how the investigation in the United States is going," the older one asked.

"It's been filed in the archives, of course. Natural causes."

"Perfect. May I deduce that no trace of evidence was left at the location?" The older man revealed his calculating mind. He's not given to imponderables or last-minute surprises.

"Complete security. I collected everything before the authorities arrived. His age also helped to close the case rapidly," the younger man explained in a cold, professional tone.

"Perfect."

They continued eating in silence. Anyone noticing the tone of the conversation wouldn't characterize it as an interrogation, at least at this stage, although this wasn't a friendly dinner, either, but a meeting with an agenda planned by the older one. Both ate slowly, taking small forkfuls and pausing to chew without hurry.

"The second part of the plan begins immediately," the older man began. "It's going to be more and more demanding. There can be no mistakes."

"There won't be," the younger man, quite confident, assured him.

"How's the team?"

"Already in place for several weeks, as you directed. All the subjects are under constant surveillance, except one."

"Good, very good." He would've rubbed his hands with pleasure if he were a man given to expressing himself with gestures. He guarded his emotions and never shared them. "And in London?"

"Our man has privileged access to the subject," the younger one explained. "As soon as I give the okay, the way is open."

"These are the hardest parts of the plan to implement. London and JC," the man with his back to the dining room said firmly.

"Hasn't he shown his face yet?" the younger man wanted to know.

"No, he's an old fox, like me. But we have to make him appear; otherwise the plan is compromised."

"We'll make him appear. London will bring him out."

"Yes. As soon as he emerges, don't think, act. If you give yourself the luxury of thinking, even for only a second, by the time you're ready to move, he'll have already won."

The young man couldn't imagine such a situation. He was prepared for everything. The idea that they were up against such fast-thinking people seemed unlikely to him. Besides, we're talking about an old man more than seventy years old. What danger could he represent? He didn't reveal such thoughts to the old man seated at the table, or rather, his table.

"I know what you're thinking," the old man warned. "All humans have weaknesses. Mine is the Church, yours is self-confidence. It's a flaw. Take your ego out of the equation. That's the only way to guarantee you won't fail."

"I will."

"You must. If things don't work out, you won't be the one looking at *their* corpses. In London, honestly, it won't be easy."

"I have a very efficient man there who'll clear the way for me to do my work."

"Let me clarify something before we continue. At the moment I have no reason to criticize or censure your work. One hundred percent efficient, but you haven't yet dealt with what you'll have to contend with this time."

"The plan is practically infallible," the young man dared to answer back.

"There's no such thing," the other argued. "You have a plan where everything has to come together precisely and you can't make a mistake. Infallible? Not even the pope."

"Of course, but—"

"To finish my point," he interrupted, "just a little warning." He waited for the young man to look him in the eye, holding his complete attention. "JC is the man who murdered John Paul the First in 1978, and, even so, he was unable to kill the pope in London. He, too, had never failed."

The young man took in his words and thought about them for a few moments. The old man was right. Overconfidence was the enemy of avoiding mistakes. That was the message the other man wanted him to get.

"I understand. I won't give anyone a chance to try something." He also realized that if he failed, he wouldn't survive. Whether through the intervention of JC or through this frequent client of the restaurant located in the unnamed city, he wouldn't live to see the next day. It was time to change the subject.

"What about Mitrokhin?"

"I'm on that," the old man replied. "My contacts in Moscow are taking care of it at this very moment."

"What about the Turk?"

"Let him stay a prisoner. He won't be hurting anyone. Don't forget, we won't communicate again until the plan is concluded."

"Yes, I understand. I won't forget. Only one thing is missing—"

"The Vatican," the older man interrupted. "I'll take care of them personally." For the first time the old man smiled faintly.

Everything has a beginning.

2

—

WOJTYLA
May 13, 1981

Among those twenty thousand people, not one would be able to say with certainty if it rained or the sky was clear on that thirteenth day of the fifth month of the year of Our Lord 1981. Perhaps if they made an effort, they could say with some degree of certainty that it was a day of brilliant sun, pleasant spring warmth, in spite of its having rained a little in the middle of the afternoon, not much, barely five minutes. Of those twenty thousand people, more than half wouldn't remember the pleasant spring warmth or the sun, but they would not forget the rain. They'd feel it wetting their bodies, soaking into their bones, just as it did on the day in question. Some would even doubt it had rained only five minutes. No. Five minutes doesn't soak you like that. But those twenty thousand people wouldn't remember the rain or sun. They would feel the tears running down their faces, and the sharp sound of each shot still vivid in their minds, one, two, three, four, five, six. And the impact that tore the flesh and made twenty thousand people scream with sorrow, as much as the victim himself. That they would remember. What does the sun or the rain matter in a calvary like that? What does the exact hour matter, if the pope could have died?

Twenty thousand people waited for him that day in the majestic plaza of Saint Peter's Square, the reception hall for the Catholic world. Of the large number of a billion Catholic believers who, according to statistics, are spread over the globe, only a few million can say they have seen the pope. Of these even fewer can swear they saw the pope at an identifiable distance. And only a very small number of these thousands can prove they touched the pope or exchanged some words with him. For most, the pope is never more than an image on television or in a photo. For the young man of twenty-three who waited in the crowd, with his hands in the pockets of his jacket, the Supreme Pontiff, Karol Wojtyla, was only a job.

He'd been in Rome for three days and expected to leave the country that same thirteenth of May, after completing the job entrusted to him. It wasn't easy to pull off, but the challenge thrilled his young heart. If he overcame these obstacles, everyone would look at him differently, with respect and admiration, even some envy—well, those within his own circle would, obviously. Society, however, would never know of his existence or his central role in the act that would change the Catholic world forever. Killing a pope was not really new; others had done it in the past. The former pope, Albino Luciani, was proof of that, as he well knew, but never had anyone done it before the eyes of the world in plain daylight, without waiting for the silence of the night to later blame a weak heart. This murder was much more daring: killing and escaping, in the middle of twenty thousand people in broad daylight at five in the afternoon.

The afternoon rain gave way to the sun that shone on the city and the small Papal State with pleasant spring warmth. The rain might be a good ally. He could hide his movements behind the open umbrellas. On the other hand, John Paul would have to have an assistant holding an umbrella over him. Worse, he might have to ride around in a closed vehicle. With sun, the universe conspired in his favor. The perfect crime is not one that doesn't look like a crime, but one for which no one is caught.

His orders had been precise, kill and leave, shoot and flee. If he was captured, they could do nothing for him. But everything was going to go well. Full of faith in himself, he squeezed the handle of the revolver in his jacket pocket. Fifteen more minutes . . .

. . .

A FEW BLOCKS from Saint Peter's Square there is another admirable temple of Christianity, the Basilica of Santa Maria Maggiore, the most ancient place of worship on earth dedicated to the Virgin. It is also known as Santa Maria della Neve, or Liberiana, in honor of Liberius, a fourth-century pope, to whom the Virgin appeared in dreams and whom she asked to build a chapel in Rome in a place where it would snow in a few days. Such a climatic miracle happened in fact in full summer on the night of the fourth or fifth of August in the year 358 on the Esquiline Hill. As pope, Liberius forgot the Virgin's humble request and sketched out a plan in the snow for what would be an enormous sanctuary. It would not be until a century later, during the papacy of Sixtus III—immediately after the Council of Ephesus, which confirmed the divine maternity of Mary and made official what had been known for five centuries, the existence of the Son of God, conceived without sin—that the basilica was constructed. It was even larger than had been planned in the initial project of Liberius's sanctuary, to whom it was consecrated. This same sacred edifice, restored above and below, stands today over the Esquiline Hill and every fifth of August is flooded with white petals symbolizing the snow that never again fell in full summer.

At five in the afternoon that thirteenth day of May, a man in purple entered this domain and walked with slow steps around the portentous apse, ignoring the faithful and the tourists, as well as the dazzling mosaics of the Franciscan friar Jacopo Torriti, dating from the thirteenth century, which depict the Coronation of the Virgin. Nor did he pay attention to the ancient columns of Athenian marble that support the nave and have served as a model for many other, similar structures in the Catholic world, or to the tomb where Gian Lorenzo Bernini rests for eternity. Nothing disturbed the concentration of the bishop, who continued toward the altar.

"Does Your Eminence need anything?" one of the Redemptorists asked ingratiatingly. He had placed himself in the path of the prelate, not discourteously, but rather wishing to be of service.

The man in purple stopped a moment on seeing his way blocked and, after some thought, avoided the brother responsible for the confessions that day.

"Out of the way," he muttered, almost pushing him, something he probably would have done had the brother not stepped aside. "All I needed was a Dominican getting in my way."

His destination was a few feet farther, next to a bronze baldachin, where he descended the steps that led to the crypt.

The Crypt of Bethlehem, also called that of the Nativity, is a sacred place with great religious and historical significance. It holds, according to tradition, the relics of the Holy Land, including the wooden boards belonging to the cradle Jesus slept in. All these can be seen in this crypt where Ignacio de Loyola celebrated his first Mass on the twenty-fifth of December, 1538, before founding the celebrated Company of Jesus. The man in purple descended to the holy place, got down on his knees, and crossed himself.

"Forgive me, Father, for I have sinned," he prayed, lowering his head in submission and genuine repentance. "The flesh is weak, I am weak. The devil tempts me daily, and I don't have the strength to resist."

Tears sprang from his eyes like springs opening new furrows. His suffering was not insignificant, nor the load on his shoulders, making him implore God the Father Omnipotent for His sacred divine mercy. Let him who is without sin cast the first stone at this sorrowful bishop of the Roman Catholic Church, since not even the saints were able to live lives immune to evil temptations, although they resisted more than common mortals. Popes and doctors of the Church are buried in this crypt. The bishop came to ask clemency and strength from them, since the weight of the load was too much for one man alone.

"Help me, Saint Jerome, intercede for me with the Infant Jesus," he prayed, asking favors from the saint buried there, since a bishop should be attended to before the other faithful, one of the privileges of serving God. "For the sake of all the most sacred, take this weight off my shoulders. Let me breathe." He got up and took out a key hanging on a gold chain around his neck. He inserted it in the lock of the door and turned it. It wasn't opened often, but it showed no deterioration, perhaps because gold is immune to the ravages of climate, history, and the madness of men.

The key turned the interconnected mechanisms that opened the ark. From within his cassock, the prelate took out a large yellow envelope, which he placed inside. His pensive expression lasted a few moments. Sweat mixed with tears—the same salt for different sensations. He closed his eyes as he turned the key, closing the ark that guarded the secret until history decides to judge it in another time, neither better nor worse, but different from this age, far off, when no one with ties to such a secret would remain in this earthly city.

Calmer now, he backed up a few steps with his head lowered, submissive but not humble.

"Our Father, forgive me for what I have done," he said in a grave, sorrowful voice. He opened his eyes, still damp, and crossed himself before leaving the crypt. "And for what I have ordered done."

AT THE SAME TIME the bishop left the Basilica of Santa Maria Maggiore, where he had expiated the sins that tormented his conscience, John Paul, the second Shepherd of the Shepherds with that name, made his appearance in Saint Peter's Square before the twenty thousand people present. A passage, opened up among the faithful by the security forces, indicated the path of his pope-mobile, specially purchased for these occasions. The crowd cheered the Holy Father, creating a deafening clamor that spread over the plaza, adjacent streets, and alleys. He was the pope, the holiest among the holiest, the voice of God on earth. What would one not pay for a moment like this, to be able to see him, two or three steps away, gesturing, smiling gratefully for the attendance and faith of the crowd?

The twenty-three-year-old waited for the right moment. The caravan was still more than a hundred yards away, approaching slowly. The Polish pope truly wanted to be seen by each of his beloved faithful. *Enjoy your last ovation*, the young man thought to himself. *From here you go directly to the tomb.* He breathed the confidence of youth, excessive and stupid, which ends with time, or not, depending on the life each leads and the force with which life bends us to its will, without mercy, without thought.

Fifty yards separated life from the valley of the shadow of death, misfortune from brief glory, Wojtyla from Mehmet, the latter being the name of the beardless twenty-three-year-old with his hands hidden in his jacket pockets, despite the warm day. Nothing united them in that moment, an assassin disguised as a worshipper and the greatest penitent of them all, unaware that he was the target of a boy, a professional gunman, prepared to add the crowning touch to his career, for which he would never be forgotten.

At forty yards, the people began to crowd together more and more tightly, elbowing one another with the selfish hope of gaining a better position to see the pope. Who knows, maybe they'd even snatch a glance and beneficence from the Holy Father, a personal gesture not to be shared. What greater fortune could happen than to go to Rome, see the pope, and be seen and greeted by him, from two or three steps away. They were perfectly aware the Supreme Pontiff would never remember them in his dreams, conversations, discourses . . . but none of that mattered.

The thirty yards between the pope and the shooter revealed a problem the boy hadn't foreseen and couldn't control: the pressing crowd made movement impossible. Ironically, one of the things that made the plan infallible, a shot coming from the middle of the crowd, fired without anyone's knowing from where or by whom, seemed instantly problematic. It was as if the twenty thousand people, unconsciously of course, wanted to protect their pastor from something they could not foresee, not even in their darkest thoughts. Or perhaps it was their God directing such an outcome from each of those present. Certainly such a thought passed through the shooter's mind, but as soon as it unexpectedly appeared, it left. It was time to act, to focus, and to neutralize his target.

Twenty yards. The euphoria grew with every step, an experience of authentic and sacred faith that filled Saint Peter's Square with commotion. Indifferent to that mystical experience, Mehmet mentally reviewed his own life, feeling recognition and admiration, even glory, approaching. He was jammed between an old, weeping Polish woman who cried out incomprehensible words in her native language, two Germans, an Italian soldier with his medals from a lifetime taking lives in defense of his country, a cripple in a wheelchair from Naples, and five Consolata missionary sisters. They all added to Mehmet's confusion. He couldn't find, as hard as he looked, the desired clear line of fire. He only needed a few inches of space, even less, and no one would catch him, but he could barely even draw his pistol from his pocket. "Damn," he cursed. His target smiled at the crowd.

Ten yards. Mehmet could make out every feature of Wojtyla's face and body. He could see his benign smile, the gestures of gratitude to the crowd, repeated over and over from the beginning of his route, but appearing always new, captivating, heartfelt. The pope emanated joy, radiance, hope, and all this created a psychological echo in those present, a redoubled encouragement, a hope so strong that everyone desired a little part of the glance and the sacred gestures of John Paul II. Mehmet needed only one second of less crowding to do his job successfully. The rain would have been a better ally, but a good executioner doesn't look for excuses at the moment of truth. He would get out of there one way or another, or not. That was the risk, but the job had to be done.

This was the moment. If the pope moved on, Mehmet would fail. *You escaped once*, he thought, remembering the recent past. *Today you are mine.* He calmed his mind as much as possible and drew the gun from his pocket. He squeezed the trigger once, twice, three, four, five, six times, until he was tackled by the people surrounding him. They disarmed him, and he was lucky not to be lynched as well. The security forces arrested him, while the pope-mobile accelerated away as fast as possible with the wounded pope helped by his assistants toward the protective walls of the Holy See. In booking Mehmet, they found a piece of paper with a phrase written in Turkish. Later someone translated it: "I am killing the pope as a protest against the imperialism of the Soviet Union and the United States of America and against the genocide they are carrying out in El Salvador and in Afghanistan."

Handcuffed and dragged before the police, Mehmet screamed out loud in his native tongue, while people looked on at him incredulously, sorrowfully, impotently, and with hearts filled with sadness and worry for the Holy Father.

The completion of the job resulted in the arrest of a poor, unrepentant

Mehmet and the wounding of three innocent people. Two of the injured were peaceful spectators free of any guilt, and the third was the pope himself, who received four bullets in a body not made to receive any. Stomach, intestine, left arm and hand, they were wounds that might have taken his life.

"I have no respect for human life," Mehmet shouted, smiling, satisfied by his completed task. It was five-fifteen in the afternoon.

Sixty-four years earlier, the same day and hour, a thousand miles from Rome, the Virgin appeared for the first time to the three Shepherd children at the Cova da Iria in Portugal.

3

JERUSALEM

The view over the Holy City is amazing when seen from the seventh story of the King David Hotel, situated on the street of the same name. One sees the dome of the Church of the Holy Sepulchre in the Christian and Armenian quarters, where it is believed Christ himself was buried more than two thousand years ago, and rose again on the third day. The golden Dome of the Rock of Hara mesh-Sharif stands out against the sky in the Muslim quarter. It protects the sacred rock on which it is believed God asked Abraham to sacrifice his son, Isaac. A little more to the right one can make out the smaller dome of the Al-Aqsa mosque, in which today, Friday, at noon, innumerable faithful will assemble. And one sees the Jewish quarter, farther back, with the arch of the ancient synagogue of Hurva, the only part that remains from the immense edifice after the battles of 1948 between the Israelis and Arabs.

The man looking out over the city in the morning light, leaning out the window, was very worried. He had landed at Ben-Gurion near Tel Aviv at mid-afternoon of the day before and immediately made his way to his destination, before going to the hotel. He entered the Old City through the busy Damascus Gate, built by Suleiman the Magnificent, and continued walking in front by the El-Wad, going with the flow of the crowd. In his hand he carried the black briefcase of a businessman. Farther along he turned to the right, entering the Via Sacra, against the flow of tourists completing the third and fourth Stations of the Cross, where Jesus, carrying the cross on his shoulder, fell, and where he saw his mother.

The Western tourists were swept up in mysticism, looking around, absorbing the energy, remembering the history they had heard since birth and finding its scale much smaller than they'd imagined. He'd felt the same on his first visit many years ago. The narrow streets and small houses contrasted with the magnificence Christ's story demands. Without discounting the importance of the historical events the place had witnessed or underestimating its picturesque beauty, this smaller scale revealed humility and faith, the elements common to the three great prophets who founded the three great monotheistic religions. Simplicity appeared all around, more so than in any other sacred place.

He continued his travel through history, filled with houses and stores, leaving the rest of the believers back in the Via Dolorosa. He passed, without a second glance, the first Station of the Cross in the Monastery of the Flagellation, where Christ was condemned and brutally tortured by the legionnaires in the pay of Pontius Pilate.

A little farther ahead the man turned left into the Qadisieh, filled with low houses and closed doors. He called at the door of the third house on the left side. There he would ask directions. A woman with a dark face opened the door. Her face didn't escape his attention though her veil allowed little to be seen. The Muslim tradition demands that women show nothing, since men must not be tempted by the flesh of a woman. If they are, the blame is hers.

"Excuse me," he said. "Would you be kind enough to tell me where Abu Rashid's house is?"

The woman slammed the door, leaving him looking at the wood chipped by the years. Perhaps this was not the house of Abu Rashid.

As he was about to leave and try another door, he heard heavy footsteps from inside the house. The creaking of hinges revealed a strong man with a gray beard and mustache in a red tunic, signs of an honorable tradition.

"Good afternoon," the foreigner greeted him. "Can you tell me where the house—?"

"Yes, yes," growled the bearded old man impatiently, spraying the air with particles of saliva. He looked at the middle-aged stranger in his black suit and turned around, leaving the door open. "Leave your shoes at the door."

He wasted no time obeying and took his shoes off. He felt a little sweaty and in need of a bath, but he wasn't going to abandon his business because he felt uncomfortable. His well-being was low on his list of priorities. He entered the house respectfully, since early on he'd learned that showing reverence for others would be rewarded. The sun penetrated the skylight that let the air enter and ventilate the hallway and rooms. He felt feminine stares behind him, without seeing them. He heard shy laughter behind some curtains. He stayed in the middle of the hallway. He didn't want to be indelicate and enter where he shouldn't. He waited for the old man to invite him.

"Tea?" he was asked from a room farther back in the illuminated area.

He walked toward the voice and found the older man seated in a rocking chair smoking a cigar. A woman without a veil fanned herself by his side, driving away the sudden heat of the late afternoon and drying the drops of sweat forming on the old man's head with a handkerchief. Surely his wife or one of them.

"Yes, I'd like some," the stranger answered. "Thanks."

A slight gesture to the young woman. She left to get it, leaving her handsome husband in the possession of the hot afternoon.

"And cover your head," he shouted loudly. "We have a visitor."

The stranger looked at him for a few seconds, worried about being an inconvenience. An aura of mystery surrounded the old Muslim that made any first move difficult.

"Sit down," the man ordered, pointing to another rocking chair like his own.

The stranger obeyed, almost without thinking. He left his briefcase on his lap.

"You want to meet Abu Rashid?" the old man asked.

"Yes," he answered. "Do you know where he lives?" he found himself asking, like a child asking for a candy.

"He comes by here all the time," the old man said. "What do you want with him?" he asked bluntly.

Despite not wanting to reveal what needed to be protected, the foreigner decided not to keep his intentions secret. Besides, he was increasingly aware of a feeling that, if he lied, the old man would know it.

"I've been sent from Rome." His serious tone showed his professionalism and competence. "I've come to investigate the alleged visions of Abu Rashid."

"Alleged?" The old man leaned forward, grasping the arms of the rocker with a questioning, mistrustful expression. "Perhaps Rome thinks it's a fiction."

"In Rome they don't think anything. That's why they've sent me," the stranger explained, sitting on the edge of his seat, trying to keep his back straight. "There are several stories about Abu Rashid's visions. I'm here to evaluate the case and recommend opening an investigation, if necessary."

The unannounced return of the young wife, carrying a tray from which the smell of steam and mint leaves flooded the room already filled with odors of musk, imposed silence. She hadn't forgotten her head covering. She left the tray on top of a small, round table next to the wall, and tipped the mouth of the teapot over her husband's cup, pouring out greenish liquid and adding six spoonfuls of sugar. Devotedly, she placed the saucer with the cup into his hand. He took it without a glance at his wife, who, only then, began to prepare a cup for the visitor.

The old man sipped a little of the tea, showing no discomfort with the hot temperature and not taking his eyes off the foreigner, who received from the wife an identical porcelain cup.

"And do you consider it necessary to recommend this commission?" the old man asked as soon as his wife left.

"I don't know yet. I just arrived, and this is the first stop I've made."

"I understand. But surely you've made your own judgment about what you've heard about Abu Rashid," the Muslim continued. "Do you believe it's necessary?"

There was a certain sly humor about the owner of the house that disquieted the stranger. His questions, his looks, seemed insolent, and as incredible as it might seem, a captivating aura of mystery surrounded the old man, invisibly, powerfully. *Who is this man?* the foreigner thought to himself. He decided to answer the old man.

"It's true the stories seem a little fantastic. We are talking about someone who might have the gift of curing the medically incurable. It seems he revived thirty people who drowned. He himself drowned and then resuscitated himself. There are innumerable examples in history of people with the gift of healing, some more believable than others. . . . As far as that goes, until I see and judge, I can't offer any evaluation." He took a careful sip of tea so as not to burn his tongue. It was too strong and sugary.

"I know Abu Rashid very well," the old man began at last, searching his memory. "He's a saintly man, able to cure the living . . . and the dead."

"The dead?" The stranger squirmed uncomfortably in his chair. "That doesn't sound likely to me," he dared saying.

The Muslim's voice changed. His rational, critical tone was replaced by something more introspective, dreamy, as if he were gazing into another reality, while he reclined in the rocker.

"Ah, but it's true," the old man insisted, gazing into space. "Completely true."

"I'll have to confirm that," the foreigner countered evasively.

"How can you consider resurrection improbable if you believe your Messiah did it for himself and Lazarus?" The old man appeared to have recovered some power of reasoning.

"That's why. He was the Messiah. No other person has had the power since then," the foreigner declared firmly.

"Allah said, 'As for the unbelievers, whether you admonish them or not, they will not believe.' I know very well what I'm talking about, since I've died and he brought me back to life."

The foreigner felt sudden interest. "What are you saying?"

"I've been dead and he brought me back to life," the old man repeated. "You're not going to find lies here."

They let the conversation lapse, each one concentrating on his cup of mint tea. Enough time had passed to cool the liquid and make it easy to drink. The owner of the house had already swallowed most of his while it was burning hot, the way he liked it.

"What intrigues me," the old man continued, speaking more frankly, "is why this sudden concern in Rome. To recommend an investigation or not. Why? What does this have to do with Rome?"

"You know the Church always defends her faithful and her saints. It may be that Abu Rashid will merit beatification and canonization, after his death, of course. This is an opportunity to document this now. Anyway, the miracles he's done in life are not valid. Only those after death."

The old Muslim gave a laugh that brought tears to his eyes.

"Oh, then, so that's it," said the old man, leaving his empty cup, in danger of falling, on the arm of his chair, swallowing back a guttural chuckle. "You can stay for dinner. You can begin your investigation with me. But it is not going to help you at all," he said, after he stopped laughing.

"Why?" asked the astonished foreigner.

The old man looked at him seriously.

"Since when have Christians prayed with Muslims?"

"No one said he was a Muslim. The stories mention a true Christian who sees the Virgin." The foreigner couldn't accept what he had heard. "Are you sure?"

"Absolutely. He's not a believing Christian. But he sees the Virgin Mary." The old man got up, approached the other, and extended his hand. "Abu Rashid. Allah be with you."

This man watching the city in the light of dawn through his window was very worried.

4

The church Dei Quattro Capi is called that because it is next to the bridge of the same name, formerly called the Fabricio Bridge and still known by that name if one decides to ask for it. It was named in honor of the master builder who laid the first stone in the year 62 before the birth of Our Lord Jesus Christ. This makes it the most ancient bridge in Rome. Before it was given the name Four Heads—derived from two busts with the sculptured heads of Mercury situated at one of the ends—the bridge was called the Pons Judaeorum for its proximity to the Jewish ghetto.

In the travertine of the arches that have supported the bridge for more than twenty-one centuries inscriptions are engraved on both sides that recall the builder, Fabricius, who wished to leave his mark on posterity. But the truth is, nobody remembers him; no historian is able to verify his first name with any certainty, except that it begins with L, as the inscriptions attest. People cross the Fabricio Bridge, forgetful or ignorant that it was once more than a footbridge and tourist site, a bridge for the passage of provisions, goods, valuables, and vehicles into the sublime capital of the great Roman Empire . . . but that was in the beginning.

Today people only cross it to go to the church, like this priest, uninterested in bridge engineering. Like all the houses of the Lord spread around the world, the small church of Saint Gregory of Divine Mercy, its official name, in the parish of Sant'Angelo, welcomes all the faithful who wish to hear and feel His Word, lay down the burden of life for the interval of the Eucharist, and unite themselves in faith.

This Tuesday morning was no exception. Several people were entering the small church, most hardly bothering to admire the facade, perhaps accustomed to it, as if it were only one more familiar fortification, like the city itself where they live. Perhaps the Mass, which had already started, made them hurry. The few who looked at the facade were undoubtedly tourists, admiring the painting of Christ Crucified, wept over by Mary and Mary Magdalene, the common scene reproduced from diverse angles and artistic and subjective interpretations of the mother and spouse who weep for their dead son and husband who will rise again on the third day. Above the portico is a plaque that reads: *Indulgencia plenaria quotidiana perpetua pro vivis et defunctis*—a priestly and papal pronouncement of daily privilege for the living and dead within this sacred temple. The priest, who had just crossed the bridge, entered the church. Its interior reflected something of its exterior simplicity, though it possessed priceless relics, although fewer in number compared with those in other Roman churches.

This is not the first time Father Rafael Santini has celebrated Mass here, although it's not the parish assigned to him. That lies to the north of Rome in a small village he barely knows—for reasons that don't concern us.

This cool morning they were celebrating the silver anniversary of Father Carrara's appointment as parish priest. He was Rafael's friend of many years and colleague in service as priest and in other matters we won't mention now. Rafael, though a priest, liked people, especially women, as has been common since the High Middle Ages. Men like Rafael look as old as they wish. We could be specific and say thirty-eight years, completed on the sixteenth day of April, but who can know with certainty his age and birthday? Anyone seeing him celebrating the Eucharist now at the altar of Saint Gregory of Divine Mercy could not fail to notice a certain indifference, unusual in a priest. The speed with which he read the missal bordered on a senseless mumble. He read the sermon without emotion, like a public official reading a traffic code or a student reciting the multiplication tables in front of the teacher.

What might seem to the common believer a lack of vocation was not really so. Let the man who has just entered and seated himself in the last row speak. His black cassock and clerical collar identify him as an ordinary priest. Notice his elderly appearance. He could say much about Rafael Santini's vocation in the zealous service of the Holy Mother Church, although he has never made his acquaintance before entering this church. Everything that guarantees the loyalty and competence of Father Rafael is based on trustworthy, eyewitness accounts that, in his opinion, leave no room for doubt.

Let the celebration of the Eucharist hurry to the conclusion when Rafael utters the phrase desired by some and not by others, "May you go in peace," sometimes "Go in the peace of the Lord," or simply "Good-bye."

"Amen," said the chorus of faithful present, making the sign of the cross. Morning Mass was over. Everyone got up to leave. The priest, who had entered during the reading of the Epistle of Paul to the Philippians, followed Father Rafael to the sacristy. Once inside, he was surprised by the emptiness. Not the lack of decoration, since this is perfectly within the Roman parameters, but the human absence. Rafael, whom he had seen a few minutes ago heading in this direction, was not there. . . .

"To what do I owe the honor?" he heard a voice from behind him.

"Ah, Father Rafael. How are you?" he greeted him after turning around. "You frightened me."

"I didn't mean to."

"I know. They warned me you were unpredictable."

"What brings you here?" he asked directly. One of Rafael's peculiarities, without categorizing it as a defect or virtue, was to waste no words on banalities. This visit could only mean one thing. They could dispense with formalities, though that didn't mean he'd be impolite.

"Father Carrara's not here?" the visitor asked.

"He'll come to afternoon Mass."

"Good. My name is Phelps. I am an English priest assigned to the Vatican. James Phelps. It's a pleasure to meet you." He held out his hand and received Rafael's strong, firm grip in return.

"Rafael Santini."

Father Phelps couldn't hide his embarrassment. He was not accustomed to these affairs.

"Relax, Father Phelps," Rafael reassured him in a serious tone. "It's all very simple. Just give me the information they gave you or where to find it, and your work is over. The rest is my problem."

"Yes. I wish it were so simple. We have a serious problem."

"They all are."

"My orders are to take you immediately to the Holy See."

"Seriously? What an honor. It'll be charming to see the Vatican. Who are we going to see?"

The Englishman wasn't pleased with the sarcasm, but his respect and admiration for Rafael, picked up through stories told by people in the know, were too much to allow him the luxury of feeling irritated.

"His Holiness Pope Benedict the Sixteenth."

5

THE MEETING
February 1981

There are some who say that the meeting between the two men did not occur in 1981, but earlier, in 1979 or 1980, or even in March 1982. Others confirm a meeting in 1981, but disagree about the month, saying August, September, or November, with no evidence to support that claim. Some of the defenders of the month of February disagree over the exact date of the meeting, and scarcely two voices are in accord about the content and tone of the conversation. As far as the location, the majority claim it took place in the office of one or the other. Another point of historical discord is the discussion itself. One faction defends a calm, cordial conversation, while another precisely the contrary. There are even those who reject all these theories and claim that such an encounter never took place. With history it's all a question of point of view and imagination.

In fact the supposed meeting between the two men occurred in the office of the first, at eleven o'clock on the morning of Tuesday, February 3. The second man showed up very early at the door of the office, not knowing that the American slept very late. He should have known his habits, since the man whom he waited for was not exactly a novitiate. At that time he had exercised his duties for more than ten years. No meeting was officially recorded.

Thus, after two and a half hours of waiting, the American finally appeared at the office.

"Good morning, Your Eminence," said the assistant who opened the door promptly so the American wouldn't dirty his chaste hand on the doorknob.

"Good morning." The harsh voice of someone who has risen too early. The best time in bed for this man was during the morning, the warmth of the sheets, the sound of daily movements, no guilty conscience. . . . Someone was sitting inside his office.

"The cardinal has been waiting for you a long time," the secretary told him quickly, nervously. The American had temper tantrums, especially in the morning. This time, though, he restrained himself from throwing any accusing look at the unlucky functionary. What could he do? Refuse a cardinal of the Holy Mother Church?

The other was seated in front of the desk, his face expressionless, absorbed in the documents he'd brought with him. The American went to his desk without looking at him once.

"Good morning, Your Eminence," the recently arrived one said in a neutral tone. "I don't recall that we had an appointment this morning."

"We didn't," replied the other without raising his head.

Two dogs sniffing out each other's fear—if you will pardon the metaphor. Take the canine allusion as merely a metaphor to help understand the scene, not a gratuitous insult to either of those present.

"Then I'm going to have to ask you to leave and make an official appointment," the American said coldly, sitting down and taking a Cuban cigar from a gold box on top of the mahogany desk.

"Has Bishop Marcinkus forgotten how to behave with his superiors?" the cardinal asked, lifting his eyes for the first time.

"Not at all, Your Eminence. I am only doing what my duties demand. All meetings should be previously scheduled. Besides, in this department my superior is His Holiness."

"I know, I know," the cardinal said without taking his eyes off Marcinkus. "And how far do you think you are going to get?"

"I don't understand."

"Do you believe His Holiness is going to help you when the Italian and American authorities start applying pressure? Do you believe that he, in good faith, is going to stand by you?" The cardinal got up and leaned on the desk, looking intently at the bishop.

"I don't understand, Your Eminence."

"Come on, drop the act. You don't have to play dumb with me. I already know everything."

"What, Your Eminence?"

"Everything. Everything. The financial machinations, the money laundering, the losses at the Ambrosiano. I know what's behind it all."

It was Marcinkus's turn to stand up and look at the cardinal from his imposing height of six feet.

"I'll have to ask you to schedule this meeting for another time. Do me the favor of leaving." His deep sigh failed to disguise the fury he wanted to show.

"That won't be necessary, Bishop." The cardinal took his hands off the desk and moved toward the door. "His Holiness is informed."

Before the cardinal could leave, he heard the American's reply.

"That's good, Your Eminence. You never know what could happen in the future."

Showing no reaction to these last words, the cardinal left and closed the door.

All the theories end with the closing of this door, witnessed by the employee in the outer office.

Marcinkus ordered no interruption whatsoever until further notice, a decision the employee noted without understanding why. With the American you listened, shut up, and complied.

Inside, the bishop grabbed a phone and dialed a number.

"They're tightening the circle," he told the person on the other end of the line, not bothering with a greeting. It wasn't the time for protocol. "We have to act quickly."

The bishop listened for some time to the person he'd called.

"I don't want any mistakes or excuses. I want this resolved as quickly as possible. The German, Ratzinger, just left."

6

Solomon Keys was an American. In itself this was neither a fault nor a virtue, just a fact. He was eighty-seven, and those times of excessive patriotism, of America, land of opportunity, liberty, and so on, were long gone for him. Let it be clear, Solomon Keys did go for all of that in the past even until very recently. He was born in the District of Columbia—named in honor of the discoverer of the continent—the center of world politics since 1800, and Solomon Keys fought in the war of his generation, World War II, "fought" in quotations, since he never saw a front line, death, wounds, or anything similar. His field of operation was in London, in the Office of Strategic Services, decoding German messages, and, perhaps, while hurting his back as he leaned over his desk, he had saved some lives. He escaped the Blitz that darkened England's nights and days in 1940 and 1941, for he arrived in the English capital in May 1943. Be that as it may, he served his country with dedication, competence, zeal, and obedience, like a good American.

When he returned home, he set off to New Haven, Connecticut, to enroll at Yale, where he studied law. Of course a young man born in the nation's capital, who had served in the OSS, which, at the end of the war was converted by order of President Harry S Truman into the Central Intelligence Agency, didn't take these steps as easily as they are described.

Everything depended on knowing the right people at the right time and place, including his initiation into the secret society of Skull and Bones in 1948 in the same group as the forty-first president of the United States. Every Thursday and Sunday night there was a meeting in the Tomb, where the not-very-secret society met for notoriously secret activities, from dignified mud wrestling to the celebrated and awkward moment in which the future member was called on to reveal some secret he'd never revealed to anyone, after which and from that day on he was treated as a "bonesman." They are the men who will be most influential in the country and even in the world, linked to one another by rites and secrets, blood brothers, in mutual service for the rest of their lives. The "gentlemen," as the members call themselves, are chosen for taking power, for molding the "barbarians" to their will, "barbarians" being their term for all nonmembers.

But all this was part of Solomon Keys's rich past. After decades of work and dedication, he decided to set off to meet the unknown, solely for pleasure without destination or ambitions, as these had already been abundantly achieved. And now we find him, far into his travels, in downtown Amsterdam hurrying to catch the Go London tour, which included a train to the Hoek van Holland Haven station, followed by a ferry to Harwich and, then, a train from Harwich International to London with arrival at Liverpool Street station. The trip was called the Dutchflyer, and Solomon Keys had a return ticket to Amsterdam, on this same service, departing in three days. From there he would leave immediately for Eastern Europe to explore the former Iron Curtain countries.

It's a little embarrassing to explain that this great man found himself with his pants down in one of the station toilets, answering nature's call. He had ninety minutes before the train left for Hoek van Holland, and it was always better to go here rather than take a chance on the train's dubiously hygienic WCs.

Solomon Keys's calm was interrupted by someone shoving open the entrance door, followed by noises that ended in the stall next to his until . . . until the noises continued with a light banging he couldn't figure out. It would be indelicate to describe these actions and leave the elderly man ignorant of what was actually happening. Therefore, instead of making ourselves voyeurs, let's remain next to Solomon Keys, who was trying to decipher the sounds reaching him from the other stall, as if deciphering a code in wartime. In his eighty-seven years this might have been the first time the American had listened to someone copulating like that so close by. It's not our place to confirm or deny the theory that Skull and Bones promoted orgies or other similar activity. If they did, it never happened in his presence.

Filling the sounds reaching Solomon Keys's ears and stimulating his imagination, the stifled moans of a woman allowed him to imagine the pleasure and passion of the two. The sliding of clothes and smacking of bodies suggested their unbridled enjoyment. A few minutes later, the frenzy died away, and the moans changed to sighs of pleasure, masculine as well as feminine, and the words we cannot repeat. The wall separating Solomon from the passionate couple began to tremble more intensely, as if something or someone were being pushed against it. A change of position? *Good God*, thought Solomon, who was not religious. He remained seated, quiet, his pants around his ankles, his heart hammering. He had never given in to the clutches of matrimony, not that he hadn't enjoyed sex, of course. But he had never heard such dirty talk during coitus.

While their activities continued with the promise of a quick climax, the door of the stall the couple occupied opened suddenly. Two muffled sounds changed that giddy excitement to sudden silence. Solomon Keys heard the sound of the bodies falling lifeless on the floor.

What the hell? thought a frightened Solomon Keys. Firm, heavy steps approached the door of his stall. Excitement gave way to panic. Solomon Keys stretched out his arms against the sides of the stall and rose quickly from the toilet bowl.

Two shots passed through the door. The first hit the tiles behind him; the second, his chest. Gripped with pain, the American felt like everything was coming to an end. Whatever he had done or deserved in the past, or the simple uncertainty of life, was over today, now. He heard nothing from the other side of the closed door. Neither steps, nor breathing. Only silence. Maybe he could still get out and look for help. With great effort he raised one hand toward the latch on the door. It seemed enormous, like the heavy

7

—

MARCINKUS

February 19, 2006

You can't administer the Church with Ave Marias.

—PAUL MARCINKUS *to the* Observer, May 25, 1986

A lot could be said about Paul Casimir Marcinkus, archbishop of the Church of Rome. Over many years, more than a decade, he was the most influential man in the Vatican. How could a man who never became a cardinal become more powerful than the pope himself? Well, that's another story.

What truly mattered on this day of February 19 was the solitude. The solitude of Paul Marcinkus, after sixteen years away from Rome, exiled in his own land of birth. He'd lived in Rome more than two-thirds of his life, cutting off practically all ties with his own country. Paul Marcinkus belonged to no side. He was a citizen of the world and at the same time estranged from it. For Paul Casimir Marcinkus, only his own world mattered; other people were no more than marionettes to be manipulated at his whim until no longer useful.

Sent back to the diocese of Chicago in 1989, he was obliged to forget all the opulence and power that had surrounded him for so long. The only thing left for him was solitude and, more seriously, the realization that he had no friends, only acquaintances. Friendships based on power crumble away almost instantly when that power is lost. Returning to Chicago, after sixteen years, he realized for the first time he'd always been alone, always an orphan. Even today, having turned eighty-four in the last month, living in Sun City, Arizona, a city of around forty thousand inhabitants, he was alone.

Now he practically never left his bedroom. No more celebrating the Eucharist in the parish of San Clemente in Rome. He spent the day with memories, ever more vivid in his mind, or looking at papers and photographs. The popes Peter, Calvi, and Gelli in the good times, the scoundrels Villot, Casaroli, Poletti, the bastards Luciani and Wojtyla . . . Emanuela . . . the beautiful Emanuela. How sad not to have a photograph of Emanuela. How could he? He, an archbishop of the Roman Catholic Church, married to God, Whoever He might be, administrator, for many years, of the accounts bequeathed by Him on earth, he'd managed to triple his investments, some claimed in a risky, harmful way, but that was malicious gossip. A picture of the sweet Emanuela? How could he justify it? How marvelous to have a photo of the beautiful Emanuela. How many years had passed since she . . . twenty-two? Twenty-three? To think he had become the king of numbers, calculations, financial operations. But nonsense, eighty-four years is a lifetime. The dead make better company than the living.

Two knocks at the door took him out of his dreamy state of thinking about the distant but vivid image of Emanuela . . . of God, if you will permit the correction. He took his time getting up from the desk and getting to the door. He didn't hear another knock. Either it was someone very patient or old Marcinkus was now hearing things. But as soon as he opened the door, he was relieved to see someone on the other side.

"Good afternoon, Your Eminence," a young visitor greeted him. Since the term "young" has a wide range, one should reduce it to between twenty-eight and thirty-three years. The young man was somewhere in that range.

"Who are you?" Marcinkus asked rudely. Congeniality was never his strong suit.

The young man didn't seem the least impressed with the importance of the man or his lack of manners.

"I'm Brother Herbert. I called at the parish to say I was coming," the young cleric informed him. Black pants, black shirt and jacket, and a collar identical to what priests wear. Marcinkus deliberated. The young man was carrying a writing case with papers and a bottle.

"No one's told me anything. Why are you here?" Marcinkus shot back. He hated visits, especially from people he didn't know.

"I'm coming from Rome. I'm doing my doctorate. Excuse me for bothering you, but my thesis is about the financial world and the Church. And who better than Your Eminence to inform me about that?" the young man continued, submissive and well mannered.

"I can't help you. Good afternoon," Marcinkus replied, starting to close the door.

"I'm not going to take much of your time, Your Eminence. I promise you," the young man hastened to argue. "I brought you a present from Italy." He raised his hand with the bottle of Brunello di Montalcino, a marvelous red nectar from Tuscany, full-bodied with an intense flavor, which should not be confused with the more common Rosso di Montalcino from the same region.

Marcinkus thought for a few seconds.

"Let's do the following." The young man changed strategy, negotiating, the difference between a good thesis and an excellent one, the gateway to a great career. "The bottle stays with you, and I'll return at a better time. Is that all right?"

Marcinkus looked at the young man awhile longer.

"Come tomorrow after dinner."

"Thank you, Your Eminence. I'm eternally grateful."

"I'll collect on that gratitude."

"It will be a privilege." The young man started to turn around. "Thank you, Your Eminence. Until tomorrow."

"Wait," Marcinkus ordered. "That stays here." He took the bottle from the young man's hand.

"Of course, of course. A thousand apologies. Until tomorrow, Your Eminence."

"Don't be late." And he shut the door, with a slam that almost knocked the plaster from the wall. Marcinkus returned to his memories, to the specters that waited for him from the other side, whatever that was, where the dead live, waiting for time to pass for us. No one has ever returned to tell us what this other side is like, but Marcinkus was going to remember those dead, awaken them, even if only in his own memory. What he didn't know was that today the dead who had accompanied him for eighty-four years would demand he join them.

"Rest in peace, Your Eminence," the young cleric said. Paul Marcinkus didn't hear him.

Time runs out. The archbishop, stretched out on his deathbed, knows that his problems are starting now, when he will be called to account by the God he fears so much and forgot on so many occasions. The true banker of God sees himself before the Omnipotent, showing his books of assets and liabilities, what is owed and what is owned, explaining why he committed frauds, convincing Him of the necessity of diversifying the investments and laundering the money of organized crime. In the fever and anguish of death, Marcinkus sees God like the chairman of a board of directors, incapable of recognizing that everything His servant did over eighty-four years was for the good of the Enterprise.

On the floor of the bedroom, beside the bed, an overturned bottle and a broken glass.

8

―

Raul Brandão Monteiro knew this day had to come. It was not that he had the soul of a mystic or had had some premonitory dream. A retired captain of the Portuguese army didn't permit himself, at the risk of his professional reputation, to seek foresight in anything other than reason. As much as he tried to convince himself and others that the past was past, he knew a day would come when the past would claim its own. That day was today.

First an old man with a cane came in. His hand covered the cane's golden lion head. Then a younger man in an impeccable black silk Armani suit entered. If the cane with the lion head supported the old man, it also wouldn't have been inappropriate for the younger. His pronounced limp revealed a past accident or wound to his left leg. Only a few knew the origin of the injury; perhaps the captain himself, Raul Brandão Monteiro, had some idea of what had happened. The man in the impeccable Armani suit, now a cripple, was not a person who divulged things from the past or raised questions of karma. Everyone must play the cards he's dealt.

The sudden tension was out of place in the serene Alentejan mountain in Trindade, near Beja, where the captain had decided, several years ago, to take off his boots and enjoy retirement, with his wife, Elizabeth, English by birth. Better that Elizabeth wasn't in the house, though, with these people. This old man with so much power, capable of bending the CIA to his wishes, knew Elizabeth had gone to the city to shop.

"My beloved captain. We meet again," said the old man, stopping before Raul.

The cripple, ignoring manners, brought a chair over so the elderly man could sit down and catch his breath. Age is a stepmother and time a stepfather. Together they have no mercy; they are implacable, bending down the strong and the oppressed, nobles and commoners.

The captain looked from one man to the other, weighing the possibilities. The old man sitting down was an easy target, despite being the one who gave orders. The other was a different story. His defect was in his leg, not his hands. He wouldn't hesitate two seconds in pulling a gun, and he'd do it coolly enough to aim well. The fact that the old man had taken the trouble to travel to the meeting clearly indicated important interests at stake, so likely the shot or shots would not be fatal.

"What do you want from me?" the soldier asked abruptly.

"Oh, my good man, where are your manners?" the old man protested without altering his neutral tone. "We are in good wine country. I know you have your own production for home consumption. We can begin there." Let no one be confused by the polite tone. That was an order, not a suggestion. These men were not given to friendly requests. Their world is not governed by congeniality.

Raul went to the kitchen under the close watch of the cripple; since as yet he has no other name, we'll continue to call him that. Not for a moment did he let the soldier out of his sight. Some people only need a second, one opportunity to get away, but not today, not now, not under his watchful eye. Only one man had ever escaped easily and caught him unprepared in the past, leaving a permanent mark. That wouldn't happen again.

Raul returned with glasses and a bottle. Without ceremony he put them on top of the table in the entrance room in this house in the middle of nowhere, filled the glasses with red wine, and left the rest to the old man, who stretched out a hand for one of the glasses and sipped a mouthful.

"Magnificent," he commented. "One of the jewels of your country is undoubtedly the wine." He turned to the cripple. "Have a drink." Then he turned again toward the soldier. "Take a glass yourself." Savoring a fine wine was always good for moving conversation along.

"I don't want one," Raul told him as coldly as possible.

"Our future time together will teach you many things, one of which is that I don't like to repeat myself," the old man stated categorically and raised the glass to his mouth again. The cripple, too, took small sips from his own glass, showing neither delight nor disgust. It was difficult to imagine what he was thinking. He was a professional who never took his eyes off his target, in this case, the Portuguese captain. Work was work, port was port, and, even sipping wine, he didn't let himself be distracted, whatever the quality of the vintage. It was not the time, and the old man didn't forgive distractions. Nor did he.

"Truly magnificent," the old man repeated provocatively.

Raul went to look for another glass in the cupboard in the kitchen. He poured a little into it and drank it. The Portuguese knew that nothing would be gained by forcing things. He wouldn't get answers just by asking. Not with these people, not that the expression "these people" insinuated anything offensive. These people only meant these people. The best strategy was to wait. Eventually they'd come around to saying why they'd come.

The old man finished his wine and didn't ask for more. The cripple didn't finish his own. Both set their glasses down, the younger always watching Raul, and the older one looking around the various corners of the large, comfortable room. It was decorated with rustic handicrafts, honoring the Alentejan region in which they found themselves, the breadbasket of Portugal, a flatland in contrast to the broken terrain of the center and north. A cart wheel dominated one wall, in all its height, varnished, with various glazed tiles along the spokes, some with verses, others with historical figures. It took some time for the old man to turn his eyes from such a picturesque object and fix them on a cow horn. He seemed in no hurry. Perhaps his advanced years made him placid, or, purely and simply, his psychological makeup. There could be no question about his manipulative genius and his skill in deceiving, always for the good, of course. What could be more important?

Ten minutes of silence. Ten. Not a word was spoken, only the heavy breathing of the old man and the rustle of Raul Brandão Monteiro's clothes, when he shifted in the chair where he was sitting uneasily. Nothing more.

9

—

THE SECOND CONCLAVE, 1978

Now that God has given us the papacy, let's enjoy it.

—LEO X, *letter to his brother Giuliano*

Monday marked the third day of the conclave. Already there had been six sessions of scrutiny without conclusion. One hundred and eleven cardinals under eighty years of age were participating in the vote, the same ones who six weeks earlier had chosen Albino Luciani, the deceased John Paul I. After only thirty-three days in office, his heart stopped, according to the official history, which was permanent . . . until the contrary was shown to be true.

Work was suspended for dinner, increasing tension in the Polish Cardinal Karol Wojtyla's shoulders. For two nights he had prayed intensely in cell number 91, which had been assigned him, that God would inspire the conclave with His infinite knowledge in the just conduct of the voting. Why was it so difficult to be a man of the Roman Catholic Church? If only the great beyond could communicate more directly with the earth . . . how to understand the signs, what was true and was not? The sudden death of Luciani still weighed on him, his genuine smile, his intrinsic goodness, his sanctity. . . . He had never thought to return to the Sistine Chapel again in his own lifetime to choose another pope, certainly not in the same year.

Now he bent over his cannelloni without appetite, afraid that God would see in him the successor to Luciani.

How was it possible that the conclave began that Saturday with a surprising six votes for him, and by the sixth round, before lunch, he'd received fifty-two? During the days of preparation for the conclave several cardinals calmed the partisans by hypocritically announcing during dinners and other holy encounters they were not candidates. Wojtyla and the others knew who the favorites were: Siri and Benelli—the first an ultra-conservative with a very bad reputation, the second in the liberal line of his friend John Paul I. He went over to discuss the chances of the Genovese and Florentine with Koenig, the influential Austrian cardinal.

"The conclave is for those runners who come from behind, Karol," Koenig answered him. "Those who enter the conclave as popes normally leave as cardinals."

"I know that, Franz. But I don't believe that this conclave will have the surprises of the previous one," Karol offered sincerely. Both spoke the living language that they shared between them, Italian. Koenig with a German accent and Karol as flawlessly as a native speaker.

"One never knows," Franz Koenig said, giving him a pat on the shoulder. "One never knows."

The first vote revealed a trend plainly along the lines of the Pole's thinking. Siri ahead with twenty-three votes, followed by Benelli with twenty-two, Ursi with eighteen, Felici with seventeen, Pappalardo with fifteen, and . . . Wojtyla with five, probably out of goodwill, five souls whom he had treated with prudence in the recent past. Let the fact be noted we are not dealing with a sporting event or other competition, but with something done in the most sacred spiritual togetherness, and any resemblance to a disorderly dispute is false. These are saintly formulas for electing a saint. The method of communication with the Father and the description of the results are merely illustrative. When it is said Siri leads with twenty-three votes, one shouldn't imagine fans shouting his name.

In the second round of Saturday, Benelli had forty votes, Felici thirty, and Siri had fallen to eleven. Ursi maintained eighteen votes, Pappalardo dropped off the list, and Wojtyla, somehow, had raised his stock to nine. At that moment he didn't worry about it; those votes would be out of sympathy, nothing sustained or sustainable. In a little while he'd drop off the list, like Pappalardo. He'd be back in Krakow by the end of the week at the latest.

Sunday would start with three sessions, although Benelli shouldn't need them all. He would be pope by the end of the day or before, Karol Wojtyla thought naively, unaware of the machinations of his great friend. The first session of the day, third of the general conclave, gave forty-five votes to Benelli, twenty-seven to Felici, an unusual eighteen votes to Ursi, and the same nine to Wojtyla. Thirty more and Giovanni Benelli would obtain the two-thirds plus one necessary, not very problematic.

In the following round, Benelli, still ahead, achieved sixty-five votes, Ursi four, and Wojtyla advanced to twenty-four. A new candidate emerged, Giovanni Colombo, archbishop of Milan, with fourteen votes.

Before the last vote of the day, Cardinal Colombo presented a petition asking not to be considered in the subsequent sessions. So, Benelli had seventy votes, five less than needed for the papacy, and Wojtyla received forty. He returned to cell number 91 after dinner with some anxiety, but not much. Benelli was close to the votes needed to become the next Supreme Pontiff. By morning everything would be resolved in favor of the Florentine. Wojtyla prayed for Benelli to obtain the necessary enlightenment to guide the Church in its next years. With the third pope in the same year, they needed stability.

So Monday morning and the sixth round surprised Wojtyla on hearing his name fifty-two times, while Benelli saw his number reduced to fifty-nine votes. As conclaves go, when one lost ground, one never recovered.

Now you know why the cardinal from Krakow looked at his cannelloni with no appetite. His nerves gripped his stomach, and he was left pale, breathing hard.

"The conclave is for dark horses, Karol," the Pole heard. It was Franz Koenig sitting down by his side. Karol's compatriot, Wyszynski, was with him.

"This is your work," Wojtyla accused him, looking at his companion.

"Mine?" the Austrian replied with a smile. "No, Karol. This is your work."

"Everything is going to turn out well," Wyszynski added in support.

The three men got up and went to the chapel. Wojtyla's plate remained untouched through the entire meal.

"Do you remember what Willebrands said to Luciani in the last voting?" Koenig asked in a low voice.

"I was not close to him in the last conclave."

"I was. And when Luciani began to panic at his imminent election, Willebrands told him a great truth: 'The Lord gives the burden, but also the strength to bear it.'"

"Don't wish to be in my place, Franz. I hope Benelli recovers and puts an end to this right away."

They got in line for the orderly entrance into the chapel. Nothing in this place was disorderly, everything according to the standards of God the Father Almighty, Creator of Heaven and Earth. Karol Wojtyla closed his eyes and took a deep breath. Everything would be as He desired. Benelli or him. What shall be shall be.

A little farther behind in line Franz Koenig rejoiced in his work. Since the beginning, he had carried out a strategy that would lead to the election of Karol Wojtyla. He had spoken with the majority of his non-Italian colleagues, given them works by Wojtyla to further convince them. Nothing like a little publicity, not deceitful, since Wojtyla was a serious man with integrity. All this with Wojtyla completely unaware. Enough of Siri, Benelli, and Felici. They all had their good qualities, of course. All right, Siri might not have any, but it was a moment for change. The time of the Italians must come to an end. The seventh session of voting, the same ritual of eight centuries, the days of black and dirty white smoke, the suspense, the frustrated, expectant onlookers in Saint Peter's Square. Two hundred thousand people in that place, on constant watch, and a million ears pressed to the radio and eyes glued to the television. There were also all the experts and the curious, unmotivated by religion, and those fond of spectacle. The recount threw seventy-three votes to Wojtyla and twenty-eight to Giovanni Benelli. Two votes more and Karol Wojtyla would never see Krakow with the eyes of a cardinal, but only as pope on brief visits. This thought daunted his heart and his eyes watered with emotion.

At five-twenty in the afternoon, according to the watches, whether more or less on time, Wojtyla became the first non-Italian pope in more than four hundred fifty years of history. The last one was a Dutchman, Adrian VI, elected in 1522, very unpopular in Rome for defending and referring in one of his works to the *haeresiam per suam determinationem aut decretalem asserendo,* which meant that the popes could commit errors in matters of faith. Sacrilege. Sacrilege. He died little more than a year after his enthronement, leaving behind no desire to remember him.

The two hundred sixty-fourth pope of the Catholic Church put his hands to his head and began to weep, spreading emotion through the chapel that turned into moderate applause. Cardinal Jean-Marie Villot, chamberlain to the pope, and the equivalent of interim pope, a duty that only exists from the death of a pope until the election of the successor, approached Wojtyla with a frown, a sign of solemnity.

"Do you accept your canonic election for Supreme Pontiff?"

With wet eyes Wojtyla raised his head and looked at everyone. Tears slid down his face.

"With obedience to the faith of Christ, Our Lord, and with confidence in the Mother of Christ and in the Church, in spite of great difficulties, I accept."

A sigh of relief ran through the chapel, especially around the Austrian, Franz Koenig. Electing a pope was easy. Accepting the duty was up to the elected one alone.

"By what name do you wish to be called?" Villot continued. The same question that only six months ago had been asked the unlucky Albino Luciani, later found dead in his apartments in the early morning of the twenty-ninth of September, the pope who died alone, according to the official version. Some claimed it was a shady death, that he'd been murdered because of his reformer impetus and total incorruptibility. They even talked of poison or a pillow that suffocated him in the silence of the night. But that was the story of Pope Luciani. What is important now is the story of the Pole, Wojtyla.

Karol Wojtyla thought for a few seconds and smiled for the first time.

"John Paul the Second."

The opening of the chapel was ordered. The brothers Gammarelli came in to robe the new pope in the sacristy. They had made three spotless tunics. One of them must fit the Pole.

The papers were burned in the way that produces the famous white smoke, but the problem wasn't in the chemical compounds, but in the dirty chimney that hadn't been cleaned in a century. Onlookers were not sure if the smoke was white or black. A few spectators stayed uncertainly in Saint Peter's Square. Others delayed returning to their homes or hotels, to their own lives.

Two hours later the bells rang announcing the good news and the doors of the portico of Saint Peter's Basilica opened. The plaza seethed with the faithful in silence for Pericle Felici to pronounce the same words of August 26, substituting only the name of Luciani's successor.

Annuntio vobis gaudium magnum, habemus Papam! Eminentissimum ac Reverendissimum Dominum, Dominum Carolum, Sanctae Romanae Ecclesiae Cardinalem Wojtyla, qui sibi nomen imposuit . . . Ioannis Pauli Secundi.

10

Sarah Monteiro knew she was one and only one of the wheels in the greater set of gears. Journalist, Portuguese/British, daughter of the captain of the Portuguese Army, Raul Brandão Monteiro, and of Elizabeth Sullivan Monteiro, she realized that her position depended on her work serving the greater interests of those who controlled the gears.

If someone had told her months ago that today Sarah would be the editor for international politics for the prestigious *Times* of London, they would have provoked a guttural laugh, blunt but true, followed by a loud "You're crazy!"

But those who controlled life, the gears, wanted it so. Sarah was the respected editor of international politics, a position immensely sought after and envied, one that she'd never expected to reach. The way she managed to get exclusive information or foresaw consequences was astonishing. Other editors of international politics followed her, waiting for her to show the path. In England that respect and admiration among colleagues had earned her the nickname "Bob Woodward."

As always, there were some greedy naysayers who, out of incompetence, misfortune, or pure malice, never succeeded in reaching Sarah's level of professionalism and who sullied her good name by inventing a supposed lover she had in the secret services. The truth was that someone did give her information, which always turned out to be correct, but it was not a lover or any agent in the secret services of any country. It was very much beyond all that.

To understand how Sarah reached this position, we would have to go back several months, almost a year, to a night in her old apartment in a house on Belgrave Road, right next to the stop for bus 24, which goes from Pimlico/Grosvenor Road to Trafalgar Square, and tell another story. We would have to speak of secret Masonic lodges and spies, assassins and assassinated priests and cardinals, documents lost and found, a pope mysteriously dead before his time.

"That's another book," Sarah protested. "It's for sale in the bookstores. You don't need me to tell you. This is a new story."

"Is it published?" Simon asked curiously.

"What?"

"That book."

"Don't be so literal," she explained. "And don't think the world revolves around you. I wasn't talking to you."

Simon looked around.

"There's no one else here."

"I have a lot to do. Come on, let me work."

Simon, Sarah's intern and assistant, recruited from Cardiff, with a thick accent difficult for even English to understand, left the office with his head down. Sarah was a mystery to him in every way. She was considered extremely attractive by all her peers. She hired him after only two questions, the first to confirm the name of Simon Lloyd and the second if she could confide in him, dissolving all the fears and afflictions, cold sweats and nerves that surrounded the day before an interview. He was prepared for something more intense in which he'd have to show his worth, self-confidence, and self-esteem, but, unexpectedly, before he even settled into the chair, Sarah gave him her hand, telling him to show up the next day at nine in the morning prepared to work. He often asked himself in the few months he'd spent in that newsroom what made her offer him the job. He tried also, many times, to know more about his corporate superior, but without success. Sarah fiercely guarded her privacy and always made clear that going in that direction was like hitting a brick wall. If a door existed in that wall, it would open when and if she wanted to reveal it.

The truth was that these last months were going well for him in every way. There are those phases in life in which we seem unstoppable, everything works out, nothing seems impossible, and the future seems very easy to reach. A job at the best British newspaper could not have come at a better time. At the same time a new love affair full of passion had appeared by chance the night he celebrated his new position, a blessing. Simon was full of calm and confidence, courage and passion for life. He felt capable of everything and emanated love, for himself and his new lover, as well as gratitude and admiration for his mysterious boss, who gave him, without knowing it, all that professional and emotional stability.

The phone rang on his desk—yes, he had his own desk outside Sarah's office, turned toward the noisy editorial office always overflowing with frenzied activity—shaking him out of that happy daydreaming and recalling him to work.

"Simon Lloyd," the person on the other end of the line said.

"Hello, my love." A wide smile gradually spread over his lips as soon as he recognized the voice. A blush colored the skin of his face and stirred other corporal reactions, normal in this case. "I wasn't expecting a call from you."

A conversation began at this point between lovers that is not worth following, topics like "Did you sleep well? You're an angel," and even "I didn't want to wake you, so I left quietly." Let's move on to the persistent ring of the phone five minutes later, another call that required his attention.

"Hold on a minute. I have another call on the line," Simon said. "Just a minute, angel. Kiss, kiss, kiss." He forced himself to press Hold.

"Simon Lloyd," he answered professionally, although he let some irritation show in his voice.

"Good morning, Simon," he heard a voice say in a not very friendly foreign accent. "I want to talk to Sarah."

"She's busy. I'll have to see if she wants to take the call. Who's calling?" he asked while he looked at the nails of his right hand, analyzing whether they needed to be trimmed. Image was everything in this business and in this city.

"Tell her it's her father."

"Oh, Senhor Raul. How are you? I didn't recognize your voice. I beg your pardon."

"No problem. I'm fine, and you?" If it weren't for Cupid's arrow, Simon would have noticed a certain impatience in the captain's voice with talking for the sake of talking.

"Very well. I'm very well." The same stupid smile spread over his mouth, a smile of happiness. "I'm going to transfer you, Senhor Raul. Have a good day." If it hadn't been for his lover on hold on the other line, Simon would have started a long conversation with Sarah's father, whom he had not yet had a chance to meet. Better that he chose not to. Better for the two of them, of course.

He pressed the buttons to transfer the call to Sarah without telling her first, since his instructions were to send any family calls through directly.

"I'm back, my love," he said with the same stupid grin and blush covering his face. "It was my boss's father. Nothing important."

Let us leave the love affair on that side and move on to Sarah's office, where the telephone began to ring. It was not Simon; that would sound different—the marvels of technology—it was an outside call, and a glance at the screen identified the familiar number of the family home of her parents in Beja. She stopped the work she was doing and answered immediately.

"Hello?"

"Sarah?"

"Hi, Papa. Is everything all right?"

"Are you all right, Sarah?" One question followed another, as he completely ignored his daughter's first concern.

"I'm fine." *Something's wrong.* Her father's voice didn't reflect his customary calm. The last time she'd heard this tone there was a man at the door of her old house in Belgrave Road preparing to kill her. And the only reason he didn't was—

"Sarah, you need to pay attention to me," her father ordered in a serious voice.

"What's going on, Papa?" An anxiety returned that she hadn't felt for a long time, a disagreeable sensation she hoped never to feel again.

"Listen, Sarah," her father repeated. "Listen carefully. You have to leave London immediately—"

"Why?" she interrupted, her heart suddenly thumping with alarm. "Don't treat me like a child. This time I want to know everything."

Silence on the line, not total, punctuated by clicks and static electricity. Confusion and alarm spread through Sarah. The past was at the door like on that night. What the hell was going on?

"Papa?" She said his name to bring him back to earth.

"Sarah." She heard a different voice that flooded her with panic and nervousness. *Oh no. It can't be him. Is it?*

"JC?" she asked fearfully, hoping she was confused and had heard wrong. *Please, no. Don't let it be him.*

"I'm honored you haven't forgotten me."

It was him. Her legs gave out; if it weren't for the fact she was seated, she would have fallen on the floor.

"How are you since our last conversation in the Palatino?" he asked just to make small talk, something that was not part of his personality and awakened distrust in Sarah. She thought back on the conversation she'd had with JC in the Grand Hotel Palatino in Rome and the promise they would talk again. Almost a year later, this call kept that promise.

"What do you want? What are you doing in my parents' house?" Sarah cut the formalities as she regained her reason. She couldn't show her fear, no matter how much she felt it. This was the way to fight with people like this, without mincing words. JC was in Portugal, at her parents' house, if the caller ID on the phone didn't lie.

"Where are your manners, dear?" JC protested without hiding his sarcasm. "I'm having a pleasant conversation with your father, accompanied by a magnificent wine. We are at the most crucial point of our reunion, the reason he's called you."

"What do you want from us?" Her voice came out hard, as she wished, in spite of the inner turmoil that tormented her.

"I'm going to simplify things to make myself understood completely with no room for misunderstanding."

"I'm all ears."

A second of silence to get Sarah's complete concentration. The old man knew how to get his listener's attention. A gun to the head wasn't always necessary.

"Leave London now. Bring what I left you in the Palatino and do not talk to anyone, warn anyone, or wait for anyone."

"And if I don't do what you ask me?" Sarah confronted him.

"In that case your father can prepare to ship your corpse back here because you'll be eliminated today."

11

———

Here we find the mortal remains of the patron of truck drivers, tunnel workers, hatmakers, pharmacists, haircutters, gentlemen and pilgrims, pilgrimages and roads, from Chile, Peru, Mexico, Colombia, Cuba, Guatemala, Nicaragua, Galicia, and Spain, and, to cut the long list short, the Spanish army. He is known by many names, Iacobus, Jacob, Jaco, James, Jacques, Jacome, Jaume, Jaime, but that which inspires most believers is Santiago. Santiago the Greater, apostle of Christ, killed by Herod's sword, brother of the other apostle, Saint John the Evangelist, both sons of Salome and Zebediah.

The exact date is lost, thanks to the uncertainties of centuries when parchments were lost or consumed by the fire of despots or by the simple, implacable passage of time. In the year 813 or 814, Pelagius, a Christian hermit, told Teodomirus, the bishop of Iria Flavia, here in Galicia, about a star shining on a hill. There are also those who in this part of the legend, or truth, depending on how you see it, substitute strange lights or a sign from Heaven for the star. Whatever it was, it fell upon a specific place, an uninhabited hill, as if someone wanted to reveal something hidden. In this way Teodomirus found a tomb, and inside, a headless corpse with a head tucked under his arm, presumably his own. All the clues pointed to the corpse belonging to the apostle Santiago the Greater, forever immortalized as Santiago de Compostela, not to be confused with Santiago the Lesser, one of the other twelve followers of Christ. Legend or not, millions of people have visited this sacred place. For twelve centuries.

Here in the Praza do Obradoiro, Marius Ferris was moved by the silence of the place. He looked at the ornate facade of the cathedral, back to back with the Pazo Raxoi, occupied by today's Xunta de Galicia, a neoclassical-style building, built by the Archbishop Raxoi, in the same century in which the building of the cathedral of Santiago was finished, the eighteenth, which one ought to represent with Roman numerals naturally. The other buildings were ancient, as well. Marius Ferris ignored them as he continued looking closely at the facade of the cathedral. The history did not matter to Marius Ferris, not even the paving stones trod by commoners and nobles. One who knew him, and there were not many who could presume so, would know he was remembering the more than twenty years since he last saw the cathedral, separated from this place that was his home. His thick white hair crowned an entire life, years of absence, spent in other places much more cosmopolitan. He had exchanged a small Galician city of eighty thousand people for another of eight million on the other side of the Atlantic. This was the cost of being a priest and following orders. A priest wasn't asked to move to New York for twenty years. He was ordered. The life of a priest was determined by the bishop, the cardinal, and, of course, the pope. Never God. He was involved in the first calling; the organizational machinery of the religious authorities took care of the rest. And of course, since His Holiness was the emissary of God on earth, everything was connected.

That was what happened with Marius Ferris, exiled to Manhattan, a dream for many, but not for him. While he looked at the facade, he smiled. His exile was over. Not that he hadn't liked the Big Apple. In some ways he'd loved it: the cultural, ethnic diversity, the museums, the theater, everything for every taste, as is often said. Yes, he was in a pleasing city and served the pope, the great John Paul II, with zeal and ability. Even now there was nothing negative his superiors could use against him. The opposite was not so true. After a year serving Benedict XVI, he'd decided to ask for a dispensation, for reasons that are not important here, but which led his life to an unstable, dangerous situation, in his own modest estimation. The truth was that he was almost killed by someone and that shook him.

This was the first day of his new life. Returning home, he came to pay a visit to the Apostle Santiago. How appropriate that this was the first thing he did, since twenty years ago, it was the last thing he'd done, before leaving for the New World.

Marius Ferris, retired priest, went up the steps of the immense cathedral. It was time to pray, to render account, to come to an understanding with his God, unaware of the man who, a few yards behind, followed him into the cathedral.

12

————

I never thought I'd know a member of the Holy Alliance."

"The Holy Alliance doesn't exist," Rafael answered abruptly.

"It doesn't exist?"

"No, it's a myth."

"Then, what organization do you belong to?" Father James Phelps asked, settling into his seat aboard the Airbus A320.

Rafael turned to look out the small window. From 32,000 feet one could make out the blue of the sky, but everything else was unconnected, blurry, like the doubts of the priest with him. Other times, even with a colleague, especially one in particular, Rafael would have responded with a categorical *I am what I am*, changing the subject. In this case, with someone on a mission whose outcome was still unknown, he shouldn't create resentment.

"I'm something else," he concluded evasively.

The cabin was carrying 139 souls, business class included. They had taken off a little more than an hour ago, which meant they still had ninety more minutes of flight. Food was being served for those who wanted it.

Rafael wasn't wearing anything that identified him as a member of the Church, while James Phelps was dressed in a sober gray suit with a telltale clerical collar. There's no shame in wearing clothes that express your belief, whether a cassock or collar, a turban, a chador, a burka, a *niqab*, a long beard or hat, a star or tattoo, but there are a small number of situations that call for forgoing those elements that might attract undesirable attention. This was one of them.

"As soon as we land it'd be better for you to take off the clerical collar," Rafael advised. It went without saying the tone of recommendation was no more than that, a tone. James Phelps was intelligent enough to pick that up.

"And later?"

"Later is simple. Follow my instructions."

"Naturally," the older man agreed. "I'm not at the age to step into quicksand."

"You're already in it, Father. Now it's necessary not to sink to the bottom."

"I trust you." He smiled.

"Better to trust in your God. More certain."

The Englishman looked distrustfully at him. "Our God, dear friend. And don't make me more anxious than I already am."

Phelps remembered the encounter with Rafael in the Apostolic Palace of the Vatican. He'd come in alone and left twenty minutes later without even stopping long enough to wait for the emissary of the Church of Saint Gregory of Divine Mercy to get up from his red velvet chair. He was still in the process of doing so when he heard a *Let's go* coming from the hall Rafael had gone down. *Where to?* he murmured to himself.

Rafael hadn't said a word about what went on in those twenty minutes in which he'd disappeared through the enormous door that separates the papal apartments from the rest of the palace. Nor whom he had spoken with. Could it have been the pope himself? Secretary Bertone? Or some other person less mentioned and revered? Rafael was not the kind of person you could ask about something like that, just as Phelps was not the man to ask, for all that he felt tempted and even had the right to, once he had to go along with him. Everyone has his business and his weaknesses, and, if the stories he had heard about Rafael's past were true, as he believed, he knew what Rafael was capable of doing. Phelps was sure that if Rafael considered it important for him to know the tenor of the conversation or the instructions, he would tell him. Until then he would live in ignorance, following the journey to the unknown through the air at four hundred miles an hour.

"Would you like something to eat?" the flight attendant asked, offering something edible wrapped in plastic, probably a sandwich with some kind of processed meat.

"Yes, thanks," Rafael answered, letting down the tray on the back of the seat in front of him, one of the ergonomic marvels of aviation, finding space where there was none.

"And you?" the attendant automatically asked James Phelps.

"No thanks. I'm not hungry." The pleasant man passed his fingers under his clerical collar, with a sensation of discomfort, a sudden pressure, lack of air, his face turning livid. *What have I gotten myself into?* he thought. "But I'd like a glass of water, please."

"Of course." The attendant picked up the bottle and poured it into a glass. "Here you are, sir."

The priest took the glass and awkwardly set it on the tray, grabbing at his left leg. A pain like a knife stab pierced through his thigh. He controlled himself as much as possible to avoid crying out, suffering, breathing deeply and swallowing his groans, turning them into painful pants of breath.

"Are you all right?" the attendant asked, her hands full of aluminum covers and a glass of orange juice.

"Yes. It's nothing. It'll go away, thanks," he answered, leaning his head back on the seat and shutting his eyes for a few minutes. Small drops of perspiration covered his face.

Rafael, unaffected by his companion's discomfort, attacked his sandwich, ham with something unidentifiable that didn't much go with it, not that that was important to him. He bent over his orange juice to drink. Perhaps he was one of those rare human beings who liked airline food.

The menu ended with coffee for Rafael. Phelps, recovered from the sharp pain, asked for another glass of water, which he drank in one gulp.

"You're making a mistake not eating," Rafael warned.

"I'm really not hungry," the Englishman excused himself. "And airline food isn't very good for you. You really like that?" He pointed at the crumpled-up plastic that a few minutes ago wrapped the sandwich.

"When you have gone days without eating and without knowing when you will eat another decent meal, this will seem like the best food in your life."

Phelps swallowed saliva. Not so much for the hellish scene suggested, but the coldness of the voice.

"What are we doing?" he asked curiously, nervously. The anguished feeling returned to his lungs. *What have I gotten myself into?* he thought once again, while he took out the white fastener from the collar of his shirt and opened the first button.

Rafael took his time answering. His thoughtful expression showed he was choosing his words and, at the same time, adding to the English priest's tension second by second.

"It depends," he answered at last, opting for subterfuge, but forcing another unequivocal question.

One could see more and more alarm in Phelps's eyes. Seventy years, adding one or subtracting a couple, spent almost completely in devotion to Christ in study, with everything carefully planned, from *a* to *c*, passing over *b*, with the most detailed schedule possible, no adventures or hungry days. And now this. A trip, the unknown, dark and dangerous, and what most dismayed him, the calm of his companion in the seat beside him, looking out the window into the empty air, after calmly eating. But it was best not to think of that, since everything had started with a visit to the papal apartments and whatever they are going to do had the endorsement of the Vatican, perhaps of the Supreme Pontiff, the great Joseph Ratzinger. At the moment what most tormented him was the sparse reply to his last simple question.

"On what?" he insisted. It was logical that something that *depends* is subject to variables that can be explained.

"If we arrive on time . . . or not."

13

The tracts, testimony, medical examinations, bureaucracy, conditions, evaluations, impressions, interrogations, positive or not, that form part of the process of beatification or canonization are countless. Laws and rules exist, rigorous in most cases, that have to be followed scrupulously by the functionaries, emissaries, and prelates of the Holy See responsible for the case. A miracle, just one, is enough to unchain the machinery of verification. It can take years, sometimes decades, to legalize the facts, depending on the candidate in question and the interest of the Church in the matter. Much interest results in a faster process; little interest in delays capable of blackening and pulverizing the stones of the paved road. Preferably the candidate for sainthood should have been dead for more than five years in order to initiate the process of beatification, except in certain cases of sanctity in attitude or way of life. The venerable Mother Teresa of Calcutta is an example; in life she was more holy than many saints after death. Abu Rashid, the Muslim, seated on a narrow chair in a room on the seventh floor of the King David Hotel, might also fit that description.

Through the window the foreigner watched the ancient city, polemical but peaceful. Today was Friday, not yet noon, but already loudspeakers were heard calling to prayer from the tops of the minarets of the Al-Aqsa mosque. In former times it would have been the muezzin who called the faithful for the hour of prayer to Allah, facing the sacred city of Mecca.

"Tell me everything, Abu Rashid," the man asked, not taking his eyes off the church cupolas of the Christian and Armenian quarters.

"What can I say that you don't already know?" he answered.

The foreigner remembered the previous day and the fortunate visit to the Muslim's house, as well as what happened afterward.

"You brought back the dead and whoever was with you in the Haj, after the monstrous flood that drowned thirty people, around . . ." the foreigner repeated for the fourth time. "Where are these living dead?" he asked sardonically.

"Around," he said. "I don't walk around counting the life of each one."

"That we'll have to see . . . we'll have to see," the other replied. "Can you imagine the work you've made for me?" An almost imperceptible look of irritation crossed his face.

"You're more than used to it. Someone has to do it." The voice remained calm, unaltered. Somewhat patient.

The foreigner left the window and sat down on the edge of the bed. He watched Abu Rashid with a certain reverence he wished to hide, which left him even more upset. He felt himself blush. The color rose in his cheeks. He hated this happening, especially when he was working on something important.

"When did you see . . . the Virgin?" Not without some fear he evoked the name of the Mother of God.

"Every time she appears."

The foreigner reacted as if it were blasphemy. He felt as if Abu Rashid were insulting his own mother, which is true, since the Virgin is the heavenly mother of every Christian.

"And when is that?" He decided to calm down. There was nothing to gain in losing control.

"It depends."

"On what?"

"On what she has to say to me."

"She's the Mother of Christ, a Christian icon. Do you believe in her?"
Don't lose patience, don't lose patience.

"I believe because I see her."

"It could be no more than a hallucination, man of God . . . of Allah," he corrected himself.

"Allah is God," the Muslim countered.

"But not mine," the other replied decisively.

"Only one God exists. Mine could be yours."

"Leave the dogma. You believe because you see her."

"Correct."

"But she could be only a hallucination," he suggested.

Abu Rashid shook his head, denying it.

"No. Hallucinations are like mirages. They deceive."

"And she doesn't deceive?"

"Never. Everything she tells me is always true." The word reflected the respect he had for the visions.

The foreigner got up again and paced from one side of the spacious room to the other. He sighed deeply, his hands behind his back.

"What has that vision told you?" he finally asked.

"Oh, many things . . ." He smiled.

"For example," the foreigner insisted.

"She spoke to me of the flood and the drowning."

"How many years ago was that?"

"Ten."

"You've had this vision for ten years?"

"More," the Muslim agreed, with the same smile on his face.

"When did you have the first vision?" the foreigner inquired, halfway between the bed and the door in his nervous demand. "Do you remember?"

"As if it were today," Abu Rashid announced with a melancholy, nostalgic look, and remembered that day, his birthday, the eleventh, when she appeared at his side on the Mount of Olives, dressed in pure white, so brilliant that he had to shield his eyes with his hand. He was running back to the city to the same house he lived in today on Qadisieh Street to go with his father to pray at Hara mesh-Sharif.

"Where are you going in such a hurry?" she asked him in a calming, melodious voice.

Contritely, respectfully, the boy explained his duties to God and his family.

"God is always within you. It is enough to hear and feel Him," she replied like the song of a nightingale. The melodious reply had made the boy stop to see her better.

"Who are you?"

"I have many names. Maria of all wishes and ideas. The Virgin, anything you want to call me, including Lady."

The boy found that very strange. A lady with any name you want to call her?

"Okay, okay, okay," the foreigner said, calling him back impatiently to the present. "So, according to what you're saying, she's appeared to you since you were eleven years old," he summarized.

"Correct."

"Is there some specific day, some ritual you have to perform so that she'll appear?"

"No."

"Can you calculate how many visions you've had?" He sighed. He was losing patience.

"That's easy."

"It is?" At last there was hope.

"It is. All I have to do is count the days since the vision on the Mount of Olives."

"I don't understand." He returned to sit on the edge of the bed, attentive.

"It's simple. She's appeared to me every day since then."

The foreigner stared at him incredulously. "Are you saying the Virgin appears to you daily? That would be thousands of times."

Abu Rashid confirmed it with a nod of his head.

"And this fact hasn't converted you to Christianity?"

"As you can see, no."

"Why?"

"Because the Virgin has never asked me to."

"And would you convert if she asked you?"

"She wouldn't ask," the old man affirmed with certainty.

"But suppose she did?"

"She wouldn't ask."

"And what is it she tells you?" The foreigner changed the subject.

"I've already answered that."

"But I didn't know you'd experienced thousands of visions of Our Lady. This changes a lot of things. Okay, give me some more examples." His tone of interrogation and challenge was obvious.

"She told me you would come."

The foreigner gave Abu Rashid time to continue.

"She told me everything that's going to happen to you and me."

"And it's turning out true?"

The ring of a telephone interrupted them. It was the foreigner's cell phone. It couldn't be anything else, since Abu Rashid hadn't given in to the marvels of technology.

"Yes," the foreigner answered, getting up and going over to the window. He spoke in whispers so as not to be heard by the Muslim, still not convinced of his visions. Anyway, it was unlikely that Abu Rashid understood Italian.

The conversation lasted several minutes, always in the same nasal tone. He couldn't be too careful. The foreigner tried to be as evasive as possible, letting unconnected words be heard, like *problem, prove, certainly, I'll do what I can* . . . Suddenly he looked back at the chair where Abu Rashid was sitting and couldn't help thinking that he understood, or rather that nothing was news to him. He concentrated on the words of the person he was speaking with, setting aside the ideas distracting him. He couldn't let himself be influenced by words. Only facts counted. The call ended with a click on the other end. He would never dare to hang up first.

"Did you get your instructions?" Abu Rashid asked suddenly.

"It was a private conversation," the foreigner protested.

"About me," he asserted.

An ironic smile crossed the foreigner's lips. "I didn't know you knew Italian."

"I don't, but I've known the content of that conversation longer than you have to live," he said powerfully.

The attitude in those words struck the foreigner. Something was going on here. "Well, do you know what's going to happen next?"

"We're going to take a trip," he continued with a serious expression.

"What else has she told you?" He tried to change the subject, lightly, ignoring the old man's hitting the mark.

"That neither she nor her Son worry about communism or any other political conviction. They never divide the world between good and evil people. Everything bad in the world is created only by us, by our free, spontaneous will. So that when one prays to God to protect us, one really ought to pray to man to defend him from himself."

The foreigner got up and went over to Abu Rashid, looking down at him from his almost six feet of height.

"Careful what you say," he warned.

"I'm not afraid."

"I see that nothing is news to you."

"Well, no."

"Is there anything else you want to tell me?"

"I know what they did with the body of the Pole," Abu Rashid said.

Confused, but trying not to show it, the foreigner put the gag that hung from the neck of the Muslim back in his mouth and made sure that the ropes tying his body to the chair were tight to prevent him from escaping.

14

NESTOR

August 18, 1981

I'm so happy to see you recuperating, Your Holiness."

"Thank you, Marcinkus."

The two men were sitting on a scarlet sofa in the papal office. Wojtyla had seated himself with difficulty. The scars of the attempt on his life remained engraved in his body.

"To what do I owe the honor?" the Pole wished to know.

The American sipped a little tea that the Holy Father had amiably sent for, the plate in one hand, the cup in the other.

"A subject I fear will not please you, Your Holiness."

The High Pontiff frowned, showing complete attention.

"Tell me."

Marcinkus arranged his black cassock on the sofa before speaking.

"Well, I'll be direct and concise, as the Holy Father deserves. I've been contacted by a man who calls himself Nestor and claims to belong to the KGB. He's informed me that he was behind the assassination attempt of a year ago, and you can prepare yourself for others if you don't comply with his demands."

The pope's face took on a look of disgust and suspicion.

"And what are these demands?"

"That you immediately stop financing Solidarity and stop pressuring the Iron Curtain. Suspend all the audits of the IWR. Increase investments in South America in a way he'll specify."

The pope closed his eyes and sighed.

"Is that it?"

"Immediately," Marcinkus replied.

"And why did he contact you?"

"Because I represent the IWR. I manage the money. He was specific," Marcinkus warned, taking a more serious tone. "Cease the donations immediately or you could be the victim of a new attempt and, he guarantees, this time—"

"I understand," the pope interrupted with a raised hand. "What's the time limit?"

"The first offer was fifteen days, but I've managed to get a month."

"I'm grateful to you," offered Wojtyla, who got up and walked painfully through the office.

With his hands behind his back, cold sweat made the pope tremble, but Marcinkus didn't notice. Being pope was more difficult than one thinks. Besides countless obligations, his life was always in danger, always.

"What did you say this agent calls himself?"

"Nestor, Your Holiness."

"Nestor, yes."

"Have you heard his name, Your Holiness?"

"No, no."

The pope walked slowly to the red sofa and looked at Marcinkus.

"A month. We'll talk again."

"Naturally, Your Holiness."

Marcinkus got up, kissed the ring of the Fisherman, and left the office.

The pope let him leave in silence and remained silent for some time. Later, he got on his knees in the middle of the office and kissed the rosary he always carried with him.

"Help me, Mary."

15

Geoffrey Barnes was the CIA man in Europe. This was the simple way of explaining countless responsibilities and tasks. The specific name for the imposing position is the Director of Operations and Manager of Intelligence for Continental Europe. The principal headquarters was in the city of London in a perfectly normal building, very central, and for which we cannot give an address for reasons of national security. Thus, we designate it the Center of Operations only.

Geoffrey Barnes had hundreds of people in his charge spread over the continent, from subdirectors to department chiefs, agents, technicians, and collaborators, all on Uncle Sam's salary. Their pockets were filled with money to keep them dancing to his tune. He who can, can, and he who cannot, quits. Like it or not, the best secret information always came from this side of the Atlantic, to be sent later to be expurgated in Langley, a place that can be publicized without fear of reprisals since it is of public, and even historic, knowledge. Barnes had only two superiors in the chain of command, the director general in Langley and the president of the United States. There was also intelligence sharing among other agencies, in particular Mossad or other secret entities generously patronized by them.

Today the problem was the agency's alone, the death of a longtime agent in the central station of Amsterdam in doubtful circumstances. The trip to the Dutch capital had been quick, without incident. The distance from London to Amsterdam was negligible. Accompanying Barnes was Jerome Staughton, promoted to Geoffrey Barnes's personal assistant a year ago, who found his old position of data analyst in real time more to his liking. Being towed in Barnes's wake was like carrying a tunneling machine on your back, subject to his caprice and mood swings, his deep guttural voice full of contemptuous reproach, and his desire to feed his gigantic body at all hours. Beyond the evident differences between being an analyst and an assistant, working on the ground was always more dangerous than being seated at a desk. It was career progress that wasn't always welcomed, except for the pay at the end of each week. In any case, in spite of the seriousness of the situation, Barnes has been calm, in no way truculent, even convivial, not a very natural trait in a man who has to protect great secrets.

On landing at Schiphol, they found the cars waiting for them. Everything was planned to the minute. The cars were middle-range models to avoid raising suspicions, and they would obviously not appear to be CIA but rather FBI agents trying to learn more about what had happened and offer their service to every extent possible. One of the disadvantages of the disguise was their having to drive in the middle of traffic instead of opening a free lane. If they had been in the States or even the UK, they would have swept everything out of the way, but here they had to preserve appearances and good conduct, since the Dutch were known not just for tulips but also for hospitality. So the trip took them an hour. As soon as the station was in sight they noticed the presence of Agent Thompson, who had come ahead of time to survey the situation.

As soon as they got out of the cars, Barnes put his hands on the small of his back, stretching as if to make some discomfort or cramp go away.

"This screws me up," was all he said. "This job is going to kill me."

"You're going to bury us all, Chief," Thompson said, holding out his hand to Barnes and then to Staughton. Chain of command trumped good manners. "How was the flight?"

"It's taken us longer from the airport here than from London to Schiphol."

"It's the time of day."

"Let's get to business," Barnes ordered abruptly. "I want to get home in time for dinner."

"Over here." Thompson motioned to go inside the station.

"What have you found so far?" Barnes wanted to know.

Staughton was known to speak little, so his silence wasn't a surprise. He was assimilating everything he heard and saw in order to process it later. He was good at this, in summarizing the parts, always trying to restrain the director's impulsiveness.

The station wasn't closed. Only parts were cordoned off by police tape, so civilians were constantly moving about.

"They didn't close the station?" Barnes inquired.

"They didn't consider it necessary. The bathroom is in a corner away from the center of the station, so they decided to close access to that area and not affect normal functions," Thompson explained. "The trains weren't even late."

"Efficiency."

"Our man was named Solomon Keys," Thompson began. "Born in 1920."

"Solomon Keys?" Barnes marveled. "He's a legend at the agency. I remember seeing him once or twice. He was part of the establishment since the beginning. He came from OSS, if I'm not mistaken."

"Affirmative," Thompson continued, checking a note he had written in a small notebook with a hard black cover. "Member of the OSS from 1943 until the end of the war, recruited by the agency when it was founded."

"One of the founders," Barnes remembered, speaking more to himself than the others, remembering his own career up to now, to director of the CIA, here at Amsterdam Centraal. A lot of sweat and blood spilled, life in danger many times, and the loss. The loss of everything, family, women, normal life . . . *The company demands exclusive commitment.* It was what he was in the habit of thinking on lonely nights to justify what he had lost. The truth was he wouldn't know how to live any other way. When a man had a level of information as elevated as Geoffrey Barnes, with the power and responsibilities inherent in the position, he no longer had a life of his own. *It's a cross to bear.* His cross, the cross everyone carries each in his own way, some heavier than others. No one had any notion of what it was like to be a Geoffrey Barnes, what it was to have his work, what it was to know what he knows. No wife, dedicated as she might be, would have the temperament to wait endless nights, trying not to think about whether she would see her husband alive again. It was hard to work for the agency, but just as hard being the wife of an agency employee. As Jerome Staughton could attest, with his two failed marriages, thirty crappy years. You had to be a son of a bitch, as mean as a cobra, a bastard until the day you said "enough."

"Right," Thompson noted. "He studied law at Yale at the same time he turned into a valuable resource for the CIA. He left the service in 'ninety-two and traveled around the world. Ah, and do you want to know something interesting?"

"That's what we're here for. For tragic events I could have stayed home."

"He was a member of Skull and Bones. Initiated the same year as Bush the father."

"What an SOB."

"Who?" Thompson asked curiously.

"Neither. It's just an expression," Staughton explained, always prepared to save Barnes from his own mouth. "If I say you're an SOB, I'm not insulting you really. Understand? It's just an expression."

"Okay."

"A member of Skull and Bones," Barnes repeated thoughtfully.

"What is Skull and Bones?" Staughton asked. "Some club? A fraternity?"

"What do you mean, what is Skull and Bones?" Barnes was scandalized by such ignorance.

"I wasn't hired for my knowledge of culture," Staughton replied by way of excusing himself.

"Skull and Bones is a secret society. Or better, *the* secret society of our country," Thompson explained.

"Like P2?"

"No, not at all," Barnes answered. "No. P2 is different." He reflected for a few moments. "If we ranked every secret society, P2 would command them all, including Skull and Bones."

"But, according to Thompson, Skull and Bones has influential members. I heard talk of a president," Staughton argued, truly curious.

"Yes. In truth there are two. Bush the son has been a member since 'sixty-eight," Thompson added.

"Let me see if I can make myself understood." Barnes stopped to moderate the question.

The allusion to P2, the Italian Masonic lodge whose complete name was Propaganda Due, had to do with a case that occurred a year earlier that brought together these three men in a massive investigation that ended in nothing, according to Barnes. Propaganda Due was one of the most cited special collaborators with the agency, and the millions in funds they had received from Langley for more than thirty years gave their leaders a privileged relationship, often confusing as to which one was in charge of the other. The power of this lodge was enormous, greater than some presidents, prime ministers. In reality P2 had enough power to install governments or bring them down when they didn't serve their interests. They disposed of lives as it served them, including popes, as John Paul I would testify, if he were still with us. Skull and Bones was a minor league club, a game for rich students, compared with P2, even though it consisted of influential members always under the control of those who really gave the orders. And those people didn't appear on television reports.

"But the chief said P2 commands *almost* all the rest," Staughton interrupted. "The 'almost' is missing."

Barnes looked down on the two men from his imposing height. They resumed walking to the place where the crime was committed eighteen hours ago. Dutch police tape set off the area, including the door to the bathroom. A uniformed officer was on guard at the door to ensure that only those authorized entered.

"All right, you fools, who orders everything and everyone?"

"Who?" Thompson asked, unable to answer.

"Opus Dei," the chief concluded.

He showed his FBI badge to the guard and entered the crime scene, leaving his subordinates with their mouths open looking at each other.

"Opus Dei?" they both said at once.

They finally joined Barnes moments later, not knowing if what he had said was true or not. It was time to set aside the general subject of power and concentrate on finding the assassin or assassins of Solomon Keys.

"Here we are," said Barnes, looking at the ample space. Urinals to the right, stalls with doors to the left. A passage separated them. The yellowish tiles couldn't hide the passage of time. Once they were pure white, an indisputable choice for bathrooms, a symbol of health and luxury at the same time. They found the objects of their investigation in the fourth and fifth stalls. Blood spread from the walls to the floor, more in the fourth than the fifth. The door of the fifth had three bullet holes that formed an irregular triangle. A bloodstain lay over the wall that supported the water tank. A few tiles were broken on the left side of the same wall.

"This is where they killed our man," Thompson informed them.

They all stared in silence, looking for clues. The smallest detail spoke to them, intent on answering their questions. Who? Why?

"What a shitty way to die," Barnes vented his feelings.

"Yeah, it is. And, according to the Dutch report, with his pants around his ankles. Literally," Thompson added.

"You can't even shit in peace," Barnes said, closely examining the place.

"Here in the other stall was an English couple. Like our man, they were waiting for the train to Hoek van Holland."

"When I die, I want to go like that," Barnes joked, flashing a sarcastic smile.

"How do you know that's what they were doing?" Staughton asked.

"I'm a quick study," Barnes advised. "There aren't any same-sex bathrooms here."

A light went on in Staughton's mind. Of course, it was obvious.

"And these shots in the door?" Barnes questioned Thompson.

"It seems Keys was killed with the door closed. At least it was found locked from inside. One shot hit his chest, the other his head, and the third buried itself in the tiles."

Barnes looked at Thompson and then at the doors.

"The door was closed?" He shut the door with the bullet holes and analyzed it more carefully. Then he passed to the other door. "Where did the other two get the shots?"

"Oh, one shot each in the head. Very clean," Thompson told him.

An open door, a shut door. Barnes's mind seethed with equations and hard thinking. Things were never what they appeared. There were always variants and exceptions, accidents and imponderables, things difficult to connect and understand.

"What are you thinking, Staughton?" his chief asked him.

A professional, Staughton was unfazed. With Barnes he always had to be on top of things, fearlessly decisive, prepared to take the shots, figuratively of course. Field work had never been Staughton's strong suit, and his contribution was to present solutions without having to be in the place where they were worked out in concrete detail. Obviously he'd prefer never to leave London, the Center of Operations. But excursions like this to Amsterdam didn't bother him. There were much more dangerous things in this world.

"If the report is correct, and everything happened as we hear—"

"Don't bullshit," Barnes interrupted. He had no patience for playing around.

"I'd say Mr. Solomon Keys was collateral damage," he concluded.

"He was what?" Thompson said, astonished.

"It looks like it to me, too," Barnes supported his associate.

"How can you come to that conclusion?" Thompson insisted, still stunned.

"Staughton, do us the favor . . ." Barnes authorized his subordinate to present the theory.

"It's not a conclusion, obviously, just a theory," Staughton cautioned. Things should always be explicit in order to avoid confusion and mistakes. "If the facts you've given are correct"—he looked at Thompson, who affirmed with a nod the trustworthiness of his facts—"we are dealing, almost certainly, with collateral damage. The door of the toilet where the couple was found was open and doesn't show bullet holes. Besides it doesn't show any signs of being forced. The lock is intact, as it should be." He pointed at the catch on door number four, which showed no sign of violence. "That is, whatever they were doing . . ."

"They were definitely fucking," Barnes murmured to himself while gesturing toward Thompson with a vicious smile.

". . . they must have been so immersed in their affairs, they didn't bother to lock the door from the inside. The other door confirms that it was closed from inside, and the murderer didn't trouble himself to throw it open. He let off three shots, and everything was over."

"I don't know where you are going with this," Thompson said, confused.

"It's simple, Thompson. Whoever did this was not worried about the old man. He didn't even take the trouble to make sure he was dead, or see who he was. It didn't matter to him. I say Keys was already inside when the couple entered. Later the murderer entered, opened their door, and shot them. Since Keys's door was locked, he assumed there was someone inside. He got off three shots and got out of there. In summary, this was for them"—Staughton pointed to door four—"and not for him."

"Do you know their identities?" Barnes asked Thompson. He obviously supported Staughton's theory.

"It's here," Thompson announced, handing him a paper with the identifications.

Barnes looked at the names. Two unknown people, male and female, both dead in the course of their pleasure. Barnes didn't hold back his smile, imagining them releasing their fluids and energy, and, suddenly, *poom, poom,* or better, *puff, puff,* since no one in the entire station heard anything resembling a shot. He was carrying a silencer. Solomon Keys on the other side, trying to be as inconspicuous as possible, maybe even excited, to the extent permitted at eighty-seven, by the madness he must have been listening to and trying to imagine, and then suddenly, nothing. Probably he heard the bodies falling helplessly, and, later, silence, only silence. He bet not even breathing was heard from either of them. What a fucked-up way to die. A man who gave everything for his country. There was no justice. Barnes felt humiliated for Solomon Keys, for himself, since no one knows how he's going to cross over to the other side. Dead, that's for sure, you arrive dead, but the ultimate moment, that last moment, of the last breath, how many are going to have the serenity, the perspicacity to feel it, to know it has arrived and to say good-bye? The moment of *poof, poof,*

poof, for Solomon Keys with his pants down. The bastard finished him off. There was no justice. He was collateral damage, in the wrong place at the wrong time. There was no worse luck than being in the wrong place at the wrong time. Everything was tolerable except that. But who had the power to divine what places are wrong or right? The English couple was the reason for the crime. The killer was after them.

"Oh, shit," Barnes cursed.

"What's the matter, Chief?" Thompson wanted to know.

"Do you recognize one of these names?" Barnes asked, passing the identification page to Staughton.

Not waiting for an answer, Barnes took out his cell phone and made a call.

"Oh, no," Staughton let escape.

"What's going on? Somebody tell me," Thompson kept asking, angry at not recognizing any of the names.

"It's Barnes." He identified himself as soon as the call was answered. "I want to report a homicide." He waited a few moments. "Call him, please." For a moment he appeared to be listening to what the party on the other end of the call was saying. "I don't care if he's busy. Call him immediately and cut the shit. There has been a murder, but that's the least of our problems."

16

Let us return to the gears and solitary wheels that only know their part, ignorant of the final result. Let us speak about Sarah Monteiro and the whirlwind that invaded her, the call from her father and JC, strange and worrying, the two together in the same house. How anxious must Raul Brandão Monteiro feel? Certainly her father's voice sounded stressed. She sensed no sorrow, but who knew the reality of anything concerning JC? He was the one who seemed to know everything and everyone and disposed of everything and everyone as he wished. He was the designer of the gears, the engineer and constructor, the one who created the movements of toothed wheels, chains, belts, now toward one side, now another. Everything danced to his music; Sarah was sure of that. She owed her position as editor of international politics at the *Times* to him, as well as the correct news forecasts. Even absent, he was always present during the last year, whispering stories in her ear, the shadow that dissipated when she looked over her shoulder. But not today, not now when she heard his voice again. To stay to see his sentence carried out was not an option. Better to comply with his instructions and figure it out later.

The taxi took her to her new place in Chelsea, a two-story house with lots of space and a dream view for someone who liked buildings and the river with its brown water. After that night a year ago, she hadn't been able to set foot inside her old house in Belgrave Road again. The scenes constantly came to mind, and she recalled them all too intensely. How everyone looked suspicious, even ordinary pedestrians she saw through the window. The man with a garbage bag, the woman talking on a telephone who was always looking out the second-floor window of the Holiday Inn Express, in front, the 24 bus stop, the black car with tinted windows parked in the street, the man who broke into her house with a gun pointed at her, and the two mysterious shots that left holes in the window of her old bathroom and two deadly wounds in the man who came to bring her down. Only later did she realize who'd helped her, who killed the assassin who came to kill her. She thought about him often, although she'd never seen him again. He appeared to her every night freeing her from the nightmares, from the image of JC, from the other well-dressed man, from the shots, the deaths, the malignant laughter, the evil acts. It was always him coming to lie down with her, every night, murmuring lullabies in her ear, until Sarah woke up in the morning, calm and serene, a smile on her lips, alone, with no one. The monsters returned every night, the same images, people, faces, the same bullets, deaths, the last night in the house on Belgrave Road, the gun pointed at her, the final moments of a short life, and he who returned to her side, murmuring lullabies until she slept again. After that she went to live temporarily in the studio apartment of her friend and colleague Natalie Golden on Pentonville Road. Later she rented another studio on Polygon Road, until her recent employment gave her the financial security to lease a new place. She wouldn't have it if it weren't for him, or be in this taxi, nor would Simon Lloyd be her intern seated at her side with a look of happiness in his eyes.

Sarah wouldn't feel right leaving without word, so she'd informed her editor in chief about her brief absence. A journalistic coup, at the last minute, an exclusive worth investigating, would justify her trip.

"In that case, take Simon with you," the editor ordered her, and she hadn't been able to argue against it. Perhaps another time, more calmly, she could have persuaded him not to send Simon, without questioning his competence, but her mind was occupied with more urgent problems.

"What are we going to do in your house?" Simon was curious and impressed by the speed the taxi was making through the streets of London, despite the late afternoon hour.

"I'm going to look for some investigative files," Sarah explained. "And afterwards you're free to go," she concluded.

It was worth trying, but she was certain Simon was not going to follow such a suggestion.

"My orders are to go with you. Don't think you can get rid of me so easily," Simon replied like a man. Bravo, young man.

"I give you your orders. Have you forgotten?" she returned.

"With all due respect, I always follow your orders, but these have been given to me personally by the editor in chief," he argued, pointing up as if he were speaking about God Himself. "What do I tell him if I show up for work and he asks about you?" Simon scored a point. " 'Ah, sir, she excused me.' Do I tell him that?"

"Okay, okay." Sarah gave up. Better to go along for the moment and see about later. She would never forgive herself if something happened to him because of her. "Pay attention to what I'm going to tell you. Do whatever I tell you to do. Do you understand?"

Simon looked at her, his feelings hurt. "That's a little insulting, but you can count on me. I won't make problems. We're a team." He smiled.

A little flash of temper, there, Sarah thought with irritation.

"And now, can you tell me where we're going?" Simon asked curiously.

"We're going to my house, as you know," she replied dryly.

"Yes, and after that?"

Sarah still hadn't planned that part. The phrase *Leave London* pounded in her mind like a pneumatic drill, but leave for where? Where could she go? There were a lot of choices. London was connected to the world by land, water, and air. That was not the problem. But where? An international flight to the States, for example. Would that be a safe place temporarily? Or should she stay in Europe close to her father with more flexibility and independence to move? She hadn't been given any other instruction than to get away as fast as possible without looking back. They were following her. Don't let yourself be caught. And later? It would be best to stay close, she decided. Besides, her last experience on the other side of the Atlantic was so traumatic, it seemed better to face the dangers of this side.

"After that, the train to Paris," she announced.

"Paris?" Simon repeated with his face glowing. "I've never been to Paris. That's fabulous."

"Simon, this is work, not vacation," she warned. "What are you doing?" Sarah asked as she saw him frantically dialing his cell phone.

"I'm sending a message to my sweetheart. You know how it is. Do you have a boyfriend?" Maybe now he would find out something about his boss. Unexpectedly. He was curious how everything changed in seconds; perhaps this business trip would end up bringing them together and change the conventional work relationship into a nice friendship.

"We've arrived," Sarah informed him, ignoring his question. Her house was situated at the end of the street, and she wouldn't give any more information about it to protect her privacy. It was important that episodes like that on Belgrave Road were not repeated, for her own mental health. She needed room to breathe.

After they paid off the taxi, Simon and Sarah crossed the street, and she opened her purse, looking for the key to the solid white door. She thought of a trip to Paris in the Eurostar, the high-velocity train that crossed the Channel tunnel and arrived in two hours and thirty-seven minutes. The last time she made this trip she went with him, her savior, with an immense weight on her conscience, forced by destiny, like now. They'd left behind a scene of destruction, it was true, a sea of tears, of broken homes, projects canceled or postponed, separated lives, on the last trip on Eurostar to the City of Lights. No, this time was very different. There were no deaths or wounds, at least that she knew about, only a warning and an order to get out of there. She'd see what happened next.

Sarah found the toy donkey on her key ring and fit the key in the lock just as a shadow darkened the whiteness of the solid wooden door. She looked behind her and saw a London bus stopped in front, letting passengers with normal lives get off and on. If only she could be the same. Instead she had to remember things like the place she put the dossier that JC, or someone working for him, more probably, had left in her room on the seventh floor of the Grand Hotel Palatino in Rome.

"Sarah Monteiro?" she heard a voice say in her ear. It wasn't Simon. She looked at a man dressed in a black suit with a scar on his face from his right eye to his upper lip. He looked like a typical bad guy from pulp fiction. She felt panic, among her other feelings, but to her surprise, she managed to control it enough not to let it show.

"Who wants to know?" she asked, showing no nervous trembling in her vocal cords.

"My name's Simon Templar," he replied succinctly. "I need you to come with me." One more thing to deal with. He gripped her arm as he showed his identification, a card inside the wallet with his photograph, a few years younger, with his affiliation printed underneath. SIS. Secret Intelligence Services.

"Why?" Sarah asked, flushing. Her nervousness gave her chills. Was this really happening?

"Affairs of state. I can't tell you more," he concluded, showing some irritation. The State with a capital S is above everything. Faith, race, profession, personal life, nothing matters when it concerns the State. You can't question it. You just comply.

The agent, Simon Templar, whose name seemed to have come out of some 1960s television series, took Sarah's arm, like a prison guard, alert for any unforeseen or illicit action.

"I don't need a guide. I know how to walk, thank you," Sarah told him, freeing her arm and looking confidently at the agent.

They walked to a black car with official markings, somewhat reassuring for Sarah.

"Sarah," the other Simon called, running to join her. Her assistant had been in shock, not reacting, but soon had recovered his quick thinking. "What do you need me to do?"

"Ah . . . I don't know how long this is going to delay us, so . . ." She thought hard. "Go in my house and in the bookcase in the hall look for a wooden box with a bottle of vintage wine, Oporto 1976. Behind it is a dossier. Take it with you and wait for me to contact you," Sarah concluded, getting into the backseat of the vehicle.

"Will do, Sarah," he calmed her. "Anything you need . . . anything."

The government car took off fast, its interior hidden by tinted glass. Simon, a well-trained employee, approached the solid white door. The key was still in the lock. In the unexpected confusion, Sarah had forgotten to take it out. The refrain of Michael Jackson's "Bad" began to sound on Simon's phone. He didn't let it reach the third verse.

"Hello, my love," he greeted his lover. "You'll never believe what just happened. I'm right in the middle of things. . . . I'll tell you later." He listened to the voice of love on the other end of the imaginary line. "We're going, I mean, we were going . . . we still have to go, as soon as she's free." More conversation. "Free is just a figure of speech. As soon as she's ready . . . I'll tell you more . . . Now? Now I am going in her house."

In order to explain why two seconds later Simon was lying on the ground between the sidewalk and the asphalt with the door broken in half on top of him, it is necessary to use a slow-motion camera, since two seconds have been enough to separate the last words from all the rest that follow. And, if two seconds seem very little, they're more than enough for the key to turn in the lock of the solid white door, for the door to hit him, forced by an explosion from inside, and throw him several feet through the air, striking his ribs against a double-decker bus that was pulling away. He'd crushed the vehicle's body in a little without breaking the windows. The explosion had taken care of that, not only in the bus, but in a radius of hundreds of yards. Almost all the cars and houses had seen their windows disintegrate into thousands of pieces, thrown in all directions. Simon was on the ground with his feet on the sidewalk and his head in the street, next to the bus, showing no signs of life. He didn't notice the flames erupting from Sarah's house and reaching the ones next door. Incoherent cries resounded through the street. They recalled older and more recent attacks on the lives of normal people. Lives ended, without appeal or grievance, without pity.

Simon opened his eyes for a moment, blood running over his face and body, splinters of glass, wood, and ashes on top of him. The boards that were the door had split over him. His unfocused eyes tried to see, but couldn't make out anything. Where was he? Was he dead? Was he entering heaven? He felt no pain. He sensed shapes moving closer. A second, a millisecond, and something in his own mind, a fleeting focus on one of the shapes, provoked a smile before he lost consciousness, murmuring.

"My love, my love."

It was curious how everything could change in seconds.

17

Having just passed through the automatic glass doors of the entrance, let us continue ahead to the elevators. Except for Sunday, it's very crowded all week. Since today's Thursday, we can understand the movement, at first sight chaotic, of all those who work here, on every side, in the elevator, going up the stairs, walking up and down the maze of hallways, everyone with a plastic identification tag hanging on jacket, shirt, or low-cut blouse. Each person is an important piece, a part of the whole system. Once in the elevator, we press 3. Once there we come across a long hallway, take a right and cover a hundred yards, more or less, where we come upon a pair of aluminum doors. They're closed, but open with a push. Twenty or thirty yards down, where the hallway makes a sharp ninety-degree turn at the corner of the building, is another pair of aluminum doors with a burnished plaque engraved with the word "Pathology."

Inside are three stainless steel gurneys, as well as a number of monitors, utensils, and cabinets. A whole wall is covered with steel and eighteen square doors, uniformly arranged, three rows of six covering the length and height of the wall. These are refrigerated chambers that hold bodies that left this world under doubtful circumstances. We are speaking of the autopsy room of the Nederlands Forensisch Instituut, the place where the dead await their final judgment.

Here we see the three Americans enter, Geoffrey Barnes, Jerome Staughton, and Thompson. They've come to view the bodies of the two English fornicators and Solomon Keys, and they don't have much time.

Unlike conventional morgues, rooms vary in temperature between fifteen and twenty degrees centigrade below zero in order to totally interrupt decomposition, preserving as much forensic data as possible. In hospital and funeral morgues the intention is not to stop decomposition, but slow it down, so they keep the rooms between two and four degrees centigrade above zero. These are two different ways of preserving the departed long enough to say all there is to say about the causes of their death, before sending them to their last resting place, wherever that may be.

A man in a white gown, a coroner, according to his name tag, was cleaning one of the tables with a fine hose shooting out liquid antiseptic, preparing for a new autopsy, free from any old germs contaminating the new tests. He looked at the three big men who'd just come in while he washed the blood into the adjacent drains. How many corpses have passed under his scalpel today to suffer the ultimate incision, the most invasive of all, which will relate everything, the vices and virtues without omission or lies or half-truths, in black-and-white, in the entrails, the arteries, the veins, and other organs whether vital or not? After observing everything, annotating, noting, measuring, disconnecting inside and out, he would close the skin together again and sew it up, depending on the particular results, with or without all or some of the organs put back inside. A former life was now filed away in one of the refrigerated compartments awaiting the funeral, cremation, identification, or claim by the family. Everything society has to show ended up in these chambers: happy families struck down by an accident, victims of crimes of passion who miscalculated the risk of a spur-of-the-moment affair, John Does, and criminals who saw their deals turn bad. Whatever a human being is capable of doing to his fellow man, his family, his friend, neighbor, or stranger because an argument got out of control, or even for profit.

"Are you Dr. Davids?" Barnes asked impatiently, in English obviously.

"Yes, I am," the other answered in the same language, continuing his routine.

"Lieutenant Balkenende gave us permission to come in," Barnes continued. "We want to see three bodies."

"*Ik wil ook veel dingen,*" the other said in his own language. I also want many things. "Wait a minute, please."

"*Wij willen deze dode drie zien, nu,*" Barnes demanded irritably, shaking a paper in his hand. We want to see these three bodies, now. He was not truly multilingual, but an understanding of basic phrases in the most important European languages like Spanish, French, Italian, German, Dutch, Portuguese, and Russian was required for his appointment to a position in Europe. "And don't make me grab you by the neck and shove you into one of these compartments," he concluded in English.

"*Amerikaanen,*" the doctor let slip between his teeth, grabbing the paper out of Geoffrey Barnes's hand. *Always arrogant.*

He read the names written on the paper, turned to a computer installed on a small square table, and pressed the keys that made the first name appear. Solomon Silvander Keys, the victim's complete name. After he pressed the Enter key, detailed information appeared on the monitor with the certificate of autopsy attached, and many other facts of little relevance to Barnes and his agents. What Davids wanted from this procedure was to know the location of the victim, which appeared immediately in the lower right screen, number 13. Since the count was made starting from the top and left to right, we know that the thirteenth door Davids is heading toward, or Dr. Davids, we should say, is in the bottom row on the left side.

The doctor opened the square steel door and slid out the rack he found inside, where the corpse was lying stretched out, inert. A container that held Solomon Keys's life of eighty-seven years. The tone of the skin, noticeably ashy, was a result of the temperature to which the body was subjected, interrupting completely the decomposition, but giving him a cadaverous, supernatural, vampiric look. If three of the men hadn't been used to dealing with the most revolting scenes, they might have doubled over with fear or vomited their guts out, as we see Jerome Staughton doing at this moment into a blue plastic bucket.

"Go outside, Staughton," Barnes ordered. He had no time for his subordinate's weakness.

Staughton went gladly, with no desire to be heroic. Barnes knew perfectly the strengths and weaknesses of those who served him and what they could tolerate. Otherwise he would've made him stay there for the entire observation. Staughton was good at other things, as he'd already proved in the bathroom at Amsterdam Centraal. To observe and deduce, summarize and process facts. Yes, no one could compete with Jerome Staughton in analysis.

A serious Barnes looked at the body. Totally naked of clothes and prejudices, sanctified by death. There were two entrance wounds corresponding to the police report, one in the chest and the other exactly in the center of his head, brown, lifeless, since even the blood loses vitality.

"Do you have the ballistics report?" Barnes asked without taking his eyes off the body of the old member of the agency.

"Yes, wait a minute," the doctor answered, reluctantly returning to the small table, where he looked at the monitor. "Nine millimeter."

"Nine millimeter," Barnes repeated. "Of course. It had to be." He continued looking at the corpse. "Were all of them killed with the same gun?"

He couldn't take his eyes from the body. He knew that one day it could be him stretched out on another gurney in some other morgue, with a bullet in the head and wrinkles cut with age, if he made it to Solomon Keys's age. Solomon's world didn't exist anymore—the time when people trusted strangers who came out of nowhere suddenly, manipulating them at their will, paying generously for information, eliminating those who had to be, and avoiding risks to those who took care of that. Today things were more dangerous, the criminals much more intelligent, cautious, always two steps ahead of the intelligence services, and never thinking twice. Besides, double or triple or totally invented lives, as in his time, didn't make sense now. Everything was done at a distance on the Internet or other wireless technology. The demand was much greater. Communications were encoded, and millions of dollars required to validate or decode a message, with no certainty it was trustworthy. That was one of the reasons the company opted for surveillance on everyone, not just those who might be considered suspicious, since in reality they have no idea who is or isn't. After an information scan in which the supercomputer uses key words such as "president," "attack," "bomb," "United States of America," "menace," "gas," among others on a long list, via Internet, audio, and video, from time to time they manage to catch someone. No, Barnes wouldn't make it to Solomon Keys's eighty-seven years, nowhere close. The shot to the temple was practically guaranteed. Hence the compassionate look he gave the deceased old man.

"Yes. All with the same gun," the doctor concluded.

"I want to see the other two," Barnes demanded.

More fast finger movement on the keyboard, and the information appeared on the computer screen. Doors 15 and 16 held the bodies of the English couple. Davids went to 15 first and slid out the rack to reveal . . . no body.

"This is unexpected," Davids uttered, paralyzed with surprise.

"Are you sure this is the right one?" Barnes asked.

"It's what the computer says," the doctor informed him.

He opened 16. Nothing.

"Fuck," Barnes swore. "Do you see this?" He whirled around to ask Thompson.

Irritated, impatient, Barnes started opening all the refrigerated compartments and sliding out the racks.

"Hey," the doctor protested.

"Keep quiet," Thompson warned, also opening the compartments and reading the tag attached to each corpse's toe.

Thirteen corpses later, some compartments empty, they still hadn't found a sign of the English couple. They reviewed the list, and everything seemed to be in order with the rest.

"Who could have taken them away?" Barnes asked the doctor.

"No one. The bodies aren't even prepared for transfer yet."

"And when will that be? Who takes them?"

"In this case, since they're foreigners, the family or a representative of their country of origin, but always accompanied by a family member."

"Could there be an error? Could they already have been handed over and the information not yet entered in the computer?" Thompson wanted to know.

"It seems strange to me, but I'm going to find out," Davids informed him, much friendlier now than in the beginning. It was the morbidity of the situation. Irony. Irony.

He picked up a telephone attached to the wall next to the entrance door and punched three numbers, an internal extension. Three seconds later he started a conversation in his nasal Dutch that ended with violently slamming down the receiver, leaving it dancing on the end of the cord.

"He's coming," he explained.

"Who?" Barnes and Thompson asked.

"The boss. Dr. Vanderbilt," he explained. *"Zoon van een wijfje"*—son of a bitch.

The reasons for his blasphemies were his own, of no interest to us, nor to Barnes, Thompson, or Staughton, who came in white as a cauliflower, cleaning his mouth with a cloth handkerchief and covering his nose with it.

"Everything is sterilized. It doesn't smell of anything," Davids pointed out, fed up with all the interruptions. They were going to set his work back. Staughton paid no attention to the remark. He looked at the open doors of the gigantic refrigerated bay and the thirteen corpses slid out from the compartments. He looked at Thompson curiously. The latter, seeing him, turned his eyes away.

"Don't ask," he advised.

Meanwhile, the doctor, who must have been the previously mentioned Vanderbilt, Dr. Davids's boss, came in. He was wearing a blue suit with an indigo tie underneath his open white gown. His posture radiated confidence and arrogance. He cut short the *"Goede nacht, heren"*—Good evening, gentlemen—upon seeing the macabre spectacle. It looked like someone wanted to buy bodies, or parts of them.

"Davids, sluit alles, nu," he shouted at Davids, the equivalent of ordering him to close up all the shit, without the profanity, but inherent in the tone he used. "What's going on, gentlemen? Are you trying to screw things up?" he offered in a joking tone.

Barnes gestured to Thompson to place himself in Davids's path and keep him from carrying out his chief's order.

"Stop there, Davids," Barnes said. "Nobody is touching anything in here until you tell me where the two missing corpses are."

"But what's going on, gentlemen? Where do you think you are? In your own country? Here you don't give orders about anything," Vanderbilt made clear, abandoning his conciliatory tone.

"This American was murdered in your country in this city. If you knew how important he is for the United States, you'd think twice. If we were able to get to Baghdad in three weeks, we can easily get here in three days."

"Okay, okay. You needn't get all worked up. Besides, you're under Dutch jurisdiction. That body isn't going anywhere unless I give the authorization."

He's put us in our place, Barnes thought.

"Very well. Where are the corpses of the English couple?" he asked.

"They've been reclaimed. They're on their way to London at this very moment."

"It's not in the computer," Davids told him, surprised.

"Because I haven't put it in. I just did the transfer forty-five minutes ago."

"Who took the bodies?" Barnes's voice cut through sharply. Something had gotten away from him. What?

"A family member."

"Name," Barnes demanded.

"He knows perfectly well that the matter is under investigation and secret—"

"The name." This time he shouted to leave no doubt about who was giving orders here.

Dr. Vanderbilt went to the computer and entered several codes and other input. An instant later he turned the monitor so they could see the name. His face was unfriendly, but it didn't matter. What was done was done.

Barnes approached the monitor and read the information. Staughton and Thompson did the same.

"What?" an astonished Staughton exclaimed.

"Son of a bitch," Geoffrey Barnes swore, not wanting to believe the name he read.

18

God, whose only begotten Son, who with his life, death, and resurrection obtained for us the gift of eternal life, grant us, who celebrate these mysteries of the Holy Rosary, follow Him and attain what He promises. For Christ our Lord," the priest recited.

"Amen," the believers responded.

So the service was celebrated in the great chapel of the cathedral of Santiago de Compostela, where the largest incensory in the world, the *botafumeiro*, hangs motionless, without incense but commanding the greatest respect. For seven hundred years they have followed the tradition of using the great incensory, not this one, which is a little less than a hundred and fifty years old, but others, the idea being to purify the surroundings spiritually, although, in regard to smells, it was an effective means of repelling the odor that emanated from the pilgrims, after hundreds and thousands of miles of pilgrimage for their faith.

Marius Ferris had spent the entire day here attending all the rituals of the daily liturgy. He had visited Jacob's Crypt, where the remains of the apostle lie. He remained kneeling in prayer for more than an hour in the narrow place, ignoring the passersby who approached that place below the altar, with its entrance through a narrow door that opened onto some even narrower stairs. Marius Ferris had continued to pray to Santiago the

Greater, kneeling on the prie-dieu, with his eyes shut, forehead contracted, feeling every word he offered. From time to time a tear formed under his eyelid and ran down his cheek to evaporate.

Now he was sitting in the nave, listening to Father Clemente's last words, while night had fallen for over an hour already. A few dozen faithful were scattered among the pews, old and bent over, just come from their jobs or business, grateful for the grace obtained or probably asking new favors or substituting more recent ones for old ones, like a service provided from above to someone who knows how to negotiate.

In the last row sat a young man in a black suit, and anyone who had noticed him during the day would never guess Marius Ferris was the reason for his presence. Just the opposite. The way he walked around the cathedral, avoiding the crypt when the priest was praying earnestly, would have convinced the most suspicious that we were dealing with a historian or a passionate admirer of sacred art. He'd lingered in different corners, appreciating some of the relics open to view, not all, since a day, even a lifetime, wasn't enough for that. He paid special attention to a gold crucifix, originally from the year 874, that contained, it was believed, a piece of the True Cross on which Christ was crucified. Is there really a piece of the wood in it? He had reflected on this for several long minutes for lack of any other interest and place to go, but had ended up concluding that, even if such provenance were confirmed, an object didn't become holy merely because it subjected Christ to death, causing him pain, torturing him for hours until the last breath.

Later he'd gone down into the crypt when it was empty and analyzed the narrow place. Three small, latticework doors, the middle one guarding the silver sarcophagus with the sacred relics, the bones of Jacob, at the end of a small passage with a floor covered in black-and-white mosaic. The other doors guarded the mortal remains of two of Santiago the Greater's disciples, San Teodoro and San Atanasio, gathered together with those of their master in life and death.

This personal pilgrimage over, done more out of obligation than to avoid the task assigned to him, he'd gone to sit in the last row where he had remained since Mass began.

"In the name of the Father, and the Son, and the Holy Spirit," Father Clemente intoned, raising his right hand over his head when he said "Father" and over each shoulder when he said "Son" and "Holy Spirit." "Go in peace, and may the Lord be with you."

Another celebration of the Eucharist was over, the fifth he'd attended today. It was time to end his martyrdom and begin that of others. Things were going well on the various fronts of the operation.

He saw Marius Ferris walking toward the priest, who was heading toward the sacristy, but didn't attempt to get up. It wasn't time. His instructions were specific.

"Don Clemente," Marius Ferris greeted him in a quiet voice, in accord with the sacred place.

The other, also with white hair, stopped and examined him. That face was not unfamiliar. But the white hair . . .

"Marius?" he asked a little doubtfully.

"You still remember me," the other replied.

"Oh, Marius."

The two men of the Church embraced, gathering together all the years of separation in that gesture.

"How many years has it been?" Don Clemente finally asked, astonished to see his friend and countryman again.

"Many," Marius Ferris answered. "It doesn't matter. How are you?"

"As you see," the other replied. "In the Grace of the Lord. I wasn't expecting to see you again. How are you? What have you been doing?"

"I've returned," Marius Ferris informed him, adding no more than he had to. Enough was enough.

"I heard you were in New York."

"Yes, it's true," he answered evasively.

"And now, have you returned for good?"

"Almost," Marius Ferris said. "I still have one last journey. But I wanted to begin here first."

"Of course, of course," Don Clemente added. "First those closest to us."

"Naturally. I've spent many years away from my homeland." These last words were pronounced with a certain melancholy and an empty stare.

Time passes through its orbit, without mercy, what goes, goes, is ended, is past, and will not return to the present, ever, for all that he mourned. It was a sorrow that overcame him when he recalled the time that he had lost. But a life dedicated to the ideals of the Church was not to be regretted, much less by a person in Marius Ferris's position. He could feel pain for a life far from home, for the heart that remained behind when he went away twenty years ago, but not for the deeds and essentials, for the propagation of God's Word and for his word, he being the Shepherd of Shepherds, His Holiness the pope, the many whom he had served all this time. "I will also go to Fátima, Lourdes, and visit the Holy See. Only then will I come back for good," he concluded.

"A truly personal pilgrimage," said Don Clemente, admiring him.

"I've needed this for a long time."

"I believe it. I believe it," the priest said. "I'll be waiting here for you when you return. You always know where you can find me."

He laid a hand on Marius Ferris's shoulder in a gesture of affection and then continued walking to the sacristy.

"Actually," Marius Ferris began, interrupting Don Clemente's steps, "I've come here for another reason, as well." His expression was serious.

"Oh, really?" He waited for his friend Marius to explain, but he said nothing further, only continued to look serious. "All right. What is it?"

"I want to make a confession."

The oppressive tension Marius had created was cut off by Don Clemente's strident laugh.

"Is that all?" Don Clemente asked, while wiping his tears on the sleeve of his cassock. "For a moment I thought you were going to ask me for money."

It was Marius Ferris's turn to smile.

"No, I only want confession."

"Very well."

Silence extended through the whole, practically empty, cathedral. Only one person strolled through the Pórtico de la Gloria, absorbed in the magnificence of the place. Marius continued looking at his friend.

"Now?" Don Clemente asked. He hadn't realized the request was for immediate action.

"Yes," the other confirmed.

Don Clemente consulted his watch. He frowned and looked at the great door of the cathedral.

"Wait for me here. I'll be right back," he decided.

And with these words he turned his back and walked off. Marius Ferris sat down in one of the pews looking at the altar.

Normally, a priest never makes confession in a confessional. It is said and known that one of the privileges of his office, if one wants to consider it such, is never to have to enter the claustrophobic cubicle to bare the soul, murmuring through the screen to the priest on the other side. When a priest confesses to another, he does it face-to-face, eye-to-eye, unburdening himself of past sins, purifying his spirit, in whatever way possible. The disadvantage, if there is one, is that, contrary to common belief, a colleague in office can't tell another his most profound secrets. It's not that there's an exception for priests; confession functions the same way—closed, inviolable, not transmissible. Every word spoken can never be told to a third person. The problem is that the sinner is a priest, as is the confessor, and for one to have to guard the secrets of another son of the Holy Roman Catholic Church, depending on the secret and the sin, might give one man an advantage over the other. Everything depends on the other's character. For this reason, when a priest confesses, he has to be very careful.

Don Clemente returned a little later dressed for the occasion with his clerical collar under the shirt signifying his calling. He sat in the pew and waited for Marius Ferris to approach.

"Tell me, Marius," he asked. "Purify your soul."

Marius Ferris came closer to his friend and looked at him for several moments, eyes moist with emotion. What he wanted to come out would be the total truth, without evasion, today, right now. Marius Ferris was going to open his heart without weighing his words. There would be nothing held back, no secrets.

"You've known me for many years, Clemente," Marius Ferris began. "You know I was always devoted to the Lord, always followed His teachings, in His infinite wisdom, without any doubting."

Don Clemente nodded in confirmation.

"I have done all I ought to have done, according to what was demanded of me, within my capabilities and values, sometimes with much sweat and sacrifice. Not everyone understands the paths of God as you and I do, you know that well."

The confessor listened with his eyes fixed on the speaker, showing no judgment about what he was hearing.

"I can't complain about anything. Leaving Compostela twenty years ago was probably my greatest test. Galicia robs the soul, holds on to us with claws and teeth and doesn't let us forget her. There were many nights when I cried over being away from her and not seeing the cathedral or eating *navajas* at Don Gaiferos. I wept, yes, but in the room of my luxurious apartment on Seventh Avenue a few blocks from Central Park. I celebrated Mass in the comfort of my home in a room set up for that service for only a few well-to-do friends who had that privilege. I amassed a lot of money for God's work." He spoke in a restrained tone, appropriate for the atmosphere of the cathedral; for all that, there was a noticeable harshness in his voice. "Last year some things started happening that made me anxious."

"What were these things?" Don Clemente asked, caught up in the story.

"I received some documents from a Portuguese Monsignor Firenzi. Have you heard of him?"

"I recognize the name," Don Clemente answered, settling himself on the pew, "but I don't think I know him personally."

"You may have heard about him when they published the notification of his death," Marius Ferris explained.

"Perhaps," the other acknowledged with that thoughtful air of someone searching his memory for a name or event. "Of course," he remembered now. "They found him in the Tiber last year."

"Correct," Marius Ferris agreed. "Valdemar Firenzi was murdered because of those documents. He was the one who sent them to me to hide in a secure place."

"And what documents are those?" Don Clemente's avid curiosity was well known.

Marius Ferris was silent for a minute, which further encouraged Don Clemente's gossipy tendencies. The former was organizing his ideas, but not weighing his words. Everything had to be said.

"Documents written in the hand of Pope John Paul the First, which disappeared the night of his death," he concluded.

Don Clemente stared openmouthed, but soon recovered his senses.

"But . . . but . . . what documents are those? Where are they? Isn't that a myth?"

"No, I've seen them. I've had them in my hands and read them. Apparently Valdemar found them by chance in the Secret Archives of the Vatican, where they had been for twenty years. Apparently it was the murderer himself who put them there."

"But how? Is he one of us? How is it that you have access to all that information? Is it reliable?" The torrent of urgent questions that burst from Don Clemente didn't appear to bother his colleague or friend or whatever they were after twenty years of not seeing each other.

"I had the misfortune of finding out about it last year."

"Who? The murderer of Pope Luciani?"

Marius Ferris made an affirmative gesture.

"Marius . . ." Don Clemente stared at him in astonishment. "Do you realize what you're saying?"

"It's the truth, Clemente. Completely true. He found out that I was guarding the papers and found me. I barely escaped."

This confession began to become more of a conversation, a revelation, than an actual explication of worldly sins committed by the faithful Marius Ferris, follower of Christ.

"Go on," Don Clemente told him. "If I keep interrupting you, you'll never finish."

"I was captured and held with a group of people who in one way or another also knew about the papers written by the pope. There were four of us. The only ones left. The others had already been murdered. The worst was awaiting us. But thanks to an emissary from the Vatican and a Portuguese journalist who forced an agreement, we all managed to escape, some more wounded than others. Thanks to the Good Lord, I got out unharmed.

The papers I am telling you about are valuable only for historical reasons. They contain no information capable of shaking the foundations of our beloved Church. They are the thoughts of a liberal man already dead now. Nothing more. We are all free to think."

"What you're telling me is dreadful," Don Clemente added, still astonished. "Nevertheless, I still haven't heard a single sin in anything you've told me." A smile spread good-naturedly over his features. "Incidents of destiny, yes. Imponderables of life, also, things that escape our control. But not one sin."

"Now we're getting there," Marius Ferris warned him. "Now," he repeated.

Don Clemente took the opportunity to rearrange his obese body on the pew, while his friend organized his thoughts.

"During this last year, I've done a lot of thinking. I've analyzed all my years of work and devotion, as well as those of others. I've discovered that there are many people taking advantage of the Church for their own gain, Clemente."

"I know that well, Marius. But what can one do?"

"Many things. One can change everything." Visibly irritated with his friend's resigned attitude, Marius Ferris reproved him. "The work of God has to continue."

"The work of God serves only the interests of a few."

"How can you dare say such a thing?" The heat of anger spread over his face. "Over the years I have heard slander, but I never expected to hear it from an intelligent person like you."

"Marius. *You* know what is true. You may be well intentioned, Marius. I don't have any doubt about that, but you yourself said the same thing a little while ago. You celebrate the Eucharist in the comfort of your apartment for a few privileged people."

"Don't you understand, Clemente?" He looked hard at him. "Don't you understand that the soldiers of Christ have to reach every level of society?" He looked around the majestic nave of the cathedral. "Your purpose is to win the poorest. Mine, the richest."

"Soldiers? Conquer? This isn't a war, Marius." His reserved tone reflected an attempt to calm the troubled waters of the conversation.

"There you're deceived. This is a war. A strategic war. We have enemies outside and inside the Church. And we have to eliminate them all."

"Listen to yourself, Marius." The attempt to calm him had not worked. The dialogue had broken down in this confessional conversation. "War? Eliminate enemies?"

"The experience of the last year has made me realize that there are other groups operating in the inner halls of the Vatican. Our Holy See is scheming with these people. And what do they offer us? Nothing. They are not even believers. They only want the money and power they gain from this collaboration."

"Very well, Marius. You are here to confess, not to complain. Go on, please." Don Clemente offered these words coolly. *No one changes anyone,* he thought. *As much as you might think the contrary.*

Marius Ferris continued, irritated with not having been understood.

"Forgive me, Father, for I have sinned," he said coldly.

"Tell me that sin," the other said.

"I was an accomplice in the death of a man."

Silence. Don Clemente gestured for Marius Ferris to go on.

"And what evil did this man do you?"

"He attacked our Holy Mother Church."

"And in what way did he commit this act so offensive to our Holy Mother Church?"

"He repudiated the teachings of the Lord and sold his soul to the devil."

Don Clemente moved about impatiently on the pew. He didn't like what he was hearing, but so many complaints had passed through the confessional already, on such different subjects, in his long years of service that his mind and heart were immune to shock. What perturbed him was that it was a friend, though long separated from daily familiarity by his work, who offered this nonsense.

"And how did he repudiate the teachings of the Lord?"

"He tried to kill a pope. One of ours tried to murder the Supreme Pontiff. Do you believe it?"

"What are you saying?" Don Clemente must not have heard right.

"You heard right. He tried to murder a pope." He added nothing more, although the confessor continued to stare intently at him.

"Well . . . today you don't cease to amaze me." He didn't know what to say.

"What type of penitence does such an act merit?"

Don Clemente pondered the question for a long time. He would never have imagined seeing Marius Ferris again that day, nor that he'd tell him so many things he would prefer not to know. That Pope Luciani was murdered wasn't news. And the way the Vatican handled the matter was reprehensible. But that was thirty years ago, and Don Clemente was not the sort of man to question the actions of his superiors. It was also widely known that plans to attack the pope continued to this day. Every pope had been a victim of attempts, even if only in thought, on paper, as a project. In practice few had succumbed or been wounded in one. Nevertheless, out of the last three popes, two suffered attacks, one dying and the other gravely wounded, but this was general knowledge. Which of these was Marius Ferris speaking about?

"It isn't considered a sin when the cause is the sacred institution of Holy Mother Church. So, although complicity in a murder is a grave sin, I can't assign any penitence for the act," Don Clemente decreed.

"Thank you, Brother. That is what I wanted to hear," Marius Ferris said, kissing his hand. "How's your nephew?"

"He's well," the other answered with an expression of appreciation for the memory.

"In that case I won't take more of your time and will say good-bye. Until we meet again."

Don Clemente got up, seeing the other do the same, and walked toward the great door of the cathedral.

"Good-bye, Marius."

Marius Ferris didn't look back and left the sacred building. Don Clemente, staring vacantly at the door where his colleague had left, remained in the pew, his mind in turmoil. He didn't notice the man dressed in black approaching him.

"May I help you," he asked when he noticed the visitor.

"Yes, thank you," the man responded cordially, while he took something from inside his jacket. "I want you to tell me where the dossier on the Turk is."

"The what? I have no idea what you are talking about," Clemente answered, confused.

"Then I don't need help."

"In that case, good night." And with that Don Clemente turned his back on the visitor, shrugging his shoulders.

"It's not considered a sin when the cause is the sacred institution of Holy Mother Church," the man said. Don Clemente turned around toward him in time to see a Beretta with a silencer in his hand.

19

In the room where Sarah Monteiro waited, daybreak couldn't be seen, only deduced. There were no windows, only clocks. The ever prudent Simon Templar had brought her to the installation at Vauxhall Cross, the general headquarters of the SIS, Secret Intelligence Service, the complete name of the British secret service, more commonly known as MI6, its previous name. During the Second World War the British secret service was divided into various departments charged with different operations. These were denoted by MI, Military Intelligence, followed by the number that identified the service; they went from MI1, charged with breaking codes, to MI19, in charge of extracting information from prisoners of war. In the middle were the famous MI5, charged with security within the border, and MI6, which took charge of intelligence abroad. The names changed, but the conduct and objective were the same, aided in the present by technology exclusively. Simon had asked whether she wanted something to eat and drink, but she'd declined the offer. They asked her to wait. This had been almost nine hours ago.

The room where she waited was bare of any decoration, only the essential furnishings, a square table, big enough for two people on each side, but at this moment with only three chairs.

Sarah was seated on a small black sofa, uncomfortable, since it tipped

back. Five clocks hung on the walls with plaques lower down identifying the place to which they referred. From left to right, it was three hours
and three minutes in the morning in London, four and three in Paris,
twenty-two and three in Washington, six and three in Moscow, and the
same time in Baghdad. Time may be different, but it never stops.

Sarah's sigh expressed fatigue and discomfort. The hours of waiting had already been long. She had no idea why. Now she wished she'd
accepted the offer of food, but since Templar had left at six o'clock, no one
else had bothered to offer any. Sarah spent the time sunk into the sofa or
pacing. She tried to call Simon Lloyd and the paper, but the calls wouldn't
go through, in spite of a signal for the network on the cell phone. Luckily
the room had a small bathroom, clean, thank God, that Sarah used twice.
If the idea of all this was to break her down psychologically, it was working.
She would have said anything they wanted and signed whatever they put in
front of her. She had looked at the door several times without approaching
it. The numerical key box next to the lock required a code to open it, but
Sarah hadn't wanted to see whether the lock was in fact activated. It was
a way to avoid feeling like a captive. During the first hours she went over
the possible questions they might ask her. There were many things. She
couldn't think of a reason why they might be concerned with the murder
of Pope Luciani. No, that secret was well guarded, and it was not in JC's
interest that the British interfere in that subject. It had to be something
else. But what? Six digits were pressed into the keypad outside the room.
Finally, the answers were coming.

Two men entered. Sarah immediately recognized Simon Templar.
Sarah jumped up, as if her body automatically knew how to react.

"Sarah Monteiro," said the man she didn't know. "Come and sit in this
chair, please," he said, putting his hands on the back of the single chair
across the table.

Sarah complied as if the request were an order. The agent pulled out
the chair for her like a good waiter at a high-priced restaurant. She couldn't
help feeling nervous after so many hours of waiting, but she tried to hide
it as much as possible. She couldn't show weakness at a moment like this.
Simon Templar had already sat down in one of the chairs across from Sarah

and waited for his colleague. An atmosphere of cooperation had been created. A file was placed on the table. The letters on the label stuck on the cover were too small for Sarah to read.

"Sarah Monteiro." The same man opening the dossier spoke again. "The lady is a very mysterious woman."

"I am?" The only words that came to mind.

"Yes, Sarah," he confirmed in a friendly tone. "A woman of many secrets."

"I don't know why you say that," she dissembled.

"Yes you do," the agent pressed her. "But before we debate the subject that has brought us here, I'd like you to take a look at this." The unnamed agent pulled some photographs out of the dossier and slid them over the table to Sarah. "You covered the city in dust a few hours ago."

Sarah looked at the first photograph in A4 format that showed a London bus with its windows blown out and dents in the body. Other vehicles were in the same condition. Glass and debris were scattered across the street.

"Do you recognize the place?"

The second photograph showed a house, completely destroyed, or at least it seemed so, missing doors and windows, only the skeleton of walls remaining and the street number over what had been the portico.

"But . . . but . . . this is my . . ." Words failed her.

"It's true," said the only agent speaking at the moment. "This is what's left of your house."

"But how?" She was unable to take her eyes from the photograph.

"Really, you should thank Agent Templar for being so solicitous when he went to find you."

"I don't understand," Sarah continued, astonished, eyes wide, examining every inch of the photo.

"As you can see, all this damage was done by an explosive device triggered by turning the key in the lock. It could have been you, Sarah."

Sarah reflected on this for a few moments, completely devastated. Someone had tried to kill her and gone to enormous lengths to do it. It could have been her turning the key in the lock, as the agent pointed out. It could have been . . .

"Oh, my God." She raised her voice nervously. Simon. She remembered her intern. He was the one who opened the door. She told him to. She hid her face in her arms, leaning her head on the table. This couldn't be true.

"He's alive," was all the agent said.

"He is?"

"He suffered some scrapes, some broken bones, but he'll survive. It could've been worse. He's in the Chelsea and Westminster Hospital," he informed her.

A wave of relief passed over Sarah. Scrapes and broken bones could be dealt with. Death could not.

"We have to go into this more deeply," the agent alerted her. "But, as you know, this isn't the reason we've invited you here," he said as he took the photographs back from Sarah.

Invited me? He calls this inviting? He's crazy, she thought.

"My house has been destroyed. What else is there to talk about?"

"I understand your reaction, but, believe me, right now there are more important things."

"Yes, Sarah." The first words Simon Templar had spoken since he picked her up nine hours ago. "Let Agent Fox ask the questions. Later we'll talk about what happened to your house."

"It's natural for the lady to be worried about what happened to her house, Simon," the recently baptized Agent Fox added.

"Sure, but with all due respect to Miss Monteiro, we have more important things to talk about. You know that, John."

"More important than putting a bomb in my house, and wounding my assistant?" Sarah was furious.

"In fact . . . there are things much more important than that," Agent John Fox informed Sarah, while handing over three more photographs to her. "Recognize any of these people?"

This time there were three portraits in three-by-five format. The first, an older man with immaculate white hair. Sarah's hand caused the glossy paper to tremble. Her nerves were on edge. Of course, they'd blown her house away without a thought, and she'd been the target. Almost a year later, her life was again hanging by a slender thread that could break at any moment. The photograph was taken when the man was getting into a green taxi with Arabic script indicating somewhere in the Middle East.

"I don't know him," she concluded.

"Are you sure?" Agent Fox pressed her.

"Absolutely," Sarah insisted. "I've never seen that man." She looked again at the old man in the photograph. "Why? Should I know him?"

"It depends on your relations with CIA operatives," Simon Templar cut in bluntly.

Sarah didn't expect this. What would the old man in the photograph have to do with the CIA? In moments like this she doubted what she could say or not, what they knew or acted like they knew. It was difficult to handle these connections. What was certain was that she didn't know the man in the photograph and they couldn't accuse her of anything . . . until she knew different.

"I have no relationship with the CIA, as you ought to know." She decided to protect herself. "I have as much as I have with you."

If they suspected something, they'd continue following the same line of questioning; otherwise they'd move on. This was how they worked, and Sarah knew it. They throw out the bait and wait to see what they reel in.

"That man was named Solomon Keys, and he was a longtime CIA agent," John informed her.

"Was named?" *Now he's not?*

"He was killed two days ago in Amsterdam."

The men looked at Sarah as if expecting a confession or a comment.

"If you think I had something to do with that, several people can con-firm I was covering the G8 summit in Edinburgh." She hastened to clear herself.

"We're up to date on where you've been. Don't worry," John Fox informed her. "What about the rest?" He pointed at the photographs remaining in her hand.

Sarah hadn't even remembered to look at the others. She assumed they were of the same person, but realized not, when she looked at the next photo. A blond man about thirty-five. The last photograph showed a woman about the same age, an idyllic smile on her lips, with blond hair falling over her shoulders to breasts covered by a tight blouse. What did all this mean?

"These I know," she said.

"Who are they?" John Fox wanted to check.

Sarah resisted answering for several moments. Didn't they know? Yes, in all certainty. It wouldn't be difficult to discover their identities, affiliations, professions, prior records, and political leanings. She decided to trust them. She had nothing to gain by concealing things.

"He's Greg Saunders. She's Natalie Golden."

"And what's your relationship with them?"

"We're friends and professional colleagues. Natalie works for the BBC, as you know, and Greg's a photojournalist. Now he's doing animal photography and travels frequently to Africa on assignment with *National Geographic*, as you ought to know from his passport."

John Fox and Simon Templar exchanged uncomfortable glances. Sarah picked up on that and a chill ran down her spine.

"What's going on?" she asked.

"Do you know what the relationship was between them?" John Fox asked, leaning on the table.

"The relationship between them?" Sarah didn't like the turn in the conversation.

"Yes, the relationship. Were they lovers? Friends? Engaged?"

"They're not the marrying kind," Sarah said, smiling a little as she imagined the scenario. "They might've had a roll in the hay, but nothing serious."

"And these affairs were frequent?"

"It depends. I'd call it a casual relationship. When the occasion happens." *Where is this conversation going?*

"I understand." Simon Templar took a cigarette out of the pack and put it in his mouth. "Do you mind if I smoke?"

He didn't wait for Sarah's reply, but flicked a silver lighter and immediately touched the end of the cigarette, lighting it. Two deep breaths made the cigarette glow, and he released a mouthful of smoke into the air.

"Are those encounters still going on?" John Fox asked.

"I haven't seen them for two or three weeks, but I presume so."

John Fox got up and started to walk around the room.

"Sarah, there's no good way to say this, but—"

The telephone rang at this precise moment and made Sarah jump. The strident, continuous sound came from the cell phone on John Fox's belt. He finally took the device and put an end to the loud torture.

"Fox," he said into the phone. He listened to what they were saying on the other end of the line for several moments and began to show tension in his muscles. Whatever it was, it was not good news, that was certain. A dry sound marked the end of the call.

"Let's go," he ordered, closing the file and taking the photographs out of Sarah's hand without ceremony or courtesy.

"Her, too?" Simon Templar asked.

"Yeah, all of us. Let's go," the other replied, heading for the door.

Simon got up, Sarah, as well, confused.

"Where are we going?" she inquired.

"To Redcliff Gardens," John Fox informed them.

It took Sarah a couple of seconds to realize.

"What are we going to do there?"

John Fox punched in the code on the keyboard of the lock and opened the door before looking Sarah in the eye.

"They've found a body inside your bedroom."

"A what?" She gasped.

"What I said," he repeated and turned toward Simon. "As far as the corpses of the others . . ."

"The ones from Amsterdam?" he asked in confusion.

"Exactly. They disappeared from the morgue."

Sarah listened to this exchange of words attentively and felt a chill run up her body.

"Corpses? What corpses?"

20

THE ARCHBISHOP

September 26, 1981

The paper was stamped with the pontifical seal of John Paul II, two crossed keys, one gold, the other silver, joined by a red cord, below an azure ecclesiastical shield with a yellow Latin cross. The papal tiara with three gold crowns above the shield and keys.

Paul Casimir Marcinkus, titular archbishop of Horta and secretary of the Roman Curia, was a step away from being named vice president of the Pontifical Commission for the State of Vatican City, making him the third most influential man in the Church. The only thing lacking was the signature of Karol Wojtyla, who had his gold pen poised in his hand.

"Are you completely sure?" the German asked.

With a sigh the Pole set the pen on the desk by the side of the paper.

"He seems like a capable man."

"Think a little more." He sat in a chair in front of the majestic papal desk. "He doesn't inspire confidence in me."

"You don't trust anyone, Joseph."

"I do. I just think we're being manipulated."

"That's what brought us here," the Pole added.

The German cardinal looked at his friend and superior condescendingly. He was right, as usual.

"I understand, Karol," Joseph agreed. "But it troubles me to see him with more power. It seems we're giving him full powers. I'm sure with a little more time . . ."

"I made a promise when I was elected, Joseph. To protect *our* family," he said emphatically. "I'm not going to wander from that road," he asserted firmly.

Joseph knew it wasn't worth contradicting him. Nothing was going to prevent him from keeping the promise. He'd made a commitment to God, and no one in his right mind reneged on an agreement with the Creator.

"Many people write about my actions, as you well know. I cannot take a step without being judged by someone, archived for posterity. When I announced I had pardoned the boy his act, everyone criticized it. It's hypocrisy. He's only saying it to look good. He's trying to be a saint. Not for a moment did they think, Who am I to judge the actions of others? Not for a moment did they say, Look, there's a sincere gesture. . . . *As we forgive those who trespass against us.*"

Silence spread through the immense papal office. The major decisions of the Catholic world were made here. A simple signature on a sheet of paper with the papal seal had the power to change consciences, begin revolutions or inspire them, alleviate in a small way hunger in the world, poverty, provide shelter for those without homes, protect those whose forefathers rejected them. Here were created priests, bishops, archbishops, monsignors, cardinals, missionaries who carried the name of Christ to every corner of the world, a friendly word, a piece of bread, a glass of drinkable water, a smile accompanied by a kiss of peace. Here what couldn't be said was omitted, and truth embellished. Only in this way, complex, accustomed to concessions, negotiations, strategic accords, could the Church exist. The pure simplicity associated with the image of Jesus Christ was not possible to implement in the world of men, unless by a superior man, like Christ himself.

"After all they managed to blame on the Turk . . ." the German cardinal defended him.

"That's precisely why I'm doing this. If in fact he was implicated, he won't suspect our distrust. Later we can investigate at our leisure."

"Perhaps you're right," Joseph conceded.

"When possible, I want to talk to the Turk personally."

Wojtyla took the pen at the exact moment the door opened and the secretary announced the arrival of archbishop Paul Marcinkus.

"Tell him to come in." He turned to the German cardinal. "Give me a minute, Joseph, please."

Thwarted, Joseph got up from the chair and left the office through a side door, at the same time the American bishop entered.

"Holy Father," he greeted him, making a motion to kiss the ring of the Fisherman on Wojtyla's finger, but the latter didn't extend his hand.

"Sit down, please." He received him seriously. "Would you like something?"

"I don't need anything, thanks," he answered with a smile.

"Have you had news from Nestor?" the Supreme Pontiff asked.

"No. Anyway, we still haven't finished what he required, Your Holiness."

"Yes, yes," he agreed misleadingly. "Remind me what he asked of us."

"They're interested in increasing the investment of IOR in South America and Switzerland," Marcinkus explained. He adopted a confidential tone. "In reality he's pressuring me. But I didn't want to trouble the Holy Father. I've made excuses for the preparation of the trip to the United Kingdom, and, at the moment, I've managed to keep it apart. But I always live in fear they'll make an attempt on you again, Your Holiness. It's a torment."

"Of course, of course. I appreciate, my good man, all you've done to protect me," the Pole said. He thought for a few moments.

"You can start investing in South America as you consider best."

"That couldn't be better news, Holy Father." Marcinkus smiled sincerely. "I'll make intelligent investments that won't hurt your good name."

"So I expect. I don't want another Ambrosiano, Marcinkus," he replied firmly. "But I haven't called you for this."

"No?" *There is more to come?* Marcinkus thought.

"No." Wojtyla got up and looked out the window. "I want to tell you I'm going to name you vice president of the Pontifical Commission for the State of Vatican City."

Marcinkus looked at him incredulously.

"You honor me greatly, Holy Father. I'm speechless."

"You'll have more responsibilities, but I'm sure you'll manage them."

"Thank you, Your Holiness." Marcinkus was truly surprised.

Minutes later, alone, Wojtyla sat down in his chair again and signed the sheet of paper with the seal.

21

The dark Mercedes van traveled down the E19/A1 expressway at great speed. Greater than the maximum of sixty miles an hour. Few drivers complied with the speed limit, and this Mercedes was no exception. It was traveling at ninety miles an hour, passing the rest of the vehicles using less gas.

"Do we need to go so fast?" James Phelps asked with a pale, uncomfortable look from the passenger seat.

"Time's a-wasting, my friend," Rafael answered without taking his eyes off the road. "We have two hundred miles to go and four hours to do it in."

"Where are we going now?"

"You'll soon see."

It'd been like this since they left Rome by plane, and now this black Mercedes van.

The sparse information provided by Rafael in only small, ambiguous portions, without going into detail deeply, or at all, affected the mood of James Phelps, always so calm and circumspect. His displeasure seemed out of place.

As soon as they'd landed, Rafael ordered him to wait for him right there in the airport terminal.

"Don't contact anyone, don't talk to anyone, unless someone talks to you. If they ask, say you're waiting for a family member to pick you up."

"Who's going to talk to me?" Phelps asked, astonished.

"I don't know. I'm only giving you these instructions as a precaution. You never know," Rafael explained calmly. "Take the opportunity to get something to eat. Two hours from now go to the door for arrivals and wait for me," he concluded, walking away through the crowd.

"Wait. Are you going to be so long?" James Phelps asked, but Rafael didn't hear him, losing himself among the crowd of just-arrived passengers and reunited families in the arrival area.

Phelps strolled through the terminal for several minutes with a worried look on his face. He didn't want to eat anything, despite the advice, and, after an hour, bought the *Times* at a news kiosk. He looked it over carefully since he had nowhere to go in the next hour and nothing else to do. Night had fallen and the display screens spread through the terminal showed eight o'clock at night. He tried but couldn't concentrate on reading. To think that in the morning everything had been fine, calm, organized, and a few hours later . . . If he at least knew what had been said in the papal apartment . . . it would probably lessen his anxiety. *He's very intelligent*, he thought. *With so many vultures surrounding him, this was the only way to manage all this without going crazy. Meetings behind closed doors, secret encounters. He is a brave man, a brave man*, he reflected while trying to read the paper. *Assuming it was he Rafael had talked with, of course*, he continued speculating. *That has to be it.*

He pursued these frenzied thoughts to fill up the wasted time without paying much attention to what he was reading. He glanced at the page, reading the headlines, until stopping on a story that caught his attention, for whatever reason something grabs our attention or doesn't.

An English couple murdered in Amsterdam.

An English couple had been found dead in one of the bathrooms at the central station in Amsterdam. According to the few details given by the authorities, it seemed to involve some sort of execution, since both had been killed with a single shot to the head. Their identities had not yet been released by the Dutch authorities, who had joined forces with Scotland Yard to investigate the causes.

Lives mown down without pity. Someone had to gain from this, certainly, but was it worth the price? What would something taste like bought with human lives? Probably it would be tasted without caring, without considering the method used; otherwise no one would do it.

Two hours had passed, and James Phelps, always keeping his commitments, even those he had not made himself, showed up outside the terminal arrival doors to wait for the strange-acting Rafael. Five minutes passed before a black Mercedes van honked at him. At first he didn't pay attention, but when the automatic window on the passenger side rolled down and he saw Rafael in the driver's seat, he realized the beep was for him.

"What's this?" was his first reaction.

"A van," Rafael replied.

It took them around an hour and about sixty miles from the airport to the E19/A1 expressway. They had, as Rafael informed him, two hundred miles to get to a destination only Rafael knew.

"I don't like traveling at night," Phelps complained petulantly.

"Don't worry. Everything's going to be fine."

A little quick braking, harder than normal, but not too hard, caused a bang against the separator between the trunk and passenger compartment. Something had bumped against the metal divider.

"Are we carrying something in back?" Phelps asked curiously. He looked through the small window of the divider, but could see only darkness in the back of the van.

"It must be the jack or spare tire rattling around back there," Rafael answered, watching the road.

But Phelps wasn't convinced. What had struck back there was something larger and more solid than a jack or a spare tire. There was something mysterious back there . . . or maybe not.

A few miles farther on Rafael interrupted the silence to let Phelps know he was going to stop at the next service area. Looking closely at the exit signs before Rafael made the signal to turn right into the rest area, Phelps saw a sign that said eight miles to Antwerp. What were they doing in Belgium? And where were they going? He must find that out as quickly as possible. He couldn't continue being a puppet. Besides, he had his whole life on hold. He was no secret agent, no spy in the service of the pope. That was Rafael's role. He was assigned to the Holy See to serve, he believed, the faithful as best he could as a pastor and guide, not an active agent of the Holy Alliance, or whatever the Vatican secret services were called. Active in the sense of being there because, if anyone asked him what he was doing, he would not know how to answer, since he didn't have the slightest idea. He was discombobulated, out of place, and hated not being in control of things. They could take everything from him, except that. He needed to have the idea that everything was going as planned and organized, without danger and the unknown. Not like this.

As soon as they came to a stop, Rafael got out of the car and started filling the tank. A few moments later he knocked on the window of Phelps's door. Phelps lowered it.

"It's filling. I'm going to the men's room."

"All right," Phelps replied.

One, two, three, four, five seconds, the time he estimated for Rafael to take going into the station and disappearing into the restroom. Phelps left the van and went to the driver's side to reach the switch to open the trunk. It confirmed his suspicions. It was not a spare tire, much less a jack.

"Damn," he cursed furiously. "It can't be. It can't be," he kept repeating. "This is—"

"Father, control yourself." He heard Rafael's voice from behind him.

"What is this?" Phelps asked, startled and indignant. "Is it what I think it is?"

"It can't be anything else, can it?"

"Enough secrets. I want to know everything." His voice changed. Phelps was truly angry. "First you leave me waiting two hours in Schiphol, then you appear in this van with no explanation. Now we are in the middle of Belgium, and I see this. Two coffins?"

"Correct, my friend," Rafael admitted impassively.

"What's going on?" He was furious. "Are there people inside?"

"Of course," the other answered. He climbed into the van and opened the two caskets. A woman was laid in the one on the right, a man on the left.

Phelps remembered the story he had read in the paper a few hours earlier. "English Couple Murdered in Amsterdam." This was no coincidence. He couldn't say for sure this was the same couple, but it was highly probable, confirmed by the holes in their foreheads. *This is not okay,* he thought. He noticed the agonizing pain in his left leg had returned. He touched the spot in the middle of his thigh. These were the signs of age in his body, attacking by chance without compassion or pity. In health and sickness we are all the same; no matter what treatments we receive, no matter how healthy we are, time and chance will put an end to everything and everyone. The pain made him almost double over and moan, but he managed to control himself. A few more moments and the pain went away completely.

"You ought to go and have that leg looked at," Rafael advised without displaying any kind of compassion. A neutral tone completely out of place in someone watching someone suffer like Phelps.

"It's nothing," the other replied. "Who are they?" he asked in a weak voice, looking at the cadavers. The pallor of the corpses extended to his own face. He used a handkerchief to wipe away the drops of cold sweat that pearled his face.

"They are the bait," Rafael answered, looking at him seriously.

22

Nights were the worst part of the day, when he was on a high state of alert, like today. The sky was filled with stars, though, a scene he had rarely enjoyed, having been born and raised in a big city, with high buildings, many cars, people, competition, and little time to admire the sky day or night. This would be a magnificent view if he were susceptible to the majesty of the universe. He was preoccupied with the pain in his left leg that acted up on dry nights. The pain didn't bring climatologic or esoteric foresight, it just hurt . . . nothing more. But someone had to make the rounds, watch over the property, although it was highly improbable their enemies knew where they were, and, even if they knew, it wouldn't be easy to find them on that mountain in the middle of nowhere. Beja in Alentejo, the heart of the Portuguese plains, a little more than forty miles from the Spanish border. His Prada shoes were full of dust. Not the right shoes for this terrain. His Armani suit wasn't right, either, but if it had been raining, it would be much worse. The sound of rain would make it impossible to hear someone approaching, to say nothing of mud getting in his shoes. The dust was better.

It was three hours before dawn. Everything was calm. He had established a surveillance perimeter of fifteen hundred yards that he covered personally every two hours. In other times he would have had several men distributed at key points, chosen by him, prepared to give the alarm and neutralize the menace. All of a sudden Kabul, Budapest, Sofia, Ramallah came to mind. Today he was alone, hindered by a bad leg, but no less lethal for all that. He got off the seat of the tractor where he had rested for a few minutes after the fourth round and covered the distance from the barn to the house.

On top of the table were three plates with leftovers from the meal, half a ham, stuck on the carving board, several glasses, some with wine, others empty but with the reddish bottoms, remnants of an apparent banquet.

Raul Brandão Monteiro rested on the sofa, covered with a light blanket. He had prepared one of the three bedrooms for the old man, JC, but refused to sleep in his own. His military background didn't permit comfort at times of crisis. That, and his wife, Elizabeth, had given him a dirty look when she arrived home and learned the identities and intentions of the illustrious visitors. She blamed Raul for what was going on and she was right, in so far as his past was the reason for this situation. His initiation as a rebellious youth into a Masonic lodge was the cause. The effect: JC was the present Grand Master of that order and had interests that interfered with their lives and their daughter's . . . for the second time. She was in danger, and he could do nothing. They were all in danger. This time Elizabeth was not going to forgive him.

The cripple sat down on a chair next to the wall with the wagon wheel on it surrounded by Alentejan handicrafts. He would rest for an hour, with one eye always open. He wouldn't let the devil catch him napping, in a manner of speaking, of course, since the saying assumes the devil exists.

"There's another bedroom available. You can rest there," the captain suggested, stretched out on the sofa without opening his eyes. "I'll keep watch."

"I'm used to this. There's no need," the cripple answered, leaning back on the recliner and shutting his eyes, as well.

"As you like," the captain replied. "Any news?"

"Not yet," he said, nothing more. He forced his knee to flex. It seemed to ache more and more. Some days the pain interfered with his thinking. At least today was not one of them. He'd had to live with this pressing, permanent, implacable problem for almost a year.

"I'm worried," the captain confessed with his eyes still closed. It was evident he couldn't sleep. His daughter never left his thoughts, his daughter and his wife.

"You're not helping anything with that," the other said harshly. "You can only hope."

"She should have spoken with my contact." He opened his eyes and sat up with the blanket covering his legs.

"Don't start talking about that," the cripple interrupted. Raul's mere mention of the contact provoked so much anger he forgot the pain that punished his leg.

"I understand your anger. Believe me, I understand, but this time we're on the same side," Raul tried to explain.

"Don't talk nonsense. We'll never be on the same side," the cripple shot back.

"There is only one side," they heard a voice say, "mine."

They both looked in the direction of the voice and saw JC in a bathrobe, next to the door of the bedroom. He was leaning on his cane and walking toward the sofa, where Raul made room for him at his side.

"Can't you sleep?" he asked Raul.

"I'm not the only one." The military man looked at the cripple.

"Him? He seems awake, but he's sleeping," JC said, leaning on the cane.

The cripple made no response. He continued with eyes closed, stretched on the recliner, aware of the inside and outside. His capacity for keeping watch was amazing.

"Your wife hasn't reacted well."

"How could she?" Raul sighed. "If someone told you your daughter's in danger, how would you feel?"

"I don't have children. Family is a weakness," he said coldly.

"You believe that?" Raul looked at him, horrified. Without descendants, without family, there was no humanity.

"Has it never crossed your mind that without us this world would be paradise?"

Raul didn't answer. Now he understood why JC had no respect for human life. He considered it dispensable, unless it had some momentary utility. Only his side mattered.

"Who's shown the courage to make the terrible JC, assassin of John Paul the First, flee?"

"Oh, my friend. Don't attribute crimes to me that history doesn't consider such."

"We all know history is made by daring." Raul returned to the attack.

"It's what we have and what we respect," he deliberated calmly. Raul's words hadn't upset him, if that was their intention. "In regard to your question, we are dealing with an unfavorable strategic combination, nothing more."

"When you put it like that, it seems simple."

"And it is. Consider, yesterday's allies are today's enemies. That's the way the world works. There are thousands of examples in history to illustrate this, and you don't have to look back far."

"And enemies are turned into allies?"

"Of course." He lay back on the sofa and leaned his cane on its side. "You don't have to be a genius to see this easily. The relationship of the Americans with bin Laden, for example."

"He was always the eternal enemy."

"Or the eternal ally?" A quick question to throw Raul in doubt.

"No way is he an ally of theirs," Raul returned.

"My dear captain, there are innumerable ways of cooperation. If I attack you, I am not necessarily your enemy. I can be an ally whose role is to seem like an enemy. But I am talking too much, excuse me. That example does not illustrate what I am saying. Look at Pakistan or Saudi Arabia. They are allies and enemies of the United States, depending on the best interests of whoever's in power."

"And what is your relation with those countries? Ally or enemy?" Raul touched a sore spot for JC.

His first response was a dry laugh followed by a suppressed cough that left him choking. At his age it was difficult to get enough oxygen.

"No one has the luxury of having me as an enemy, Captain. If you knew me, you'd know that."

"That's not what it seems. If so, you wouldn't be here." The soldier was in fine form.

"They don't know me, either. Soon they'll take note of that," the other answered in the sure, serious tone of leaders.

"And the CIA, where does it fit into all this? It has a lot of power over them."

"We can't count on the CIA for this battle. They'll be on the other side of the barricades. They're going to understand that, but not lift a hand to prejudice either side. It's a strange way to function, but the only way to survive."

A vibrating sound, followed immediately by Beethoven's Ninth Symphony, filled the room. The cripple's cell phone, which he answered without opening his eyes.

"Yes."

Twenty seconds later he hung up without saying another word of good-bye, not a "so long," least of all "thanks."

"They've blown up her house. They still haven't made anything public," was all he said.

A terrible feeling, worse than a hot knife, slashed through Raul.

"And Sarah?"

"There's no word about her."

"Good God." Raul put his face in his hands despairingly. A feeling of impotence filled his soul, while he tried to imagine his daughter, thrown to her fate, uncertain, including death in the most awful way. Professionals didn't have compassion. If her death was confirmed, he hoped it had been fast.

"Don't worry," he heard JC say. "If something happened to her, we'd know already."

"How can we be certain?"

"Because that would be a message they'd want us to get immediately. It would already be on television. You can be at peace. All is well," the old man explained calmly. Such coldness sent chills down Raul's spine.

"How can they hide an exploding house from the media?" He didn't understand. JC's words, such as they were, calmed him. Sarah was okay, he forced himself to think positive, and felt a little better.

"Circling off the area or saying it was a gas explosion. Right away they lose interest," he explained. "What matters is blood and terrorism."

"All this has to do with the murder of Luciani?" the Portuguese wanted to know.

"Ironically, no."

"No?"

"No."

Silence fell over the room quickly. Raul waited for a conclusion that didn't come. The old man was irritated.

"Well then, what does it have to do with?"

"Hot tea."

"What?"

"Hot tea is what sounds good to me now. Do you have any?"

Raul couldn't believe that in this disorienting moment the old man could be thinking of tea, but he should have been used to it. Most of the time Raul saw him as a normal human being, a fragile elder like so many around there. Nothing could have been more of a false impression.

"Do you have any?" JC asked again.

"Herbal," the military man replied.

"That'll have to do. But I suggest you renew your stock of Earl Grey or Twinings for tomorrow."

Raul got up and looked at him from above before going into the kitchen to make tea.

"Aren't you going to answer me?"

"This has nothing to do with Pope Luciani," JC said without looking at him. "It has to do with the Pole."

"Wojtyla?" Raul looked at him incredulously.

The old man nodded.

"Do you consider all the popes enemies?"

"Wojtyla was not my enemy. Never. He was an old man without balls, but not an enemy."

This reply left Raul in shock. The mystery intensified. So this had nothing to do with what he thought. It was completely beyond what was happening around him. One thing was sure. There were not many people who could make someone as influential as JC retreat to a place like Alentejo to find refuge. What was happening had to be very serious to make this brilliant strategist leave the comfort of his villa in Italy. Another thing that shook him was the older man's attempt to protect his daughter, although he had done nothing specific except warn her. He had a faint hope in his heart that he had done it in time and that she was able to get out of the city.

"While you put the water on to boil, call your contact."

"Sir," the cripple cried out, awakening with his pride wounded. "Not that."

"Sit down," the old man ordered in a firm voice. There was no doubt about who was in charge here. "We need someone closer to what took place. Because of our strategic retreat we don't have anyone in place to be our eyes and ears. This is the best solution." His austere look showed that everything had already been decided and explained.

The cripple—an epithet used with no intention of insult, only an allusion to something about someone who doesn't like to reveal his name—didn't hide the anger in his face, but ended up sitting down without saying more.

"Who's after us, then?" Raul asked. He had not yet gone to put the water on for the tea.

The old man threw the blanket that had covered Raul over his legs. Warmth was a necessity he should never scorn at his age. Raul waited for a reply, which was glacial, unfeeling.

"Opus Dei."

23

There are a lot of things happening under our noses, and I'm not happy we don't have even minimal control of the situation," Geoffrey Barnes shouted as he came into the Center of Operations of the CIA in London.

He walked through the enormous room, filled with monitors, computers, and a large screen that filled an entire wall where a map of the world appeared with various symbols that would have meant little to the common person, although they had much to do with the lives of these common people, shouting and gesturing, red with anger. Here in this station only a few lives were important; the rest were disposable, always or whenever necessary.

The printers vomited pages and pages of information and added to the agitation that reigned in the Center of Operations. No one paid attention to the director's angry words. There was no time or patience. He himself would stop if he thought anyone should listen, but he didn't. Geoffrey Barnes entered his office, separated from the Center of Operations by a thin structure of aluminum and glass. The director had a privileged view over the room. Nothing escaped his attention, as he wished, but if he wanted to enjoy a few minutes of privacy, all he had to do was lower the inner blinds and no one could see in. Staughton and Thompson followed him into the office and closed the door after them, shutting out the noise from the outer room completely.

The chief sat down and put his feet on the desk. Staughton and Thompson only watched him as he swept aside some papers to arrange his legs better and enjoy some ephemeral rest. He didn't dare mistreat the three telephones lined up on the mahogany desk on the right. Not these. One green, another red, the other beige. The green was direct contact with Langley, the headquarters of the CIA in the United States; the beige, his colleagues at the agency. Barnes avoided answering that phone, whether or not he knew who was on the other end of the line. The people who used that phone were very powerful, some even more powerful than the man who used the third, red phone, the president. When it rang, it meant someone from the Oval Office, or the president himself. It had rung only once since Barnes had assumed his responsibilities more than seven years earlier, the morning of July 7, 2005, when terrorists detonated explosives in the London transportation system. He remembered flushing when the phone began to ring. It had never crossed his mind that the phone even worked, he was so used to seeing it silent. On answering he realized it was some assistant to the president wanting to know more details firsthand to inform the chief of state. Barnes was not caught off guard and gave him the official version, to which anyone had access. Sometimes the truth was not for the ears of the president.

This is not to say Geoffrey Barnes wasn't patriotic. Anyone who didn't want to see his life laid wide open should never say so where he could hear them. Geoffrey Barnes was one of the few men privileged to sift through intelligence information and sort it into categories, the essential, the important, and the normal. The important was given out to others. The country had so many crooked dealings that certain things couldn't reach the knowledge of the president. Everyone understands, surely.

"We're fucked." He was recovering, still furious. "Set up a meeting for six-thirty."

"So early?" Staughton questioned timidly.

"I'm awake, aren't I?" Barnes yelled. "So no one else better lie around in bed." He saw that Staughton wasn't going to object.

"Okay," Staughton replied, opening the door to carry out the order. For a few moments noise filled the office, shattering the quiet in there.

"Thompson," Barnes called.

"What, boss?"

"I want a report in a half hour on my desk with all the facts and events we know up to now."

"It's done," the other obeyed, immediately looking for the door out.

"You should warn all your contacts," Barnes ordered.

"All?" the other asked with his hand on the doorknob. All he could think about was the cigarette he wanted to smoke as soon as possible.

"All." Barnes got up with difficulty and leaned on the table. "How much time do you need?"

"I just have to make a few calls," Thompson replied thoughtfully. "Fifteen minutes. I want to know what rumors are going around now."

"Do that."

Thompson opened the door. Now he could already anticipate the bitter tobacco calming his nerves, refining his olfactory pleasure, his fighting instincts. Things would be hard from now on.

"And don't forget to bring me the report in half an hour," Barnes warned, turning his back and looking over the city. He hated not having control over situations. Worse, he hated not understanding shit about what was happening. Three murders in a public bathroom in Holland, one of them an old CIA agent. The memory of him with a dark, purple cavity right in the center of his head marking the end of his life. Whoever killed him was a son of a bitch, since everything indicated only one killer, and statistics don't attribute crimes of this sort to women.

The city was an immense lamp of yellow lights, punctuated below by the red taillights of cars. London was also a city that never sleeps, never. At this hour he'd rather be taking breakfast at Vingt Quatre on Fulham Road in Chelsea. Being known there saved him from having to stand in the long line of people waiting for a table night and day. The thought of some scalloped eggs with fried sausage made his mouth begin to water. To hell with those who came between his proud gut and the possibility of filling it with nutritious substances. He'd have to leave it for another night. It was lucky Vingt Quatre hadn't moved.

He forgot the city and picked up the phone. Someone was waiting on the other end of the line, his secretary, Theresa, who asked him what he wanted.

"Hello, Theresa. Bring me a double burger with cheese, pizza, and a Carlsberg, as quick as possible." Barnes's mouth watered at the thought of all that in front of him. At the same time he listened to his secretary's solicitous questions. Barnes always showed respect and never raised his voice with her. "I prefer Burger King, but if you can't find one open, it can be anyplace else, don't worry about it." And he hung up.

He turned his thoughts back to the situation at hand. Once again Jack Payne or Rafael, or whatever he called himself, had crossed his path. The difference was that this time Rafael wasn't going to get the best of him. There wouldn't be deals to save him. Why had he carried off the two corpses in Amsterdam? For what? The bodies were useless, or were they? He needed a clue as soon as possible. That was it. He picked up the telephone, but this time pressed three numbers. Two seconds later someone picked up and spoke his last name, the organizational rule for avoiding "hello" and "who's calling?"

"Staughton," said the recipient of the call.

"I want you to put a team on Jack's trail. I want him in front of me before the morning is over."

"After Jack Payne, really?" There was no room for misunderstandings in this profession. One was playing with human lives, and errors were costly.

"Of course Jack Payne. Who else?" Jack had a gift for leaving him irritated, and, consequently, hungry.

"Okay. I'll take care of that," Staughton replied, disconnecting without waiting for Barnes to give him more instructions. Giving orders was fine, if you didn't have to carry them out yourself.

Barnes hung up also, a little stupefied. He looked at the room beyond the divider window. A continuous stream of men and women moved back and forth, people swinging their arms with their hands full of papers, others shouting into the phone, some listening attentively but not to music. The more distracted or less familiar with this scene might imagine they were dealing with the stock market on Wall Street or in London, working overtime. The apparent disorganization was deceptive. Everyone knew what they were doing inside that room. On the large screen that filled the wall, the map of the world had changed and now showed only the Old

World. New circles of various colors blinked psychedelically over certain places. Each color identified a certain activity, whether a listening post, a long-term or short-term operation, or mere positioning of agents in a territory or wherever. They were indicators that meant something only to those who worked here, although many secret services or other less scrupulous individuals would love to get their hands on that information.

Although it seemed like no one gave the screen a second look, the instructions contained there were vital to the agency. The actions of the people running around inside there were identified and classified. With a simple click they could access anyone's personal data, previous criminal records, bank accounts, weddings, children, if there were any, and every imaginable and possible fact. If it was necessary, they could block the same accounts or modify them, alter former records, innumerable possibilities that were done every day on people, though not on Barnes, of course. Up to now he'd been considered an active, competent agent in his yearly evaluation.

If he made the effort, from where he was in the office Barnes could see a red circle blinking over Amsterdam. Information was still scarce, but soon it would be coming in.

"My fucking food still hasn't come," he complained.

At that moment a shrill sound resonated without stopping. He shivered. He looked at the green telephone on top of the desk. A green light winked on and off. The alert was impossible to avoid. Langley wanted information on a secure line. This wasn't standard. The beige phone also went off, making an amalgam of ringing sounds. An orange blinking light announced the sound. Barnes silenced the telephones to clear the atmosphere and his own head, leaving the pulsing lights as a signal the calls continued. What was the protocol to follow when two telephones on secure lines sounded at the same time? It didn't exist. He chose his patrons at Langley. Ultimately they were the ones who paid him.

"Barnes."

The sound of the other phone could be heard in the office. Barnes sank into his chair without taking his eyes off the telephone. The endless sound might fool him, but the blinking red light of the emergency signal left no room for doubt. The president's telephone was showing signs of life, too.

24

The gas explosion at an address not necessary to mention had left the place unrecognizable. Its owner could testify to that; she knew well how it was before and now entered the destruction. She'd like to forget the last few hours. Her eyes were swollen from tears, recent or about to start again, since a tear was running down her cheek. She couldn't say whether for this unhappy sight or for the sorrow she felt over losing two friends. Natalie and Greg were dead. That was inconceivable, no matter how much she tried to convince herself. She knew death would happen to all of us at a certain hour on a certain day, maybe without warning. What most affected her was the way they left this world. Surely they didn't even realize they were dying. In one second they were alive, making love, according to what the agent John Fox had described; in the next, dead, cadavers, lifeless, inanimate. It was cruel. And as if this weren't enough, she now had to face this shredded house, without personality, in ruins. Surely both sorrows merged in the tear. This hadn't been an easy day for Sarah Monteiro.

"Are you sure Simon Lloyd's in the hospital?" she asked uncomfortably, remembering with a shiver what she'd come to see.

"We're sure. Relax," John Fox assured her. "This is someone else."

"I hope I don't know him," she confessed selfishly, more for her own sake than the agents'.

They put on gowns and wrapped their shoes in protective covers that tied at the ankle to avoid contaminating the crime scene, although Sarah Monteiro's DNA would surely be found all over the place.

"Don't touch anything," ever-friendly Simon Templar warned her. "I want it on record that I'm against your presence in this place."

"It's on record," John Fox affirmed, making clear who gave the orders, if this was still not understood. "Let's continue."

The place was lit with spotlights. Metropolitan Police technicians were scattered through the rooms of a once tastefully furnished house. Some walls still stood untouched by the blast of fire, stroked by the hot lights of the projectors reflecting off their clean surface.

They almost needed a map to see where they could step, since work was going on. There were still inaccessible areas where forensic technicians bent over small objects with a fine hairbrush, like archaeologists patiently uncovering bones from the Cretaceous period. The work required patience, dedication, and attention.

"Where's the body?" John Fox asked one of the technicians.

"In the living room," he answered without even raising his eyes.

John Fox looked at Sarah as if asking her where the room was.

"Ahead and to the left," she said. "I think."

Slowly they went along the blackened hallway, full of debris on the floor, officially sealed off with the crime-scene tape police use to enclose those areas that require more hours, perhaps days, of intense work. Luckily the public relations department had concealed the true cause of the explosion from the public, at least for now. This relieved the pressure on the forensic technicians. If the criminal origin became public, there'd be many more agents assigned to the investigation, and the phone calls would be pouring in, demanding a guilty party or scapegoat. This way there was time for work to be done with certain results, if necessary.

John Fox entered the living room first. Shelves, sofas, forty-inch flat-screen television, DVD player, dining table and chairs. At first sight nothing seemed in one piece. Everything showed signs of flames and explosion.

"I wasn't expecting you today," the coroner grumbled, anxious to hand over the corpse to the legal process and free up the rest of his day. "Can't you see it at the morgue?"

"If we could or wanted to, we wouldn't have told you to wait here," Simon Templar snapped back, ready for a fight.

"Drop it, Simon," John Fox ordered. He turned to the doctor. "It'll be quick."

The body was laid on a stretcher in a closed body bag.

"Let's get this over with." The doctor ran the zipper down to open the bag. The sooner the better.

John Fox looked at Sarah and didn't need to say anything to prepare her. She came forward slowly toward the stretcher until the interior of the bag was in her field of vision. She didn't have the courage to look at the face right away. She began with the chest because that was as far as the doctor had opened the zipper. She confronted her fear, turning her look closer to the side of the face. He was a large man, corpulent, who reminded her of Geoffrey Barnes, a bad memory. He was wearing a shirt and white jacket, both heavily damaged by the explosion, ripped and burned in some places, but intact enough to still be identified as a jacket and shirt. The body was in reasonable shape for someone who'd been the victim of an explosion.

"What was the cause of death?" Sarah asked.

"Who's the lady?" the coroner asked rudely.

"I'm the owner of the house," she answered. "I'm a journalist."

"That's great," the coroner let slip. "Now is when everything gets fucked up."

"Watch your language," John Fox warned. "Miss Monteiro is here as a witness, and she's not going to make public any of our conclusions unless it's in our interests," he concluded.

Sarah looked at last at the face of the corpse. Pale but calm. He seemed like the victim of a peaceful death.

"Homicide," the doctor pronounced. "A blow to the head, but only the autopsy can confirm that."

"Do you have any information on the identity?" John Fox asked seriously.

"We do. Judging by the documents in his wallet. Look for yourself," the doctor said as he handed over a paper.

"What's this?"

"A printout of the facts related to the victim. The wallet has been sent to the lab. They couldn't wait for you." He gave a laugh.

John Fox took the paper and began to read out loud.

"Grigori Nikolai Nestov, fifty-one years old, Russian from Vladivostok, he is . . ." The words stuck in his throat. "Is this true?" he asked the coroner.

"It hasn't been disproved yet," the other responded, chewing some gum that showed every time he guffawed, like now. The situation amused him. The effect of working daily around death—forget sorrow.

"What's going on?" Sarah was curious.

John Fox passed the paper to Simon Templar.

"Do you know him?" he asked Sarah.

"No. I've never seen him before," Sarah replied without a shadow of doubt.

"Are you sure?"

"Absolutely."

"RSS?" Simon Templar asked.

"That's what it seems," John Fox replied.

"RSS?" Sarah asked curiously. "What does that mean?"

"That the victim was an agent in the Russian Secret Service."

"Russian Secret Service?" Sarah's jaw dropped. "What was he doing in my house?" she asked, half incredulous, half scandalized.

"Okay, I'm going to leave you to your problems and go on with my own work," the coroner let them know, as he zipped the bag back up. He whistled at the door to call the technicians to carry the body to the ambulance. They were ready and began carrying it out, one on each side.

"Be careful on your way out. We don't want to appear on television or in the papers," the doctor warned as he looked at Sarah. "Good night, gentlemen," and he went out behind the stretcher men.

Without the body the room seemed emptier, floodlights illuminating the space, the remnants of what was once solid construction. Sarah had moved so recently, and now she'd have to move again . . . if she survived. Something caught her attention. An object out of place. A small wooden box had survived the holocaust without a scratch or scorch. Although she couldn't see inside from where she was, she knew what she'd find there. A bottle of port, vintage 1976, the year of her birth.

She stepped around the box thrown on the floor, in the midst of the debris. Such a small, fragile box had escaped the explosion and fire. What were the odds of that? If a body couldn't even survive a blow to the head. . . . Sarah knew the front part of the box was glass to show the untouchable nectar contained inside. Simon Templar's words came to mind, *Don't touch anything.* That wouldn't be necessary. She could see inside, through the intact glass, and she was startled to see the bottle wasn't where it should be. The box was empty. She bent over it.

"Don't touch anything," Simon Templar warned.

Sarah got back up thinking about a simple bottle of wine, as old as she, gone from the surviving wooden box. She looked at Simon Templar, to whom she'd decided to say nothing, and realized he hadn't taken his eyes off her, was watching her closely.

She was. Sarah was a woman full of mystery.

25

The last pitiful look had always had such a devastating effect on him that he'd turned it into a bad habit. Most of those in his vast experience were pleading but the reactions were different in every case, depending on what came to mind for each victim in the final moments. Don Clemente fell into the category he most disliked. He had confronted the gun with a calm, peaceful smile, and so it had remained, even after . . .

Normally when one killed, one took from the victim what he most prized, but there were people like Don Clemente from whom one took absolutely nothing. He deferred his need to feel guilty after squeezing the trigger that summoned Death. He hadn't let himself look at Don Clemente when he'd fallen back and knocked over a row of pews with his robust body. The priest hadn't felt a thing, he was certain, as he'd placed the shot perfectly so Don Clemente would be dead before he hit the floor.

But this ordinary-looking man, a notable advantage for someone in his profession, wasn't given to introspection. Don Clemente was gone, born and dead, his body lying more than a thousand miles away in Galicia, perhaps in some morgue trying to tell the coroner the story of his death. To hell with Don Clemente, Galicia, and Santiago de Compostela, city, cathedral, and saint, all of them.

He had time to catch the last flight to the English capital, where the plan for this phase was playing out. The days had been long but pleasant with countless trips, Rome, Amsterdam, Compostela, and now London. The boss pursued another agenda, as foreseen. Two more days and they'd have the final resolution.

He rode through the city in one of its famous London taxis. There were still targets the Beretta must erase from the map. Once he was the faithful owner of a Glock of the same caliber, nine millimeters, but this Beretta 90two had a different feel. It was like a projection of his hand, the bullets spitting from his fingers. The Glock was more brutal, made for war, and, despite causing the same destruction, it kicked back on each shot, too much for a perfectionist professional like him. He'd opted for the less temperamental Beretta. Guns don't have a conscience, only the person who uses them. They serve their owner blindly.

The vibration of his cell phone could be felt over that of the car going over the irregular surface of the street. He took a wireless hearing device out of his jacket, placed it in his ear, and pressed a button to take the call. He listened wordlessly to the demand.

"I'm on my way," he said in French, then he frowned slightly.

"That's not good."

The lights of the city shone in the backseat while the cab went farther into the city. They came and went, invading the compartment, dispossessing him, making another presence in an unending play of yellow light.

"I'll take care of that. Everything will go according to plan. I have people on site. I'm certain they'll act appropriately." He disconnected.

He took the phone and pressed four numbers. Two rings later, someone picked up.

"Where are you?" he asked brusquely. "Perfect. I'm coming. Don't leave."

He turned the cell phone off and permitted himself a slight smile. Things were going well, after all. The team was good. He pressed the button that let him speak to the driver.

"Change of plans. Take me to the Chelsea and Westminster Hospital."

26

Certainly Abu Rashid's face had seen better days. Cut lips, a swollen eye, some internal and external bruises, especially on the body hidden under the white tunic. In spite of everything, he didn't flinch and kept the same calm expression of knowing a greater truth.

The foreigner went to the lavatory, and then sat toward the back, in one of the luxurious, cream-colored seats of the private jet flying over Bulgarian territory. The plan had been to return by commercial flight from Ben-Gurion airport with a stop in Frankfurt, before the final destination, Rome. Abu Rashid's words so disturbed the foreigner's superior that he immediately ordered a private jet prepared and a change of route. They left from Kefar Gallim in order not to raise suspicions, and Abu Rashid cooperated at every step. Perhaps that was why his face was in the condition we witness. The blood on his lip had dried, but his swollen left eye seemed to get worse with each passing moment. All this because he wouldn't recant the words he allegedly heard from the mouth of Our Lady in a vision. Because he was Muslim, this greatly aggravated his situation. There was no mention in religious history of a Catholic saint appearing to a believer of another religion, let alone the Mother of God in person. The situation was far worse when the Virgin's words, communicated to the world by an Arab, could cause a split in the Catholic world.

The foreigner thought through the various possibilities as he looked out the tiny window. There was nothing to see, since it was dark; night had set in for the rest of the flight, which wouldn't be long. As God was his witness, he didn't want to hurt the old man, but if he opened his mouth in public, everyone would suffer. He needed to be silenced, discredited, which was not difficult. A Muslim who sees Mary should be seen as a joke, cause only for laughter in the Catholic and Muslim worlds. The problem was what he was saying. If someone more intelligent were to think deeply about his words, he might easily find the truth behind them. And that couldn't happen. They had to force the man to recant. Even if he actually saw Mary. She had to understand. There were Catholics and others, no mixture, and there never had been. The day this happened religions would come to an end. This was serious, very serious.

He got up again and went over to Abu Rashid's seat. He rested with his eyes closed, smiling slightly.

"I know it perfectly," the old man said without opening his eyes.

"What do you know?"

"I know where we are going. You were going to ask me that."

The foreigner sat down on the seat beside him and sighed. He looked at the black briefcase strapped to the seat. Besides Abu Rashid, another of his responsibilities was that black case. These premonitions were unreal. Not for a moment did he think it was really the Virgin helping the old man. He'd lose all power and control if he let this idea take over. It would be her way of saying she couldn't count on him or any other Christian. Or that in reality everyone was equal. *Shit, shit, shit.*

"It might not seem so, but I'm here to help you," the foreigner claimed. "If you cooperate, it'll be good for you and for us."

"I haven't done anything but cooperate," Abu Rashid declared with his eyes still closed.

"I need more on your part, Abu Rashid," he observed. "Give me what I need to intercede with my superior, and you can go free."

A smile stretched the Muslim's lips.

"What you want is for me to lie."

"I want you to cooperate."

"I'm cooperating," Abu Rashid insisted. "It's not my fault you've chosen the wrong side. But that's your right. There are always two sides."

"Are you saying you are defending those who want to harm the Church?"

"I am Muslim. I couldn't be less interested in your Church." He opened his eyes wide. "I am on her side."

"I am, too," the foreigner claimed.

"You are on the side of the Church."

"The Church that represents Her. That has made her image, made her what she is."

"Precisely," Abu Rashid offered, turning his eyes toward the window with a sad expression.

"What do you know specifically about the place we're going?"

"I know everything I have to know." The old Muslim stroked his beard.

"Can you be more explicit?"

"Do you know what happened the thirty-third day after the death of the former pope?"

"I don't know," he sighed. "But, according to my contacts with my superiors, I don't think you know, either."

"Maybe it would be better for me not to know anything," Abu Rashid confessed.

"Does that mean we are coming to an agreement? You can forget everything you believe you know?"

"My friend, you're a politician and work for politicians. I can't trust you. You're capable of selling the Mother of Heaven herself."

The foreigner got up and rolled up his sleeves. There were still a few hours of flight remaining.

27

LÚCIA

August 31, 1941

Lúcia was not a pretty girl. The only thing attractive about her face, which was not repellent, were her two black eyes below thick eyebrows. Her hair, thick and black, was parted in the center and fell over her shoulders. She had a snub nose, thick lips, and a large mouth.

—FATHER JOHN DE MARCHI, *The True Story of Fátima*

There was a certain urgency in the writing. The words surged forth, under pressure, hurled out by the ink of the pen, sliding in a precise, correct form, without unacceptable blots. These weren't characters written with pleasure, elaborated or adorned in execution. It was work, a duty, an obligation. A copy of something already written by someone else. It lacked the spirit of her own creativity. The pages were white, unlined, some written on, others about to be. Those filled with the mother tongue, Portuguese, were separated into two piles, set on the left side. The reason for this separation was unknown, but it had an intrinsic curiosity that would call the attention of more perceptive persons, if there were any in the room. The pile on the right presented a beautiful handwriting, innocent, nothing scratched out, born of a pure hand, perhaps ingenuous, young. The other was like this page that was now being written, under pressure, captive to a vague obligation, as if she knew she shouldn't transcribe those words that weren't hers. The two stacks of manuscript pages were written in the same hand, but the difference between them stood out.

Why?

The same woman was writing them, seated in a dark wooden chair, bent over a small table, by the light of a candle, her head looking at the sheet of paper from a few inches away, though she didn't see it clearly. Not that this was the reason for the difference in handwriting. The page at her right side was what needed to be copied in her hand.

The emissary in a black cassock came into the narrow cell, silently, with quiet steps toward the woman and deposited another pile of pages on the right side.

"These are the last, my daughter," he said in a low voice to avoid disturbing her.

"You can leave them." The young woman stopped writing and gave the man a worried look. "Are you sure about this? It doesn't seem right to me."

"Don't worry, Lúcia. You are doing the right thing under God's direction, through His intermediary, His Eminence Don Alves Correia da Silva."

"But I don't understand this secrecy. Our Lady—"

"Calm yourself," the emissary interrupted. "The faithful have to be led. We have to be very careful how we pass on the information so that we don't risk ridicule, while we reach the most people."

"I don't understand. You speak of secrets. Our Lady has never spoken of secrets."

"I am going to explain it to you again. The pope has decided to divide the revelations into three secrets. First, the vision of Inferno. Second, the end of World War One and the prophecy of World War Two, if we continue to offend God and Russia does not convert. Third, the secret we haven't succeeded in interpreting. I ask you not to write about that one now."

"I understand. But Our Lady has never shown me any vision of Inferno, nor spoken about the World War Two, nor of Russia's reconversion . . ."

"As I have told you, it is necessary to prepare the faithful. Trust the Holy Father. He knows what to do."

"I trust him," Lúcia declared.

The emissary settled into a chair.

"Has Our Lady appeared to you?" he asked timidly.

"Every month."

"Don't forget to put down everything she tells you. It could be important."

"Everything Our Lady says is important," Lúcia muttered.

"Of course . . . That's what I meant to say," the man mumbled. "But the way the message is communicated to the world has to obey the orders of the pope. Only he knows how to divulge it to the faithful."

Lúcia agreed with a nod.

"I shall follow the instructions of the Holy Father and the bishop. Please, tell them that which . . ." She reflected. "That which they call the third part of the secret should be revealed no later than 1960."

"I'll share that with the bishop," the emissary continued. "Everything Our Lady communicates should be put on paper and sent through me to the Bishop of Leira, who will decide how to proceed."

Lúcia listened attentively. She understood nothing of the rules that regulated the Church. Things should be simpler. When Our Lady appeared to her, wrapped in an aura of peace and happiness, simplicity reigned. She didn't ask for secrecy. In truth she didn't ask for the Church's direction. This happened on its own, since it was natural the clergy would want to be cautious. Still, she'd never thought the control would be so intense, guarding her from public life, alleging she needed protection, instructing her what she should say about herself and the Virgin. She had nothing against that, no criticism. She even liked the obsequious attention she was shown by the Church. They treated her like a fragile glass bubble that might break with the slightest touch. There were days, though, when she couldn't avoid the feeling of being a prisoner, suffocated. It was the destiny God reserved for her and couldn't be attained without sacrifice.

What bothered her wasn't the control the Holy Father and Bishop exerted over her visions, but the fictitious elements they attributed to Our Lady, which she never mentioned in her apparitions. The emissary's explanation was satisfactory. They knew better than anyone how to spread Our Lady's message.

"Don't forget. Never talk about this with anyone whatsoever. You'll return to Portugal soon and enter the order of the Carmelite sisters. That's the will of God and Our Lady."

She would obey the vow of silence. Meanwhile, she'd write what they asked her with the certainty that soon Our Lady would appear again, and she'd be able to put on paper the felicitous words the Virgin offered. Those were the happiest moments in her life.

28

The ferry ride was no added relief for James Phelps. Three and a half hours of travel had left his seat numb.

The breeze was a little chilly, but that didn't matter. The sky was clear and full of stars, which he admired, since people rarely look at the stars in the sky unless they are astronomers, amateur or professional. He'd felt absorbed into the forces of the universe for some time. Rafael was talking to the captain of the boat inside the tiny pilothouse. In the darkness he could make out the lights dotting the coast of Dover, the beginning of the British Empire. He had all the ingredients for feeling at peace with his God, but he was uneasy. Rafael was a man of mystery and didn't confide in him; that was obvious. Otherwise he would have told him about the bodies they transported in the van. At least they sleep the sleep of the just.

They hadn't exchanged a word since the service station in Antwerp, but Phelps had worked out his own plot, hundreds of guesses and theories, trying to understand even the smallest part of the puzzle. Still, he only managed to feel his seat get more numb as each mile went by. They had entered France and covered the north coast to Calais at high speed, where this ferry waited for them. Everything very well organized and Phelps, as always, a spectator involved in the plot but completely outside the plan.

"Enough," he heard himself say in the emptiness.

He reached decisively into the inside pocket of his jacket and took out his cell phone. He had a right to have the latest technology, unless it was a corrupter. It had advantages when used with sense and moderation, like everything. He ran through the list of numbers for the name of the person he wanted to call. As soon as he found it, he pressed the green button that began the call. He glanced over at the bridge where Rafael continued a friendly conversation with the captain, who apparently was an acquaintance.

"I'm still completely in the dark," he said the second someone answered the phone. "I don't know anything. They ordered me to accompany him, but he doesn't open his mouth about anything. It's difficult like this. If he doesn't talk, I think Monsignor has a duty to inform and alert me." He gave the said Monsignor an opportunity to accept the suggestion. It might seem by the decisive tone of voice that Phelps had had enough, since it would never cross his mind to give orders to anyone, let alone a monsignor. "Yes, of course. I beg your pardon, but I've been in the dark since we left Rome." Pause. "It was not my intention," he excused himself submissively. "I beg your pardon, but please understand, we are carrying corpses with us. You have to agree that is not normal. I'm not used to—" He was interrupted on the other end of the line. "You heard right, Monsignor. Bodies. According to what I know, an English couple." A new pause. Surely he had pricked the curiosity of the prelate. "In the English Channel on the way to Dover."

He felt a painless pressure on the back of his hand that made him open it, involuntarily, and release the cell phone into another hand, Rafael's. He hadn't heard him come up.

"How dare you?" cried Phelps, reddening. He couldn't tolerate this man anymore. He hadn't the least respect for people or for age, which surely deserves dignity.

Rafael threw the phone out in an arc that was lost in the darkness of the night. It fell into the waters of the channel, causing an inaudible splash confused with the noise of water thrown up by the prow of the ferry.

"Are you crazy? How dare you?" Phelps was possessed, looking at the water where the voice of the monsignor had just drowned.

Rafael looked at him with that indifference characteristic of his style. He said nothing, unaffected by his companion's anger.

"I . . . I . . . I . . ." Phelps insisted in his shocked litany.

He regained his customary calmness. His reproaches dried up quickly before his tongue was tired. The flush of fury would certainly be worth seeing, if the light was favorable, since even a gentleman like Phelps has the right to be carried away by passion by an insult like this. Or no? It was a cell phone, his own, and he was in the middle of a conversation. There could be no greater insult.

Rafael put a hand on Phelps's shoulder and looked him in the eye seriously. "Turn the other cheek," he said. "Turn the other cheek." He returned to the bridge to resume his conversation with the captain.

Exactly fourteen minutes later, Rafael was sitting behind the wheel of the Mercedes van again, and Phelps, silent, in the passenger seat, prepared to continue on to the unknown destination, unknown at least to all the Phelpses of the world.

Phelps consulted his watch, which Rafael hadn't yet thrown overboard, or in this case out the window. It was still on Roman time, an hour ahead of old Albion, an easy calculation. It was 3:03 in the morning. The night was half over, as was his anger. If things continued like this, he was going to lose respect for his calling, dishonor Almighty God the Father, and slap this Rafael in the face . . . or maybe it would be better not to start down that road. Surreptitiously he prayed his bad thoughts away. It was incredible what this man managed to arouse in him. The road in front was deserted, marked by the light poles on the sides. Only the noise of the van's engine disturbed the harmony of the night.

"When are you going to stop treating me like a puppet?" he asked finally in a calm tone to try to get some information in another way, although it was clear nothing mattered to this man driving the Mercedes.

"I'm not treating you like a puppet," Rafael answered without taking his eyes off the road.

"No?" For a moment he lost his self-control, and this negative reply left his lips louder than he intended. He continued to appeal to calm to reunite his efforts and take back control of his body and spirit. "I don't know where we're going or who the corpses are we're transporting or what's going to happen to them. It's a sacrilege, you ought to know, to profane corpses in this way. They deserve eternal rest." He enumerated with his fingers, remembering not to raise his voice. How could Rafael maintain that cool posture? That was another thought that went through his mind and upset his serenity. It was irritating. "You had the gall to throw my phone in the channel." Here his voice began to change. Simply remembering brought back his anger. "I can't tolerate this situation any longer." He vented his feelings. "I feel lost, I don't know what I'm doing here . . . I want to help, don't get me wrong, but I don't know how." He sighed. "If you want to know the truth, I feel like a prisoner. I'm in your custody, and I don't know why, or what punishment awaits me."

A sudden slamming on of brakes scared away Phelps's thoughts and left him shaking with anxiety. The van stayed perfectly stopped in place.

"What's going on?" Phelps asked, his instincts awake, looking around on all sides.

Rafael was imperturbable and calm.

"Is something happening?" Phelps wanted to know, unable to make out anything out of the normal.

"I'm waiting," Rafael declared.

"Waiting for what?"

"For you to get out of the van."

Phelps stared at Rafael in astonishment.

"You want me to get out of the van?"

"No. It's you who feels like a prisoner. I'm showing you that you can go whenever you consider it convenient."

The two men looked at each other in silence for a few moments. Rafael was not a man to leave things unresolved. When there were doubts, he preferred to clarify some and leave others to develop further. The message he wanted Phelps to get was that this mission would go on with or without him.

"Keep going," Phelps decided.

"Is that your wish?" Rafael pressured him, since that would ensure that the problem remained resolved.

"Go on," Phelps repeated.

The Mercedes accelerated in the direction of London. The tension in the cab of the van had disappeared.

"You'll know at the proper time why you're with me. Only then will I tell you what you have to do. As far as the rest, it's better you not know, for your own safety."

"Why so much secrecy?"

"It's not my part to explain all the ins and outs of the operation."

"But what's all this for? Are we following something or someone?"

Rafael left Phelps's question hanging, a suspenseful pause to arouse his curiosity, common to all master manipulators.

A phone call broke the silence. It could only be Rafael's cell phone, since Phelps's lay on the bottom of the channel. Rafael looked at his watch, and, for the first time, Phelps saw him show doubt. Whoever it was had some effect on him.

"Yes." He finally paid attention.

Sixty-one seconds passed in which he didn't pronounce one word, but his indifferent attitude abandoned him. His frown revealed his tension. *He's human after all*, Phelps thought.

"You don't have more information?" Rafael asked over the phone. He listened to the reply. "I know who can help us. I'll take care of it . . . if we're still on time." He disconnected the phone. Phone conversations between people like this are always as brief as possible.

Something had disturbed Rafael; his indifference seemed to have vanished. His mind was an engine working at high speed. Even Phelps could understand that.

"You didn't finish telling me," Phelps interrupted when he thought enough time had passed. "Are we following someone?"

"John Paul the Second," Rafael answered dryly.

"What?"

29

This bedroom community on the outskirts of Washington, D.C., can influence everything that happens in the world. It's like a vital organ of society that, if functioning badly, can cause great problems. We are speaking of Langley, Virginia, the headquarters of the Central Intelligence Agency. Here is where intelligence information is gathered from all over the world and presented to the political powers of Washington, when justified.

Invented or trustworthy, fictional or real, the truth is that the confidential reports that go out from here have the power to start wars where they don't yet exist, suppress any political movement, here or on foreign soil, or modify the routine of thousands of people at a specific point on the globe, only because, according to preliminary studies, it could benefit the American economy.

Nevertheless, after sixty years, the company was beginning a new era. Other institutions, in particular the NSA, the National Security Agency, for many years called the No Such Agency, uses technology that always reaches farther and faster than the human resources the CIA relies on, contributing to its decline and even discredit. Besides, machines are always more trustworthy. The age of spies has changed suddenly and without warning.

The night shift has just come on, and that irritated the assistant subdirector since it meant extra hours, the sacrifice of family time again, the third time that week. For Harvey Littel, country came before anything else, and perhaps this explained the elevated rate of divorce among those working in this branch, though not yet in his case.

He'd covered a lot of miles through these corridors. He punched in at seven in the morning. The sun hadn't yet risen, and now he returned crossing them toward the elevator to the east wing. His thirty-minute run every morning before coming to work gave him an enviable physique that enabled him, at fifty-three, to endure the daily pressure to which he was subjected as assistant subdirector.

Harvey Littel's function could be explained fairly simply. He carried out all the dirty work for the subdirector, who could present it to the director as his own work, or, if Harvey Littel, by some chance, screwed up, everything could go to hell, but only one head would roll . . . his.

He glanced at the windows that reflected the darkness of the night, noting how he'd spent one more day unable to take advantage of the sun. At five in the afternoon, he'd told his wife, Lindy, not to count on him for supper.

"Harvey, it's the third time this week," she complained as soon as she was able to get to the phone, out of breath. Harvey didn't even need to tell her why he was calling. "See if your boss will let you off. This is what happens when your husband does more than everyone else." She continued to complain, more with herself than with him, speaking faster. She was a lonely woman, now that the children had gone their own ways. She believed her husband was too busy with his work in the computer store where he was head of the sales department. Lindy couldn't figure out why her husband thought he was saving the world every day. Nor did Harvey imagine that her protests over his not showing up for dinner were made from on top of the bed, his bed, where she'd been romping at five in the afternoon with her lover, Stephen Baldwin, who, by chance, happened to look like the famous one, and who, by another coincidence, also worked at the agency, in the commissary. Stephen Baldwin was at Harvey Littel's house at five in the afternoon every Monday, Wednesday, and Friday, without realizing that Lindy's husband was the assistant subdirector of the CIA.

Once in the elevator, Littel swiped his card with level-two clearance and punched in the code assigned to him. The elevator read the order and began to descend to the second basement floor, buried well underground, where they waited for him. These clearances went from the lowest grade, six, to one, and controlled the security and information each individual could access inside the building and in other branches around the territory. The security system was able to monitor in detail the work of everyone associated with the agency. So, if it was necessary, it would be possible to consult the dates and know that Harvey Littel descended in elevator number twelve to the second basement floor at twenty-three hours, forty-five minutes, and twelve seconds today. The cards assigned to the employees not only cut off access to classified information, but also the entrance of all whose card didn't permit access. If anyone inattentively tried to enter where he shouldn't, he'd see the door stay closed, the elevator immobile, and would be called soon to Internal Security to explain himself.

But these are the house rules, of little interest to most mortals, and only serve to entertain us while the elevator takes Harvey Littel to his floor.

A soft braking came before a male voice announced the obvious, "Door opening." Harvey went down the dark hall, with hidden sensors that turned on fluorescent lights as he walked with a firm, energetic pace.

After turning once to the left and twice to the right, he came out into another hallway, narrower, with a bluish light and a door at the end. Harvey swiped his card through the scanner on the wall and entered the code. Once he was on the other side, the door closed behind him, separating one world from another.

The light created an eerie atmosphere, as if transporting the passersby to another dimension. Several doors ran along both sides, all closed. The one Harvey Littel wanted was the third on the right side. He passed his card through the scanner. It was surely one of the movements he performed most often during the day, facilitating access to places he wanted to go. The door opened as soon as he entered the code, and, taking a deep breath, he went in. There were seven people inside awaiting him.

"Good evening, gentlemen," he greeted them, his tone appropriate to his professional role.

Almost everyone got up from around the large rectangular table the participants barely filled. Only the old colonel, Stuart Garrison, didn't. Not because of the born arrogance that made him insufferable but because of the wheelchair in which he sat. These were the wounds of war that remain for life, received, as he never tired of telling, in March of 2003, on the outskirts of Nasiriyah, during the second Gulf War, when the allied forces were marching at top speed through Iraqi territory on the way to Baghdad. A rocket launched by some Shiite fighter at the Humvee in which he was riding took away from him any capacity for movement from his waist down, affecting his sexual ability, as well, although nothing affected his strong character. That act of terrorism earned Colonel Stuart Garrison the Medal of Valor. In colorful terms the report said that Stuart Garrison, trapped in what remained of the frame of the twisted Humvee, was able to destroy the menacing fighter about to give the coup de grace with another rocket. A sure shot to the head of the insurgent saved the lives of the six occupants of the vehicle, although one didn't survive his wounds and died on the way to the field hospital, after waiting five hours for a rescue team. What the report didn't mention was that the shot killed a teenager less than fifteen years old whose action was revenge for the allies annihilating his innocent family. These were the atrocities of war, implacable for both sides. Once removed from the battlefield, Stuart Garrison was invited to join the agency because of his privileged contacts in the Middle East, making him the most imbecilic, arrogant, and deficient man in the CIA—words not spoken out loud by those who knew him.

Having explained the trivia of why some get promoted and others not, let's move on to the rest of the group in hierarchical order. They were seated three on each side, leaving the head of the table for the assistant subdirector, Harvey Littel. If the subdirector or director had been here in person, they would have been at the head. On the right side, from the point of view of the assistant subdirector, we have Colonel Stuart Garrison, responsible for communications with the Middle East and Russia, followed by Wally Johnson, lieutenant colonel, liaison with the U.S. Army, intrepid and proud, some forty years old, although still in puberty in regard to military careers. Across from them, Sebastian Ford, diplomatic attaché, politician by profession, one of those who seem to have excellent judgment, but, when you squeeze their words, seem to have no juice, nothing there. He was the demagogue who connected the department with the president, always prepared to sacrifice anyone for the good of his career . . . and, of course, national security. The others were not important enough to name, since they have little relevance for the unfolding of our story. But let's not forget the woman who wasn't seated at the table. She was next to the wall, behind Harvey Littel with a notebook ready to take her frenetic notes. She was Priscilla Thomason, Harvey's secretary.

"Have we managed to connect already?" Littel asked no one in particular.

"Yes," someone responded.

"Good. Barnes?" He spoke into the phone in front of him. There was no answer.

"Barnes?" he tried again.

The same response.

Littel raised the earpiece to his ear. He dropped it immediately.

"We've been disconnected. Put it through again," he ordered.

He was surprised when no one moved.

"Are you waiting for me to do it?" He was irritated by such a lack of zeal and picked up the phone again.

"Dr. Littel," Priscilla called from behind him, getting up. At least someone was attentive. "The connection has been made, but . . ." She lowered her eyes.

"But?" Littel urged her.

"He's hung up." Stuart Garrison finished the sentence.

"He's hung up?" His expression showed amazement. He thought for a few seconds. "And you've tried to reconnect?"

"Several times," the assistant standing by his side told him. "He's not answering."

Now Littel understood the pensive mood when he entered. His mind seethed with theories and possibilities. Barnes had disconnected the direct, secure line that connected London and Langley. This was a serious breach of protocol, with the risk of disciplinary action and possible dismissal, if it couldn't be justified. Barnes lost his temper easily, nothing was ever good with him, but from that to jeopardizing his service record through his own actions was a big step. He was active, highly esteemed, a true pack mule who took on an entire continent and the outskirts of another two. This couldn't be. Something must have happened to make Barnes disconnect. Something serious. Unless . . .

"Has anyone called the Center of Operations?" He assumed the attitude of a leader. There was hope.

"No," Stuart replied.

"It didn't cross our minds. Geoffrey Barnes's conduct is very serious," Sebastian Ford added. "I'll have to tell the president about this." He seemed to have difficulty opening his mouth to utter these words. His hair plastered with gel, a pen in hand, held vertically, his back stiff, he seemed conscious of each gesture, each word as well. Everything was calculated. The politician in true form.

"He wouldn't be able to answer if the building has fallen on top of him, for example," Littel argued. "Call the Center of Operations."

The diplomatic attaché's threat irritated him. He'd sold out, a self-proclaimed patriot who didn't even know the story of the founding fathers. If there was anyone Littel would put his hand in the fire for, it was Barnes. He'd have a plausible justification . . . there was no doubt.

Priscilla took the telephone and pressed four numbers. The beeps resounded in the office from the speaker, while everyone watched apprehensively. Finally they heard a static noise that preceded the connection and a nervous voice, probably because of where the call was coming from. They didn't receive a call from the "cave" every day.

"Staughton." More like a question than an identification.

"Good evening, Agent Staughton," Littel greeted him affably. "This is Harvey Littel. I'm sure you've heard of me . . ."

"Yes . . . yes, sir," Staughton replied quickly. His discomfort was audible.

"I'm going to get directly to the point, Agent Staughton. I need to speak, urgently, with your superior, Geoffrey Barnes." His manner was serious now.

"Well, I'm not with him, but . . ." he stumbled, excusing himself.

"Do me a favor. Look for him."

"Of course," Staughton answered respectfully. "I'll call you back in five minutes." Again more question than statement.

"No, no, Agent Staughton. You don't understand me. I want you to look for him now. Now. Understood?"

The silence proved that Staughton didn't expect that order. If he had known the large audience listening to him, he would have buried his head in the sand. They all listened attentively to Staughton's panting breath. If his eardrums weren't ringing with the beating of his heart, he might have heard the sighs from thousands of miles away.

"Agent Staughton, are you listening to me?" Littel pressed on. Time was wasting.

The answer came ten seconds later, when Littel was about to repeat the question.

"The chief's in the office."

Littel felt relief as if he were taking a cool shower. Wonderful.

"Perfect, Agent Staughton. Please pass him the phone."

"Ah, that's not going to be possible," Staughton refused.

"Why not? Do what I tell you." Although he was being rude, Littel knew why Staughton couldn't pass him the phone. Barnes had another priority.

"What petulance," Colonel Garrison muttered.

Littel got up and raised his hand for silence.

"It's just . . . it's that . . ." Staughton stammered.

"It's what, man? Spit it out."

Except for Littel, everyone in the room was holding his breath. What the hell could Barnes be doing that his agent couldn't pass him the telephone?

"He's on the direct line with the White House."

Everyone turned red except Littel, who saw his thinking rewarded. He looked at Sebastian Ford, careful not to let his inner smile show. It was always good to see those who think the worst of others have to retreat with their tails between their legs and eat their words.

"Excellent, Agent Staughton," Littel continued. "Tell your superior to call me as soon as the call from the White House is over."

"Okay, sir." Staughton's voice recovered its confidence. Maybe someday he'd even get used to receiving these calls.

The call ended on the American side, leaving a heavy silence in the air. Everyone chose a neutral or indistinct point on which to fix his eyes. Most preferred the mahogany table, the phone in second place. Littel was the first to stir the waters, as he ought to be. The time for thinking was past.

"It's obvious the situation has escaped our control," he asserted sadly.

"In an alarming way," Wally Johnson concluded.

"Sebastian," Littel said. "Prepare the crisis committee."

"When?"

These politicos could only deal with appointments and schedules.

"Within a half hour," Littel answered curtly.

Ford went out with his two assistants, who'd been seated at his side.

"Colonel?" Littel turned to Garrison this time. "Who do we have in Russia?"

"Nestov and Litvinenko."

"Didn't Litvinenko die of poisoning?" Wally Johnson was astonished.

The colonel and Littel looked at him with disdain.

"There is more than one Litvinenko in the RSS," the old soldier explained.

"Try to contact them. This is going to get hot, and we have to be prepared."

The colonel wheeled himself back and then was helped by an assistant around the table and into the hallway. Littel, Priscilla, and Wally Johnson remained. Littel and Johnson exchanged looks silently, and immediately burst into laughter, leaving Priscilla astonished.

"Get us two coffees, please, Cil," Littel asked, wiping his eyes from laughing. "It's going to be a long night."

Priscilla went out to fulfill their request, leaving the two men alone.

Wally was the first to break the silence.

"What do you think the president wants with Barnes?"

"A recipe for cod in sauce," Littel responded seriously, provoking a laugh from the soldier.

"How does it happen that that son of a bitch Keys gets himself killed so far away and in a bathroom?" Wally Johnson wanted to know.

"That is what we have to find out. The idea of collateral damage doesn't convince me."

"Do you think anyone suspects?"

"No," Littel answered without a shadow of doubt. "It's going to be a bombshell."

30

A door saved Simon Lloyd from certain death. That irony was lost on those whose steps echoed in the dark hallway, disturbing the silence that had fallen since night began. This was the orthopedic wing of the Chelsea and Westminster Hospital, and moans caused by iron staples that pierced the flesh and fixed the bones couldn't be heard only because the doors were reinforced and closed. So Sarah's loud footsteps and John Fox's quieter ones at her side left no impression on the patients stretched out on beds who could be seen inside the rooms, where they tried to endure another night of pain, hoping for a better day soon.

Sarah avoided showing the weakness she felt. It wasn't a good time, walking next to an SIS agent, although John Fox acted reasonably friendly. Simon Templar preferred to stay in the car, thus his absence—better to stare at the steering wheel than serve as a lady-in-waiting for the Portuguese woman.

As soon as the coroner had taken Grigori Nestov's body out of the ruins of Sarah's house, Agent John Fox had tried to excuse her. Enough things had happened, enough surprises, for one day. They could call her if they needed to make further contact. Conscious that the orders she'd received from JC were very explicit, she decided to go to Waterloo International, the train station, and catch the first Eurostar for Paris. Once there she would call her father. She remembered her duty to visit Simon Lloyd. It was the least she could do for all he'd gone through. So she decided to visit the hospital, close to her house, before heading out for Wellington. She asked John Fox for someone to go with her, and he offered to do it himself, as we see. It was a way of checking on Simon Lloyd's condition for giving a statement. By coming with Sarah, he would gain Simon's confidence sooner and be able to arrange a visit the next day.

Sarah's worried expression didn't leave him unmoved. He sympathized with what he had seen of her, not just as a woman but also the mystery she carried within her. This woman knew a lot, although he didn't know what or how. He had read the articles she wrote for the paper, sometimes of great help to various SIS departments, as well as foreign agencies, he well knew. It was as if Sarah were sending messages to the various factions, Western and East European, as if she knew them all, their true, secret identities. She would be a valuable asset as an ally; for that reason, John didn't understand Simon Templar's suspicions. Was it because it was a woman who possessed the information they all would like to have? It didn't matter. He, John Fox, was ready to invest in this contact, not pressure her, show himself a friend. Later he'd see. Good things could come out of artifice.

"Don't worry," he tried to calm her. "He'll be all right."

"I hope so." Sarah took a deep breath and answered with a timid smile.

But it's not him I'm thinking about, she confessed to herself. Her mind went back over the past year, remembering everything. He was at her side, the protégé, in spite of his irritating tendency to not tell her anything, or tell things in bits and pieces according to a logic only he understood. How much she missed him at moments like this. She felt alone, unprotected, although she didn't feel truly in danger despite all the deaths around her, some close enough she didn't want to think about them, as with the explosion in her house, JC's alarming call, and all that. Not like that night a year ago when they'd broken into her house and put a gun to her head. Maybe today's bad guys, whoever they were, knew she was with SIS agents. That was obvious. The short ride to Waterloo International would be tense, since she didn't plan to accept John Fox's amiable company again. They couldn't find out about her intention to leave London.

"What's the room number?" Sarah had forgotten in her nervousness.

"Twenty-five," John Fox told her. "We're almost there."

Their steps closed the distance to the room, where, according to the reception desk, the patient from emergency number 259475, listed under the name Simon Lloyd, was assigned. They passed 19, 20. Unconsciously Sarah slowed her pace, feeling defensive about what she was going to find.

She breathed deeply. . . .

21 . . .

Breathed deeply . . .

22 . . .

She hung back even more, letting John Fox get a few feet ahead.

23 . . .

She let herself close her eyes for a few seconds. Why was this happening all over again? No one should have to go through this twice, or once, for that matter. Simon Lloyd, another victim of the power of men who didn't care what means they used. All because of her, her father, his past . . . last year . . .

24 . . .

"Do you feel all right?" John Fox stopped, waiting for her three paces ahead.

Natalie and Greg. Dead. Why? She didn't want her mind to wander through these dark subjects, but she couldn't avoid it. So many doubts, so many questions, no answers. She thought about her own life in danger. Natalie and Greg punished by someone without the least respect for the existence of others. Let alone fear of God. They were the most dangerous. She could think of one reason why they were killed. Yes, it existed. Practically inoffensive but real. That must have been what killed them. Good God, capable of killing for so little . . . if only he were here . . .

She opened her eyes.

"Yeah, I'm okay," she replied in a weak voice. If the light hadn't been so dim, almost nonexistent, John Fox would have seen the dark ocean in her eyes.

"Ready?"

Sarah's apathetic look restrained him. "I'll go in first and call you in later." It was an order, not a suggestion, and John Fox had to accept it.

Sarah opened the door carefully to make as little noise as possible and closed it as soon as she was inside. The room was brighter than the hallway.

She dried her eyes with her hands and looked at the bed where Simon was sleeping, leaning against the head of the bed, his head hanging to the right side. Saliva ran from his open mouth onto his hospital gown. Somebody must have been visiting him, and he had fallen asleep watching television, remaining in this position, half sitting, slumped over, not quite one or the other. The television cast an irritating glow in this moment, brighter, darker, great contrasts of tone, depending on the image from the horror film that filled the screen. Simon slept on, oblivious to all this, giving a slight, almost imperceptible snore of pure exhaustion.

Sarah took a deep breath and approached her colleague cautiously in order not to startle him.

"You're back?" she heard Simon say without opening his eyes, in a drugged voice.

"It's me, Sarah."

She looked him up and down, inspecting him carefully at first glance to see if he was all there. She saw nothing more than a bandage on his left hand. Of course the light blanket covered his lower body from her inspection.

Simon opened his eyes and smiled alertly.

"Hi, boss. What time is it?" He looked at his wristwatch on top of the table. "Damn. So early," he exclaimed. "What are you doing here at this hour?"

He pulled himself together to sit up completely.

"I've come to see you." She intended to maintain a normal voice with the intention of sending a subliminal message that everything was all right. "How are you?"

"Considering the circumstances, I couldn't be better. My hand was burned, as you can see, and a leg. I'm in a little pain. It seems I hit a bus, but I'm ready for more."

His shining eyes suggested a certain pride in having passed a test and survived.

"What really happened? Was it really a gas explosion?"

Sarah was not prepared to discuss this. Besides, she didn't have answers to Simon's questions. The less he knew, the better for him, at least for now.

"Yes, that's what it was," was all she said. "A problem with the installation. I apologize for that," she excused herself awkwardly.

"You don't have to apologize. It's over," Simon replied a little condescendingly. "We can continue the trip tomorrow." He changed the subject
with a smile.

"You'd better stay here and recover. I'll take care of everything."

"No way," he protested. "I'm fine."

Journalistic perseverance. A hazard of the profession. One of the first
things one learns if one hopes to survive in the job.

"Besides, there are people who are going to want to ask you questions
in the next few days," she added. She wasn't going to give in. The danger was
real. She had to be alone, not dragging more innocent people along with her.

"More?" He moved his hand in irritation more than he should have
and let out a moan. "I'm sick of answering stupid questions."

"Careful. Calm down," Sarah replied, going over to him and passing
her hand through his sweaty hair. "Who's been here?" she asked, as if this
were only a normal conversation.

"Scotland Yard, the FBI, also MI6," he sighed with annoyance. "They
were right here at my bed when I woke up. After the doctors, they were the
first people I saw."

"And what did they want?"

"To give me instructions, but I think I can tell you. We're in this together."

Sarah brought a chair over to the bed and sat down to listen carefully.

"I've been the victim of a gas explosion and that's what I have to tell
anyone who comes here. If they ask me about you, I'm to say I don't know
where you were. I went to the house alone."

"And have you complied?"

"Of course. With others it's been easy. The hardest has been convincing
our editor."

"He's been here?"

"Yes. And asked about you. Haven't you gotten his calls on your cell?"

"Where I was I couldn't get calls."

"I don't know if he was convinced, but I told him we'd split up. I'd gone
to pick up some stuff at your house, while you were buying some clothes
you needed. We had agreed to meet at the station. If he asks you, this is the
official version. Don't get me in trouble." He offered a timid smile.

"Don't worry. You can relax. I'll call him and confirm the story." She carried on in a friendly manner with Simon, although her mind was seething with other matters more pressing than convincing the editor.

"I never thought I'd be a media star. All because of a gas leak. They even apologized to me."

"Who?"

"The MI6 people." Maybe the late hour caused Simon to mix subjects of conversation, perfectly understandable. "For giving me instructions, but under the protection of the terrorism law, they didn't want a different version of the story released to the public, based on conjecture and sensation." He pushed himself up a little straighter, remembering not to use his injured hand, which made the movement more difficult. "Explosions scare people."

"And the others? Were they friendly, too?"

"Not at all. They were assholes." He was truly indignant just thinking about it.

"What did they want?"

"To know how everything happened. If I was smoking, carrying some kind of explosive, including something solid, liquid, or gas or any other substance. They're arrogant shits and don't seem to believe what we're saying."

I know the feeling well, Sarah thought.

"In bad moods. Especially the Americans. They think it all has to do with them." He continued complaining. "It seems we committed a crime to make work for them. Imagine if it had been an Al Qaeda bomb. I'd be a prisoner now." He swelled with anger.

"Shhh. Everything's fine. Just the fact you can complain is a good sign."

"How is it they let you come in at this hour?" Simon asked.

"I came with an SIS agent," she answered without thinking. "They wouldn't have let me in otherwise."

"Yes, it's true. A secret service agent." He looked thoughtful. "Sorry. I didn't think of that. How has everything gone? Do they think it's a terrorist act?"

"Don't worry about that," she answered evasively. "He's outside waiting to be introduced. Are you up for that?"

"You're the boss."

"I'm not here casually. I'm your friend. It's up to you."

Simon didn't take long.

"Tell him to come in."

Sarah got up and went to the door. She opened it and looked around the hallway. There was no sign of John Fox. Strange. It didn't make sense he would leave without letting her know. Maybe he'd gone to the bathroom. She went out into the hall for a better look, but she hadn't been mistaken. She didn't see him anywhere around. Sarah, worried, went back in the room. *Forget it. He'll show up.*

"He's not there. He must have gone to the restroom. Have you had other visitors?" Sarah tried to make conversation.

She decided to wait for John Fox for fifteen minutes. After that, so long.

"Well, my parents came, all upset, as you can imagine, but they left more relieved. My sister was here also. But that was just the time the FBI men arrived, and she had to go. They're so rude, arrogant . . ."

"Forget it, Simon. It's over now. It's not worth being in a bad mood over people like them," Sarah advised him.

"You're right." He took a deep breath. "You're right." He smiled, a pleasant thought replacing his bad memory. "And my girlfriend visited. That was the best visit, except for my family, of course. She's shy. She only came after the others left."

When Simon got going, he didn't shut up. He would tell his whole life story to whoever was there. Poor listener. Sarah thought about this as she saw her colleague coming to life in front of her eyes. Good. One less thing to worry about.

"Look at the present she brought me." Simon reached over to the table and got something. "What do you think of this?"

Sarah gazed, mouth open and astonished, at the bottle of old port, vintage 1976. It couldn't be. It couldn't be.

31

With every step Geoffrey Barnes wore out the blue carpet covering the floor. His imposing figure, the product of the good restaurants that abound in this part of Europe, contributed to this, as well as nervousness about a phone conversation he'd had with the White House not five minutes before. We ought to amend this last information, since the telephone the color of blood, or victory, was linked to the office of the president of the United States of America wherever he was, not just in the White House. This time, the red phone was on board *Air Force One*.

Barnes was furious with worry, not his usual reaction after speaking with the president in person, instead of his tame lackeys.

Staughton opened the door and felt the bad vibes coming from the chief. His curiosity would have to wait for a calmer time. It didn't bode well, if the communication had left him in this state. But he needed to give him the message to avoid being called on the carpet.

"Chief, the guys at Langley want you to call them." He braced himself for a scorching blast of words.

"What do those sons of bitches want?" This contemptuous reproach was uttered without raising his voice, but still showing irritation.

"It was Harvey Littel who called. He asked that you call him as soon as the call with the White House was over."

"How did they know I was on the telephone with them?" Barnes raised his eyes to Staughton.

"He wanted me to pass you the telephone. I had to give him a reason."

"You did well. You did well," Barnes affirmed, sitting down in the chair and exhaling with relief. "I'll call shortly. Let them wait. Fuck them."

Theresa came in with the order. Double burger with cheese, pizza, and a cold Carlsberg. Just in time. Drench his disgust in beer and fill his belly with carbohydrates. Thompson came in behind her with a stack of papers in his hand.

"News?" Barnes asked, appraising the containers Theresa was putting on the desk.

"Big." Thompson shook the papers.

"Is it going to ruin my appetite?" Barnes asked, sounding put out. "If so, you can wait outside."

Thompson paid no attention to his boss's words. They were typical explosions, nothing to interfere with the work. What he had was important information, and Barnes would thank him for it later. That's the way it worked.

"Several hours ago there was an explosion in a house at Redcliff Gardens, near Earl's Court," Thompson began, as enthusiastically as a reporter with an exclusive story.

"An explosion?" Barnes inquired, just for the sake of asking a question, his mouth full of the double cheeseburger he was savagely chewing. Immediately he raised the neck of the Carlsberg to his mouth to help him swallow the mouthful.

"Anything else, Dr. Barnes?" Theresa asked from the door.

"No thanks, Theresa. I'm fine."

She went out and left the three men alone in a silence broken only by the loud chewing and tenacious swallowing of enormous bites. In three tries, the burger disappeared. He moved on to the pizza.

"What about this explosion?" Barnes asked with his mouth full.

"The authorities are talking about a gas leak."

"Then there's no story," Barnes concluded.

"No," Staughton agreed.

"My men have been to the site and put together some information. It wasn't a gas leak. It was a bomb," Thompson threw out dryly, immediately capturing the attention of the other two. Barnes stopped chewing.

"Are you sure?"

"Absolutely. And there's more. MI6 is involved in the cover-up of everything."

"Why? What do they gain from that?"

"I don't know yet. But they know the way we are. We like to sniff around . . . and what have we discovered, off the record?"

Barnes and Staughton waited in suspense for him to finish his statement.

"They found a corpse in the debris. It belongs to Grigori Nestov. Do you know the name?"

"Grigori Nestov," they repeated, searching their memory.

Staughton gave up. "I have no idea."

"I've never heard the name," Barnes said with certainty.

"Nor I," Thompson finished with a triumphant smile. "But it turns out Nestov is part of a unit of the RSS."

"Wow!" Staughton responded. "RSS?"

Barnes and Thompson looked at him reprovingly. What's so special about being RSS when they were CIA?

"We have the RSS in the middle of an explosion. What does that mean?" Barnes wondered, raising the last piece of pizza to his mouth.

"But it gets better, and this will get you out of your seat," Thompson anticipated.

"What?" Barnes asked expectantly.

"The house. It's in the name of Sarah Monteiro. Does that tell you something?"

"What?" This question came in a deafening shout with Barnes on his feet leaning on the desk.

"Wow," Staughton repeated. "Confirmed?"

"Completely confirmed," Thompson clarified, holding out the papers and handing over the first page to Staughton so he could see with his own eyes.

"What bastards," an enraged Barnes said. "Who are these English? Who do they think they are? They're only good for wiping our asses, and now they want to leave us out of the picture? Assholes."

"What's happened to the girl?" Staughton asked, as he handed the paper to Barnes, who grabbed it roughly out of his assistant's hand.

"Her location's unknown. There's one injured, checked into the Chelsea and Westminster Hospital, but it's not her."

"Go there immediately," Barnes ordered. "And I want her in front of me before the morning is over. Find out what a Russian agent was doing in her house. That's top priority. Understood?" He didn't wait for an answer. Of course he'd been understood. "Is there news about Jack?"

"On my part, nothing," Thompson said with some frustration. "Payne is a stone in our shoe and knows how to irritate us."

"Not much," Staughton replied with some confidence. "We've located a reservation for a Mercedes Vito van rented out at Fiumicino and left at Schiphol."

"Amsterdam," Barnes said out loud to himself. He sat down again looking thoughtful.

"The reservation was made in the name of Rafael Santini," Staughton continued.

"Rafael Santini?" Thompson asked. "Do you think that could be him?"

"It's him," Barnes affirmed with certainty. "His real name, it seems." Anger rose in his voice.

"Why haven't we discovered this before?" Thompson asked curiously. The individual had always caught his attention.

"Because he hasn't wanted us to," Barnes clarified. "A good double agent, infiltrated, a traitor, a son of a bitch, only reveals himself when it's good for him." He turned to Staughton. "Where is he?"

"We don't know." He looked down.

"We don't know?"

"No. He's been seen in Antwerp, Dunkirk, and we've lost all trace of him after that."

Barnes raised his hand to his chin, thinking.

"He's heading this way," he said at last.

"What?"

"How?"

"He's coming here," Barnes repeated. "He picked up the van in Amsterdam, went for the bodies, was seen in Belgium and France. He's coming here, and I want a welcoming committee to meet him when he arrives. No mistakes."

"How can you be so sure?" the ever-calculating Staughton asked.

"Because of something we don't have the luxury to fight at this time."

"What?" his assistants wanted to know.

"The fact he's scattered the clues so we can easily pick them up. That bothers me. He wants us to find him." Barnes changed the subject. "Go to the hospital and see what condition the injured man is in. I want a thorough interrogation. His mouth can't be injured. Make him spill everything. It's time to satisfy Langley."

"What about the White House? Anything worth mentioning?" Thompson asked. He had held that question back since he came into the office, waiting for the right moment . . . this one.

Barnes took a last swallow of Carlsberg before answering.

"A weapon of mass destruction, my friends. A weapon of mass destruction."

32

W ho . . . who gave you that?" She couldn't look at anything but the bottle. "Can I see it?"

Sarah took the bottle from his hand before Simon could reply. She analyzed it in detail. Even the provenance was identical, Real Companhia Velha. It couldn't be.

"My better half." Simon was puzzled by his boss's behavior. Sarah was a woman full of mysteries. One of them was the way she was examining the gift bottle. "Does it remind you of Portugal? I didn't realize you were so sentimental," Simon teased, discreetly, fearfully. Little by little he was regaining confidence. Little by little.

I wish it were just sentimentality, Sarah thought. With the bottle in hand she went to the door and opened it a little. She looked around the hallway with all senses alert. No one. No John Fox. Panic gave her goose bumps. She closed the door slowly and confronted Simon, who looked at her inquisitively.

"Your girlfriend gave you this bottle?" she asked again. "You're sure?"

"You could say that," Simon answered, beginning to react, still puzzled.

"Either she did or she didn't." It was not worth getting annoyed with him. She had to remain cool in order to think logically. Quick thinking meant staying alive.

"It was . . . not my girlfriend."

"You said it was from your girlfriend," Sarah interrupted. "So who was it?" The hell with this guy not getting to the point. It must be the medication.

"I know what I said. . . . He's my boyfriend," he explained reticently.

Fear thickened in Sarah. That explained a lot.

"You have a boyfriend?"

"Yes."

"And he gave you this bottle?"

"I've already told you yes." Simon observed Sarah for signs of disapproval, but didn't detect any. Only confusion . . . in both of them.

"Simon, do you trust me?"

"Of course," he answered without a trace of doubt.

"Good." She looked at him seriously. "Get up and let's go."

"What?" What a ludicrous suggestion. "When?"

"Now."

"Sarah, what's going on?"

Sarah went over and put her hand on his shoulder to encourage him.

"Simon, trust me. Our lives are in danger. If we don't get out of here right now, we're going to die. I don't know how else to say it."

Simon was unable to say a word. Doubts swept through him, making him collapse back on the bed. Sarah would have to explain better than she had.

"Simon, do what I tell you. Get up."

Simon didn't move.

Sarah sighed and shut her eyes before making a decision.

"It wasn't a gas leak." *Thy will be done.* "It was a bomb set to go off when the key was turned."

"What?" he blurted out, astonished. "Who would do that?"

"Who doesn't matter at the moment, Simon. If we wait here to find out, it's all over for us."

It took Simon two seconds to decide. The new facts were relevant. He got up, put on the hospital slippers, and dragged himself to the door. Sarah would have to support him. He leaned against her side. It'd be easier for Simon, slower for the two of them. There was no time to waste.

"Wait here," Sarah told him, helping him to a chair at the side of the door next to him. Simon preferred leaning on the arms to sitting down. Sarah opened the door slightly and looked from one side to the other. The way was clear.

"Let's go."

Sarah returned to serve as a crutch for her injured colleague, and they started down a dark, deserted hallway. All the groans, cries, and whispers of the patients and machines were a catalyst for fear. One step at a time, a sweaty, dragging pace, looking around in search of danger. The end of the hallway seemed to stretch out forever, eliminating hope of getting outside. Even their shadows made them afraid someone would jump out of the darkness, without warning, and put an end to everything.

"Are you sure?" Simon whispered, afraid.

"I am. Do you think I'd take you out of your room and jeopardize your recovery if this were a game?"

Of course not. Sarah would never do that. Damned hallway that seemed never to end. A metallic noise clanged behind them. Some object dropped or thrown. Sarah and Simon paused. They looked back. They didn't see anyone. Maybe they should try another way, but Sarah knew only this one she'd come down with John Fox. They started down the hall toward where the noise had just come from. Better to be in known territory. Their hearts beat harder. Simon, leaning on Sarah, his body trembling, asked to rest. The sound of her heart beating in her ears interfered with her thinking. Ironically, the end of the hall was closer with every step, since their fear of what was around the corner, next to the elevators, was palpable.

Finally, they took a left at the corner and saw the elevators. The source of the noise was a metal tray, fallen from a cart left against the wall. Surgical instruments were scattered on the floor, scissors, scalpels, forceps of various shapes and sizes, and other objects not easily identifiable at first glance. They moved cautiously toward the elevators, avoiding the repulsive metal. Sarah could see dark stains on some of the cutting instruments, but the dim light didn't reveal colors. Her imagination suggested red blood, which made sense with the scalpels. Still, it didn't seem plausible that a doctor or nurse would leave all these instruments without sterilizing them.

She put those thoughts out of her mind and hit the elevator button. It was interesting how something as natural as the presence of blood in a hospital could seem out of place. This was a theory Sarah could analyze later. Right now they had to get out of there.

A loud sound signaled the elevator was arriving on the floor and the doors would open. There were three possibilities, left, right, and straight ahead. It turned out to be the center elevator. The doors opened, revealing agent John Fox inside, looking at Sarah.

Simon dug his fingers into her arm so hard that, if it were not for the adrenaline pumping through her body, she probably would have cried out.

"This is Agent John Fox, who came with me," Sarah, relieved, let him know.

Simon loosened his fingers, sharing Sarah's relief.

The agent was silent and kept staring at Sarah.

"I've something to tell you," Sarah began, raising the bottle of port she carried in her only free hand. "They . . ."

John Fox took an uncertain step forward and supported himself against the open doors like Samson between the columns of the temple.

". . . are here," Sarah finished without thinking what she was saying.

They both stared at John Fox, who was concentrating on the two of them in a strange way.

"Get out of here," he managed to whisper before blood gushed out of his mouth. He took two steps forward like a zombie, terrifying Sarah and Simon, who moved back to give him room without taking their eyes off him. John Fox swayed for a few moments until his body fell heavily on the cart, knocking it over and spilling the rest of the instruments on it. From his back there protruded no less than six scalpels.

Sarah gave a silent scream and pulled away from Simon's hand.

Steps. They heard steps in the hall they had come down. Without stopping to think about it, they stepped into the open elevator. The steps got closer each moment. Firm and cadenced, neither hurried nor slow, provoking horror in Sarah Monteiro. They kept pressing the button marked zero, but it could as well have been any other, as long as the doors closed and the footsteps no longer were heard.

"Close, close, close," Sarah pleaded in a vain attempt to hurry the process with words.

A shape rounded the corner of the hall and ran toward the closing doors.

"Simon. Simon," they heard shouted.

Impelled by a voice he recognized, he looked for the button to open the doors and pressed it.

"Simon, no!" Sarah shouted. "Don't."

Simon paid no attention to his boss and kept pressing the button. The doors promptly opened to light up the shape and reveal a spruce gentleman, older than Simon, closer to Sarah's age.

"What's going on, my love?" the unknown man asked.

"Oh, God, it's been horrible. Someone's killed this man." A tear ran down Simon's face from the fear and disgust of having seen what he'd never forget. "They're after us, Hugh."

"What? Who?" The man seemed lost, looking at the body and Simon, not looking at Sarah at all. "Who's done this?"

"I don't know. I don't know." Simon was weeping.

"Oh, my love, don't cry." Hugh comforted him, placing himself inside the doors in a way that prevented the sensors from shutting automatically. He embraced Simon. "Okay, it's all over." He kissed him tenderly on the head. Simon broke down in a torrent of held-back emotion. "It's okay. Okay. It's over."

The two men turned in their fierce embrace so that Simon was outside the elevator and the other inside with his back to Sarah, who watched indecisively. She didn't know what to do, or, she did, but feared the consequences. The embrace cooled, although the men continued holding each other. Simon's eyes were closed and moist, enjoying every second.

"What are you doing here at this hour?" he asked. "How did you get in?"

The man hesitated a moment, but the embrace hid this doubt from Simon. Only Sarah saw it, even though he had his back turned to her. It helped her make her decision. And this was the right time to act. She hoped it worked.

"Uum . . . I have an acquaintance here. I couldn't bear thinking about you."

The force of the bottle of old port, vintage '76, striking Hugh's head, shattered it at once. Only the broken neck remained in Sarah's hand.

"That's for stealing what doesn't belong to you, *Hugh*." The emphasis on the name showed her suspicion of its veracity.

What a waste of good wine streaming down the head of Simon's boyfriend.

Before Simon could perceive what was happening, Sarah grabbed him by the arm and pushed him inside the elevator, while she took advantage of Hugh's momentary stunned condition to shove him outside. She was surprised to see him leave the elevator so easily and fall to the floor. Magnificent. In a single action, since the sensors were unhindered, the doors closed to carry the occupants to the ground floor. Mission accomplished. Sarah's excitement was such that she didn't notice the small hole appear in the mirror behind her, caused by the badly aimed gun of this supposed Hugh.

"What are you doing?" Simon cried. "Are you crazy?" He pressed the button for the floor they'd just left. "Fuck. How could you do something like that? You can't suspect everyone in this way." He was completely beside himself.

"Shut up, Simon," Sarah ordered firmly. "This bottle." She shook the neck that remained in her hand, as a defensive weapon, lacking something better. "When this was a bottle, it was in my house. Do you remember where I told you to look for the file?"

Simon managed to think with difficulty. He remembered her instructions. To get a file that was behind a bottle of vintage port.

"And?" he questioned. "Is it the only one? Aren't there more in the store?"

"The box was intact in what remained of my house. The bottle was not inside it. Can I make things any clearer?"

Tears returned to Simon's eyes.

"It can't be. It can't be. He must have an explanation." He saw his life falling apart in front of him. "It must be a coincidence." He grasped at this hope. There were other bottles of vintage '76 port. It was a present from Hugh, nothing else, without all these complications. He remembered Hugh's shape at precisely the moment he lost consciousness in Redcliff Gardens. It could be a confused vision, a hallucination, a trick of the mind that made him see his lover just then.

"I'm sorry, Simon. He's probably not even named Hugh. I'm very sorry."

The elevator reached the floor, and the doors opened. Waiting for them was Simon Templar.

"I'm glad I found you," Sarah said, panting. "They've killed your partner and they're after us."

Sarah helped Simon leave the elevator, and they walked toward the exit, sixty feet away. Except for Templar, no one was in sight.

"Where do you think you're going?" Templar asked in a roguish way.

Sarah kept dragging Simon Lloyd toward the doors to the outside. They heard an electronic sound similar to a walkie-talkie. Sarah quickened their pace, pulling a groggy Simon.

"James, you are truly stupid," they heard Simon Templar say over the radio.

A hiss passed the ears of Simon and Sarah and shattered the marble floor, raising dust and stone. A shot with a silencer. Sarah looked back and saw Templar, gun in hand, aiming at them. Simon seemed not to care, but Sarah felt panic and frustration. A gun pointed at her again a year afterward.

"The next one's in the head," Templar warned, putting the radio to his mouth again. "James, come down. I've got them."

33

You're kidding me."

"No, I'm not."

"Are you telling me that we're running around pursuing a dead man?" Father Phelps expressed disbelief. "I went to His Holiness's funeral two years ago."

"Me too, along with more than four million other mourners."

"Less than a month ago I visited the Crypt of the Popes and prayed in front of his tomb. Peace for his holy soul." He ignored Rafael's observation.

"Some people don't die."

"Sure, historically, intellectually, culturally. Caesar, Emperor of Rome, will never die, Henry the Eighth, Christopher Columbus . . ."

"John Paul the Second," Rafael completed the list. He concentrated on the few miles remaining on the M20 to the outskirts of London.

"John Paul the Second," Phelps admitted. "Then we're on the trail of his legacy."

Rafael turned toward Phelps and looked at him gravely before immediately returning his eyes to the motorway and the red lights from the vehicles in front of them heading for the frenzy of the capital, neither confirming nor denying Phelps's conjecture. All in due course.

Although Phelps was driven by morbid curiosity about Rafael's orders from Benedict XVI, sleep began to overcome him. He'd been awake for almost twenty-four hours, and the movement of the van and engine noise began to sound like a cat purring. He closed his eyelids against his will.

When he noticed Rafael change direction, he opened his eyes.

"Are we there yet?"

"Not yet," Rafael answered. He was looking at the side mirror. "Someone's following us."

"Seriously?" A lump formed in Phelps's throat, dispersing sleep completely. "We're being followed by someone?"

Rafael accelerated the van in the direction of a secondary road. Phelps bent his head to look in the side mirror at the white lights shining at the van. His heart pumped blood faster through his body. His breathing tightened.

"Are you sure?" he asked fearfully, without taking his eyes from the mirror.

"Absolutely."

"What are you going to do?"

"Nothing," Rafael said. "Keep going."

"Where are we going?"

"A little farther and we'll know."

Phelps undid the top button of his shirt, suspicious, distressed.

"I'm not feeling well," he announced. "Rapid heartbeat."

"It's nerves," Rafael said. His attention was on the road and the car following them, without any sign of worry.

"You . . . you're not scared?" Phelps asked with his mouth crying out for something wet to placate his thirst.

"Afraid of what?"

Rafael insisted on not looking at him and assumed an insensitive tone highly discomforting to Phelps.

"Of them." He pointed behind them.

"No," Rafael replied dryly.

Phelps looked at the side mirror again, estimating the distance that seemed to have shortened more each time he looked, according to his eyes, not very trustworthy at this hour.

He wanted to ask more questions, but Rafael's expression wasn't encouraging. Best to wait to see if this passed; let's hope it did with God's help.

These doubts disappeared when Phelps saw the lights of the pursuing car almost bumping the van, leaving him worried and full of panic. The speed of the two vehicles wasn't fast, less than fifty miles an hour, and every time he looked at Rafael, he didn't seem willing to go faster.

"Don't you think we should speed up?" he asked at last in a voice heavy with fear.

"There's no danger."

"No?"

"No. Whoever's watching isn't going to let us see him."

"Are you saying they aren't following us?"

The vehicle behind signaled the van with its lights. Phelps understood less and less what was happening. And still less when Rafael came to a complete stop.

"What are you doing?"

"Stopping."

"Isn't that dangerous?"

"No." Rafael unfastened his seat belt and opened the door. "Stay here."

Phelps wanted to protest, but Rafael closed the door, leaving him stamping his foot. He used the side mirrors to try to see what was happening. The lights of the other car were turned off, and he saw two men getting out and approaching Rafael, who waited for them calmly, leaning on the back of the Mercedes. They shook hands, which was a relief. Bad guys didn't greet their future victims. If it wasn't a trick. Rafael talked to the two men for a few moments. A little later one of them gave him an object Phelps couldn't identify. Rafael turned to come back, and the Englishman managed to hear the men saying good-bye with an "À bientôt." Strange.

Rafael climbed into his seat, started the engine, and took to the road again without offering one word of explanation.

The silence was deafening, which infuriated Phelps. Who did Rafael think he was? Someone incapable of showing the least sign of confidence in him. He was a worthy inheritor of the tricks and intrigues of the Vatican. He would make an excellent member of the Curia and had everything necessary to become one. He always kept the best to himself and deliberately weighed his words. He created an advantage over others that confounded allies and enemies, like a puzzle in which he alone knew the position of each piece in the total shape.

"So it turns out no one was following us," Phelps said, keeping his eyes on the road. An insult to his dignity as a man and a prelate that he didn't care to call attention to.

"I never said they were following us," Rafael explained. "I said that someone was coming behind us."

"One has to watch his words with you," Phelps replied, holding back his disgust. "Not everything is what it seems."

Nothing more to say. Silence took over for the rest of the journey, unpleasant, uncomfortable, always there. The great city of London spread before them, with more traffic. Even so, Rafael managed to pass slower cars.

Rafael's cell phone rang. He looked at the screen identifying the caller and answered.

"*Alors,*" he said into the phone, indicating he knew who was calling. He listened to a message that lasted for some time. He showed no sign of interjecting either a thought or agreement. Seconds later he disconnected and, without warning, pulled the Mercedes around in a U-turn, making Phelps hit his face on the door window. He took off now at high speed in the opposite direction in the wrong lane.

"Are you crazy?" Phelps protested.

"It makes more sense with the wheel on this side," Rafael answered, dodging vehicles coming from the other direction on the correct side, protesting vehemently with their horns and swerving away as they could. Some ended up crashing into vehicles pulled over to the shoulder of the road.

"Careful!" Phelps cried out, holding on to the seat.

Rafael continued driving, indifferent to the insults or admiration from other drivers. Phelps shut his eyes and said no more. He crossed himself and prayed silently, *Our Father, Omnipotent, free me from this black sheep, separated from the flock, and put him on a better path. . . .*

Many horns and insults later, the van came to a stop at the entrance of a Victorian building in disrepair. Rafael scrutinized the surroundings carefully on all possible sides. Phelps wanted to discover where they were, but was still too upset to speak reasonably and calmly. Besides he was from Newcastle, in the north, and not obliged to know where things were in the capital of the empire.

"Where are we?" he asked Rafael.

Rafael ignored the question and took out the package given to him by the two unknown men, under the cover of night.

"What's that?"

Rafael answered by tearing off the paper that covered something inside.

"Good God. What do you need that for?" Phelps asked, surprised.

Rafael checked the chamber of the Glock and took off the safety before looking at Phelps.

"Not everything is what it seems." He left the van and went toward the door of the abandoned building.

34

What hurt him most was the slap, backhand, that knocked him to the floor. The physical pain was nothing compared with the empty heart and the loss of dreams of a wonderful love, beautiful, idyllic, and innocent, destroyed by harsh reality. For Simon Lloyd the idea of life as beautiful came to an end with that blow. Rage overwhelmed him, but a kick in the stomach made him rethink his priorities while the pain spread through his body. Anger could wait.

Sarah hadn't received the same treatment because those were the orders received by Templar and his associate.

"Herbert's coming. He says not to touch them," Templar warned when James or "Hugh" or whatever the son of a bitch's name was was about to apply another round of blows.

"He'd better get here soon," James protested.

Sarah and Simon Lloyd now found themselves shut in a small windowless room completely sunk in claustrophobic darkness. Simon had received more slaps from his ex-lover, who was enraged by the bottle Sarah broke over his head. And since the asshole couldn't take the insult out on Sarah, he hastened to do so on Simon. He, Simon, was only a job, something that guaranteed a paycheck. . . .

Sarah heard Simon snuffling or trying to disguise his crying by mumbling in a low voice. It made her feel completely discouraged. Another victim paying for something she'd done.

"What are they going to do to us?" Simon asked, breaking the silence.

"To you, nothing," she said confidently. She'd do everything to prevent his paying for being with the wrong person. No one ought to suffer for that.

"I was so deceived, so deceived." A damp sound confirmed the tears that still ran down his face unseen.

Simon meant Hugh as the target of these words, but Sarah applied them to herself, since she felt them deeply. She considered herself a disappointment for everyone, beginning with the people she loved, always in danger, pleading, wounded, dead. So she repeated, "They won't do anything to you." She would strongly resist cooperating with this Herbert, unless he agreed to release Simon. She might be tortured, but she'd only talk when Simon was out of danger. Even if it was the last thing she did, which was possible, she intended to save Simon. The worst was if this Herbert didn't want information from her and was only coming in order to personally carry out their killing. If that was the case, Simon would pardon her, if her lack of power wouldn't permit heroic acts. If she found Herbert willing to negotiate, only one of them would survive. This was hard reality, not the stuff of detective novels or films. The good die before the end.

"What's happening? What have we done to deserve this?" Simon lamented in the darkness of the room that blended into the mental darkness overwhelming him since he'd turned the key in the unlucky door of the house at Redcliff Gardens and summoned the unknown.

"You haven't done anything, Simon," Sarah said with shame. "This . . . only has to do with me and me alone," she confessed. "Last year a price was put on my head," she began to explain.

It was impossible to see anything, but Simon straightened his back against the cold wall, sharpened his ears, and waited.

"My godfather, whom I hardly remembered, sent me a list of names belonging to a secret Italian society. It contained the names of some very important people in politics, the judiciary, religion, and all at the international level. Even my father's name was on it. I found out later that that list was in John Paul the First's hands the night he died . . . and I knew that he was murdered."

"What?" Simon could barely believe what he heard.

"Just what I said. The sect, called P2, and the CIA started to persecute me."

"Good God," Simon exclaimed. "Are they the ones trying to do us in?"

"No. This is something else entirely. I still haven't figured it out."

Simon stopped talking in order to let Sarah spill her guts.

"Things poured out in such a torrent that I couldn't process all the information given to me. Even today I don't understand how far-reaching it all is."

"Sarah, we're prisoners in a basement or whatever this is. There are two armed men outside prepared to give us a passport to eternity."

Despite all that was happening, Simon seemed more in control of himself. The power of resignation has this consequence. We accept what has happened and look for better times to come. Of course the fear was always present. A quick death was preferable to torture, though obviously the best result would be if they opened the door and let them go with apologies for what they'd done, regretting a terrible mistake in identification, accompanied by a farewell dinner in some luxury restaurant. Ah, the power of the imagination, unconquerable, even in the face of imminent death.

"Let's try to make a deal with everyone," Sarah continued.

"What kind of a deal?"

"We won't turn them in, and they won't hurt us."

"Maybe they've repented," Simon suggested.

"They'd have a lot to lose. Besides it's the Holy See that protects this agreement," Sarah said thoughtfully. She wanted to put the loose pieces together to see if they made some sense. "That is something else."

"One thing not missing is crazy men with power," Simon revealed his feelings. "Do you think they're going to leave us here the rest of the night?"

"Long enough to soften us up." It was Sarah's turn to sigh. "They're specialists in that."

"I don't know about you, but I'm softer than a marshmallow."

Two bursts of laughter filled the small room, completely out of place given their situation. Fear can even make a person laugh.

The sound of the lock turning put a stop to the laughing. Seconds later the light from the hallway filled the dispensary and blinded Simon and Sarah, who blocked the light with their hands.

"It's nice to see you feeling so good," James mocked them from the door, where they made out his silhouette. "Get up. It's time."

Simon swallowed saliva. His heart still went cold when he saw this cool killer who looked at him with curt indifference.

Without waiting for them to obey, James yanked Simon up brutally by his shirtfront. James had executed his job in an exemplary way. Now he wanted to make his scorn for Simon plain.

If Simon wanted to fool himself into imagining a sweeter scenario, a joke in tremendously bad taste, maybe, but still forgivable, two hard punches James had the pleasure of giving him in the face drove that fantasy out of his mind. Simon swallowed his impotent rage in silence. When all was said and done, James had the gun pointed at the head of his ex-lover.

"Leave him alone," Sarah cried, calling attention to herself.

The result was immediately visible. James turned on her with contempt. He looked her up and down in such a hateful way that Sarah lowered her head, nauseous. James took a short step toward her and put the barrel of the pistol under her chin, forcing her to lift her head. A bad man knew how to recognize the hate that emanated from her eyes.

"Your time has come," he said scornfully. He followed up with a punch to Sarah's face that split her lip.

"You son of a bitch," Simon immediately cried. "Without the gun you wouldn't be so brave, you bastard." Indignation overwhelmed him.

"Simon, shut up," Sarah ordered. One should never irritate men like these, especially James, who seemed very temperamental. "Please, Simon."

James returned slowly to Simon. He put the gun in his back pocket, covering it with the lower part of his jacket so Sarah wouldn't get crazy ideas. He opened his arms, showing off.

"No gun," he said sarcastically. "And now what are you going to do?"

Simon stayed leaning against the wall, in the same position James had left him. James paused for a few more seconds, awaiting Simon with his enormous open arms.

He ended with a guttural chuckle, triumphant. He had dared, and he had won, as he knew he would one way or another.

"You're a little faggot, Simon," he offered with a self-satisfied laugh over his little joke.

Simon just lowered his eyes. Not looking at James laughing in his face meant he could be laughing at anything. At least he could give himself that freedom. All he wanted to do was cry.

James interrupted his own laugh, almost mechanically, as if it were something he fabricated, manipulated, an actor improvising.

"Enough joking around. Come on. In front of me," James ordered in a voice of military command.

Simon and Sarah could do nothing more than obey. Even so, they were pushed down the hallway, not necessarily to make them walk faster, but simply to show who was giving orders . . . and who had to follow them.

They advanced along the dim corridor, their faint hope disappearing with each step. The jabs in the ribs, to one and then the other, with the cold barrel of the gun served as a catalyst for their negative, fearful emotions.

"Left," James ordered. He touched Sarah's shoulder with the gun.

They saw a closed white door. In the middle a sign read that only authorized persons were permitted to enter.

"This doesn't seem like a hospital," Simon said in a whisper. "I don't see anyone. Where are the doctors and the rest of the personnel?"

"This must be how it is at night," Sarah supposed in a murmur.

"And security?" Simon continued. "There's no security here?"

"It's better not to have anyone, believe me," Sarah warned.

"Quiet," James shouted. "Inside and keep your mouths shut."

Sarah pushed open the door to what had to be an unused room for interns. The space was big, a double bed stuck in a corner, enormous windows all along a wall, in another corner an open white cabinet. Long ago they'd gotten used to the antiseptic smell penetrating their noses. Right in the center, seated in a plastic chair, Simon Templar, gun in hand, looked at them gravely. The moment had come. Herbert must have arrived.

"Here are our little doves," James sneered. "I'm anxious to have a little fun with them," he said with his mouth right next to Sarah's ear. She closed her eyes. He stuck out his tongue and wiggled it a few inches from her skin. She didn't show it, but Sarah felt a convulsive nausea overwhelm her. If James didn't pull back, her stomach would turn over, and she'd end up vomiting on him.

"And now?" James asked, turning toward Templar, who looked like someone who had just heard bad news.

Templar ignored the question and continued to look at Sarah, or at least it seemed so.

"What now, man?" James asked again. He didn't like Templar's glassy stare.

The behavior of his colleague in service, butcher or mercenary, in the pay of whoever opened his wallet most generously, seemed abnormal also. James approached Templar, seated on the plastic chair, put his hand on his shoulder, and gave him a push.

"Well, then?" he said. "Are you sleeping with your eyes open?"

The gun in Templar's hand went off. Luckily it hit the ceiling where it was pointed. The vigorous push made him fall to the floor on his stomach without moving. James leaned over him in shock. Two holes in Templar's jacket explained the rest. James looked at the chair where the two holes were repeated with a smear of Templar's blood, dark red, the sign of death.

James panicked.

"Don't move," he cried. "Don't anyone move."

Confused, he aimed the gun randomly, turning toward every side, alert, looking for the source of danger, the origin of the bullets. He couldn't find the shells, which meant someone had retrieved them or the shots hadn't been fired inside.

"Don't move," he shouted again. "The first person who even breathes gets a shot in the head."

"Okay, okay," Simon agreed, uncomfortable with the panic reflected in his ex-lover's eyes. "Be careful with that thing."

Sarah looked around the room, trying to understand what was happening. When one lost control, one lost all dignity, she thought, watching James's contortions.

James approached the huge window slowly and looked out, holding himself back to look at the glass.

"Oh shit," he exclaimed.

Seconds later he was thrown back and fell on the floor. Simon let out a scream, more a howl, and saw, as did Sarah, a thread of blood flowing from James's head. His eyes were full of panic as he died.

"Fuck," Simon exploded. "Did you see that?"

Sarah didn't reply. A strained, out-of-place smile came over her face as she looked out the window.

"What's going on?" Simon asked, looking out the window for the reason for this smile.

In the glass, three small holes.

35

THE POLE AND THE TURK
December 27, 1983

The Holy Father never exhibited again the bright glow of former times. *The Lord gives the burden, but also the strength to bear it.* He thought of Franz Koenig, the enterprising Austrian, responsible, admittedly, for his election in October of 1978, as he climbed the stairs of the penitentiary in the direction of the cell. With him were the faithful Stanislaw, Dziwisz, his secretary, as always, and the director, some priests, and a few guards. A rigorous security perimeter was set up. There was no room for distractions after what happened two years ago in the foreign territory of Italy. *The Lord gives the burden . . .* The phrase returned to his mind. He'd thought about it a long time and come to a conclusion. What was important was not to carry, but to endure. He'd been the Shepherd of Shepherds in the Catholic world for five years and could confirm, better than anyone alive, that the papacy ages one and kills slowly. It was a constant weight, incomparable to anything else, and one had to endure it, not carry it, until one . . .

He climbed the stairs with difficulty, helped by Stanislaw. Age was another kind of burden. But it was the bullets that weakened him like this, making other such obligations and pleasures difficult.

The last step was like a victory without particular savor. It marked the beginning of recovering his strength, his breath. Wojtyla let himself be led through the gray, ugly hallway toward the cell where the young Turk paid for his notorious crime against the life of the pope, the very pope who was walking to see him.

"Are you all right, Holy Father?" Dziwisz, who'd devoted his life to the pope for many years, asked.

"Yes, I am," the Supreme Pontiff replied, panting.

"Do you want to rest, Your Holiness?" the director asked at his side.

"Let's keep going," Wojtyla said good-naturedly. A slight smile accompanying this wish could be taken as evidence of his sincerity.

Some dozen feet ahead they stopped in front of a gray, iron-plated door, where two guards were standing at attention, one on each side. The director ordered one of them to open the door. The subaltern obeyed quickly, not without first going down on his knees before the Holy Father and kissing his hand, as respect for the clergy demands from the faith of common men. He turned the key in the lock and entered the cell first, while his companion remained alert by the side of the door.

"Please, Your Holiness." The director extended his hand, indicating the way in.

Wojtyla entered, followed by Stanislaw and the director, leaving the rest of the delegation at the door.

Inside, the young Turk was on his feet looking at the Pole with an ashamed expression. He couldn't maintain it for long. He lowered his eyes at once like a good boy who has done mischief and awaits punishment.

"Holiness, take as much time as you wish," the director instructed. "A guard will remain here at all times with the safety off on his gun."

"Perfect." The secretary acknowledged the security instructions.

Wojtyla had already entered another level looking indulgently at the young Turk. They waited for the director to exit the cell. They heard the lock closing from the outside, followed by silence, oppressive for some, but not for Wojtyla. He looked at the Turk, who lowered his face submissively. The pope approached him, spontaneously lifted his wrinkled hand to the Turk's face and raised it. The dead-looking eyes of the young man had nowhere to hide, nor could he close his eyelids. They remained open, naked before the man who ought to have died two years ago, been wept over, buried, and replaced, since life continues and only those who are here matter, like these two now who must overcome cultural, religious, ideological, and other more deadly differences.

Suddenly the Turk allowed some life to revive his pale eyes. They filled with tears and seemed to give in to the pope's scrutiny. Wojtyla's hand lifting his chin was firm as a rock. There was neither censure nor reproach in his expression, no sign of visible condemnation, only a man, the holiest of them all, looking into the depths of the other's soul and understanding everything without saying a word or showing emotion.

As soon as Wojtyla let him go, the young Turk knelt at his feet with such devotion the guard almost fired on him. The pope raised his hand, as if saying lower the gun, and the guard obeyed.

"Forgive me, Holy Father," the Turk pleaded with his head bent over the feet of Peter's worthy successor.

Wojtyla crouched to lift him up and placed his hand on the Turk's head.

"Get up, my son. What has to be forgiven was already forgiven a long time ago."

He helped the Turk up and led him to the bed.

"Now, sit down," he ordered. "Take a deep breath and tell me everything, my son."

36

Harvey Littel entered the crisis office room with the confidence of a sovereign handing down laws to his people. Certainly Littel didn't make laws or carry out regulations. His world was a world apart, a world of intelligence, counterintelligence, military, civilian, industrial, and political espionage. There was only one rule on this battlefield: conquer at any price. Imbued with this spirit, Harvey Littel took his place at the table as the windows of the door automatically darkened to block the view from outside.

"Good evening, once again, gentlemen. Any news?" he asked, taking his seat in a comfortable leather easy chair.

"We have the Russian contacts on permanent alert," Colonel Garrison informed him. He took a cigar from his pocket and put it in his mouth.

"Perfect. Excellent." Littel raised his hand. "I'd appreciate it if you don't smoke in my presence. Thank you." It was obviously an order, not a courteous request.

Stuart Garrison looked at him with the Cuban cigar unlit. He put it back in his jacket pocket for a better time.

"And Barnes? Has he given us any information?"

"He's on the phone at this moment, Dr. Littel," Priscilla hastened to inform him with her notebook at the ready.

"Wonderful," Littel responded. "Let's not make him wait any longer," he decided. "Cil, put him on the speakerphone."

"Geoffrey Barnes?" said Priscilla, whose affectionate diminutive was only for her boss's use and no one else's.

"Yes?" They heard Barnes's guttural voice filling the room from the speakers placed in the ceiling. The phone, as in the previous room, was near Littel on the table.

"Barnes, how are you?" Littel greeted him with audible friendliness.

"Littel, good, thanks. You? Shut up in the second basement without seeing the full moon?" His voice expressed confidence, which in itself calmed everyone who was listening.

"You know how things are. We just get by. I bet you're sitting at your desk on the sixth floor watching the lights of the city, knife and fork in hand, ready to devour some roast pheasant."

"You're mistaken about the food, but it's a good idea."

"Well, all right. How does it happen that one of our own has been killed in Amsterdam?" He suddenly took a serious tone of voice.

"My people have been there. I was, too, last night, and I can affirm that the victim, Solomon Keys, was in the wrong place at the wrong time."

"Solomon Keys. It's confirmed." Littel corroborated the information Barnes gave him with what he already had.

Some sighs were heard in the room in recognition of the name. Most had heard him spoken about. Others knew him personally. Peace to his noble soul.

"Yes. Well, he died because he was in the Amsterdam Centraal station, in one of the restrooms, specifically when a British couple came in to satisfy their carnal desire."

Some listeners began to laugh nervously. It was humorous to hear Barnes tell a story like this with complete professionalism.

"Someone came in to eliminate the couple, and Keys paid the price," Barnes concluded.

"Okay, in any case we're going to ask for his service order to confirm whether the motive of his trip was tourism or an operation," Littel said, while gesturing for Priscilla to carry out that task. She agreed and wrote it in her notebook.

"He was over eighty years old," Barnes commented in the sense of excusing the old agent of the company of any blame.

"It wouldn't be the first time, Barnes," Littel clarified. "Sometimes they return to activity for a mission or two."

Although separated by thousands of miles, both of them imagined the same thing. Little old men with canes, arthritic and breathing with diffi-culty, but, if the agency needed them . . . That was their life, the best mar-riage they ever made, until death do them part.

"I agree," Barnes said. "But you probably won't find anything. The sub-jects of this operation were two English journalists, Natalie Golden and Greg Saunders."

"Who are they?"

"Prestigious journalists."

"Is the motive known?" Littel asked.

"We're tracking that down. We'll know something soon."

"Natalie Golden and Greg Saunders," Littel said to the room. "I want you to find out everything about them, from where they were born to who they hung out with. The smallest detail is important. Get working on it."

A group left the room to follow up on the order.

"Barnes, what else do you have for me?"

"There's been an explosion this afternoon here in London."

"In . . ." Littel consulted his notes on the table. "Redcliff Gardens. We're current on that."

"Okay. The explosion was of criminal origin and resulted in a death and an injury."

A certain uneasiness filled the room.

"We're already trying to question the injured party."

"And the death?"

"An agent of the RSS, a certain Nestov."

"Nestov?" Colonel Stuart Garrison exclaimed. "This was why he wasn't answering his phone." The colonel looked pale.

"Whose house was it? What was he doing there?"

Barnes didn't answer. A murmur rose in the room.

"Silence," Littel said. "Barnes, are you there?"

"I am."

"Then do me the favor of answering. What was he doing in the house?"

Barnes again showed no sign of answering. When that happened, it could only mean one thing. Littel understood and picked up the receiver of the phone while disconnecting the loudspeaker.

"Okay, Barnes, now it's just you and me."

It was clear the other listeners didn't like the idea of being excluded from the conversation. It meant greater secrecy, increasing their curiosity.

Littel listened attentively to what Barnes was telling him. His face began to change from perturbed and dark to an expression of irritation and unease.

The others noticed this change of mood and felt even more frustrated.

"Is this the president's position?"

Hearing Washington mentioned, everyone perked up his ears in vain. They continued hearing the same thing: nothing.

Seconds later Littel put down the receiver and disconnected the call. They could see a couple of drops of sweat running down his face. And it wasn't the fault of the air-conditioning. Something was bothering Littel, and if something worried him, it would soon worry everyone.

He drummed his fingers on the table for a few minutes, making the others, who kept silent in frustration, very nervous.

"Wake up the subdirector," he ordered at last. "And get a plane ready."

37

"This isn't very clear," Staughton protested from the passenger seat as Thompson got to the end of Montpelier Street and turned left toward Brompton Road.

"That's how the services function. If everything were clear, we wouldn't have a job."

"That's for sure," Staughton admitted. Uncomfortable, he took a deep breath. "But someone could be wrong."

"No, they couldn't."

"No?"

"No," Thompson repeated. "They're working with us. We work with them as long as it's in our mutual interest. We understand that, and they do, too."

"Yes, but according to the president."

"The president acts according to the interests of the United States of America. That's all he has to be concerned about. And according to those interests he swore to defend, he helps whoever can give him the most."

"It doesn't seem right," Staughton confessed.

"You're still a beginner in operational work in the field, so let me give you some advice. There are Americans, that's us, and the others. Don't ever get too friendly with the others because the day will come when they're our enemies. Do you understand?"

"It's still not right."

"Forget about being right. The world is not fair. Take my advice, and you'll never have a problem when the pieces change sides. Precisely because they're the 'others' "—he made quotation marks with his fingers—"they're mere accessories and the first to go when things change."

"I understand."

The two men continued the trip in silence. Staughton took in the moral lesson given by his colleague, who should be his friend, given the hours they spent working together every day. Maybe they were friends without knowing it, ready to give their life for the other one if the need should arise. It was curious how they spent nights together, traveling, on surveillance, listening, but continued to be strangers, perhaps because each one erected a wall that prevented any closeness. One of the things this profession had taught them and they never forgot was, contrary to war, in which your life is entrusted to the man next to you, here no one trusted anyone. Even your own shadow wouldn't hesitate to inform against you.

"Let's get back to Sarah Monteiro and Jack Payne. Don't you remember anything?" Staughton asked.

"You ought to remember something yourself. Or did that blow you received in Saint Patrick's leave you with amnesia?" His irritation was obvious. It wasn't something he liked to remember.

"I'm not proud of it, I agree. Nobody likes to end up out cold." He pointed at Thompson. "But I wasn't the only one. I won't mention any names, but I take note." He smiled, trying to break the bad mood the memory created. "On the other hand, I'm glad things turned out the way they did."

"The way they did? Why?" Thompson even took his eyes off the road to look at his partner, amazed to hear this stupidity.

"Because we would have had to justify three or four unnecessary deaths. Both sides reached an agreement by talking, and no one died," he concluded.

Thompson looked at him without knowing what to say, at least until he recovered his reason, and his irritation.

"They reached an agreement through blackmail. *Keep quiet or we'll publicize this.* And I should remember that the author of this blackmail died fucking in a bathroom in Amsterdam, next to your colleague, who was guilty of nothing and probably didn't know what she'd done. And they did it in front of him." He spat with anger.

"And now someone who has nothing to do with this shit has decided to even the score. And Uncle Sam—"

"Leave Uncle Sam out of it," Thompson interrupted. "Uncle Sam always knows what he's doing even if it doesn't look like it. Let's stop making him always the reason."

Staughton shut up. It wasn't worth arguing. Thompson was an agent with the vices of working in the field, in multifaceted operations, used to assuming personalities that had nothing to do with his identity. A true spy, a chameleon of a thousand and one colors, capable of convincing his mother, if she were still alive, that he was her husband.

Staughton was a very different case. Recruited by the information section for electronic surveillance, he had always operated inside. With a mouse and a telephone there was no adversary to confront. Operations took on an air of fantasy when everything was done with eyes on a monitor that determined the results, like a computer game that paid a real salary at the end of each week. Now, since he'd been with Geoffrey Barnes in the field, he understood that the shapes on the screen signify real places and the color points show flesh-and-bone people, like himself and Thompson, who was driving in a bad mood by his side. The mission accomplished described only one of the parts. There was always someone who lost, and usually much more than he expected.

Thompson accelerated, a reflection of his irritation, entering Fulham Road a little faster than the speed limit; there were no policemen around. He turned off rapidly to the right and drove faster. Staughton breathed heavily. He knew that any moment the hospital would come in sight on the left.

A mile and a half later the hospital appeared, as anticipated. Chelsea and Westminster Hospital, two ambulances parked in front with no one around, except a Mercedes van parked on the street with the lights on and engine running. Thompson turned around completely to pull up behind it.

"Look there." He pointed toward the entrance.

Staughton was also looking. A woman he immediately recognized was leaving the hospital with an older blond man and a young man dressed in pajamas.

Thompson stopped the car and got out, gun in hand.

"Sarah Monteiro," he called in a loud, commanding voice, pointing the gun at her. "Don't move."

Staughton got out of the car, confused, but without taking his gun out. His partner had the situation under control and was more used to pointing guns at people and even . . . shooting them without hesitation or conscience.

Sarah and the others obeyed promptly and even raised their hands, as film directors require, without receiving the order.

Thompson smiled, seeing the scene unfold under his direction, and looked at Staughton confidently, like a teacher showing his willing student the art of apprehending one or more individuals. But his expression changed as soon as he turned his eyes toward his partner and saw a red dot moving up his chest toward his head.

"What?" Staughton wanted to know. "What's going on?" Fear made his voice tremble.

"Don't move," Thompson ordered, looking across the street, the probable location of the shooter. Several buildings with the lights out made it practically impossible to tell.

Thompson pointed the gun at the three people with no sign of putting it down, while he watched the buildings in front, visibly uncomfortable.

"Sarah Monteiro," he shouted. "Get over here."

He could use her as a shield, getting an advantage over the shooter, whose identity he thought about. It could only be Jack Payne, the so-called Rafael Santini.

Sarah walked toward Thompson, step by step, without haste. This was not in her plans. Everything had seemed solved by the elimination of Templar and James. A noise in the window of the driver's-side door on Thompson's car broke it into pieces and made Sarah cry out and hit the ground. Thompson shook the pieces of what used to be the window off his jacket and ran to reach

Sarah, his last chance, fifteen yards away, lying on the ground, easy, easy. The asphalt jumped twice near his feet. Two shots, without doubt, that made him stop and get the message: *I don't want to kill you, but if I have to* . . . He dropped his gun and put his hands behind his head without anyone's ordering it. He had lost. In that moment he saw Rafael come out of the house in front and cross the street with a gun pointed at him.

"Make your colleague lay down his gun," Rafael ordered.

Hearing him, Sarah got up and looked at him with luminous eyes. A year later, another encounter in the same circumstances. Couldn't they meet another way? More normally. A dinner, a date at the movies, a cup of coffee?

"Do what he tells you," Thompson told Staughton in the same firm voice as always. This clearly wasn't the first time he'd found himself with a gun aimed at him. A warrior's occupational hazard, Staughton thought with respect, while he tossed his gun away from him. If they knew him well, they'd know he'd never shoot at anyone.

Rafael crossed the street without taking his eyes off the two men. He never relaxed or even glanced at Sarah, who already knew how he operated. All business. There's no diversion in the life of Rafael Santini, a sometime double agent for P2 who used the name Jack Payne.

When he got near Thompson, Rafael arched his lips in a sarcastic smile.

"How's Geoffrey Barnes?"

Neither agent answered, naturally. Thompson met Rafael's look, while Staughton lowered his eyes to avoid calling undesirable attention to himself. On the computer everything was much easier.

"Give him my best, friends," he said in a neutral tone. Of course, they'd never pass on that message, but Staughton was pleased to know that Rafael wasn't going to harm them.

"You're totally crazy," Phelps protested. "Gun out, shooting at people? You're completely possessed. My God, where are we? And who are these men?" He pointed at Staughton and Thompson, who looked at him fascinated.

"My beloved Phelps," Rafael called. "Help our two new friends into the van. It'll be a little crowded, but where there's a will . . . And don't say any-thing else."

Phelps was fuming, but Sarah's hand on his brought him back to earth. Immediately Simon and the woman walked to the van, where they'd have to squeeze three into a seat for one. Anything can be done with the grace of God.

Rafael, ever on guard, picked up the guns thrown on the ground, unloaded them skillfully, and let them fall, keeping the clips for future use.

"We'll see each other again," Rafael informed them as he walked to the van. "So long."

Before getting into the van, he pressed a pen that sent a beam of red light into Thompson's eyes. Not everything is as it appears. Then he took off as fast as possible.

The two men remained behind, confused, seeing the van leave down Fulham Road in the direction of Fulham Broadway. Their reaction came afterward when Thompson opened the door.

"Let's go."

"Where?"

"After them. Where do you think they went?"

The two men got in the car and took off in the same direction, or, at least, that was their intention. Thompson felt something wrong and slammed on the brakes. He poked his head outside and saw what he hadn't noticed pre-viously: two of the tires were flat. Rafael must have shot them out.

"What's the problem?" Staughton asked.

"Flat tires," Thompson explained, getting out of the car.

"He is," Staughton exclaimed with a sigh.

"He's what?" Thompson was not joking.

"He is good," Staughton said admiringly.

Just as Thompson was about to express his anger, a London cab stopped next to the car. A young man got out with a disdainful look.

"What happened here?" he asked rudely.

"Keep going," Thompson answered impolitely. "This is none of your business."

A sarcastic, annoying smile appeared on the man's face.

"You must be Barnes's men."

"And who are you?" Staughton asked, unhappy with the insult.

"I'm your boss for the next few hours. I have two men inside there. What's happened here?"

"Are we speaking with Herbert?"

The man nodded yes.

"Your men should be dead. We couldn't stop them from taking the woman away," Staughton confessed.

"Who?"

"You haven't heard of Rafael Santini or Jack Payne?"

Herbert recognized the name. He went over to the taxi driver's door and took out a revolver.

"I'm out of patience. So I'm going to give you five seconds to leave the vehicle."

The taxi driver sat astonished and immobile, but when Herbert looked at his watch and started to count, one, two, three, four, it only took a second for him to leave the taxi and start running as fast as his age allowed.

"Let's go now," Herbert ordered. He turned to Thompson. "You drive." Then to Staughton, "You call Barnes. We can't let them get out of the city, even if we have to get the president after them. They can't and won't leave the city alive."

38

Good Lord, who could it be at this hour?" protested the poor sister who had to dress as quickly as possible to attend the impatient person who'd been knocking insistently at the door of the Convent of the Order of the Sacred Heart of Jesus for the last five minutes. She even crossed herself when, still in bed, she looked at the clock and saw that it was ten minutes before five in the morning, fifty-five minutes before she'd get up for the first prayers before breakfast.

Whoever it was would have to listen to her reprimand since it was highly discourteous to disturb the sleep of the sisters, even more so when the evening before they'd had a night procession with candles in honor of Our Lady. The Marian Sanctuary stood some hundreds of feet from here, and today thousands of pilgrims were expected to come to show their devotion to the Virgin and her fruit conceived without sin.

The sister descended the stairs in a bad mood. It was the Mother Superior's orders to open the door at any time. All the devout faithful had the right to a friendly word, meal, or refuge in case of necessity. But it wasn't the Mother who had to get up at this hour and open the door, exposed to assault by some vagrant. No, she slept on an upper floor and said her first prayer of the day in the comfort of her room, coming down only for breakfast to give the orders of the day, which were always the same as every other day.

The sister got to the door, dressed in the pure blue robe of her order with a white head scarf she arranged to appear presentable to whoever was there. She opened a small square wicket in the door. She had to get up on a small box that once held fruit in order to reach the height of the opening, a little narrower than her head.

"Who's there?" she asked in a disagreeable voice to discourage any levity on the part of whoever was there . . . on the other side of the door.

"Good evening," she heard a man say. "Pardon my showing up at such a late hour," he began to excuse himself in a gentle voice. "I meant to arrive sooner, but I was delayed."

"Who is the gentleman?" The sister strained her eyes to make out the man who was speaking.

"I'm Father Marius Ferris. I was planning to arrive last night to sleep under the sanctified roof of this convent."

The sister was moved upon hearing his name and changed her attitude completely.

"Marius Ferris? Escrivá's disciple? My God!"

The prelate didn't see the sister jump down from the fruit box or knock it out of the way with a well-aimed kick. He did hear all the sounds that accompanied these actions as well as the key working vigorously in the solid lock to reveal the friendly sister, a foot shorter than he thought, as soon as the door opened. Not everything is as it appears, thought the white-haired man whom the fawning sister invited to enter the convent.

"Come in, please. You are welcome."

They both went up the stairs to the convent proper, Marius Ferris more quickly than the sister, whose age didn't permit her unanticipated climbs, the effects of half a lifetime shut up in those four walls, praying to the Lord, preparing three meals a day, and sleeping eight hours. In Marius Ferris one saw the results of his daily walks in New York City from lower Sixth Avenue to Central Park and back.

"Mother Superior asked me to let her know as soon as you arrived," the sister told him, trying to catch her breath.

"That's not necessary," Marius Ferris replied. "Let her rest. Show me to my room, and the sister can also rest a little more." His friendly voice charmed her completely.

"Thank you. I'm fine. I'm going to ask them not to bother you until breakfast so you can rest."

Marius Ferris smiled.

"Don't trouble yourself, sister. I slept during the trip. I only need to take a bath, make some calls, and go down to breakfast."

"Today a great number of people are expected," the sister informed him helpfully. It's not every day they had a dignitary of such importance. Only the pope himself could surpass this visit. With this holy thought, they arrived at the door that opened to Marius Ferris's temporary abode, a small brown door, similar to the others along the hallway, with a cross fixed in the center.

"I know that well, sister," the prelate replied with a friendly gesture. "Yesterday was a procession day, if I recall."

Oh, if only the sister were not a nun. What sweet words, or at least they sounded so in her honeyed ears.

"Correct. It's too bad you were delayed. The ceremony was beautiful."

"I imagine so. I imagine so. I saw it many years ago, more than twenty." His eyes expressed a nostalgia he tried to hide in vain. The past has the power of years. No one can resist it, even the boldest.

"There will be other opportunities, surely," the sister answered with good humor. It would be a good day. She opened the door and invited him in with her hand. "You know, Your Eminence, from the twelfth to the thirteenth, between May and October. Since 1917, thanks to the Virgin Mary." She bent down intending to kiss the cleric's hand for his blessing, which he didn't decline.

"God bless you, sister," he intoned magnanimously. "I'll come down right away."

"Welcome to Fátima, Your Eminence."

They said good-bye with no further words. Marius closed the door behind him and set the small suitcase he carried on top of the table next to one of the walls of the cell. Although small, it was the best room for repose in the convent. Spare in decoration, as was fitting, only a single bed, the table that could also serve as a desk sometimes, an old chair, and a small shelf with some books authorized by the Holy Mother Church.

He smiled as he examined the cubicle. How he adored being treated with deference, almost as if he were a sovereign, and certainly he was one in his own way, secretly. Of course, he wouldn't pass into history as Marius I or II, but who knows whether in a few decades he wouldn't be Saint Marius, protector of the good name of the Catholic Church? The image of the faithful praying to his image, leaving an offering, making a fervent petition, almost carried him away with ecstasy.

He checked the signal of his Nokia. The bars indicated maximum power. Let's thank the Cove of Iria, whoever Iria was, where everything began ninety years ago, and Lúcia, Jacinta, and Francisco saw the Mother of Jesus reveal to the world the three most important secrets, beginning with the end of the First World War, which occurred the following year, the fall of the Soviet Union that did so much evil to Christ and the Mother, and, finally, that which remains unrevealed and so continues with Marius Ferris, the assassination of a pope, the celebrated Albino Luciani, Pope John Paul I. The late Holy Father was a man of good and bad memory, the good being his smile and upright character and the bad, the night of September 29, 1978, in which he died in circumstances that Marius knew well. He was not a man to justify a bad act, but he adopted a motto the Church lives by: *What's done is done*, to which he added *No use crying over spilled milk*. What needed to be done was to clean up the mess skillfully and correctly without letting the evidence come to light. In that Marius Ferris was a master. He lay down on the bed to rest for ten minutes. Afterward he'd pray for the soul of Clemente, ask Santiago Mayor to forgive his sin and rescue him from the flames of the Inferno into his heavenly company. Everyone deserved a second chance, if not here, then there . . . on the other side of life.

He closed his eyes to seek within himself an image of peace, the rose or the white dove, living beings, the color of purity of spirit and of the noble values that send goodness, serenity, and all nouns of that kind.

When the first dove shook her wings silently in the ceiling, a Gregorian chant filled the cell, eclipsing the drowsy stupor Marius Ferris had fallen into. His cell phone, left on the small table, exulted the Pater Noster in male voices that didn't belong in the convent. Another person, probably, would feel soothed by the melody and embark on the sleep of the just, but not Marius Ferris, who knew the enterprise he'd undertaken and that the Gregorian ringtone was the prelude to a message of the utmost importance for the operation in progress.

He jumped up and grabbed the phone immediately.

"Yes," he said into the receiver.

He spent the next few minutes listening to how the situation was unfolding in the various locations of the operation, which he called the Work of God. One of the comments exasperated him.

"How is that?"

Something was off track.

"How could that happen?"

The silence in the cubicle was interrupted by Marius Ferris's altered breathing and frenetic pacing up and down.

"Listen to me. It's imperative they not leave the city. I'm going to make sure you'll have everything you need to make that happen." His voice was harsh and cutting. The leader was putting the train back on track. "Who did this?"

He heard the name impatiently.

"Are you sure?" He gave his aide time to answer. "Then we have a serious problem. Stay alert and prepare for everything. I don't want delays." He disconnected the call immediately to review the list of numbers in the directory and dialed another one when he found it. He waited for the international connection, and even before the first "bip," someone answered on the other end.

"Mr. Barnes, good evening," he greeted him. "Good, mine has been nothing special, either. Do I need to remind you what side you're on in this mess?" Two seconds' pause to allow Barnes's reply. "Perfect. I know we're not fighting just anyone. But my money doesn't care about sides when it comes to choosing friends. So I'm giving you this order, and I hope—" He paused momentarily to choose his words—"I know you are going to do it. So find the woman and the other accomplices and get rid of them without thinking twice. Got it?" He waited for the reaction on the other end. "Don't worry about JC. He's under control." Another pause. The silences were important to manage. "Take care of it. God wants it this way." He hung up.

It was time to pray for the salvation of Clemente's soul.

39

Somebody explain to me how we could have had those sons of bitches in our hands and let them drive off?" Barnes was almost shouting, at the head of an enormous table in the meeting room occupied by service agents.

"Well," Staughton began.

"You, shut up. No one asked you," Barnes exploded, beating his fists on the table. "I have the White House and Langley after my head because you"—he pointed at them all—"are a gang of fuckups who don't know how to do your jobs."

"And because the president owes the bastards in the clergy some favors," Thompson murmured, under the scrutinizing gaze of Herbert, who, with the exception of Barnes, was the only person on his feet, leaning on the wall.

"Do you want to know what your lousy work has done? Do you?"

The room was quiet, waiting in suspense for their chief.

"Littel is on his way. Yes, the Harvey Littel you're thinking of, assistant to the subdirector. He's coming to evaluate the quality of my agents. And you know what I'm going to tell him?" He spelled it out with his teeth clenched. "That you guys are S-H-I-T. You can't even wipe your ass," he added, turning around.

"What's Littel going to do here?" Staughton whispered to Thompson, who was sitting next to him.

Thompson shrugged his shoulders as if to say he had no idea, and, at the same time, attracted undesirable attention.

"Do you have something to say, Thompson?" Barnes inquired in an ugly way. "I'm listening."

Thompson didn't need to be coaxed. He got up and cleared his throat.

"I understand your irritation, boss."

Someone at the table coughed. It sounded like a cannon, but Thompson stayed firm, unaffected by the interruption.

"But I think I'm more useful to the agency alive than dead," he continued.

Barnes swelled with impatience. He was sick of excuses, but the real reason he was upset was not Langley, not the president, not even the inconvenient call he'd received a few minutes ago from Escrivá's disciple. His bad mood was named Jack Payne or Rafael Santini, whatever you want to call him, a traitor who sometimes served the CIA, on loan to the P2, blind to his own duplicity, a member of the Holy Alliance or whatever the secret service of the Vatican was called . . . if it ever existed. For Geoffrey Barnes, Jack Payne would always be the enemy, even though, God forbid, someday they might operate on the same side. He'd seen enough of this world to know the possibility always existed.

"To visualize better what happened, imagine a soccer game. A forward receives the ball, completely alone, with no hope of anyone getting to him. It's just him and the goalkeeper; the goal is guaranteed, but suddenly the forward's attacked by a defender who comes up out of nowhere and takes the ball away, leaving the forward on the ground with no hope of recovering it."

The room listened in silence.

"That's what happened at the Chelsea and Westminster Hospital before this gentleman arrived." He pointed to Herbert standing up, leaning on the wall, motionless, cool as a stone. Barnes sat down.

"Can you tell me what your men did to let a wounded man and a woman get away safe?"

"We're still investigating," Herbert declared, perfectly cool, his voice indifferent, insensible to the change of mood.

"Actually, it's already investigated." It was Staughton's turn to get up, half confident, half hesitant, thanks to the faces looking at him. The closest to him could almost make out a slight blush tingeing his face. "There were three bodies inside the hospital related to this case. One on the fourth floor belonging to an SIS agent named John Cornelius Fox, the other two on the first floor, Simon Templar, whose real name was Stanishev Yonsheva, a former member of the KDS—"

"KDS?" someone exclaimed. "Where have we seen anything like this?"

"First an agent of the Russian RSS, now one from the former Bulgarian KGB," Barnes reflected. "Where is this going?" He sat down in the chair, thinking. He had a strong desire to ease the lump in his throat, but a boss couldn't give the impression he was disconcerted. He turned to Herbert. "Where did you recruit that guy?"

"The Bulgarian was in our service, I admit. As far as the Russian you're talking about, I have no idea who he is," Herbert informed him.

"Go on," Barnes ordered Staughton.

"Well, okay. The Bulgarian had two shots in the back from the same gun that left a bullet in the head of James Hugh Cavanaugh, an American mercenary who had no affiliation with or interest in any side."

"He was crazy for guns and money," Herbert concluded. "A failed actor who decided to try out the real world."

"According to MI6," Staughton continued, "the shots came from the building in front, conveniently abandoned. The glass in the window had three holes that the forensic technicians are still analyzing, but we assume will correspond to the projectiles found in the bodies."

"And the one on the fourth floor?" Barnes asked. "How did he die?"

"He was stabbed with six scalpels," Staughton explained. "No bullet was found in him. The individual named James had several scalpels in his pockets, so he seems a good suspect for the killing."

"The wrong place at the wrong time," Barnes suggested.

"According to the receptionist, John Fox and Sarah Monteiro came in at four to visit the man wounded in the explosion, who's now identified as Simon Lloyd."

"Good work," Barnes praised him. He knew Staughton was good with this sort of thing. Comparing and processing information. His development in the field would be slow and complex, but once he got there, he'd be a capable agent. There was time. "What do we know about him?"

"He's an intern at the *Times*, an assistant to Sarah Monteiro. Nothing out of the ordinary."

Barnes raised his imposing bulk again to deliberate the orders. This was what was expected of a chief. Listen to the reports and decide how to bring the objectives to safe port.

"This is the situation we find ourselves in, ladies and gentlemen. We have four people beyond our control . . ." He interrupted himself. "Who's the fourth?" he asked the room.

Staughton, now seated, replied again.

"He hasn't yet been identified. He's an elderly man around sixty years old, but no more is known. A few minutes ago we received the images of the hospital exterior from security, and now we're working on the identification."

"It's not important," Herbert advised with his hard eyes.

"I'm the one who decides what's important," Barnes interrupted. "Here's the point: we have four people in a Mercedes van. They cannot get out of the country under any circumstances." A heavy stare swept the room to which he added his guttural, serious voice. "Every trail is important. If you find them, I repeat, if you find them, shoot first and ask questions later."

"The most probable thing is that they'll abandon the van," Thompson suggested.

"They can't," Staughton answered.

"Why not?" Barnes was curious.

"Because of the corpses," his subaltern explained.

"True, the corpses." Barnes hadn't remembered them. Everyone exchanged glances, while Barnes thought about plausible solutions. "Why the hell do they want the corpses?"

40

Dawn awakened with the crowing of a rooster just as it does in fairy tales. Here in this rural area, favorable to roosters and hens, pigs, rabbits, and other animals, the wake-up call was heard for a radius of hundreds of yards.

The old man slept on the sofa, a blanket protecting him from the cold that was common at night in this region.

The easy chair where the cripple had sat was now occupied by Raul Brandão Monteiro, sleeping poorly, with his eyes closed, in a very light doze, waking with the smallest chirp of a cricket or crowing of a cock, like this one. The cripple must be walking one of his disciplined rounds, since no precaution was too great when one's enemies were powerful.

Raul got up, half asleep, put on the shoes that had slipped off his feet while he tossed and turned during the night, and faced the dawn of a new day. He'd spent hours watching the phone in hope of news, ignoring the fact that the phone would be heard when it needed to be answered. He'd checked it over and over, the keypad, the receiver, to be sure the phone was working perfectly. Everything was normal. No one had called.

He went to the bedroom where Elizabeth was sleeping, but the closed door kept him from seeing how she was doing. He didn't need to see her to know she hadn't closed her eyes all night, and, certainly, she turned over in bed when he tried without success to open the door. It didn't matter. She'd come out soon to ask him about their daughter and be angry when he had nothing to tell her. *Ring, telephone, ring*, Raul wished anxiously as he returned to the room where old JC waited for him, sitting on the sofa with the blanket on his lap for security. "Already awake?" the old man said, smiling.

"I don't know how you're able to sleep as if nothing's going on," Raul said indignantly.

"The body gets used to anything, my dear captain," he explained. "Where did you see combat?"

"In Cuanza Norte in 'sixty-three," the captain answered, thinking of his induction into the army and the two-year commission he served overseas in the war between Portugal and her colonies.

"And tell me something. Did you sleep while you were there?"

He knew where JC was going. For him it was one more routine day in his long life. Nothing out of the ordinary. He adapted to periods like this when he had to change his refuge or was the target of forces as great or greater than his own. He lost no sleep over this because he knew no other reality, no other way to live. Calm and serenity, yes, these could make him lose sleep.

"There's still no news." Raul was worried.

"There will be," the old man declared calmly.

JC got up with the help of his cane and walked over to the table that still had the remains of last night's dinner on it. He sat down and looked at Raul.

"What's for breakfast?"

With a sigh, Raul went out to the kitchen to prepare the meal, normally spiced and hearty to sustain a day in the field. Today he wasn't hungry, so he'd make only enough to fill up the old man's stomach.

"Good morning, my friend. Everything okay?" JC asked the cripple, who had just come in.

"Nothing new," the younger man replied professionally and sat down at the table.

The old man poured a glass of water from a bottle on the table, took a box of pills from his pocket, selected two to place on his tongue, and helped them down with the water. The cripple watched him without saying anything.

"It's not time yet," the old man replied to the unasked question. "We're going to stay here."

The cripple got up, showing neither objection nor agreement. The old man always knew what he was doing.

"In that case I'm going to take a bath," he informed them. "This dust is sticking to me."

"Go on, go on," JC encouraged him with a certain bonhomie. Old age appeared to be having a softening effect on him, not in his combative spirit, but only in these small domestic activities he formerly would have ignored.

The cripple left the room that was now converted into an operational center for the three of them and left JC to take charge of strategy, which wouldn't change much, since he wasn't a man who liked to act on an empty stomach, unless necessary, which was not the case.

"Raul?" a female voice asked.

JC turned toward this melodious sound and found Elizabeth there. Now in the early light of morning he saw her natural complexion without makeup, and he noticed the hatred emanating from her. A perfectly natural reaction given the circumstances.

"Your *husband*'s in the kitchen making breakfast," he informed her, emphasizing the relationship that united them to show he'd perceived the strain in the relationship.

Elizabeth made no reply. Instead she began to walk around the room without taking her eyes off him. She finally sat down next to him and looked away.

"You're truly your daughter's mother," JC said in praise, although it could be understood differently.

"Is there news about my child?" Her anguish was clear.

"There will be," was all he said.

A tear slipped down Elizabeth's face, carrying all a mother's sorrow. A parent should never have to bury a child; there was no sorrow like that. JC wiped away the tear without a trace of shame.

"My father used to say that tears should be saved for the dead." He showed no condescension or sorrow for her. "You might not think so, but I also had a father at one time in my life."

Elizabeth looked at him disoriented.

"No one has died here," he said in a clear, firm voice.

"But someone could die." His certainty, for some reason, convinced her.

"We all can, my dear." That was a great truth, undeniable, unchanging.

"I can't decide if the fault for all this is her father's, if she—"

"No one is guilty," he replied decisively, as if it were a subject he'd pondered on his own in search of answers. "Is someone guilty for being born poor or with an illness or parents who neglect and exploit him? Or being born in a poor country or bad neighborhood? These are the cards we're dealt, and we have to accept them and go on playing according to our luck. No one is guilty, or we're all guilty, and fifty, one hundred years from now someone will blame us for the evil in his life." He paused so Elizabeth could take in what he was saying. "We can be thankful for being born in Europe, the most civilized part of the world, but even here there are bad things. We've inherited some of that evil. We have to shake it off, expel it, but it's hard. Only our persistence will defeat and bury it. Still, more evil will appear; we have to confront it, sooner or later."

Elizabeth listened to him closely. He spoke of certainties, not theories or idle speculation. They were intelligent thoughts about the reality of our lives.

"When will we hear from her?" Her hope increased the confidence she had in the old man's replies.

JC was silent for a few seconds without blinking or expressing any sign of doubt.

"Soon," he assured her.

"I think I'll go to my mother-in-law's house in Oporto." It was a cry for help, a motion to be approved or denied, in this case by the man in front of her.

"Don't leave us, my dear." His voice was friendlier. "Besides, we can't let you go. It would weaken our position. You're better off with us, safer, and soon you'll be able to talk to your daughter."

Raul came into the room with a tray in his hands. On top, a steaming teakettle, Alentejano bread, butter, local cheese, milk, and hot coffee.

"Wonderful. Your husband is trying to kill me with an overdose of cholesterol," he joked. "And I confess it's the best of deaths." A sign he'd eaten and drunk well in his life.

Raul said nothing. He hadn't expected his wife there, much less in quiet conversation with the old man. But JC had a gift for making others admire him. Looking like a frail old man helped.

"Are you all right?" She was the one who asked. It seemed the old man also had a gift for resolving conflicts between husband and wife.

"I'm better now," Raul confessed, passing his hand tenderly over her shoulder.

The phone finally rang, startling Raul and Elizabeth. Raul ran to it before the caller could disconnect.

"Raul," he identified himself with a hysterical cry. He listened without saying anything and closed his eyes. "Thanks," was the first thing he said when the speaker stopped talking. "Thank you very much," the second. "I have complete confidence in you. I know it's not going to be easy. You have half the world after you, so be very cautious. Call tonight so we can work out a plan. And thanks again."

The conversation ended with a press of the button of Raul's phone.

"What? Who was it?" Elizabeth asked impatiently.

"Rafael. She's with him." A smile from ear to ear. "She's fine. She couldn't talk because she was sleeping. But she's okay. That's what's important."

Elizabeth looked at JC, remembering his prophetic foresight minutes ago.

"This is just a pause, my dear. Nothing's resolved," the old man warned her.

"Yes, but it's something," Raul said.

"Where are they?" the mother asked, visibly relieved of the weight that was crushing her heart.

"In a safe place," Raul replied with a smile. "A very safe place."

41

She remembered parking in the garage of a house, but it seemed like ages ago. There was a car in the same garage, also déjà vu. He'd asked them all to get into the vehicle. Of course, that was the difference, they were not alone this time, two or three more people were with them. She didn't bother to count. They left the garage again in this other car, a new car being used for the first time; it had that new car smell. She'd gone into the backseat with one or two others, perhaps only one, thrown her head back and rested. Rocked by the motion of the car being put to the test by the city streets, the passing lights creating a dark, yellow glow, she'd fallen deeply asleep, leaning against a window, and ceased hearing the noise of the engine, the tires on the asphalt, breathing, life going on around her.

She couldn't tell how long they'd been in the car, minutes or hours, but remembered a light caress in her hair at some part of the trip that made her feel as if she were floating suspended above the ground. She'd opened her eyes a moment and saw herself levitating over some familiar, dark wooden stairs inside a house that made a shiver run down her spine. She felt a body against hers, strong arms around her, and, finally, a soft pillow and sheets shutting out the cold. Voices whispering in the distance she couldn't make out but one, both close and far away, she managed to understand, *Not now, she's sleeping,* before she gave in to the absolute rest of body and mind. Sleep, body, because the fight has only begun. It renewed her energy, relaxed her nerves, cured her wounds, and forced her fear to retreat. After a very few hours, Sarah Monteiro opened her eyes and awoke.

It was already day. Sunshine entered the room between the red curtains. She looked around trying to recognize the place, a large bedroom, antique decor. An enormous dark wooden closet, familiar, took up one whole wall. She sat on the edge of the bed and put her feet on the soft green carpet that covered the wood floor. She risked getting up and brought her hand to her mouth, incredulously. A tear in her eye showed her emotion. This was her room in the old house on Belgrave Road. There wasn't the slightest doubt. It had been almost a year since she last stayed here. Her uncertain steps made the wood creak from her weight, not that she weighed much, not at all, but it's natural that such old wood would react to the slightest touch.

"Good morning." She heard Rafael's voice. He was standing in the door. "Better?"

"What are we doing here?" she asked sharply.

"We're safe. Nobody's going to look for us here," he answered confidently. "I have breakfast ready downstairs." He left.

"Whose house is this?" Sarah had time to ask, raising her voice so he could hear her.

"Mine," she heard him say before his steps told her he was going downstairs.

She was astonished. She took a deep breath and inspected the bedroom. It was the same as she'd left it that night when life spun out of control.

She thought about what Rafael had revealed and decided he'd chosen to give her the easiest answer, the one that needed no more explanation, but he was very mistaken. He wasn't going to get away so easily.

He appeared again in her life at a crucial time. This time she wouldn't be satisfied with an excuse. She wanted to know everything . . . now.

She left the room impetuously in her night clothes, which were from the previous day, and bumped into the open door of the bathroom. Set across from a clear glass window, a bathtub challenged her decision to go downstairs immediately and demand satisfactory answers. She stopped and decided she might not have another opportunity to take a much needed bath. Better take advantage now than be sorry later. She returned to the bedroom and opened the closet. She was surprised to recognize the clothes she hadn't worn since she'd abandoned the house and sold it with the furniture and furnishings to avoid any further contact with that traumatic environment. Now, forced to but also grateful, she chose what to wear from her old clothes. It had to be practical. She picked out pants and a blouse, nothing fancy, took some underwear from the drawer, recovering little by little the habits and gestures the bedroom demanded of her when she lived there, as if she'd never left. All she needed was a towel from the bottom drawer, and she went into the bathroom, delighted by the prospect.

Twenty minutes later Sarah wrapped herself in a towel and left the bathroom, rejuvenated and smiling. Her glance crossed the windowpane, and in an instant she felt a shiver of fear. Two holes like those she'd seen in the Chelsea and Westminster Hospital, before these, that brought back the past and confirmed she was awake. It wasn't a bad dream—if only it had been. She looked around the room fearfully, much more well-lit in the morning light than on that night. She could see the body of the man fallen over her.

Forget it, forget it. It's over, she made herself think.

Everything was exactly as she'd left it, which amazed her. She'd left the house a long time ago. It wasn't normal for some change not to have taken place, especially since she'd only had the most basic furniture for someone who didn't need much, was at the beginning of her career, and wanted to save money for something better. It was all very strange.

The lower floor consisted of a living room and kitchen. In the living room where the stairs came down was a big sofa, pushed against the wall with a window. Stretched out on it was the friendly older man she still hadn't been introduced to. In the kitchen, Simon Lloyd, more relaxed, was leaning on a table reading the paper. There was no sign of Rafael.

"Do you feel better?" Sarah asked, sitting down on one of the chairs.

"Oh, good morning." He raised his eyes from the newspaper. "I'm much better. You?"

"Not bad," she replied, looking around. "Yesterday I completely disappeared. Sorry," she excused herself.

"You did well. After the night we spent . . ." He changed the subject. "Who are these people?" Simon asked in a whisper, like a child who didn't want to be caught.

"They're friends," was all she said. "Did you sleep some?" A change of subject is always useful when you don't want to say more.

"A little," he replied, scratching his head. "I spent more than an hour answering John's questions. It was an interrogation like in the movies."

"John? Who's John?" *Is he the old man lying on the sofa?*

"John Doe. The one who saved us in the hospital."

"The one lying on the sofa?"

"No, stupid. So you don't know them? That one's named James Phelps. He's a man about town. The younger one who carries a gun and carried you upstairs."

"What did they ask you?"

"Well, let's say we reviewed my whole life from birth with more emphasis on last night. Truly therapeutic."

He didn't give the impression of having been pressured in any way. He was practically cheerful, smiling.

"What's funny?"

"Who could be named John Doe?" He laughed out loud.

"Tea, coffee, milk?" asked Rafael, who had entered the kitchen unnoticed. Simon's laugh froze.

"Coffee with milk." Sarah asked for one of her morning favorites.

Rafael quickly turned to a table where everything was ready. He took a cup he'd previously cleaned and rinsed and poured a little coffee in it. Then added milk. Slipped a plate underneath and carried it to the table, where he set it in front of Sarah. He passed the sugar, offered her a clean spoon, and then went to get a tray of chocolate and nut muffins, fresh scones, bread, butter cookies, orange juice, and some slices of York ham and cheese.

"Where did all this come from?" Sarah asked, curious and marveling over the delicacies.

"From the bakery three buildings down on the other side of the street," Rafael answered. "It's fresh."

"I can back that up. I've already tasted it, and I guarantee it," Simon added, feeling much better. Rafael's presence didn't seem to cause him any fear.

Rafael created a mixture of inexplicable feelings in Sarah. It was almost a year since she'd last seen him, as she never tired of reminding herself. She felt nervous fear and shivers in her stomach, but that could mean a lot of things. What really struck her was the idea that she'd always been with him during this period of time, never absent. Almost like friends in a café or pub who see each other almost every day.

Calm down. Think about it. Stop. He's a priest.

"We have to talk. I have a lot of questions that need answering . . . truthfully." She was trying to put her slippery thoughts out of her mind.

"Eat your breakfast in peace, and then we'll all have a talk," Rafael said calmly. "Ah, and if you look back and analyze everything that's happened, you'll see that I never said or did anything that wasn't true." He got up and went out of the kitchen, leaving her with Simon and the banquet ready to be devoured.

Sarah didn't think about the food, but about his words. She was sure that what he'd said was true. He'd never lied. Perhaps he left something out when he felt he shouldn't be the one to give her certain information, but that was far from lying. He was right. She'd probably been too hard on him.

Simon got up and grabbed some clean silverware.

"I think I'm going to help. That's a lot of food for you, and you're not going to finish it."

"He carried me to the bedroom?" Sarah wanted to know, picking at a delicious-looking chocolate muffin.

"In his arms," Simon said mischievously with a scone stuffed in his mouth. "Don't you remember?"

No, she thought, but didn't say so. "I have a vague impression."

"And now, what's the next step?" He could barely get the words out of his stuffed mouth.

"Don't think about that," Sarah warned, sipping the coffee Rafael had prepared for her, prompting a slight smile.

Simon laughed and made her blush.

"What's going on?" she asked, a little upset. "What's going on?" she asked again when he didn't answer.

"The two of you aren't fooling anyone," Simon finally answered.

"Who?" She wasn't good at acting as if she didn't understand.

"You and John?" Another chuckle.

"Come on!" Sarah rolled her eyes.

"Good morning," a friendly voice greeted them. Phelps's peaceful theological studies didn't agree with this rebellious life his clerical destiny had led him into.

"Good morning," Sarah and Simon answered in unison, as required by good manners.

"Did you sleep well?" Simon asked.

"Sort of. Although actually that sofa needs some fixing up. Those springs . . ." Phelps complained, rubbing his sore back. "But anyone with a roof over his head to shelter him shouldn't complain. Right?"

"Sounds like a priest talking," Simon joked while chewing away on the food.

"Don't go," Sarah said. "There's food for one more. Sit down," she invited him in a friendly way.

"Ah, thank you," he acknowledged, sitting down at their side. "The truth is I'm hungry. I haven't eaten for hours." He didn't tell them it had been more than a day since he'd put anything in his mouth.

"There are scones, bread, butter, cheese . . ." While she was talking, Sarah passed them to Phelps, who still didn't find what he was looking for. "Do you want some milk, coffee, tea?"

"Tea, please."

"Good choice. It's still hot." She poured a little into a cup. "I'm Sarah," she introduced herself.

"James Phelps." He got up and offered his hand formally. "Nice to meet you."

Sarah got up, too, and held out her hand. She wouldn't leave him there with his hand in the air.

"Pleased to meet you."

"Yesterday was hard," Phelps said in an awkward attempt at generating polite conversation.

"If you two hadn't appeared just in time, my mother would've been very unhappy," Simon said convincingly as he joined the conversation.

"How do you know Rafael?" the older man asked politely, sipping a little tea and taking a small bite of a scone.

"I don't know anyone by that name," Simon replied immediately without thinking.

"It's a long story, James. Excuse me, can I call you James?"

"Of course, Sarah," he agreed.

"Who is Rafael?" Simon persisted without understanding.

"I would be delighted to know, if you want to tell me," Phelps continued, leaving it in Sarah's hands and ignoring Simon's question completely.

"Later," Rafael interrupted from the doorway. "I see you've all met. Now it's necessary to dot all the *i*'s and tell you your jobs."

"What jobs?" Phelps and Sarah asked at the same time.

"Do you think the danger has passed? This is only the beginning."

42

Sarah and Rafael were late. They were due in Barnes's office, ready for a not very cordial interrogation. That time had come and gone, and they didn't show, except for himself, in the office. His solitude had been broken by brief visits from Staughton and Thompson reporting on the progress, which was nothing, and as the hours passed, that was worrisome. Priscilla had passed by to check on his physical state, and he'd asked her to bring him an order of roast pork with potatoes and oregano, the cravings of a body hungry for victory.

At that moment Herbert entered.

"Don't tell me they've found a hole to hide in?"

"Don't fuck around with me," Barnes shouted with irritation. "If you were better, you wouldn't need to walk in our shadow to do your shitty job."

"Don't doubt that if I were the one giving orders, I'd do it alone, with no help. You have hundreds of agents, and not one has managed to find them. As far as we know, they might have left the country."

"They haven't left," Barnes insisted firmly.

"How can you guarantee that?" Herbert pressed, seeing Barnes worried.

"My word is enough. They haven't left the country. And I'll tell you more. They're still in the city."

Even the younger man's smile was without any feelings. More a grimace, livid, lifeless.

"You're basing that on instinct, Mr. Barnes. You Americans are very fond of luck and destiny."

"This has nothing to do with luck. I know the suspects well," Barnes said. *Besides, I know that he's going to find a way to let us know when he leaves the country.* He didn't speak this thought. You've got to have an ace up your sleeve that others don't know about, even if they're associates.

Herbert raised his hands in the air as if to say that Barnes's arguments were worthless, but if he wanted to believe them, fine.

"I've got to inform my superior about the situation in half an hour. What am I going to say? That we haven't expanded the radius of the search because you have a hunch?"

"Fuck what you're going to tell him. My men are doing their job. I don't have the least doubt that any moment now they are going to come through that door with something solid. If you want to tell him, I don't think we are going to have any news until nightfall. So prepare him and yourself. It's going to be a long wait."

"Who's the man who showed up at the hospital? This Rafael who seems to have upset you?"

Barnes paused thoughtfully before responding.

"A traitor. He infiltrated P2 in order to destroy it from the inside and almost succeeded."

"He managed to deceive JC and the CIA?" A sarcastic smile.

"You're in no position to laugh," Barnes warned, chastened. "For all I know he gave your men a good looking over three times. They probably don't even know what happened." He laughed in an offensive way that seemed not to affect the other. He congratulated himself thinking that deep down Herbert must have been angered. Nobody could be so cool all the time.

The office door opened to let in Staughton and the pandemonium of noise from the Center for Operations. Closing the door behind him cut off the exterior noise, leaving a silent movie unfolding on the other side of the window, an agitation without meaning.

"News?" Barnes asked, leaning back in the chair to give his younger colleague an impression of calm and control.

"We're analyzing the images on CCTV, but it's like looking for a needle in a haystack. We can't find any Mercedes with continental markings or the license plate in question. We see no bank transfers in the accounts of Sarah Monteiro or Simon Lloyd. . . ."

Barnes laughed dryly.

"What do you want? Everything tied up all nice and neat for you? It won't be there."

"Where will it be then?" Herbert asked maliciously.

"Rest assured you're dealing with someone who knows how we work. I get irritated, unhinged, fucked up, but we have to be rational."

"What do you mean by that?"

"That he's going to appear when and where it seems best to him."

"That's not an option. There has to be a way to find them." For the first time a note of irritation could be detected in Herbert's voice. Barnes was pleased and didn't take long to show it.

"We're doing everything possible already," Staughton told him. "We have the CCTV on constant alert, not just in London, but over the entire country. All the police and border patrol have their photographs and know what to do if they're spotted. The MI6 is working with us."

"It's okay they're helping," Barnes interrupted. "I don't much like their thinking about their own interests."

"There's nothing else to do," Staughton declared.

"What if we offer a reward?" Herbert suggested.

"Don't talk nonsense," Barnes protested. "Publicize the thing? Have the journalists and public opinion all over us? What do we gain from that?"

"Catch them sooner. People will do anything for money."

"It might not be a bad idea," Staughton put in.

Herbert crossed his arms and looked skeptical.

"We've identified the man who took Sarah and Simon to the van."

That got the attention of Barnes and Herbert.

"He's named James Phelps, an English priest assigned to the Vatican."

"The what?" Barnes grumbled. "Son of a bitch."

The three were silent for a few seconds. In this profession everything was a question of strategic analysis. Deciding what route to take to get to a determined objective, speculating about what the others would do. The more facts they had to fill in the blanks, the more accurate their speculation. When there was little information, everything was guesswork and hunches. Trusting luck was not good, but sometimes one had no choice.

"What if we leave the priest out and send out an advisory on just the others?" Herbert tried again.

"It won't work," Barnes said. "The woman has an influential position at the *Times*. It's only going to hurt us."

More silence.

"What time is Littel getting here?" Barnes asked.

"Two hours from now."

Barnes sighed.

"Very well. Two hours. Until then we won't do anything. When he arrives, we'll make a decision," he blustered again. "Get me something in the next two hours, Jerome. We're not looking good with our friends in Opus Dei." He pointed in Herbert's direction, who noticed his sardonic tone.

The door opened to let in Thompson.

"We have news."

"Spit it out." Barnes jumped up.

"Between five and six a metropolitan policeman returning to his house after his shift saw a Mercedes of the same description as our alert enter the garage of a house on Clapham."

"What are we waiting for, gentlemen?" Barnes asked as he grabbed his gun.

43

MIRELLA
May 7, 1983

At the age of sixteen the libido renewed itself every second that passed. The awakening of sensual, lustful feelings, satisfied with the simple stare of a longing male, avid for a contact that is never permitted. The first steps in the art of seduction began, the looks, the signs one body sends to another, under control at this stage or not, affected by an urgent immaturity satisfied by a simple smile, an anxious voice greeting one from a distance, a compliment shouted from a Lambretta that made one blush secretly, the more direct the better, a furtive touch, without delicacy, on a buttock covered with a tight skirt. Triumph was an invitation to go out, or a kiss on the mouth, with or without the tongue, according to what she wanted—it's always she who asks—or, the gold medal, an invitation to dinner with an older man. Not with just any twenty-year-old student, studying architecture or law, which would also be a victory, but with a man turning thirty-seven or forty, with a car, house, settled life, perhaps divorced, in fact separated, one or two children he doesn't bother to mention, desiring the new feeling of a younger woman, a woman capable of turning the clock back to former years of passion.

Mirella looked at herself in the mirror for the umpteenth time. One couldn't run risks in an encounter of this kind. Any error was harmful, able to shake the confidence of an adolescent who considered herself an adult. Of course she wasn't actually thinking of these technicalities. She acted, with an instinct for self-preservation humans can't escape no matter how intelligent they consider themselves.

Obviously, when she was sixteen, her parents were not going to permit a candlelit romantic dinner, as she imagined, with a man old enough to be her father, enchanted with her femininity, ready to smother her with expensive presents and endless gallantries. So she'd accepted his suggestion to tell her parents she was staying with an old friend from school. That way no suspicions were aroused. Not to do that invited a serious paternal interrogation that would conclude with a prohibition without appeal, tears on Mirella's part, locking herself in her bedroom for hours lamenting her bad luck and cursing her bad parents, and a long face for days until she found a new source of diversion to make her forget the previous one. But none of that was necessary.

"Where are you going to eat?" asked her mother, who had just come in the bedroom where Mirella, elegant and beautiful, was admiring herself in the mirror.

"At Campo dei Fiori. I still don't know where," Mirella replied without taking her eyes off what looked like the inopportune beginning of a pimple on her chin. "What a bother. It's starting to look red."

It was one of the dramas of adolescence. Certain bodily assaults one couldn't foresee or avoid.

"Pay no attention to it. He'll have a lot also."

"It looks really bad," Mirella protested.

Her mother took her chin and turned her face toward her, like an object she owned, which was somewhat true, according to her point of view. She examined the irritated skin of her daughter's face with a maternal expression. A small red spot could be made out on the right side of her chin, nothing serious.

"This is nothing. It's going to take some time before it breaks out," her mother declared. "You've got to learn to live with those."

"What did you do to get rid of pimples?" Mirella asked, interested in the magical formula that, at times, mothers seem to possess.

"Don't worry about it," her mother answered. "Someday you'll do the same," she finished with a smile.

The wise words of a mother or father, not always so wise, fall on deaf ears in anything related to the dramas of surviving puberty. Someday would Mirella stop worrying about the infamous pimples that broke out on her face just before her period? Never. Naturally, she wasn't, at the moment, in possession of all the information about what her future life would be, no one is, it's the rules of the game. If she were, she'd know that she'd never have to worry again about cutaneous eruptions, menstruation, classes, excuses, sensual seductions, joking, libidinous thoughts, worrying about conquests, feeling admired, the erections that her simple presence provoked, the calculated, suggestive smile, dinner with older men, her parents . . . or her life.

It was almost time, and Mirella went to the window to see if his car was already waiting there. She flashed a fascinating smile when she saw him there. He'd arrived five minutes early. A good sign. Romans were not punctual in any way. It was their style to arrive late for everything. Fifteen minutes to a half hour didn't seem bad to anyone.

"I'm going," she called from the kitchen. "See you later."

"Don't forget. Home by twelve at the latest," her mother reminded her, although the door had already closed, leaving Mirella free to go.

A mother's anxious heart told her to go to the window and watch from behind the curtain the car her daughter got into at that moment, smiling, full of light, shining intensely. She felt a heavy heart, a disturbing anxiety, gloomy thoughts, nothing she should give importance to. She couldn't see the driver's face because of the dark, moonless night that had settled over the street. She thumped her chest to rid herself of the tightness. A few seconds later she felt relieved, her soul relaxing, the bad feeling had dissipated, everything was fine.

She left the window to go serve dinner, and left her daughter and the friend to follow the road in the privacy of the BMW.

44

It was time for the Farewell Procession in the Cove of Iria, when the Virgin Mary was carried in procession among the hundreds of thousands of pilgrims back to the Chapel of the Apparitions, where she would remain until the next year. A light mist marked the blessing of the act in this place central to the Catholic world, on a par with Saint Peter's in the Vatican. Hundreds of thousands of white handkerchiefs waved in the air, marking the immaculate farewell. People wept in prayer, with petitions for help, genuine or bizarre, because no one was there for no reason, out of a pure manifestation of faith and feeling for the Mother of Christ. There was always a request, a grace, *Save my daughter. Help me in this business deal. Give me money and fortune. . . .*

To the right of the colonnade was the chapel of the Perennial Exposition of the Holy Sacrament, where the Congregation of the Religious Observers of Our Lady of the Sorrows of Fátima has prayed to the Sacred Heart of Jesus seven days of the week, twenty-four hours a day, since 1960. It's a worthy act for forgiveness of worldly sins, according to the call of the Virgin in 1917 to the chidren, without requiring anything in return except peace on earth, no small thing, comparable to a miracle from heaven. These were the teachings of Father Formigão's disciples, whom the Virgin asked to forgive sins after the prayer. All this Marius Ferris experienced, kneeling in the last row of the chapel with the sister there in front of him finishing her turn at prayer.

After making the sign of the cross, Marius Ferris got up and left the chapel. From there, under the colonnade, he could see the sea of people crowding the vast enclosure, the processions in the back, on the way to their usual site, the exact place where the oak was found that sheltered the visions of Mary.

"Do you believe that one of the bullets that threatened the life of the Polish pope in 1981 is in the crown of the Virgin of Fátima, Brother?" The voice came from behind Marius Ferris.

"That's public knowledge," Ferris replied. "We know that Wojtyla was very devoted to Mary." He quickly bowed before the man confined to a wheelchair. "Your blessing, Your Eminence." He kissed one of his hands.

"God bless you, my son," the other recited, concluding the ceremony of greeting.

The man was much older than Marius Ferris, near ninety you might guess. He was wearing a black suit and a large yellow gold cross hanging from a thick chain around his neck. A young cleric dressed in a black cassock, perhaps his aide, pushed the chair according to the old man's wishes.

Marius Ferris rose after a few moments of prayer and looked at the old man in front of him.

"I envy your physical fitness," the old man praised him.

"Don't be envious. I'll never reach your age." A smile appeared on his face.

"Only He knows that," the other observed. "Do me the favor of pushing my chair, Brother." It was a demand, not a request. With a gesture, he dismissed the young man. The conversation would be private now.

Ferris took the chair and pushed it smoothly along the colonnade toward the Basilica. The voice of a prelate could be heard resonating from the loudspeakers inside. A polyglot expression of gratitude to all the pilgrims, directly from the altar placed in front of the Basilica, at the top of the stairs, which was used in the international celebration of the Mass.

"Is it the Roman envoy?" Ferris asked.

"Yes, Sodano."

"The one the pope forgot?" A certain joking in the voice, a certain disdain.

"He always finds a way to promote his position. Besides, the German has chosen a very bad secretary of state."

"Did he choose, or was that the only option they gave him?" Ferris countered.

"Could be. In any case the present pope knows what was agreed to in his election. If he should go back on the deal—"

"What's the deal?" Ferris interrupted.

"Whatever it may be, Brother. Draw in the Church, reassert the old dogmas, combat any menace of liberal reform, stop creating this constant circus in the media. Christ is not an amusement park." A certain flush showed how deeply he believed this.

"A Church turned inward."

"How?" the man went on, having just started his sermon. "If they followed the teachings of our Church, the only, the true one, we wouldn't have half the problems society debates today. Abortion? Contraception?" His irritation grew with each topic. "Ecumenism? Why? Interreligious dialogue? There is us and there is them. There's no conversation. Yes, in some way, they attack us; we throw ourselves on them. It's always been like that. Why are we bothering now with stupid diplomacy?"

"It's going to change," Ferris predicted.

"I hope so. Otherwise we'll have to do something about the German."

"I don't think it'll come to that."

"Is everything going as you planned?" An almost imperceptible change of subject.

"Until now, yes," Ferris lied. A small lie. He didn't want to worry him with insignificant things that would be resolved shortly, perhaps already had been.

"Wonderful, wonderful," the other rejoiced. "Are you going to blame the Russians and Bulgarians?"

"They were actually guilty for a long time," Ferris asserted.

"Do you know where I was on May thirteenth, 1981?" the prelate asked.

"In Rome?" Ferris guessed.

"Of course in Rome. In the Bethlehem Crypt."

"In the Basilica of Santa Maria Maggiore?"

"Indeed," he confirmed. "Expiating my sins next to the cradle of the Infant Jesus," he confessed.

"Is Pius still praying there?" Ferris smiled, referring to a statue of the pope praying before the holy manger.

"Yes, he is. But he was a real pope. He didn't fool around with insufficient methods. He acted, made decisions, and kept everything in its place."

"Those were other times," Ferris observed.

"The times are what we make of them. For fifty years we have had movie stars on Saint Peter's throne."

Marius Ferris stopped pushing the wheelchair. He looked at the procession of the Virgin, who was now in the place where she reposed daily, adored by millions of people every year, in person or at a distance. The ceremony had ended, and it would be hours before the asphalt enclosure emptied and returned to normal. Soon they'd see worshippers again, lighting candles, praying the rosary humbly, following the path on wounded knees, doing the promised rounds around the chapel to thank the Virgin for grace bestowed or asked for, since they had to pay in advance.

"At the moment the Pole was shot in Saint Peter's, I was praying for him. The Lord wanted him to live some twenty years more, and I always obey His will, even if I don't agree, because He is infallible."

"In any case he turned out to behave himself well," Ferris said.

"We managed to control him, thank God. At least until the end of the eighties. After that he followed his whims."

"Yes, but it wasn't bad. Ultimately he couldn't go back on his word."

"It's true. But I can't forget who gave him that independence in the nineties." His voice was irritated again.

"Nor I. We're taking care of that."

"That's good," the cleric advised. It sounded almost like a threat. "I want him dead."

The man took off the chain with the gold cross, reached for Marius Ferris's hand, and gave it to him.

"In the Bethlehem Crypt, next to the manger you will find what you need. It's been there for twenty-six years waiting for you," he told him.

Marius put the gift in his pocket with as much care as if it were a treasure from heaven, which, in a sense, it was. They resumed their way as if two friends on a walk.

"At the precise time the Pole was being shot, I was praying for him in Santa Maria Maggiore," the old man repeated. "And now the bullet is right there, a few yards away, in the crown of the Virgin. It's like a curse that follows me," he confessed.

"This place is like a discount store for relics," Marius Ferris declared. "We have the three shepherds buried in the Basilica, a few feet away from here a piece of the Berlin Wall."

"A testimony to our work," the cleric observed.

"Of course. Every holy place is a guarantee of the Church's capacity to realize its mission," Ferris asserted with a smile.

"And what about Mitrokhin?" the old man asked seriously.

"What he left is controlled by the British. It's in their interest, too."

They stayed silent as they watched the faithful disbanding. At the back a little to the left there was the new Sanctuary of the Holy Trinity, with the capacity to hold almost nine thousand people. The power of the Church expressing itself in concrete.

The young attendant approached and took over the wheelchair. No one had called him, but he'd seen that whatever had to be said was said.

"Bring our ship into good port," the old man said, calmer now, with a lethargic, pensive expression, tired from so much talking.

"I can see it now," a confident Marius Ferris agreed. "We just need to tie up at the pier."

"You know where to find me at the end."

They separated with a farewell gesture. This time Marius Ferris didn't bend to ask a blessing. Everything in moderation, excess was the enemy of faith.

In spite of signs everywhere prohibiting the use of cell phones, he didn't hesitate to place a call. Those were rules for the faithful, not for the clerics—benefits of the cloth and the profession.

"Hello."

He received the report without interruptions. Marius Ferris knew how to listen. His face relaxed.

"Perfect. Attack the place. Keep me informed."

He disconnected the call and took the chain with the enormous cross out of his pocket. He looked at it with intense respect, the personification of the body of Jesus engraved in gold, the threads of energy and history that penetrated deeply in his soul and made it resound with feeling. He got on his knees, turned toward the Virgin, Mother of Christ, in the distant chapel, and lowered his head, while a tear ran down his cheek.

"They've been found. Soon they'll be in our hands. I'll avenge you," he promised. "I'll avenge you and your son."

Behind him in the chapel of the Perennial Exposition of the Holy Sacrament, the old sister continued praying through eternity.

45

"How many times do I have to repeat myself?" Sarah was irritated by Rafael's umpteenth question. "Are you trying to catch me in some contradiction? I'm being held here in custody, is that it?"

"In some way you are. I don't think you can freely walk down the street right now," Rafael advised in a neutral tone. "The only reason I'm pressuring you is to get every fact that can help us."

"Am I behaving well?" she asked sardonically.

"Perfectly." He went on to show her. "Your colleague Simon was the victim of an explosion detonated on entering your house. You had the good luck, in quotes"—he emphasized the expression—"to be warned minutes before by Simon Templar."

"Correct," Sarah agreed in the same tone of voice.

"That means they've always known your whereabouts and decided not to act until the hospital."

"But I was the one who decided to go to the hospital. No one made me. I went on my own will."

"It's irrelevant. You did them a favor. That way they could take both you and Simon."

Sarah looked at Simon. She hadn't thought of that. Maybe he was right.

"But Templar was against my going to the hospital."

"Maybe, maybe not," Rafael answered. "He could have simply made you think that. I'm sure you never suspected him."

Sarah thought about that. He was right. Besides, he did know what he was talking about. It was his profession.

"That raises a question," Rafael continued. "Who placed the bomb? Templar's behavior tells us he knew nothing of the device, in spite of being a chameleon."

Like you, Sarah thought, but didn't say. She ended up feeling ashamed for the thought. He didn't deserve that lack of respect. His way of seeming one thing and being something else had saved her life several times, as she never tired of remembering.

"Let's not forget the Russian agent who was found, and that Herbert person they were waiting for in the hospital, but never appeared," Sarah pointed out, a little more cooperatively.

"We'll worry about the Russian agent later. In regard to Herbert, there is nothing to think at the moment. He's only a name . . ."

"Like Jack Payne?" Sarah quipped. In the end her cooperation was fleeting.

"Like Jack Payne," Rafael agreed.

"Who's Jack Payne?" Phelps and Simon asked simultaneously. "I realize nobody seems to have a problem not using his real name," Simon said.

"It's a long story," Sarah said. "Some other time."

"Time is the one thing we have." Phelps's interest was apparent. "I'm very interested in hearing the story of Jack Payne."

"Jack Payne is dead," Rafael observed. "He belongs to another story. There's nothing to say."

Sarah helped change the subject.

"You mentioned a *they* just now. That have been following me. Who are they? Barnes?"

"No," Rafael quickly corrected her. "Barnes is a puppet in the hands of other interests. He just wants them to leave him in peace."

A hesitant clearing of the throat indicated Phelps's turn to join the conversation.

"I don't mean to be at all critical, but I've thought of a certain reason for the story only Sarah and Rafael know about." In spite of the diplomatic manner, his judgmental attitude was evident. He turned to Rafael. "I believe it's time to make everything clear. I don't want to get into your joint history, far be it from me to intrude on your privacy, you have a right to it, but, when I asked Rafael a question last night, I was terrified by the answer, although it was evasive."

"What was the question?" Simon was curious.

"Who are we after?" Phelps concluded.

"And what was the reply?" Sarah asked with her eyes fixed on him.

"John . . . Paul . . . the Second . . ." Phelps responded slowly, so that each component of the name weighed on them.

The silence was oppressive, and attention turned immediately to Rafael, who showed no sign of reproof toward Phelps or any sign of discomfort.

"Oh my God. The dossier on the Turk," Sarah let slip, remembering the file that JC had left with her in the Grand Hotel Palatino in Rome, the one that was behind the bottle of vintage port.

"The one I was going to look for?" Simon asked with wide-open eyes.

"Yes."

"Don't worry about that," Rafael tried to appease them. "It hasn't been there for a long time."

Sarah was angry. "What do you mean by that?"

"That it hasn't been there for a long time," Rafael repeated without a bit of emotion.

"It wasn't where?" Sarah was afraid she'd lose her mind if he said what she thought he would say.

"In your house that exploded in Redcliff Gardens, behind the bottle of port, vintage 1976," he said. "I was there to get it also, but I suspected you'd miss it."

Sarah got up from the table, red-faced, upset with the outrageous back and forth about her life, and, what was worse, without her realizing it.

"How could you?" she almost shouted at him.

"Someone had to read it," Rafael argued. It was a fair argument from his point of view.

"You had no right," Sarah continued, hurt, although she might have felt flattered knowing that he was always present and attentive to her survival. She sat back down.

"We're digressing again," Phelps complained.

"Actually, we're not," Rafael answered. "The Turk's dossier is an important element of this case."

"In what way?" Phelps insisted.

"It's a complete report on how everything happened, what led to planning the death of the Pole, who the conspirators were, what happened in the years that followed, and the consequences. An authentic, detailed account."

"And where is it?" Phelps asked like a police inspector. "I'd like to read it."

"It should be in my house," Sarah protested, although more calmly now.

Rafael smiled. The second time Sarah'd seen him smile.

"You didn't pay attention to it, Sarah. You fled from it like the devil from the cross."

Phelps crossed himself on hearing mention of the devil, provoking a laugh from Simon, who tried to hide it.

"And where is it?" Phelps asked again.

"In a safe place. It's better you not know its location for security reasons."

"For our security? What's the problem?" Phelps asked again. Ah, brave man.

Rafael confronted the three questioning looks without blinking.

"What do you think all this is about?"

"Why don't you clarify it for us?" Sarah's tone was serious.

"They want that report and to eliminate any and all threat it could represent, even though they've not yet read it," he spelled out.

Once again because of papers, Sarah thought with a strong feeling of déjà vu.

"Don't these people know they should leave nothing in writing?" she lamented. "And this has nothing to do with Albino Luciani and what happened to him?" She began to feel a certain fear. This was much more complicated than she thought.

"No. It's about John Paul the Second and what we don't know about him."

"But, who are they?" Simon asked. His body began to ache again. He needed rest.

"The saviors of the Church. Those in command of the Church."

"The pope?" Simon continued.

"No, of course not. Who thinks the pope rules the Church?"

"The conclaves, the election of a successor, the Swiss Guard, the prime minister. Choose one." Simon presented an endless list.

"The commander of the Church is and always has been . . . money," Rafael explained.

Phelps felt insulted by the remark. "Listen, Rafael. . . ."

Rafael raised an authoritative hand, demanding silence. "Money rules the Church. Think of the banking system."

Phelps sighed. What sacrilege. For her part, Sarah couldn't understand where Rafael was going with this idea.

"Banks have to obey the directors of the Central Bank. They raise or lower interest rates, set policies, regulations—"

"Where are you going with this?" Sarah was the impatient one this time.

"To what is obvious. We have the Holy Mother Church, the Vatican, which is the face and regulatory agent that manages the wealth and advises what decisions to make to promote the faith."

"For the love of God." Phelps was furious. He got up and put his hands on the table. "What are you talking about? Surely the Vatican—"

"You're mistaken. I'm speaking about Escrivá's organization."

"Holy Virgin." Phelps crossed himself again three times in a row. "Heresy."

"Escrivá's organization?" Simon was lost.

"Opus Dei," Sarah and Rafael said in unison.

"That seems like a theory without foundation," Sarah contradicted.

"An outrage," Phelps added. His voice trembled with indignation.

"Unfortunately it's not a theory, it's not even speculation. It's a certainty. That's the way it works."

Phelps sat down completely crushed. "My God, I don't believe it. There has to be something wrong."

Minutes passed without a word, only listening to their breathing, panting, fatigued, nervous.

"Okay!" Sarah interrupted the silence, recalling conversations of this kind with Rafael in the past. "I think we're all in agreement to tie up the loose threads. We want to know everything."

The other two just nodded in agreement. Yes, they wanted to know everything . . . now. Sarah looked at Rafael seriously. *We want to know everything . . . now.*

"You can start by talking about the bodies," Phelps suggested, crossing himself at the same time.

"What bodies?" Sarah felt goose bumps.

"This is getting more and more interesting," Simon said with a sour smile.

"The bodies this guy went to pick up in Amsterdam. We covered five hundred miles with them before we got here," Phelps said incriminatingly.

"Natalie?" Sarah said timidly. "The bodies of Natalie and Greg? You've brought them?" She couldn't conceive of this repulsive act, snatching two bodies, people she knew, from eternal rest.

Rafael nodded.

"Why?" Sarah demanded. This man never ceased to amaze her. She had no idea how he felt, if he considered this good or bad.

"Among other reasons . . . for this." Rafael showed them a small black object the size of a jacket button, circular, smooth.

"What's that?"

"A CD."

"That's a CD?" Simon looked astonished at the object. "They make them that size?"

"They make whatever size is necessary."

"And what does it have on it? Who had it?" That was what mattered to Sarah.

"Information Natalie had been investigating for a long time," he only said.

"About what?"

"Emanuela and Mirella."

"The girls?" Phelps asked nervously. "Good God, this is torture. I can't believe it."

"What girls?"

"My God. The girls." Phelps covered his face with his hands, paralyzed. "Information about the worst that could happen to them, I suppose."

"What girls?" Sarah asked again. The loose ends were getting even looser, instead of tying together plausible explanations. No resolution was in sight. Suddenly the conversation she wanted to have about the house seemed inopportune.

"Two adolescents who disappeared in Rome in 1983," Rafael finally told her, ignoring Phelps's comment.

"What do they have to do with this? Why did Natalie want information about them?"

"She was doing an investigation of the attempt against John Paul the Second. He deserved to die."

The image shook her, impeding her formulation of the next question. It took her a little time to recover.

"But who are those girls?" Simon put in.

"It's a delicate subject. It's enough to know they were carried off in Rome by persons connected with the Church at that time. Despite having circulated the idea they wanted to exchange them for the Turk, they killed them a little after the kidnapping for other reasons."

"And what were those reasons?" Phelps demanded.

"What I've said is enough." Rafael's expression made it obvious he'd say no more on the subject.

"And what about the other victim who died with them?" Phelps changed the subject. "Did that have something to do with the case or was he just caught up in the imponderables of life?" He was remembering the article he'd read in Schiphol airport that mentioned the English couple and another man, not yet identified.

"Are there other dead?" Simon felt he'd entered a world gone mad.

"He was the one who figured everything out. He was with the CIA, one

of the founders, in fact. He was as good as dead as soon as he started following their movements. Ironically he'd just been relieved of the case the
day before. His work was over. He'd reported something Natalie had been
looking for in Bulgaria. This man, Solomon Keys, was going to spend a
few days in London before returning to the United States. Natalie decided
to satisfy her desires precisely in the place where Solomon, who now had
nothing to do with the subject, happened to be. He probably had no idea
it was her. The shooter never knew that it was Solomon Keys in the other
toilet stall."

"How is that?" Phelps was fascinated by so much information.

"The shots were fired with the door closed from the inside."

"My God," Sarah exclaimed, imagining the scene.

"You're very well informed," Phelps commented with some reservation.
Rafael said nothing.

"The Dutch authorities didn't find the CD?" Sarah asked suspiciously.

"Of course they did," he said. "And they handed it over to the person
they had to give it to."

"I don't understand." Sarah wanted everything perfectly explained.
She had the right.

"There are behind-the-scenes games by the secret services that are not
important here."

"How did you know all this?" Sarah insisted.

"Nothing is invisible to the eyes of the Vatican," he answered conclu-
sively but evasively.

"And the girls? What do they have to do with the assassination attempt
on John Paul the Seond?"

Rafael looked hard at her to be sure he was understood.

"Everything."

The story was only getting more confusing. She wanted answers and,
in part, had gotten them, but every answer contained new questions, new
doubts.

"To summarize," Simon began, "a supposedly religious institution,
Opus Dei, does not wish known the circumstances surrounding the attack
on John Paul the Second in 1981." It sounded like a journalistic presentation.

"For that reason they initiate an operation—I imagine that's the appropriate term—the objective of which is to silence anyone who has or might have knowledge of the affair, as well as getting hold of all the documents pertaining to the case."

Everyone listened to Simon's synthesis. Sarah remained perplexed. She needed a cool head to make things fit together.

"They have the help of an enormous American governmental organization, and we're here putting off the inevitable. Is that it?" Simon concluded with a question.

"That seems about right to me," Sarah agreed. "So many things need explaining. I feel more confused than when I arrived here."

"There is a question, though, that has still not been asked," Simon said, analytically, hesitantly. "What is Opus Dei's interest? We're talking about a costly operation with a lot of resources. And what does the CIA have to do with this?"

"We'll talk about that later," Rafael decided. "Now we have to discuss what happens next."

A vibrating sound interrupted them. Rafael's cell phone. He listened without offering a word and disconnected in the same way.

"Um, by the way, I have to call home. Can I?" Phelps asked cowardly. "I have to reassure my family. I talk to them every day."

"Of course," Rafael granted. His voice was serious, professional.

"Don't worry. I know well what I cannot say."

"Me too," Rafael informed him. "But before that, Sarah has to make a call."

"Me?" She was not expecting this.

"Yes. We need to set your father's mind at rest. I told him you'd call." He put the cell phone in her hand. "And, in passing, ask him to tell his associate we need a plane for tonight."

46

EMANUELA
Wednesday, June 22, 1983

It wasn't difficult to guess the reason for those shining eyes and that wide smile on her rosy lips. It was the happiness of fifteen years parading before the marvels of life, the promises, the future, which resembled a bouquet of roses. Destiny was the color of a rose.

The reason for her enthusiasm was her first job opportunity. A small job, part-time, but honest, an opening, her first salary, hers alone. She could hardly wait to get home and tell her family. She needed to hurry because the music class had already begun at the institute. Oh, how beautiful Rome was! A salesperson for Avon cosmetics at a fashion show. Who would have thought this opportunity would be in reach?

"Emanuela has the looks for this position. She's what we're looking for," the representative had praised her minutes before on the terrace, as she was enjoying the taste of a soda.

He didn't get around to opening the black briefcase at his feet, with the handle on top, new and well cared for, the odor of leather blending with the fresh summer breeze. He was around forty, more or less, and had the confident look of someone who knew what to do as a recruiter.

"I'll have to ask my family," she'd said. But she'd wanted to accept without bothering with parental permission. "But I think you can count on me," she concluded with a smile.

"Wonderful, wonderful. But don't forget. Your parents' approval is necessary. Without it there can be no contract," he said seriously.

The man finished his drink and got up, took the briefcase by the handle, and held his hand out professionally.

"It's been a pleasure, Emanuela. I hope I can count on you."

The girl responded to the gesture with a smile, constant, delicate, passionate.

"Do you think you can give me an answer tomorrow?" he asked.

"Absolutely," she answered. "Shall I call you at the office number?"

"No," he hastened to say. "We can meet here tomorrow at the same time." It wasn't a question and Emanuela understood.

"Of course. I'll be here. Same time," the girl answered.

"Tomorrow," he specified to avoid any mistake.

"Tomorrow." The same bright smile. "See you tomorrow. I'm running late."

The farewell was quick. The man stood on the terrace with a thoughtful expression, waiting for the next meeting, in his hand the key to the BMW parked in front, another job interview, who knows. He saw her turning the corner running toward the Pontifical Institute of Sacred Music.

It wasn't hard to guess the reason for these shining eyes and wide smile on her delicate lips. It was the happiness of fifteen innocent years.

She didn't feel much like going to class, she was too excited, but she couldn't ask her parents' permission after skipping; that was out of the question. It was better to fulfill her obligations, avoid problems with her parents, and later, who knew if this job might not be the beginning of a future in the fashion world?

She entered class a little late, for which she apologized and was pardoned. Roman traffic is hell, everyone knows.

The class passed normally, new exercises to practice at home, besides the three days a week she had to come to this building to learn more material for the flute. A little after seven Emanuela called home and talked to her sister about the offer from the Avon representative. Her enthusiasm was obvious. Prudently her sister told her not to make any decisions without talking to her parents.

She walked to the stop for the bus that would take her to Saint Peter's Square and then to her house, where she'd lived since she was born. She felt the slightly longer days, the sun that stayed a little later, setting slowly behind the buildings in an orange arc, incandescent, which Emanuela didn't notice, at least not consciously. Nor did she lose time looking at the posters put up along the street with the photograph of a teenage girl, a year older than she, named Mirella, who had disappeared from her parents' house on the seventh of May. The parents were anxious to see Mirella again or, at worst, to see her body appear, lifeless but touchable, to put an end to the agony of the unknown.

At the bus stop there was a woman waiting, wrapped up in her own life. Emanuela didn't acknowledge the car sounding its horn in front of the stop, certain the horn couldn't be for her.

"Emanuela," someone called from inside the vehicle.

She heard only the second time, absorbed as she was in her own dreams, and she smiled in confusion.

"Hi," she replied.

"Do you want a ride?" the male voice offered.

"Don't worry. I don't want to trouble you," she excused herself sincerely. "I'm going to the Vatican."

"I'm going there, to Borgo Pio, for another interview." The man took his black leather briefcase off the passenger seat to make room and put it in the back. "Get in."

Emanuela took two seconds to think about it, and with the same innocent smile, opened the door and got in.

The woman waiting at the bus stop didn't even glance at the BMW that took off in the direction of the Colosseum. She remained ignorant of what was happening right in front of her. The Avon man was counting on that.

The car had already turned down Via dei Fori Imperiali and couldn't be seen.

47

Three people got out of the black car parked in front of the Holiday Inn Express. They went into the hotel for tourists on low budgets and short stays, passed the reception desk without asking for any authorization or room key, and went up the stairs to the second floor, where an open door revealed every conceivable variety of monitors, cameras, computers, and other kinds of unconventional technology, some top secret that cannot be identified, operated by a dozen agents packed into the tight space. Paying no attention, the three made their way to a room on the side. The door was closed. They opened it without hesitation and went in. They saw four men in identical suits looking out the only window in the room. Jerome Staughton, Thompson, Herbert, and Geoffrey Barnes.

"Good afternoon, gentlemen," the recently arrived Harvey Littel, accompanied by his assistant, Priscilla, and Wally Johnson in military uniform, greeted them. "I see there's been some progress."

Barnes greeted Littel with a firm handshake. He didn't try to hide his serious expression.

"Welcome."

"This is my assistant, Priscilla Thomason, and the military attaché, Wally Johnson." He gestured toward the two, whom Barnes greeted similarly with a frown.

"My assistants, Staughton and Thompson." It was an exchange of introductions that left no one unknown. "This is Herbert"—he pointed toward him—"but you should know him better than I."

"What's new?" Littel asked, putting an end to the formalities.

"We've found the van they used in a private residence in Clapham. The bodies that were missing were there, but not a sign of the woman or the—"

"And afterwards?" Littel interrupted.

"We investigated the identity of the owner of the house and discovered—"

"What?" Littel again interrupted.

"Are you going to be quiet and let me explain or do you want to find out everything on your own?" It was a warning.

"My apologies. It's your investigation. Go on." Littel was sincere.

"We've discovered that the house is listed in the name of a multinational branch of a telecommunications firm called Hollycom. It didn't take much looking to find out the company doesn't exist. It's a cover for our friends in the Vatican."

"The Vatican?" Wally Johnson asked. "What side are they on?"

Barnes ignored the question from the recent arrival.

"We did an investigation of the property registered in the name of the company and came up with a Volvo only three months old. We sent out an alert, and your associate Herbert's men here have come across it."

Barnes asked Littel to come to the window. Staughton, Thompson, and Herbert moved aside to make room. Barnes pointed at a car parked on the other side of the street, a Volvo.

"It's that car." He raised his hand toward the house in front. "And Sarah Monteiro lived in that house."

"Then we're on the right path." Littel rubbed his hands. "Let's finish this. I'll inform the subdirector, and we'll return home today."

"He didn't come?" Barnes asked.

"Bed's a big adversary when you wake someone up at four in the morning. He wants to stay informed and trusts that I'm capable of resolving the problem. Which means I can't screw up."

"It's always the same shit," Barnes protested.

Littel agreed with a glance and turned to look at the house again.

"Is there movement?"

"Yes, especially on the ground floor."

"Then let's not delay. Order them to go in." Littel dropped his eyes when Barnes looked at him from his full height.

"Whenever you want."

Barnes brought his radio to his mouth and pressed one of the buttons.

"Attention, Alpha Leader. The commander authorizes you to go in. I repeat, authorization to advance."

Several seconds later they began to hear over the radio the operation taking place. There were three teams, the Alpha Leader, the Beta, and the Gamma. Alpha would go in the front, Beta in back and from above, and Gamma remained in reserve in case they needed reinforcement. It was evident that this kind of operation didn't follow the same rules as special forces, although in part the principle was the same. Let's not forget we're dealing with forced entry into a house in broad daylight by a foreign governmental service with no jurisdiction, authorization, or knowledge by the country they're in. So what better disguise than city construction workers to attack the house from the front, the Alpha team, and electrical line workers to go over the roof and enter the back, team Beta? An operation organized in record time, without much analysis of the layout of the building, which was poor planning they'd have to ignore. They didn't expect much resistance. Gamma team was scattered along the street inside cars, reading newspapers at the number 24 bus stop, a street sweeper cleaning the sidewalk, a mailman, tourists with suitcases and a map in hand looking for a hotel.

Barnes and the rest listened in suspense as the attack by the Alpha and Beta teams unfolded. They entered with no difficulty or alarm. Everything was over in a few minutes. While the teams searched the rooms, they alerted Barnes about the situation, offering the word "free" to signify there was no one there, the area was clean. They reported just one person in the living room.

"Arrest the suspect," Barnes ordered.

Littel was present without interfering.

"Subject detained without resistance," the agent announced a few seconds later. "He says he has a message for the commander."

"Repeat, Alpha Leader," Barnes said.

"The subject has a message for the commander."

Barnes left the window and walked out of the room.

"Wait, Alpha Leader. I'm coming down."

"Received," the agent informed him.

Two minutes later Barnes was in the living room of Sarah Monteiro's old house with the entire group who had filled the room in the hotel in front.

"Who are you?" he asked brusquely.

"My name's Simon Lloyd. I'm a journalist for the *Times*, and my newspaper knows I'm here."

Barnes looked him over, and vice versa, evaluating the young man in front of him. He seemed nervous and rightly so. All attention focused on him, influential, powerful people, who with a gesture could end his life without thinking twice and later make up any reason to excuse it. Reality was a great fiction.

Simon tried not to show panic. This was the job given to him to carry out so Sarah and Rafael could complete their plan. Rafael reassured him everything would go well, but now, under so many hostile stares, he wasn't so sure. Perhaps it was just an excuse to convince him. Sarah had warned him how manipulative these people could be. Let them be. The job would be finished.

"What's the message?" the fat American asked unpleasantly.

Simon handed over a disc the size of a button to him.

"What's this?" Barnes asked, looking at the object.

"I don't know, but Jack Payne told me to tell you he'd meet you there." Job over.

Barnes's eyes filled with hate as he looked at the small disc.

48

The vehicle moved over the rough ground at a moderate speed to avoid disturbing the occupants. There were still a few miles to go on this side road until they reached the national expressway, then turned right and continued straight. Fifty-three miles on the expressway would bring them to Lisbon; in two and a half hours they'd be at the airbase of Figo Maduro, where a private Learjet was waiting for them.

Inside the car we find JC in the backseat with Elizabeth beside him, Captain Raul Brandão Monteiro in the front passenger seat, and the cripple driving, as befits an assistant.

"I don't understand why we have to go with you," Elizabeth protested.

"My dear, you can't stay because you cannot be protected. If you were caught, you could be used as a bargaining chip to blackmail your daughter. That would give them an advantage over us. Unacceptable. Unacceptable. The enemy must negotiate with the weapons they have, not with weapons we give them."

"But you spent the night in my house. There was no problem," Elizabeth argued insistently.

"Have you heard of fugitives from the law who never sleep in the same place twice?" He waited for her to confirm. "That's our case at the moment.

Being in one place and predictable is the enemy of strategy. We have to stay moving."

"Where are we going?" the captain wanted to know, turning toward the back.

"You'll soon see."

The car traveled a few miles without a word being said. They were still in familiar territory for Raul and Elizabeth. Each one thought about his life and the common purpose the present moment required of them. Except for the cripple, who still hadn't gotten over his anger at having Rafael on the same side and was still slowly fuming over it.

Raul prayed his daughter and Rafael would arrive on time safe and sound. That was the most important thing.

"So what does all this have to do with John Paul the Second? He is dead, poor man. He suffered miserably," Raul said, bringing up the subject of the night before.

"Haven't you heard it said that we suffer in proportion to the evil we do? Karma is something like that. Not that I believe in that, obviously."

"The man was a saint." Elizabeth was offended.

"A man can be a saint and a sinner. Sin doesn't invalidate his holiness. There are thousands of examples in the Church."

"But what's the connection with him?" Raul insisted.

JC adjusted himself in the seat. The rough ground had been left behind, and now there was a good road to Lisbon, straight all the way that could be seen.

"Let's say we had an agreement."

"You and he?"

"He and I."

"What sort of agreement?" Elizabeth asked.

"That's a long story."

"We don't have to be anywhere," Raul argued. "We're in your hands. Time is something we have plenty of."

JC half looked at the green landscape, yellowed by the late afternoon light that spread over the road. The immensity of Alentejo, filled with black poplars, vineyards, and endless fields of rye. The beauty of nature, untouched in some parts.

"Wojtyla got caught in a great net when he was elected pope. The Church was coming out of a traumatic event from which it took many years to recuperate." He looked Raul in the eye without contrition. They both knew what the trauma referred to; nevertheless, JC was an excellent judge of people and confident, just by a glance, that Elizabeth didn't know the twists and turns of the situation. "Of course he didn't know what had to come. He even paid homage to his predecessor, taking his name. John Paul the Second," he proclaimed triumphantly. "He could little imagine that his beloved Church would decide to run no more risks with JP the First. You know that certain . . . let me find the right word . . . certain *obsessions* overcome the chosen one after the canonic election. They come from a vague holiness."

"Well, Wojtyla was in an exceptional situation. Pope Luciani didn't even warm the seat." A new exchange of looks with Raul. "For that reason remembering and paying homage to him benefited his image."

"Are you accusing him of taking advantage of John Paul the First?" Elizabeth was frightened.

"I'm only mentioning the credit and the debt. Whether good or bad, it was well done and useful for him. The Pole was a dynamic man, taking charge, prepared to work, to fight." A sarcastic smile came over his face as he remembered. "He didn't know what was coming. He made the same mistake as his predecessor."

"What?" Raul was totally caught up in the story.

"He got mixed up with Marcinkus."

"Marcinkus?" Elizabeth interrupted. "Who's Marcinkus?"

"He was the director of the IWR, the Vatican bank, at that time and remained so for many years during Wojtyla's papacy. An American bishop John Paul promoted to archbishop, but never to cardinal, not that that would have been accepted. He only looked out for his own interests and never for others, but who am I to accuse?" He paused for a few seconds to let what he'd said sink in. "He certainly wanted the promotion. Imagine,

Cardinal Marcinkus. Your God would have a lot of trouble just removing the pride from his face."

"And what else?" Elizabeth urged him to continue.

"And then we come to 1989. The Pole had postponed the so-desired promotion time and time again. He couldn't keep doing it. For complicated reasons, which I'll summarize if you're interested, Marcinkus had a good hold on him . . . or at least I believe he did."

"The pope?" Elizabeth was scandalized. It was a scenario hard to conceive. She didn't know about the political games behind the scenes in the Church. Fighting for power, control, just like your own country and all other politicians. To think that the Vatican, a symbol of faith, was immune to these vices . . . was deceiving oneself.

"Yes," the narrator confirmed.

"This man who, if he put one foot out of the Vatican, even a toe, would be immediately arrested by the Italian authorities, who considered him a criminal . . . was he going to be a cardinal?" It was Raul's moment to try to comprehend the scale of imperfection of political systems.

"In politics, as in everything else in life, what counts is to have the advantage. Your prime minister has to dance to the tune of whoever discovered that he flunked out of his last year of college. The American president is obliged to invade Iraq because his patrons are pressuring him . . . the Saudis, who, to avoid attention, refused to let the attack proceed from their country. We're all compromised by someone, and we're always subject to someone's advantage over us."

"What was Marcinkus's trump card?" Raul wanted to know.

"Wojtyla's life," was all JC said.

Neither Raul nor Elizabeth expected that comment. How could someone control the life of a pope? There might have been other trump cards, but never one so decisive.

"How can that be? A man who has hundreds of people guarding his security," Elizabeth questioned.

The setting sun poured into the interior of the car, the last gleam of the reigning star before submerging itself in the horizon, the darkness of night extending through the Alentejano plains until they were covered in blackness. Astronomical, scientific explanations disprove the idea that the sun sinks, since it's the center of our solar system. The universe is like religion; metaphor is always more beautiful. What matters is belief.

"The attempt of 1981 was threat enough," JC said.

"What do you mean by that?"

"Think back. Marcinkus lost one of his right-hand men inside the Vatican with the death of the secretary of state, Cardinal Jean Villot, who died in March of 1979. In itself this was an enormous loss for someone trying to manipulate the pope. One day he received a visit from the German cardinal, part of the inner circle the Pole confided in, who told him his work was being investigated closely—"

"What work?" Elizabeth interrupted. "Wasn't he the director of the Vatican bank? He wasn't dealing honestly?"

Raul and JC looked at each other, Raul a little uneasy.

"Of course not. Do you know any bank that doesn't pursue its own profit?"

"Banks should pursue an honest profit. But surely this Marcinkus must have had to account to someone. The pope, for example?"

"You're right in the sense that the bank belongs to the Supreme Pontiff, but Marcinkus didn't account to anyone but himself. Because of this lack of hierarchical oversight, the business dealings of the bank touched on the scandalous."

"Touched?" Raul asked. He knew something.

"It's a euphemism. I don't want to make your head swim with financial technicalities, legal or illegal. In the end who decides what can or can't be done? Based on what assumptions? Who can deny the fact that the IWR, under the management of Marcinkus, was the owner of businesses involved in the production and sale of pornography? Or factories for contraceptives and armaments, or operations that stimulated the economy, or financed things like genocides in Africa? Who could blame him?"

"The values the Holy See defends are opposed to these kinds of businesses," Raul said angrily, although it wasn't the first time he had heard this. "I understand John Paul the First was going to close the bank. It has a bad reputation."

"It's business," JC contradicted him. "Don't be fooled by the official name of the Institute for Works of Religion. It is a bank; it needs to generate profits, make money . . . lots of money. Faith doesn't run the world . . . money does. In that the Holy See has always been in the vanguard."

"You are in favor, I presume?" Raul suggested.

"I'm not in favor or against . . . I understand; that's different. Capitalism is not a perfect system. Nothing invented by man is. It's a system of reaction. It needs medicine from time to time so that the markets will react and money circulate. Money must constantly be changing hands. It's essential. An explosion in an oil pipeline so that the price of a barrel of oil goes up, the threat of war, a real war. Everything is calculated. Nothing is left to chance."

"I never realized all this," Elizabeth exclaimed.

"Of course you didn't. No one realizes. Marcinkus knew nothing of economics, but he had infinite business sense, to say nothing of the blessing of God. With all that, there was no shortage of candidates to help him invest. Marcinkus's economic games cost the Vatican treasury a billion dollars, and he was responsible for the attempt on John Paul the Second's life."

"He was? What about the Bulgarians? The Soviets? Not them?" a stunned Raul asked.

"You know Licio was always a master of disinformation."

"Licio? Who is Licio?" Elizabeth asked in turn.

"Licio was the Grand Master of the order I preside over. Anything that was necessary, Licio resolved it. Is a new government necessary in Argentina? When? That would be Licio's question. Are arms necessary to confront the British in the Falklands? Make a list, Licio would say. I have this judge on top of me, another person would say. Relax, tomorrow the pressure will be gone, Licio would advise." His voice rose as he listed the various possibilities or memories. A man coming to terms with his past. "He had a solution for everything. And he had one for John Paul the Second."

"For being such a great defender of Licio, you don't sound very happy," Raul provoked him.

"Age begins to call for rest, my dear friend. The past remains more vivid and pursues us. You're proof of that, too."

Silence settled in. There was too much information to assimilate all at once.

Elizabeth broke the silence. "Why did you decide to tell us all this?"

JC gave her a superior look. "You can do absolutely nothing with this information, so I have nothing to lose . . . nor you to gain. Consider it a courtesy on my part."

"I think it is one of those things everyone wants to know, but prays isn't true," Elizabeth confessed.

"Ah, that is true, very true."

"So there was no conspiracy of the Bulgarians or the Soviets to kill the pope. Everything started with Marcinkus," Raul concluded.

"In the final analysis everything comes down to a group of less than five people. It's the only way to guarantee that everything will be covered up."

"And in the case of John Paul the First?" Raul asked subversively. "How many were there?"

"According to what I heard, it was his heart that conspired against him," he said sincerely. "Don't believe everything you read in books. What these people want is to sell."

"So this Marcinkus was behind everything," Elizabeth summarized, ignoring the innuendos between the two men.

"Marcinkus gave up his soul to God in 2006," JC informed her. "Licio was the mastermind of May thirteenth, 1981."

"But John Paul the Second didn't die," Elizabeth said.

"That's true. There were many mistakes in implementing the plan. And this resulted in a profound change. But it wasn't difficult to convince the Pole that another attempt could happen anytime and anyplace."

"He threatened him?"

"Not exactly."

"I don't understand."

"Ah, that's where the Bulgarians, the Soviets, the East Germans, and also the Poles come in. They were all informed by your friend that an attack on the life of the pope was imminent. There are innumerable reports that indicate the presence of agents of the KGB, KDS, Stasi, and Poles in Saint Peter's Square that day. It was a masterful move," he proudly asserted.

"He thought he was being threatened by the Eastern Bloc," Raul concluded thoughtfully.

"And he was. But not directly. For that, Marcinkus, Licio, and I fabricated a scenario of constant menace. We invented a contact with a man who presented himself as Nestor, an agent of the KGB, who used Marcinkus to contact the pope and present the Soviet interests."

"But the Soviet Union collapsed at the end of 1991."

"Yes, but that was because someone helped the Pole then. You know in this profession you can't trust anyone for long."

"Whose help?" Raul and Elizabeth asked, almost at the same time.

"Mine."

49

London is the most closely monitored city in the world. There are cameras in the streets, alleys, buildings, and public transport, constantly recording, since no effort is ever enough, and it's the nature of people, not just sworn enemies, to always test the defenses.

There is a small park, St. Paul's Churchyard, next to Christopher Wren's masterpiece, accessible through Paternoster Row, which is usually closed after eight at night. Today should have been no exception, but the black gate yielded to Rafael's push, and didn't even squeak when he opened it completely, testimony to its frequent use and the attentive maintenance of the prelates of St. Paul's Cathedral, one of the treasures of this beautiful city.

"What are we doing here?" Sarah protested. "We should go straight to the airport. It's still far off."

"We have time. It's only ten minutes."

"Ten minutes for what?" James Phelps asked.

Rafael ignored the question and rang a bell set in the side of a solid wooden door. He waited.

To get here they'd taken three different kinds of transportation. They got on the number 24 bus, from the stop in front of the house on Belgrave Road. They got off on Lupus Street and went into the Pimlico to Euston tube station. Later they took a taxi to the Tower of London. They walked the rest of the way along Cannon Street in a roundabout way only Rafael understood. Along the way Sarah had taken charge of asking JC for a plane, which he quickly attended to. Was there nothing he couldn't make happen? She'd spoken a little to her father and mother, putting them at ease, although the somewhat unusual request for an airplane had left Elizabeth worried.

"Nobody heard," Sarah impatiently said. "Ring it again."

"They heard, don't worry. We have to wait."

Sarah sat down on one of the wooden benches throughout the small but well-cared-for park. She realized her nerves were getting the better of her, as well as doubts, undermining, conspiratorial, and alarming. Unfortunately she'd experienced enough so far to know she shouldn't take time to think at these times, lest she . . .

"Will Simon be all right?" The question was more for herself than for the two men. It was a spontaneous worry.

"Better than us, you can be sure," Rafael guaranteed.

"What if they torture him . . . or worse?" Sarah insisted. "I shouldn't have visited him in the hospital," she lamented.

"Don't talk nonsense. If you hadn't gone, he'd have been worse off by far. Or maybe he'd be better, but his family—"

"I understand," Sarah interrupted, raising one of her hands to shut him up.

"How do you know they haven't hurt him?" Phelps asked, helping Sarah and, at the same time, satisfying his curiosity.

"The same way I knew we'd been found on Belgrave Road."

"Do you have somebody spying on Barnes?" Sarah got up. "I don't believe it. It can't be." She showed her incredulity and the curiosity typical of a journalist. "Who is it?"

Phelps's anxious glance moved between Rafael and Sarah.

"Do you admit it, Rafael?"

The door opened at last after a key was heard turning in the lock.

"There are various ways of knowing your enemies' steps," Rafael said. The open door revealed a bald, fat man, dressed in pajamas with tiny blue polka dots.

"What do you want?"

"Excuse the late hour, Brother," Rafael said respectfully.

Late hour? Sarah asked herself. *It's eight-thirty.*

"We came to speak with Brother John," Rafael continued.

"John who?" He was still rude. He must have been sleeping.

"John Cody."

"And who are you?"

"Excuse my distraction. I'm Brother Rafael . . . from Rome."

"Why didn't you say so," the brother gatekeeper grumbled. "Come in, come in."

Once inside the building, Sarah felt transported into another age, around the end of the seventeenth century and the beginning of the eighteenth, well after the great fire of 1666, which left the cathedral in ruins, like the rest of the city. That tragedy showed itself in this monumental building, in this medieval-looking hallway Sarah walked down with respect and admiration, contrary to the others, who only saw a hallway, like a lot of other hallways, dark, somewhat sinister, closed to the public in general, since the people who live here need their privacy.

"I'm going to take you to the sacristy, where you can wait for John Cody," the porter informed them, who in spite of his frown seemed friendlier.

"I appreciate it," Rafael said with the same respectful tone of someone who didn't want to hurt feelings or create unnecessary confusion.

The brother opened a heavy door into the immense transept, a place for visiting and prayer.

"Magnificent," Phelps whispered. "It never ceases to appear magnificent to me, and I've come here many times." He was speaking to Sarah in a low murmur in order not to disturb a holy place.

They stopped in the chancel, the center of the majestic cathedral. At the back to the west the immense nave spanned the history of centuries, witness of royal weddings and state funerals. Resting place of many of the great personalities of the kingdom, among them the Duke of Wellington; Arthur Wellesley, the great architect of Napoleon's downfall; Lord Nelson, the lamented admiral, victor of Trafalgar; Thomas Edward Lawrence, better known as Lawrence of Arabia; Florence Nightingale, to name just a few, and, ah, of course, Christopher Wren, on whose tomb could be read:

Lector, si monumentum requiris, circumspice. Above, the magisterial dome with its lantern of 850 tons below the gigantic cupola, where one could admire Thornhill's frescoes and whose exterior was featured on the obligatory postcards of the city and in television correspondents' reports. It was unmistakable. Its height of 110 feet was surpassed only by Michelangelo's cupola in Saint Peter's Basilica.

"Stay here," Rafael ordered Sarah and Phelps.

"Why?" Sarah asked indignantly.

"Because I say so," Rafael replied with a certain arrogance. "Look around. There's a lot to see," he added, his back turned to them following the steps of the brother porter.

Sarah and Phelps obeyed the order, although clearly they weren't happy being forced to the side of whatever was going on. Sarah couldn't rest until Rafael answered everything.

"And now?" Phelps asked, visibly uncomfortable.

"We have the cathedral all to ourselves. Why don't you give me a guided tour?"

"With pleasure, but let me find a restroom first."

"That's fine. I'll wait for you."

Phelps left the chancel, the vast open space below the cupola, but at the third step his right thigh cramped up, and he bent down with sharp cries. Sarah ran to help him.

"What's the matter, James?" she asked anxiously.

"Don't worry. It'll go away in a second."

"Come and sit down," she suggested, taking him by the arm and helping him to the nearest pew on the north side of the transept.

He followed her advice and let himself be helped.

"This happens to me sometimes."

"Do you know what it is?"

"Not really." He smiled like a mischievous child.

"You should have it checked as soon as possible. You can't play around with your health," a concerned, maternal Sarah advised him.

They sat in the large, varnished wooden pew. Phelps stretched out his painful leg, still holding his thigh.

"It's already going away," he repeated, more to reassure her than anything else. He'd learned to live with this pain before.

They waited several minutes in silence, Sarah at Phelps's side, attentive, forgetting their future tasks and the secrets of Rafael, someplace in the sacristy with Brother John Cody, discussing private matters, which concerned her, Phelps, and Simon. May God protect them . . . if He can.

"I'm better now," Phelps declared, getting up with difficulty. Sarah helped him.

"Are you sure?"

"Yes. This goes away as fast as it comes." He put some weight on his leg to see how it went.

"See? It's gone."

"Good, but promise me you're going to have this looked at when you have the opportunity."

"Will do. Thanks for your concern." A smile sealed the promise. "I'm going to look for a bathroom."

"I'll be here."

Let us take advantage of this voluntary separation between them to follow Rafael, who has now left the sacristy alone. Brother Cody hadn't appeared, but the brother porter's unpleasant frown had changed as soon as he found himself alone with Rafael. He remembered, suddenly, that they should look for Brother Cody in the Whispering Gallery, at the base of the cupola, not a very appropriate place for secret encounters. In any case this was the place chosen, and Rafael climbed the spiral staircase leading to the gallery. There were hundreds of steps, but he was in shape, prepared for anything and, preferably, two or three steps ahead of his enemies.

Once he reached the dais and balustrade that make up the famous Whispering Gallery and run around the entire base of the cupola, Rafael looked around. It wasn't difficult to find Cody a few feet away leaning on the rail, watching the chancel below in the center, not worried he could be seen. Rafael crossed the distance separating them until he was a foot or so away.

"This isn't really the best place," he protested. The gallery owes its name to the unusual acoustics that let a whisper be heard all over the cupola.

"Don't worry. There is nobody up here at this hour. I've made sure of that."

The two men embraced.

"Rafael," the other greeted him with pats on the shoulder.

"John Cody," Rafael responded.

"What a name you've found for me," Cody complained with a smile, loosening the hug. "I've been investigating. John Cody was the archbishop of Chicago in the seventies."

"I know."

"A real bastard."

"I know."

"A thief, corrupt."

"I know," Rafael repeated. "What do you have for me?"

"Very little. Everything is more or less under surveillance."

"More or less?"

John Cody shrugged his shoulders.

"We always have to take the unknowns into account. Things appear without warning, and we never know what they might be."

"Excuses."

"The only thing I have is a name. They are especially interested in one man."

"Who?"

"A certain Abu Rashid."

"Why is he special?"

"It seems he knows more than he should."

"And who's given you this information?"

"No idea. They don't let many people have knowledge of this affair."

Rafael rubbed his eyes meditatively.

"Where does he usually stay?"

"The last and only known residence is in the Muslim quarter in Jerusalem. But no one's seen him there for a few days."

"Which means they have him under wraps."

"I can't say that. If that's the case, it's not us," John Cody excused himself. "Do you think it's worth going to Jerusalem?"

Rafael shook his head no.

"It'd be a waste of time."

"What do we do then?"

"We go on. I already know where I'm going," Rafael declared decisively.

"And Abu Rashid?"

"Find out as much as possible about him. Who's giving him information. And what it is. Now."

With a handshake and a slap on the shoulder the two said farewell. Rafael turned his back. He'd leave first. John Cody would wait five minutes and go down later.

"Do what you have to do," Rafael ordered him before leaving through the opening onto the spiral staircase.

"Are you sure?"

The lack of response confirmed it.

Five minutes.

They could seem an eternity, especially with the immensity of the cupola above one's head in its intricate magnificence. Time for night to fall completely, letting the shadow fill the space, countered by strategically placed lamps that give everything a dreamlike air.

Five minutes.

Let us not remain with John Cody the entire time, as good a person as he seems. Let us move on for a look at what will finally take place.

Five minutes passed, and thirty seconds, for professional accuracy, essential for every agent who calls himself competent. Cody lifted his radio and pressed a button.

"Attention all units. The group has been located. I repeat, the group has been located. Number two, New Change. Saint Paul's Cathedral. I repeat, Saint Paul's Cathedral."

50

Today was one of those days it seemed better to call the office and give whatever excuse, illness or death in the family—no one very close, so as not to tempt fate—and leave the problems for others to solve. But this wasn't an ordinary job, and Geoffrey Barnes wasn't the type to run from challenges. On the contrary, his whole lunatic career, the flow of intelligence information, the next strategic game, made his adrenaline flow in sync with his changes of mood. He wouldn't trade his job for anything . . . even on bad days.

The frenetic activity in the Center of Operations was the same. The apparent chaos of dozens of people on all sides with papers in hand, answering telephones, looking at monitors, pressing keyboards, was just an illusion. Everything was governed by invisible but understood rules, so that nothing slipped by security. Anyone in the midst of this tempestuous sea would notice something out of place, an abnormal movement, a wave out of rhythm with the others and raise the alarm.

"Somebody close that door," Barnes ordered no one in particular from his chair in the office.

Priscilla was the one who closed it, shutting off the room from the noise outside. It wasn't normal for so many people to be so busy, but we're talking about an unusual day. Seated in a chair in front of Barnes we find

Littel. Priscilla was standing at his side, like a bodyguard. Herbert, behind Barnes, looked out the window at the London evening coming on.

"Where are the others?" Barnes asked.

"Analyzing the disc," Priscilla told him. It was her duty to respond to this type of question.

"Is your pal with them?" Barnes was referring to Wally Johnson and the question was for Littel, who remained seated and confirmed with a nod of his head. "I wish they'd finish with that," Barnes sighed. "What the hell's going on?"

"Do you want me to draw you a picture?" Herbert suddenly said without turning his back to the window.

"If you don't mind," Barnes replied sarcastically.

Herbert faced those present for the first time, enraged. He wasn't used to losing control of a situation.

"It's obvious you have a mole on your team."

Littel got up angrily.

"Watch your mouth, my friend."

"For stating the obvious?" He launched a verbal attack. "Gentlemen, do I have to reiterate the fact that he was expecting us? He welcomed us as if he were laughing at us."

No one denied the observation. They kept silent, accepting the reprimand from Herbert, the agent of Opus Dei in that room and, perhaps, the head of the whole organization one day.

"I don't like that he's a step ahead of us and sending us messages. We've got to review things and find the mole."

Littel assumed his position as the senior officer in the room. "This . . . what's your name?" he asked the man from Opus Dei.

"Herbert Ross."

"Herbert is right. This is not good work." He glanced at Barnes. "We have to catch this mole as quickly as possible."

"And how do you propose we do that? A mole is not caught in an hour or two," Barnes said. "Unless you know some new way, the most I can do is start an investigation."

"This isn't a question of investigating," Herbert protested, going to the door and opening it to let in the noisy adrenaline from the Center of Operations.

"Where are you going?" Barnes asked.

"To make my report. The Master's not going to like the news." He closed the door loudly.

"I am sick of Masters," Barnes snorted.

"I don't know if it was a good idea to let the reporter go," Littel confessed, thoughtfully changing the subject.

"He's of no interest, believe me. He knows nothing Rafael doesn't want him to know."

Rafael. This name still sounded false and every time he said it, it was hard to get out of his mouth. He and Jack Payne, one and the same.

"Even so . . ." Littel didn't seem convinced.

"Besides that, Roger's on our side. He'll do what's necessary. And keep tabs on the journalist," Barnes claimed.

"Who's Roger?"

"Roger Atwood," Barnes repeated, amazed at the ignorance. "The chief editor of the newspaper."

This was a valid argument to Littel and convinced him that Barnes had been right to let Simon Lloyd go free. He was of the old guard, this Barnes.

"And the mole? What do we do?" Littel asked.

"Don't worry. We'll find him," Barnes confidently asserted. "It's always been that way, and always will be."

"Priscilla, go get us some coffee, please," Littel said.

Priscilla's supreme dedication and competence were well known, so she left, leaving the two top men of the agency alone.

"How do you feel about this?" Littel wanted to know.

"Never worse," the other answered with a sigh. He stretched, cupping his hands behind his head. "Everything will be resolved one way or another."

"True," commented Littel, looking into space for a few seconds before focusing on Barnes again. "Tell me something. Have you ever heard the name Abu Rashid?"

51

Abu Rashid continued his personal calvary, his supernatural mission, a captive of the intransigent foreigner whose conscience didn't bother him. The good name of the Roman Catholic Church would always be the foreigner's top priority.

These were the options that everyone chose based on the facts available at the moment; that's how life works, a wheel of selections, of luck and lottery, where intelligence and talent have some weight, but not much.

No, the Virgin would never appear to a Muslim. This was a case for psychiatry, for internment in a hospital for mental cases. It was legitimate and normal to confuse religion with schizophrenia, visions with hallucinations, revelation with fantasy. The best thing was that he'd be able to prove it in a few minutes as soon as they had their feet on the ground again. The foreigner held on to that hope. It would serve as an argument before his superiors, and there'd be no need for execution, speaking of Abu Rashid, of course. That was never his strength. He never did it, but he knew people who'd snuffed out a human life for less reason than Abu Rashid had provided. But those were other characters and personalities, more energetic and less patient men. It was essential to always protect the image and good name of the Church, and thus the existence of those protectors with no lives of their own, angels who covered thousands of miles to fight the threats the world produces. They were called Sanctifiers and, as far as the world was concerned, didn't exist, never existed, and never would exist. They had turned over their souls to the Church, to Christ, and beyond that they knew nothing. Sometimes we find gentler souls among the Sanctifiers, like this foreigner, but the optimists and defenders of human life shouldn't delude themselves. He wouldn't hesitate, if he decided Abu Rashid was truly a threat to his beloved Catholicism, or if he received orders to do so. He'd squeeze the trigger or cut his throat without blinking. Christ always came first, second, and third. There was no higher priority in his life.

When they had landed in Krakow, the plane had been directed to a remote area of the international airport John Paul II, reserved for private planes, where a car waited without a driver, as he'd requested. Not a luxury model with a lot of horsepower, calling attention to itself, but a white Lada, more than twenty years old, with none of the conveniences of today's cars, but which passed completely unnoticed in the immense Polish territory they covered that night.

The trip was hardly fifty miles to the south of Krakow, although in the Lada it took longer than he expected. What was important was that they'd arrived, and so we see them following the well-traveled road on foot, Abu Rashid first, with his hands tied, shoved along from time to time by the foreigner, not for walking too slowly, but to remind him he was a captive. Besides a nudge in the ribs, nothing too rough.

The handcuffs fastened the black briefcase to the foreigner's wrist as if it were an extension of his body.

Anyone else would have asked where they were going, but not Abu Rashid. We can almost make out a satisfied smile on his sweaty, beat-up face.

They climbed the path up the mountain aided by the light of a flashlight that dimly penetrated the veil of obscurity. The foreigner pointed the light slightly in front of Abu Rashid's feet.

"We're getting there," he let him know almost cordially.

"I know that," the Muslim replied.

A few feet ahead, another jab in Abu Rashid's ribs made him fall to the ground this time. The foreigner was alarmed and poised for action. He hadn't used enough force to cause that reaction, he was sure of that. Something, or someone, had caused the fall.

Abu Rashid was on his knees with his head down. It was hard to tell if he was kneeling toward the Kaaba in Mecca, given their disorientation, the cover of night without stars, and the lack of a *mihrab*, but certainly the Muslim had adopted the position of prayer, strange in those hours before dawn, but who could criticize a believer for prostrating himself in a moment of affliction?

The foreigner could. Not only from his role as captor, but because that position always made him feel a certain nausea. All that submission, the abrasive demonstration of the faith of Allah, All-Powerful God, disgusted the foreigner. Not even the ordination of new priests could compare to this lying flat out, when the candidates stretched out on their bellies, kissing the floor, almost under the feet of their colleagues, and gave their lives to the Roman Catholic Church, the only true faith, no other. Nothing was more repulsive to the foreigner than this twisted gesture of Abu Rashid with his bound arms on the ground and his head beside them.

The foreigner wanted to put a stop to it as soon as possible, but hesitated, perhaps because this wasn't the typical hour of Islamic Sabah, although it was known to vary from one place to another. He decided to wait a moment, not out of respect for an erroneous belief, but out of suspicion. So much the better that only he and Abu Rashid were present here in the middle of this Polish forest, a cold wind chilling their bones, more his than the Muslim's, which was also irritating.

For a minute nothing happened, Abu Rashid on his knees on the ground and the foreigner on foot watching him impatiently.

"There is still hope," Abu Rashid said without moving.

"Hope for what?"

"Hope for you," the other replied from the same position. "There are always two paths, as I told you already."

"Come on, get moving. We have to keep going. It's not the time to pray," the foreigner grumbled, ignoring the comment and giving him a light shove in the ribs with the flashlight, as if dealing with the unforeseen behavior of an animal. His other hand was on the revolver in the holster he carried under his jacket. One never knew; one couldn't be too careful.

"Every hour's an hour for prayer, but don't worry. I'm not praying."

"Then what are you doing?"

"I'm listening," the old man declared.

The foreigner looked around uncomfortably. He didn't feel or see the presence of a living soul. He squeezed his fingers tighter on the handle of the gun, insecure. Sacrilege. Sacrilege.

"There's no one here," he said, hiding his suspicion that she was looking at him unfavorably.

"Don't be uncomfortable. She'll always love you, no matter what you do. If she should blame you, there'd be no reason for the existence of free will. The beauty of life is that we can always choose."

"Shut up. Get up and keep going," he ordered.

Abu Rashid raised his body, remaining on his knees. His eyes were open, shining, looking into space.

"Didn't you hear me?" the foreigner insisted proudly.

"You are what I don't want to hear," Abu Rashid said.

Silence fell under the cover of the night, joined by wild animals that stopped their whimpers and calls at the exact same instant, as if everything felt the presence of a superior being. Only the foreigner was unable to feel anything despite being a devotee and believer in the Virgin. No, she couldn't be there. It went against everything he believed.

"Calm yourself, Tim. Let yourself feel the positive energy of the universe. Don't live under pressure, frustration, doubt."

The foreigner was astonished. Had he heard right?

"I've never told you my name," was all he could get out.

"I know that, Tim. I've known you since long before you were born."

"Who told you my name?"

"She. Who else?" Abu Rashid was imperturbable.

"Cut the shit. Who told you?"

"The other one asked exactly the same question."

The foreigner, baptized as Timothy, took the gun from the holster and pointed it at the Muslim's head, squeezing slightly. He was losing his mind.

"What other one?"

Abu Rashid turned toward him despite the cold barrel pressing against his head.

"This isn't the time, Tim."

52

Geoffrey Barnes was confused by what he'd just heard from Harvey Littel about the individual named Abu Rashid, Israeli by nationality, Muslim by birth, resident of Jerusalem.

"It's too surreal," he finally said after thinking for a minute. "Is there any evidence to confirm it?"

"Some, considering the sources."

"We need to know more."

"He's disappeared."

"Yeah, and the other one died," Barnes added. "Do you think someone's throwing down the gauntlet?"

Littel shrugged his shoulders. "It's hard to say. I know there's no trace of the man. We have people on permanent surveillance, but nothing."

"I imagine there are plenty of people who want to find him," Barnes said thoughtfully. "And even more who want to do away with him."

"True," Littel agreed. "But imagine if he's hiding and then one day shows up here and starts talking."

"No one would believe him," Barnes asserted.

"Except his people."

Barnes made a sign with his lips suggesting his doubts.

"I don't think it'd take much to stir up religious conflict. From there a disastrous war is only a step away," Littel warned.

"That's a little apocalyptic."

"That's what they pay us for, Barnes. To analyze and think up scenarios. That's what I see."

"We have to find a way to bring him out. He has to show signs of life."

"If he's alive."

"If he's not, all the better. Case closed."

"But we need to be certain."

The two men looked at each other circumspectly and with respect. Until a body appeared, everything was left hanging.

"A Muslim who performs miracles and has visions. This would not occur to anyone," Barnes sighed. "How did they know about it?"

"Who?"

"The religious orders."

"Those guys know everything."

"And what is it that interests them?"

"Everything is of interest to those people . . . even that which is not of interest."

"It could be of interest to the orthodox," Barnes suggested.

"For what? To blackmail the Vatican? That game's over. History."

"You never know. A more ambitious priest. He hears things here and there. A Muslim miracle man who knows secrets about the Catholic Church."

"Presuming it has secrets."

"It's enough. Presumption has always served as an excuse for a lot of things. Even torture and killing."

"I don't think it'll start from there."

"If you have people taking care of that, all we can do is wait until something happens. Aside from that, we have more important things to take care of."

"We have to resolve this mess as soon as possible. Very strange things are happening," Littel said.

"You're telling me."

At that moment they heard the tumult of the Center of Operations outside the office again. The two men looked at the door and saw Staughton with his hand on the knob.

"We have a location," he told them hurriedly.

The two got up.

"Finally," Barnes protested, suddenly animated. "Where?"

"Saint Paul's Cathedral."

"They're pretty brazen," Barnes complained, putting on his jacket. "Going to a sacred place after so much blood. Those people are such hypocrites."

"Are you a believer?" Littel asked, joining Barnes as he left the office at a fast pace.

"In our work we don't have that luxury."

"Why not?"

"It's obvious, Harvey." Thou shalt not kill is hard to avoid.

They passed through the Center of Operations, ignoring the busy employees, the running around, the disconnected cries that crossed the room forming the noisy background of voices and equipment that was heard.

Staughton and Herbert joined them with Priscilla and a group of eight agents.

"And the CD?" Barnes asked Staughton.

"It's still being processed."

"Order them to finish it."

"They can't go any faster."

"And Thompson?"

"He's already gone on ahead," Staughton informed him promptly.

"Wally?" Littel wanted to know.

"Same."

They got to the elevators, the secret four that opened onto the floors the agency used, and descended to a private garage with space for eighteen vehicles. There were three other public elevators, but these four only stopped on the floors occupied by this American institution. The floors weren't identified by any sign. Everything was perfectly organized, since as soon as the doors open to the garage, we can see four black automobiles, with tinted windows, license plates covered, doors open, the engines running, and drivers at the wheels ready to accelerate. American efficiency in all its splendor.

The garage door opened as soon as they'd all gotten into the vehicles. Harvey Littel and Geoffrey Barnes traveled in separate cars, logical rules of protocol. In the case of an attack it was more probable that one of them would manage to escape, thereby avoiding a crisis of leadership and any unanticipated promotions. Another fact of no minor importance was to ride in the middle, shielded from the car's exterior by the other agents. This works for both democracy and dictatorship, capitalism and communism, the weak and the strong, intelligent and stupid—to always protect the most important person with one's body, life, and soul. All the rest, Staughton, Priscilla, Thompson, Wally Johnson, and the remaining agents in the field, were expendable. Barnes and Littel were the ones who had to be protected at all cost, although it was improbable that something would happen to these two. The generals make war far from the front; there are no differences in the field.

Barnes assumed the position of generalissimo, since Littel had given him precedence, and they communicated by way of microphones on the sleeves of their shirts. They also had wireless earpieces placed in their ears.

"What's your position, Thompson?"

Static.

"Thompson, what's your position?"

"They . . . in one . . . direction . . . Luton," were the disconnected words they heard over the phone. It was Thompson's voice.

"We have interference. Repeat, Thompson," Barnes ordered.

"The subjects have entered a taxi and driven off toward Luton," Thompson announced. "I'm behind them, near Hemel Hempstead on the M1."

"*Okay.* Did you hear, gentlemen? Go toward Luton fast."

In Barnes's car were Herbert and Staughton, who immediately began to find fault with the plan.

"Will he be waiting there?" Staughton asked.

"Who?"

"Rafael."

"What are you talking about?"

"Don't you remember what the journalist said?" he reminded him. "He'll wait for you there."

Barnes thought about it for a few moments. He scratched his head and beard and breathed heavily.

"Charades. I am sick of games," he grumbled. "Do you have something on the CD?"

"I have people working on it. As soon as they know something, they'll tell me."

"Why is that giving us so much trouble? He doesn't have as many resources, and he managed to decipher the content."

"We've stumbled on a code. He must have set it in order to delay us," Staughton answered, excusing the men working under his orders.

"Son of a bitch," Barnes swore. "How much time do you think it'll take to break it?"

"In Langley it'd already be broken with the computer. One or two hours more," Staughton guessed.

"Do it in less than an hour," Barnes deliberated. And said nothing more about it.

"Thompson here. We just lost the subjects."

Barnes raised the microphone hidden in his sleeve up to his mouth.

"How could that have happened?"

"We're here in the airport at Luton, and a truck almost ran into us. We lost sight of them." Thompson's voice constricted with frustration. He hated to fail.

"Keep searching. It's obvious they're in the airport. Look in every corner, all commercial and private planes."

"Yes, sir," Thompson obeyed. He had expected a bigger outburst.

"Gentlemen, get to Luton fast," Barnes ordered.

"They can't leave the country, Barnes," Littel advised through the transmitter. They were all in direct communication and heard everything the other said. A true technological feat.

"I know, Harvey. I know." He didn't know anything else.

It'd be complicated if they lost their trail again and they left the country. Still, there was something in all this that made him even more uneasy.

"Who was it that located them in Saint Paul's?" he asked Staughton.

"I have no idea. We sent out an alert. I think it was one of the Metropolitan guys," he replied uncertainly.

"That's irrelevant," Herbert protested from the passenger seat. "We've lost them again," he attacked incisively.

"Do you want to walk?" Barnes's nostrils flared. It wasn't a shout, more a threat without feeling, but, at the same time, full of anger, if this was possible.

"I'm sure I'd get there sooner," the other muttered, not daring to answer in the same tone.

Barnes spoke into the tiny microphone. "Thompson, inform us of the situation."

"Thompson here. We're still searching."

"Hurry up." The instruction was for Thompson, not the driver. "Look on the runway and order all the planes stopped, if necessary," he said in a figurative sense, of course, but if he could . . .

"Roger that," the other answered, conscious of what was possible and what was not.

It took forty-two minutes and eighteen seconds for Barnes, Littel, and company to reach the airport at Luton. Night had fallen, with a cold wind. Then three minutes and forty-three seconds to reach Thompson in the department of the LCDL. He was with a thin man dressed in a suit too wide for his frame, a cigar in hand with a long hanging ash burning away the tobacco. Needless to say, smoking was not permitted there . . . except for him.

"This is the director of the London Luton Airport, McTwain," Thompson introduced him. "He's placed the airport and all employees at our disposal," he added.

It can't be helped, Barnes thought. But he wasn't interested in making another enemy. He had enough already.

"Thanks," he only said.

Thompson passed Barnes a clipboard.

"This is the list of flights today," he explained.

"Anything out of the ordinary?" Barnes wanted to know.

McTwain, besides thin and a smoker, trembled like a leaf. Not out of fear, since he wouldn't be the director if he didn't know how to fight panic, but from stress. An airport can ruin anyone's nerves.

"My subordinates are looking at every detail, but so far it seems everything is legal."

"Any flight requested at the last minute?"

"Daily we have four or five requests. Among the private flights, of course."

"Any at the last minute?"

"Define the last minute."

The trembler must think he's a comedian, Barnes said to himself.

"We only authorize private flight requests a minimum of five hours ahead. Unless it's a serious situation," McTwain clarified pedantically.

"We need to know all the touch-and-gos requested in the last twenty-four hours," Herbert ordered.

"Aren't we neglecting the commercial flights?" Staughton alerted them.

"I have the team distributed throughout the airport. If they're on a commercial flight, they'll still be in the terminal and will be seen," Thompson informed them.

"Why do I have the feeling someone is making fun of us?" Barnes showed his irritation, once again, nothing new.

"What do you mean, Barnes?" Littel asked.

"It just seems to me we're where he wants us to be."

Wally Johnson joined the group waving a paper in the air.

"I think I've found them," he said.

"Where?"

"A Learjet 45 from an Italian rental company landed less than two hours ago," he told them.

"Let me see that." Herbert grabbed the paper from Wally Johnson's hand. It wasn't the time to observe courtesy. He ran his index finger down the page. "In the name of Joseph Connelly?"

"Exactly."

"What does this ass have to do with anything?" Barnes asked impatiently.

"What called my attention was not the name, but the flight code."

Herbert looked again at the page and identified the code. He passed it to Barnes.

"Son of a bitch." He turned suddenly to McTwain. "Contact the tower and see if they've taken off."

The director took the radio.

"Attention, tower. McTwain here. Code 139346."

"Code 139346. Tower here. I'm listening."

"Tower, what is the current situation with flight JC1981?"

"One moment."

The whole group was in suspense, ears fastened, in a figurative sense, to the radio.

Scarcely five seconds passed, but they seemed interminable. Finally . . .

"Code 139346, McTwain, authorization for takeoff of flight JC1981, accelerating down runway 26."

"Tower, abort the authorization for takeoff. I repeat, abort the authorization for takeoff."

"Code 139346, McTwain. Understood," the tower responded.

Barnes looked at the pretentious trembler with other eyes. It was clear why he was the director. Decision and rapid reaction, a praiseworthy quality in any profession.

More seconds waiting. Agonizing.

"Code 139346, McTwain. Negative on aborting flight JC1981 on runway 26. Flight JC1981 is at two thousand feet with instructions to rise to eleven thousand."

"Tower, Code 139346, McTwain here. Communication terminated." He turned to Barnes. "It's not in my hands, sir. As you know, my power ends when the plane takes off. You'll have to contact the NATS."

Barnes turned his back on him, frustrated but not defeated.

"Charades. I'm sick of charades."

"Order the plane shot down," Herbert suggested.

Littel interposed himself. "Don't be crazy. What's the destination of the flight?"

Barnes showed him the paper with the information. Littel turned red when he read it and confronted Barnes's stare.

"He knows."

53

THE BUSINESS DEAL
February 1969

No believer can deny that the Church is competent in its
magisterium to interpret natural moral law.

—PAUL VI, Humanae Vitae, *1968*

Two very different men shared the same room in the papal summer residence in Castel Gandolfo.

Giovanni Battista Montini was modest and reserved; he thought more than he spoke. The other wore his heart on his sleeve and expressed himself enthusiastically. He dressed well, fashionably, and if he had any fault, although he wouldn't have said so, it was vanity. He liked what was extraordinary, and always got what he wanted. He loved to be eulogized, flattered, deferred to. Not every man succeeded in reaching what he had acquired. He was the ruler of an empire in the name of God, Opus Dei. He had thousands of followers and millions of financial donations daily. He'd become the greatest and most influential prelate ever; if not, he wouldn't be here in this house talking informally with Paul VI, his friend.

"José María, things are not that straightforward."

"Of course they are. You yourself told me that the finances were full of spiderwebs. You don't know what you have."

"They're not mine. I need an inventory of the goods of the Church," Giovanni Montini answered civilly.

"The goods of the Church belong to the pope. You know that very well. They're yours. You can give and take." While he spoke, José María gestured effusively. With his loud voice the gestures made him someone who had to be listened to. "Money generates money, Giovanni. You can be the master of an unlimited patrimony, so powerful you can bend anyone to the will of *your* Church."

"The Church is not mine. I'm her highest representative, and it doesn't seem right to go investing her assets in financial operations that could go bad. That's not the role of the Church."

"For the love of God, Giovanni. It's the duty of the Church to invest the money that the faithful deposit in the offertories. They don't expect anything else. I only ask you to give this man an opportunity. Let him inventory and organize the house. Then we'll see."

They were drinking Burmester Port, vintage 1963, the year Giovanni Battista Montini was elected pope, adopting the name of Paul for the sixth time in the history of the Church. The conclave differed from others, since the moribund Angelo Roncalli, better known as John XXIII, had pronounced his name as successor. It's known that the will of the pope should always be obeyed . . . or almost always.

José María Escrivá had brought the bottle that morning, a gift to his lord, his pastor, and everyone else's.

"Who's the man?"

"A bishop who has served in other capacities. Extremely competent."

"What's his name?"

"Paul Marcinkus."

"Paul Marcinkus? He's a personal friend. Principal translator and bodyguard."

Escrivá smiled affirmatively.

"I don't know. I don't know if he has the qualifications for a responsibility like this," the pope said in a distrustful tone.

"He does, you can be confident. He's a suitable person."

"And what is the press going to say? The pope employs a member of Opus Dei to direct the Vatican bank? I don't think so."

"There's the advantage, Giovanni," Escrivá emphasized. "No one knows he's Opus Dei. Only you and I. No one else needs to know." A boyish smile spread over his lips. So easy.

"If I were to agree, everything must be very clear. He cannot invest according to his own whims."

"Of course not," Escrivá agreed.

"He'll have to spell out a concrete, clear plan for the potential of all business deals." He raised an admonishing finger. "Only after cleaning out the cobwebs in the house."

"Of course. You're the boss. Don't forget it."

"Don't say that," Paul said uncomfortably.

"But it's the truth. You may not want to understand it or see it, but it's all yours. This palace and everything in it, the Vatican State . . . Damn, one word from you, and Saint Peter's Square is closed until you say so."

Paul preferred not to think of these things. Other affairs were much more important than the administration of the State and its assets. Nevertheless, he viewed favorably the idea of someone with understanding taking on these more mundane matters and putting the house in order.

"Tell him to come and see me," Paul finally said.

Escrivá smiled. "Agreed."

"Make an appointment with my secretary. I'm going to ask Villot to come also. It'll be good to have a friend taking this on."

"Perfect, Giovanni. You'll see how I am going to show my appreciation," he declared confidently.

"And what are you going to want as a sign of gratitude?" Paul asked ingenuously.

"A statue in the Vatican after my canonization."

Paul laughed, while Escrivá remained thoughtful.

"I'm serious."

54

After a night of good sleep, bodies awaken invigorated, ready to accept new challenges, alert and active. This was how Raul and Elizabeth felt after a flight of thousands of miles over the Mediterranean, in a plane so luxurious it even had two bedrooms with king-sized beds. They felt a little guilty, as if they'd sinned by the simple act of having rested.

"How do you think our little girl is?" Elizabeth asked, truly worried. Her heart contracted again with the paralyzing anguish of motherly anxiety.

"Surely she's well," Raul answered, putting a timid hand on her shoulder.

"Where are we?"

Raul looked out one of the small windows. It had dawned, the sun shone, but they still flew at the altitude of their cruising speed.

"I have no idea."

The door of the bedroom opened slightly, enough for a voice to be heard, the cripple's, who didn't want to interfere with the privacy of his guests.

"Breakfast is served," he informed them.

"We're coming, thanks," Raul answered.

The door closed without a sound.

"If someone had told me that today I'd be having breakfast aboard a private jet that has bedrooms, flying I don't know where, I'd have called him crazy," Elizabeth said. "I feel bad about all the kind attention with no news of Sarah."

Raul hugged her.

"Relax. These people know what they're doing. And she's protected. Rafael can be trusted."

"Yes, but people make mistakes. Whoever is pursuing them must also have resources. Perhaps more."

"Think positively, my dear."

"I'm trying, but I have a bad feeling."

"Let's eat something," Raul suggested, directing her to the door.

"I'm not hungry."

Raul turned toward his wife and hugged her with one hand around her shoulder—they were like a pair of newlyweds on their honeymoon.

"You have to eat, dear. We can't let ourselves get weak. Our daughter needs us in good shape to take care of her," he argued.

"What can we do against those people?" Elizabeth observed hopelessly.

Raul led his wife over to the bed and they sat on the edge. A slight turbulence began to shake the plane, causing some unease.

"I used to think that, too, Liz. But last year your daughter taught us all a lesson," Raul recounted hesitantly. "Things come to an end and not before that. We can sit here completely deceived, crushed, without hope, with death whistling in our ears, but God, or whatever you want to call it, has given us something precious, our intelligence. And everything can change in a second." His words were deeply felt, almost moving. "This is what happened last year, thanks to our daughter. We can never give up. She's going to be all right."

Tears ran down Elizabeth's face. She could only think of her daughter as a little girl, since for parents their children are always adolescents. Perhaps it was destiny, some divine order, that exposed her path to the most lethal and shameless side of the pious Church.

"Shall we go?" Raul insisted one more time.

"Yes, I'll go," Elizabeth agreed, getting up. "We need to keep going, for Sarah."

They left the bedroom for the cabin, where six movable leather easy chairs were installed. At the moment four of them in pairs, facing each other, were separated by a table loaded with breakfast dishes. Plates of brioches, muffins, bread, a mixture of continental and English, with plenty of sausages, bacon, beans, and poached eggs. Probably prepared with Elizabeth and her Saxon blood in mind. All this with Darjeeling and Earl Grey tea, milk, coffee, fresh fruit juice, oranges, as always, and to finish up, a plate of four *sfogliatelle napoletane*, a fine puff pastry of difficult confection, but exquisite taste, in honor of the Italian travelers. Even a butler dressed in black and white was doing the honors at the table.

JC was seated in one of the chairs, eating a *sfogliatella*. At his side, the cripple made do with a piece of bread and butter.

Various plasma-screen televisions were arranged around the cabin tuned into the best news and financial channels. Elizabeth watched the one with Sky News.

"Good morning," JC greeted them. "I hope you like what I ordered."

Raul greeted everyone and sat down. Elizabeth kept watching television.

"Come over and sit down, my dear. There's no news," JC advised. "Come and eat. I've ordered scalloped eggs and beans for you."

Elizabeth sat in the only empty chair next to the table.

"What would you like to drink, *signora*?" the butler asked.

"Tea with milk, please."

"*E voi, signore?*" he asked Raul.

"Coffee."

The butler prepared the orders on a cart like those used by flight attendants.

"Thanks. You didn't have to go to all this trouble," Elizabeth thanked JC.

"Elizabeth, dear, what gets us through this life is comfort. Did you sleep well?"

"Well enough," Raul replied, spreading some cheese over his brioche.

"There was a time when I could sleep on any side and took two minutes to fall asleep," JC complained. "Now everything bothers me. I don't know if it's the engine noise or the altitude."

The butler placed the drinks in front of Raul and Elizabeth.

"Where are we?" Raul wanted to satisfy his wife's curiosity.

"In the air, my friend."

"In whose air?" he insisted. He hated evasions.

"In the air of the Lord," JC responded in the same way.

"Where are we going?" Elizabeth's turn to ask.

"To see a friend," the other informed her.

He always has his answers prepared, Elizabeth thought, a little suspiciously.

"Do you talk to the pope like this?" Raul tried a new strategy.

"A pope is not superior to any of us," JC replied, off guard.

"He's someone very special," Elizabeth said.

"Of course he is, my dear. I'm sure he'd receive you with tea and cookies." The sarcasm was more than obvious in JC's choice of words.

"You weren't well received by the Pole?" Raul insisted on knowing details.

"He was too afraid of me not to receive me well. Which is not to say he spoiled me with parties."

"How many times did you speak with him?"

"Personally? Three. Enough to change the world." He showed no unease at his pretension. It must be how he saw himself, a savior, someone so important that he could give and take at his pleasure, bring down governments, states, and substitute one ally for another.

"That's a little exaggerated," Elizabeth considered.

"You think?" JC asked, making himself comfortable in the seat and sipping his Darjeeling. "Ask the Soviets and the East Germans."

"The Soviets and East Germans don't exist anymore," Raul observed.

"Precisely," the old man concluded with a look of triumph, the brilliance in his eyes of a boy proud of having climbed a high mountain to look back on what he'd done.

"I can't believe it," Raul said, completely amazed.

"Then don't believe it," the other responded simply. "The fact that you don't believe it doesn't mean it's not true."

They both knew that it was so. And the contrary could also be considered true.

"Why can't we know where we're going?" Elizabeth risked asking, a little fearful.

"Who told you that you can't? Don't feel like captives."

"What friend is this we are going to see?" It seemed like an interrogation agreed upon between Elizabeth and Raul. This last question had come from the husband, but JC was used to operating in the line of fire.

"You'll find out."

They noticed the engines had slowed their rotation, and the plane was descending. A static noise was heard, followed by the voice of the pilot.

"*Signor Dottore*, we are beginning our descent into Atatürk."

JC pressed a button. "Great, Giovanni. Thanks."

"Atatürk?" Raul recognized the place.

"Where's that?"

The butler began packing up the table quickly. Security rules regulate takeoffs and landings. In no time he'd cleared everything off the cream-colored table.

"What's Atatürk?" Elizabeth asked again, visibly worried.

"It's an airport," JC replied, tightening his seat belt. "Fasten your seat belts," he advised, "and welcome to Istanbul," he added with one of his rare smiles.

55

There is a barbershop in Ulitsa Maroseyka, near the Kitay-Gorod metro station, that dates from the beginning of the nineteenth century at a time when barbers performed other functions like pulling teeth and resolving family problems. In politics they organized strikes, demonstrations, political revolts, coups, among many other things. Hard as it is to believe, the simple barber, scissors and razor in hand, had more power than a president.

Ivanovsky, the owner of the establishment, who inherited it in the seventies in the middle of the Cold War from another Ivanovsky, his father, has not neglected technological innovation. He created a website on which clients could make their next appointment and choose the style of haircut, as well as the barber. In spite of the remodeling the Ivanovskys carried out, this latest descendant has never let the building lose its identity. So we can experience a museum-like enchantment inside the grand barbershop, composed of pieces ranging from the first chair used by the first Ivanovsky to unique instruments that have been used over time. Anyone can visit, even if not coming for a haircut. You can enter without disturbing the busy employees and demanding clientele since the antique objects are displayed in their own room.

Despite the tumultuous history of the city of Moscow, the Ivanovsky clan never had to worry about assaults, fires, settling bills, or anything of the kind. They've always known the right side to be on and enjoyed the benefits of their choice. The preference among the political class for barbers of the Ivanovsky family has provoked cries of amazement from the curious, especially among barbers. The barbershop's location on Ulitsa Maroseyka, very near Red Square and the Kremlin, was also a factor in its popularity, since besides being near the center of politics, it was also near the most important tourist site in Russia, where thousands of people pass through every day.

"What are we doing here?" James Phelps asked Rafael for the hundredth time, tired, feeling dirty and out of place, like a refugee who'd left his home.

Rafael, Sarah, and Phelps were in Ulitsa Maroseyka, next to a souvenir shop in front of the Ivanovsky barbershop. Sarah no longer bothered to ask questions. This was Rafael's way. There was nothing to do.

"I'm going to get a shave. You can stay here. You can go in the shop and buy a souvenir to take with you," he said.

Without another word Rafael crossed the street and entered the barbershop. The chime of the bell could be heard announcing a customer.

Sarah and Phelps didn't have time to react, and, in spite of Phelps taking a step in the direction of the barbershop, Sarah stopped him by grabbing his arm.

"Let him go. If he wanted to go alone it's because that's how it has to be," she told him.

"It can't be, Sarah." There was irritation in his voice. "We can't be left out of this. It affects us, too."

"If you want to go, go. I'll stay here." She preferred not to know what he'd gone to do, even if it had something to do with her.

Feeling authorized, Phelps started toward the barbershop, leaving her alone. There are no longer gentlemen like in the old days, and even then it was necessary to be cautious of them.

It was surprising that no one had stopped them since they arrived, not only with Barnes hot on their trail but primarily because a Russian agent had died in her house. It was more than probable the Russian Secret

Service was watching their movements, so why had no one appeared? She'd asked herself that question more times than Phelps had asked Rafael what they were doing in Moscow. It was three in the afternoon. They'd traveled all night with a refueling layover in Sofia, where Rafael had mysteriously disappeared for a half hour. They had resumed the flight as soon as he returned and landed at Domodedovo a little after midday. That was the story of her day that brought her to the door of the souvenir shop in front of the Ivanovsky barbershop. She just hoped Rafael wouldn't be long.

Inside the shop we can see Phelps looking for Rafael, with no sign of him. The establishment is long and narrow with mirrors and barber chairs on the two sides. Most of them are occupied by the male customers the shop serves, not out of prejudice but rather preference. Phelps listened to the opening and shutting of scissors or clippers, according to the customer's desire. He didn't see Rafael anywhere.

"Would you like a haircut, sir?" an employee asked in Russian, his chair just now unoccupied.

"Sorry, I don't speak Russian," Phelps answered in English.

"No problem. We all speak English," the Ivanovsky owner put in, a man the same age as Phelps, well preserved, scissors in hand, doing a straight cut in the chair in front. He might be the owner, but he worked just like everybody else.

"Ah, yes?" Phelps didn't know what to say.

"Do you want a haircut?" the employee asked again, now in English.

"The truth is I'm looking for a friend who has come for one. A European, Italian to be more specific."

"Most people here are Europeans," Ivanovsky interjected again. Nothing went on in his shop without his noticing it. Eccentric, with a fine mustache and proud look, face full of talcum powder, rosy cheeks, he added, "Even most of the barbers are French, recruited from the best *coiffeurs* in Paris."

"Good. I'll come back when I need a haircut. I promise." Phelps was evasive and insecure.

"Next time," the employee agreed, tired of the conversation. An empty chair was no money coming in. Two seconds later the chair was occupied by a well-fed aristocrat in a black-and-white-striped suit, dark brown hair gathered into a ponytail the barber loosened, a goatee and Russian mustache.

"Take a look around, mister," Ivanovsky invited Phelps.

"Thanks."

The Englishman walked along the straight hallway looking at the mirrors on both sides. It'd be easier to recognize Rafael if he looked at them. They created a certain confusion in his mind from all the mirrors and people reflected in them into infinity. Considering them all, he saw that Rafael was not in any of the barber chairs or in the waiting room on the side.

At the back of the salon there were stairs leading to the basement and an old elevator with an open, wrought-iron door. He paused uncertainly for a few moments between the stairs and the elevator wondering whether to enter or walk down.

"You don't see him?" Ivanovsky asked. He must have finished with another customer.

"No, strange as it seems," Phelps replied with a timid smile.

"Maybe he's gone down to the museum," the Russian suggested.

"Do you think?" He felt a little fear.

"If you don't see him in the salon and are certain he's here . . ." the other explained, "that's the only place he can be." He took one of Phelps's arms and pushed him gently into the elevator. "This way, it's quicker."

Before he could react, Phelps found himself inside the elevator cabin, and it took him some time to realize there was no control panel to operate. Ivanovsky closed the grate and looked at him from the other side, like a jailer.

"Be careful. There's not much light down there."

The elevator began a slow descent. Phelps saw Ivanovsky rise up, although he was the only one moving, and noticed a sardonic smile before disappearing and descending into complete darkness.

The motor growled, and the whole elevator creaked as it passed down floors. Without light he couldn't figure out how fast he was going, but with his heart in his throat he calculated that thirty seconds had passed. However slow the elevator, he must surely have descended several floors.

It stopped suddenly, almost making Phelps fall. He'd forgotten his fatigue and only worried about the unknown. He opened the door of the cage cautiously—the lighting was bad—took a step forward, a second, a third, and stopped in a hallway. He tried to see enough not to bump into the walls. The hallways, except for some architectural decoration, were all the same. They crossed the building, opening into the main rooms. This one was no different, with several doors all on one side.

"This is the museum?"

A click turned on some fluorescent lights, white and strong, just above him. He was startled and stopped walking. *They must be photoelectric cells,* he thought. He took another couple of steps out of range of the light and another lit up. That confirmed it. The walls were gray and bare. Except for four doors there was nothing more, no pictures, tapestries, tables, absolutely nothing.

Phelps went forward a little more, and the lights turned on at each step, while those behind went out automatically, creating a shadowy atmosphere.

Farther ahead Phelps began to hear voices coming from inside one of the rooms off the hallway. He immediately identified Rafael's but not the other two. They spoke Russian, or some other Eastern European language, that was certain. This Rafael was surprising. The Vatican wasn't scanty with its service. It prepared its people so they could control any terrain lacking nothing, without errors or imperfections.

He approached the door in question, which was only closed a little, but understood nothing since it was all in Russian. He tried to see inside the room, but the crack was narrow. All he could see were shadows.

Suddenly the door opened, revealing a blond man with a wrinkled face covered by a week's growth of beard. He carried a Kalashnikov and began a one-sided conversation in Russian with Phelps. He shouted, spraying shots of saliva in every sense of the word. The thought occurred to Phelps that the gun was unnecessary, since his breath was so bad it could knock down any enemy.

"He doesn't understand Russian," he heard Rafael say in English.

The man stopped his babble and looked inside.

"Why didn't you tell me?"

The Russian dragged Phelps into the room. A sixty-watt bulb hung from a wire attached to the ceiling right in the center, shining down on a square table in bad shape with blotches of dried blood on the laminated wood. Phelps made out another man with a Kalashnikov pointed at Rafael, seated, but, from what could be seen, unhurt. Next to a wall was an open armory. Inside were three shelves full of various makes of guns, grenades, radios, a satellite telephone, a machine for resuscitation or torture, depending on the intended purpose. Phelps felt panic at the sight.

"Is this everyone?" asked the man who was pointing the gun at Rafael's head. He was stronger and older.

"The woman is missing," the wrinkled man said, shoving Phelps against the wall and pressing the barrel of the gun into him. Immediately he searched him minutely. "He's clean."

The older man took the radio and pressed a button.

"Everything clean. The woman's missing."

No reply was heard in the first seconds. Only the uncomfortable silence of uncertainty.

"Good work," a man's voice said at last. "The woman's with me. Take care of the others."

56

H e knows."
One of the crucial principles for secret services that claim to be competent and in the vanguard of technological development is the capacity to construct a command post wherever necessary. In spite of the fact that the enormous headquarters of the agency in Langley occupies tens of square miles and besides secret facilities spread all over the planet, each one with specialized functions, it's common to see small units organized to respond to the demands of the world of espionage. Whether below water, above it, on land or in the air, the CIA is always prepared to act.

In this case the men under the supervision of Barnes and the astute gaze of Harvey Littel found themselves at forty thousand feet flying over Poland. And don't anyone imagine they're in their seats with their seat belts fastened. Here seat belts were only buckled during takeoff and the final stage of landing. The hurried activity was the same as that on land at the Center of Operations. Men and women concentrated on monitors and keyboards, listening devices in their ears, shouts, conversations, printers spewing information. This was a unique room. Organization was maintained, rigid and responsive, adapted to the reality of the space. The airplane in question was a Boeing 727 with the registration DC-1700WJY, plain white, belonging to the CIA, not registered with any airline whatsoever. Nor could it be. The American government wouldn't permit it. Secrets of state must be guarded by the state. Besides the paraphernalia and technicians who occupied the part we'd call economy class, there was an office for Geoffrey Barnes in the business class section, strategically located next to the pilot's door.

Here in that office, shielded from the Center of Operations, we find the same people as always. Barnes, seated in a chair identical to the one he has in London, reclining with his hands behind his head at a more modest desk. Harvey Littel, also seated in an armchair, legs crossed, a thoughtful look on his face. And the rest of the team, Thompson, Herbert, Priscilla, and Wally Johnson. Only Staughton was away, directing the work in the economy section of the plane.

"He knows," Barnes repeated, more to himself than to those present in the small office.

"How can he know?" Herbert asked, irritated.

"He chose Moscow by chance? Coincidence?"

"Even if he does know, we can't risk it," Littel advised. "What do the Russians say?"

"They don't say. They've decided not to cooperate," Thompson reported. "If it were up to them, we wouldn't have authorization to enter the country. Which still isn't guaranteed. Oh, and they deny they're in Russia."

"Bastards," Barnes swore.

"Shit," Littel exclaimed. "Why have they changed their attitude now?"

"They always have a card up their sleeve. You can't trust the Russians," Barnes said.

"One thing is certain," Thompson affirmed. "They're better documented than us."

"Could they have the Muslim?" Wally Johnson suggested.

"For our sake they better not," Littel declared. "That would be terrible."

"Why?" Thompson wanted to know.

"Because we'd have to rescue him," Herbert explained. "And something would probably go wrong and they'd all die during the operation, the hostage included," he added ironically.

"If it were up to you, even we'd be wrecked," Barnes murmured just loud enough for Herbert to hear. The expression Herbert directed at Barnes in return confirmed the murmur had hit its mark.

Staughton entered suddenly, opening the door violently, something out of character for him.

"We have a problem," he said.

"Another one," Barnes exploded.

"The Russians won't permit us to fly over their airspace. Much less land in their territory."

"What?"

"Now this. Can't you do something?" Herbert asked.

"Only if your commander has friends in Russia," Barnes informed him. "And at the highest level."

Littel looked at the floor, withdrawn, pensive.

"This is all very strange."

Staughton left the door and put a file on the desk in front of Barnes.

"What's that?" he asked, abandoning his restful position and bending over the report.

"The content of the CD."

There were a few dozen pages inside the folder. A considerable pile.

"So much?" he protested.

"And I've selected only the most important."

Barnes turned the pages with no desire to read them.

"Make a summary," he ordered Staughton.

"I can't."

Barnes raised his eyes in amazement.

"Why can't you?"

"This is confidential information. There are people in the room not authorized to hear or read it," he explained with authority, resorting to the laws that guide the agency and looking at Herbert.

"Okay, let's read this carefully," Littel confirmed. "Regarding the refusal to let us fly over and land . . ."

"We could try the diplomatic route," Barnes suggested.

"No. They know something. They're going to tie our hands and end up denying the authorization."

"While we lose any trace of the woman and the others. They must already have them in custody," Barnes said in a circumspect tone.

"But something intrigues me."

"What?"

"He's left a trail of bread crumbs so we can follow him. Why?"

"He hasn't left the bread crumbs for us," Herbert asserted.

"For who, then?" Barnes asked with no patience for the colleague butting in.

"For the mole."

"The mole again?" Barnes shouted with irritation.

"There's a mole among us," Herbert insisted.

"Then leave me in peace," Barnes answered, indicating the subject was closed. *I'm not going to let you bring this up again,* his tone suggested.

"We have a problem, gentlemen. We can't enter Russia," Barnes announced in a loud voice. "What do we do? Anyone have a suggestion?"

There was silence for a few moments. No one said anything.

"Think what this is costing the taxpayers. Everybody out," Barnes ordered. "Out of my sight."

Obviously the order didn't pertain to Littel, since he remained in the same position he'd been in for a long time, seated, legs crossed.

The rest left the office silently, depressed, tired. It was the downside of this work. When you did well, no one appreciated it or said a word of encouragement, but if things went badly, the finger was pointed and the criticism never ended. In a short time only Littel and Barnes remained.

"We're screwed," the fat man said.

"No," Littel considered. "We have people in Russia. We don't need to go there personally."

With a triumphant smile Littel went to the satellite phone on Barnes's desk and dialed several numbers. He waited for the connection to be established, and the shining in his eyes redoubled when he heard a response. He placed the call over the loudspeaker.

"Colonel Garrison. It's a pleasure to hear you."

"The pleasure is mine."

"Are you where we agreed?"

"I'm having a coffee precisely in Red Square."

"Perfect. Start the operation."

"I've already started it, my friend. I've already started it."

57

A year later the same fear has returned, panic, and the feeling of impotence. She remembered the abandoned warehouse in New York, the heavy chains that hung from the ceiling to which they fastened her wrists, along with the others. Rafael, who wouldn't be quiet, trying to draw the torture to him, away from her father and the old priest. What was his name? Marius Ferris. That was it. She hadn't thought of the pleasant old man, fragile, mistrustful, chained up the same way she was. Nor had she thought of their captors, Barnes and company, but who really dealt the cards was the man in the Armani suit, and the dark, icy stare, a killer without conscience, and his helper, a Pole of the same type. In charge of everyone, incontestable, untouchable, cruel, JC, the same person with whom she now collaborated and who, a year ago, wanted them all dead. There were no absolute truths, only the moment.

Inside the door of the Russian souvenir shop, she'd had a sudden impulse to call Simon to see how he was doing. *Matrioskas*, eggs imitating Fabergé creations, paintings, jars, ballpoints, postcards, jewelry, everything you could associate with a country. It's unnecessary to add that not one of the offerings caught Sarah's eye. She felt too tired, too worried, in a foreign country, in an exciting city, showy, but not at this moment for her.

If she could have chosen, she'd have preferred to be at her parents' estate in Trindade, without roads, flight, and persecution.

Instead of that, she heard a male voice behind her, very close to her ear. She could almost hear his breathing.

"Little Sarah Monteiro." It was not a question. "Do me the favor of crossing the street and going into the barbershop. Calm and relaxed. Don't try anything stupid. If you do, you'll hurt yourself."

Her heart almost jumped out of her mouth. No matter how many times we go through situations like that, nothing prepares us. Her first reaction had been a useless attempt to turn around and put a face on the voice of her captor, but he wouldn't permit it.

"No, no, no. Look straight ahead. We don't want to be run over, right?"

He mixed a certain pleasure and sense of responsibility in his words. He spoke English with a heavy accent. Russian, probably.

"Who are you?" the journalist asked when she'd recovered her faculties.

"That's not important. Let's go. Hurry."

They crossed the street in the middle of traffic, making some cars honk in protest. At some moment Sarah had mentioned stopping, but something circular and cold poked her in the ribs and convinced her of the contrary.

A dissonant voice woke up the radio the man had fastened to his belt. He brought it to his mouth and answered something in Russian. The bright sun had faded as Sarah and the unknown man entered the barbershop. Her eyes were slow in adapting to the new conditions. Several barbers dressed in black were cutting hair. If she'd had doubts, they'd dissipated since Sarah could see she was really in a barbershop. Again she felt the cold barrel pushing her forward. No one looked at her, even with so many mirrors. The customers concentrated on their newspapers or admired their own faces reflected in the mirror, or watched the plasma televisions set above each mirror in front of every barber chair. All of them were indifferent to Sarah Monteiro and the man shoving her. In the back she saw an elevator. To the left, stairs going down.

"Go down the stairs," the man ordered.

Step by step she went down into the deep darkness. She felt danger. She saw nothing. She only felt the cylinder stuck in her ribs. Was he going to kill her? But why? Who was he? It had been stupid to stay in the street alone. Where were Rafael and Phelps?

"Wait," the man ordered her again. "Put these on."

He gave her something she couldn't identify immediately.

"What is it?"

"Goggles. Put them on."

What you don't see, you don't know. She followed his order and immediately understood why the object had seemed strange. They were, in fact, night vision goggles. The flight of stairs ended there. Another step and she would have walked into the wall. A greenish image made everything clearer. A landing supported another flight of steps that descended lower into the Russian earth. A new landing, a new flight of stairs, with many slippery steps.

"What is this place?" Sarah asked with more fear than she wanted to show.

"The stairway to hell. Isn't it pretty?" the other responded sarcastically.

Sarah regretted asking. What was certain was that in all the way they'd come there was no lamp, light, or even a candle or place for it. The place had really been designed to have no light. A shiver ran up her spine.

"Stop. Give me the goggles."

Sarah had no choice but to obey. She found herself immersed in the darkness of the stairwell. She heard some noises to the side.

"What's that?"

Silence.

A new sound, like something dragging itself along.

"What's that?"

"Be very quiet," the man said with a panting sound indicating physical effort. The voice came from in front. "It's only a little way."

The little way had been long, or seemed so. She heard the man's voice behind her again.

"Now take a step forward."

A step forward.

"Another."

Another step ahead.

"Now relax. Stay quiet."

Sarah complied and again heard the sounds of dragging repeated.

Suddenly a white fluorescent light came on, illuminating an empty hallway. The man, almost sixty years old, was in front of her with a slightly mocking smile on his face.

"We've arrived. You can go on," the unknown man said. "Keep going straight. You can't get lost."

The hallway had doors on only one side. They went in the second.

"Stay here a minute. I'm going to urinate."

The man closed the door, but there was no sound of a key turning in the lock.

Strange, Sarah thought. Could it be he didn't lock it? After a staircase in which special goggles were required to go down, this seemed amateurish. Maybe the door could only be opened from outside. That was it. That had to be it.

Spurred on by curiosity, Sarah tried to turn the doorknob, sure it wouldn't open.

She was wrong.

She spied the hallway. Not a living thing. She started to walk down it, step by step, not knowing what to look for. An exit? Only if there were a different one, because the stairs were impossible. There was no light. She had no idea where she was. The grated door of the elevator was closed and the elevator itself empty. No alarm button was visible. She tried the doors fearfully, always alert for a sound that would indicate the return of the unknown man. She turned the knobs carefully. Two were locked. She didn't need to check the one she'd left. The door at the side was ajar. She opened it slightly and saw Phelps and Rafael seated on chairs face downward on a square table. Red stains on the floor made a shiver run down her spine.

"Rafael," she whispered.

"Sarah," he answered seriously. He showed no physical weakness. "Are you okay?"

"Yes. I mean, considering the possibilities." She was happy to see him again . . . see them . . . "Are you . . . all right?"

"Yes, thanks," Rafael answered calmly.

"James is pale," Sarah realized. "Are you all right?"

"Uh, don't worry. It's nerves," the Englishman said.

"What are we doing here?" Sarah wanted to know. "Is it Bar—"

Rafael put his finger on his lips, the obvious sign to shut up.

"We are in the custody of the Russian secret service. Old guard people without technological equipment or satellite images. They're very patient and have their own training. This is one of their old methods."

"What method?" Phelps asked doubtfully.

"They leave us loose here without pressure, prepared to complain about our life, one to the other, to talk about what has brought us here and how everything has gone wrong for us, et cetera, et cetera."

In fact all this sudden freedom has Seemed Strange to Sarah. It smacked of amateurism. It might have worked if Rafael were not here.

"Would you like something to drink?" Rafael asked Sarah.

"What?" She hadn't expected this question. "Ah, if I had the pleasure of a cup of tea . . ."

"Three teas for us down here, please," he shouted at the door, startling Sarah and Phelps.

"It's not every day we receive a visit from foreigners who know our methods," a voice answered from the door. "The foreigners who know them are not usually in the world of the living."

Sarah recognized him as the man in his sixties who had led her to this basement.

"You?" Phelps offered this scandalized doubt.

"Me indeed," the man answered. He turned to Rafael. "Who are you?"

They stared at each other without blinking. They measured forces, studied each other. Every gesture counted, thus the appearance of calm. Rafael seated with his elbow on the table supporting his chin as if he didn't have a care in the world. The unknown man leaning in the doorway, a cigarette in his mouth.

"You know who I am."

A smile filled the Russian's mouth. Straight white teeth.

"Does the pope know you are here?"

"Why don't you ask him?"

"Maybe I will."

He took a drag on the cigarette and adopted a meditative expression, an empty look, supported by the silence of the moment.

"I have many questions for you, Father Rafael Santini." A slight mocking look shone in the Russian's eyes. It was time to show the cards.

"I haven't come to answer but to ask questions . . . barber Ivanovsky."

58

Inside every border there is an elite with limitless access to all corners of the territory. They are in control over the population whether the regime is democratic or dictatorial. The few that control the many, a minority who clap their hands and see one pair of hands turn into an immense national applause. Beyond the greedy ones of national influence, there are others who go beyond the borders of their own country and manage to make the greater part of other populations dance to the sound of their music. These are the elite of the elite, and of course they exist, since everything can be subdivided infinitely.

Marius Ferris could be considered one of these privileged few, someone who crosses borders without being inconvenienced, who enters countries through a special door without the necessity of explanations.

Work or pleasure? is what some border guards ask recent arrivals. A phrase Marius Ferris never hears. One word, one word alone, is what they tell him: *Welcome.* They don't even take his diplomatic passport with the Vatican seal. It's enough when they see it at a distance in the hand of a man of the highest importance.

He had arrived on a commercial night flight, business class, of course. He has enjoyed the privilege of a Famous Grouse whiskey, earphones to listen to music or add sound to the images on his individual monitor, an orthopedic pillow to sleep a little. After all, it was two hours and forty minutes in the air, and sleep has to be regularized. Twenty minutes' delay from the scheduled arrival to the actual time the plane touched down on the asphalt of Leonardo da Vinci Airport at Fiumicino.

He headed immediately for the place of his personal pilgrimage. His bedroom in the Casa di Santa Marta could wait.

He found a young driver waiting for him with a paper showing the letters M.F.O.D.

Marius Ferris, Opus Dei. The prelate smiled.

"That's me. Good evening."

"Good . . . good evening . . . Your Eminence."

He could have corrected him and told him that he was not yet "Your Eminence," but he liked the deference to religious authority. In the final account he and his colleagues were the border that separates the believers from God. And nobody got to God without passing through people like him. It was worth all the money extracted from the faithful, more or less wealthy, who deposit fortunes in their hands . . . in the name of God.

The driver offered to take the small silver-gray briefcase he carried.

"Don't bother. I'll carry it," he refused arrogantly. "Show me to the car, please."

The car was right at the door of the arrivals terminal, a rare case today, explicable because the passenger was who he was.

Once settled into the immense backseat of the Mercedes, top line, with his briefcase in his lap, Marius Ferris sighed. A sigh of relief, of peace with himself. Things were coming together again.

"To Saint Peter's, Your Eminence?" the driver asked, looking at him in the rearview mirror.

"No. No. Santa Maria Maggiore."

He had to go now. He couldn't wait any longer.

The young man drove off wiping away the drops of sweat from his face. It seemed strange the bishop wanted to go to Santa Maria della Neve. The basilica was closed at that hour, like all the sacred places in Rome. Even the saints have a right to the same nocturnal rest as the living. Thank God.

There was little traffic on the expressway at that hour of the morning. The airport itself had been empty when he arrived, only the late arrivals, the distracted, the disoriented, who didn't understand Italian or English, those who'd lost their belongings or those who'd come from late-night flights like that of Marius Ferris.

The straight fast lane with guardrails less than a yard from the outer edge on the shoulder didn't intimidate the drivers who used it. Least of all this nervous young man, who, at the wheel, at sixty-five or seventy miles an hour, forgot his anxieties with nothing on his conscience. The left lane was for speed, and he didn't change lanes until he entered the Fiumicino–Rome freeway, except on one occasion to let a faster BMW pass.

At least he's efficient, Marius Ferris thought. Driving over the speed limit didn't bother him. The faster the better.

Without delay they entered the great imperial city. Marius Ferris looked at his watch. Two-twenty. It wasn't a decent hour to enter this basilica or any basilica or church in Rome or anywhere else.

They turned onto the Lungotevere di San Paolo, ignoring the first of four basilicas in Rome, San Paolo Fuori le Mura. It was not the one that mattered, we well know, or the greatest. Destiny marked Santa Maria Maggiore as the most important tonight.

"The basilica is closed at this hour," the driver dared to say in an attempt to start a conversation. He was visibly much calmer.

"For you," Marius Ferris only replied, stressing his superior importance.

The young driver had thought this would be a quick trip, picking up a priest at the airport and taking him to Saint Peter's. He'd have time to stop by Ramona's house on the Via dell'Orso and give her a good-night kiss, maybe something more. But this detour wouldn't allow him time for that. He should cross himself and ask forgiveness for thinking sinful thoughts of lust, but he was ashamed because of the presence of the prelate in the back-seat. He was afraid he'd read his thoughts. Little did the young driver know that Marius Ferris had more things to think about than his driver's sexual fantasies, although what the old man felt, now that they'd left the Via dei Fori Imperiali and drove up Cavour, could be compared to the pleasure of carnal relations, applied to the spiritual. Marius Ferris, apparently calm, felt anxious with butterflies in his stomach, just like the blessed that look forward to an amorous encounter, a kiss on the lips, a smile.

Once on Via Cavour they turned right toward the Via di Santa Maria Maggiore. It was a steep climb that leads to the Via Liberiana. The driver eased up with the basilica of Santa Maria Maggiore on the left.

Marius Ferris opened the door with the vehicle still in motion, forcing the young man to brake hard.

"Wait for me here," he ordered, closing the door immediately and walking in the direction of the side door for authorized persons only to the right side of the basilica.

The driver closed his eyes in frustration. *Hell.* He hated the idiotic phrase *Wait for me here.* He hated it. Oh, Ramona, beautiful Ramona, you will have to wait another night for him to throw pebbles against your window.

But it's Marius Ferris who interests us. He approached the side door for deliveries and employees. He rang the bell for fifteen minutes before someone appeared. For the last five minutes he never stopped pressing the button. The person who finally opened the door was a Redemptorist brother, roused out of bed by the violent, constant buzzing.

"There are hours for visiting the basilica and the brothers," he scolded. "This isn't one of them." His eyes were red with sleep and anger.

"Get out of the way," Marius Ferris said, shoving him aside roughly.

The man didn't resist and let him enter. Brothers aren't used to violence, no matter what order.

"Where do you think you're going? Who are you?" he managed to ask.

"I'm the guy who pays you," Marius Ferris answered immediately, turning his back and walking toward the interior of the church.

The man recovered and ran after him.

"Listen, I don't know who you think you are, but you can't come in like this. Identify yourself or I will have to call the Carabinieri."

If, on the one hand, Marius Ferris loved being flattered, put on an altar, and adored, the contrary infuriated him. He stopped and looked at the Redemptorist.

"Tell Brother Vincenzo I'm going to be in the crypt for five minutes. He already knows."

"You know the prior?"

"I know everyone. If you want to continue in your position, I suggest you go to bed."

"Very well, sir. Do you know the way?"

Marius shook his head. Just what he needed. A friar acting important with him. He waited until the other returned to his room and entered the immense nave with a gold ceiling, silent, dark, holy.

He retraced the way that someone else had taken twenty-six years earlier, with the opposite purpose. He went down the center aisle, unhurriedly, a slight fear rising within as the baldachin could be seen closer and closer. He would be lying if he said he wasn't sweating. The light was dim but showed the moisture covering the rest of his face. It was dampening his suit, drops falling on the holy floor. Even great men react to great moments.

The crypt was under the altar. Two small gates on either side served as an entrance and exit. They opened onto two narrow steps that descended to the crypt where the wooden boards of the manger were found, the alleged material that formed part of the infant Jesus' crib.

When he found himself before the relic, he knelt down and bowed his head submissively. He joined his hands and whispered a litany, bursting from a heart full of doubts. He wouldn't turn his back on the challenge that awaited him. Meanwhile nothing could separate him from his encounter alone with God, from Whom he asked discernment and strength to carry out his purpose.

He roused his courage and got up from the prie-dieu. He took off the gold chain around his neck and opened the glass cover that protected the relic containing the holy boards from the altar consecrated to the Virgin. He searched in the place he'd been told to look, and . . . nothing.

No envelope, object, nothing. He tried again over and over until there was no doubt. Beyond the boards, guarded inside the gold reliquary supplied with a plastic screen to permit viewing by the countless faithful who visited the crypt daily, there was nothing more. What he was looking for had been removed already.

His sweat and nerves overwhelmed him. He'd looked forward to this moment so much, had wanted to feel a whirlwind of contradictory emotions . . . and now . . . nothing. Only the boards remained inside their protective reliquary, but, with all due respect, they weren't as important as the secret that should have been hidden there.

His doubts overcame him. Had it ever been here? He looked at the chain and the gold key hanging from it. It was the only one, he was sure of that. He remembered how the other obtained the original when it had been decided this would be the hiding place under the protection of the Holy Child. He'd had to make a Franciscan drink until he passed out. The key disappeared that night, and this was the same key in his hand now. He remained on his knees in front of the sacred memorial. His legs weakened and gave out under the weight of his disillusion.

Think. Think, he thought.

He could reach only a not very optimistic conclusion.

Treason.

He closed the glass that protected the reliquary from the implacable atmosphere and climbed the stairs two steps at a time. He jumped the small gate and ran down the nave toward the exit.

Simultaneously he dialed a number on his cell phone. Two rings later, someone answered.

"We've been betrayed. Kill them all."

59

John Paul II.

"Everything comes down to him."

"He's the beginning and the end."

"John Paul the Second is dead."

"A man like that never dies."

Where have I heard that before? Sarah asked herself, while she listened to the debate between Rafael and the barber.

They were seated at a narrow table, Sarah facing James Phelps and the barber facing the priest.

The conversation was between the latter two men alone. No one else was permitted to interrupt.

"How did you get mixed up in this?" Rafael wanted to know.

"It's Mitrokhin's fault," Ivanovsky explained. "Have you heard of him?"

"Of course. He worked in the KGB archives for forty years and put together his own archive transcribing the most important documents. Later he went into exile somewhere in the UK."

"Convenient, wouldn't you say?"

"You're the ones who have to check for double agents. Naturally he quickly became the best friend of the British."

"He was anti-Russian, an idiot, a traitor."

"He passed your greatest secrets to the enemy," Rafael said provocatively.

Ivanovsky shrugged his shoulders, dismissing his importance.

"Very few secrets. The British were the ones who took him in. The Americans didn't believe him. After a certain point, we suspected him of duplicity and decided to give him misinformation."

Rafael wrinkled his nose.

"I don't know if I believe that."

"Believe it."

"The powerful Soviet Union has an agent suspected of high treason and decides to give him false information instead of arresting and executing him?"

"That's exactly what happened. The majority of what is known as the Mitrokhin Archive is pure fiction."

"Bullshit," Rafael accused him. "He deceived them, and they made up this excuse."

"Don't forget we are talking about transcriptions, not original documents. We don't have to make up anything. Or even comment on the subject."

"But the British classified it as the most complete intelligence source in memory."

"And why wouldn't they? Imagine that an agent of the CIA or MI6 transcribed documents, whether true or false, for thirty or forty years and passed them to us. Do you think we wouldn't classify them as true?"

The two men looked at each other. Their scrutiny had ended, the analysis of each other's words and character over. From here on nothing needed to be explained.

"Everything begins with Mitrokhin," Rafael said as if thinking out loud, "who accuses you, among other things, of having planned and carried out the attack in 1981 in Saint Peter's."

"With the help of the Bulgarians, Poles, and the now defunct East Germans," Ivanovsky added.

"That's where Mitrokhin caused problems," Rafael declared.

Ivanovsky frowned.

"I see you're well informed."

"I try to keep current. If Mitrokhin thought the USSR had something to do with the attempt, it was because he was led along." A meaningful wink.

"That's right. They tricked us."

"I know."

"We knew an attempt on the pope was imminent. We filled Saint Peter's Square, and the blame fell on us."

"Who did you suspect?"

"For two years we suspected the Americans."

"Why?"

"The Polish pope at that time was enough to make anyone wet his pants with fear. It was Americans or the Iron Curtain. The Americans have done it before. They killed their own president in 1963."

Sarah listened openmouthed.

"Look who's talking," Rafael observed sarcastically. "How many did your Stalin kill?"

"Better not to go there."

"I agree."

We all live in glass houses.

"When did you stop suspecting them?" Rafael returned to the subject.

"When the girls disappeared in 1983."

"Emanuela and Mirella? Is that who we're talking about?" Rafael asked. There couldn't be mistakes.

"Affirmative."

The wrinkled one, who a little while ago carried an AK-47, came into the room with a tray filled with four cups and a teapot, a sign the meeting was friendly . . . or not.

"Who are those girls?"

The two men looked at Sarah with condescension. She couldn't stand not asking. She'd heard of the girls. Phelps had called them girls but didn't know who they were. . . .

The wrinkled one put the tray on the table and left. Ivanovsky passed the cups around and served the steaming orange tea to everyone.

"Mirella and Emanuela were two teenagers who disappeared in Rome in 1983. They were kidnapped by the same man at Marcinkus's orders."

"Why?" Sarah couldn't believe it.

Phelps picked up his cup to drink the tea, but Rafael, without taking his eyes off Ivanovsky, placed his hand over Phelps's cup.

"The Vatican received three calls from a man who identified himself as the American and demanded the immediate release of the Turk in exchange for Emanuela's liberty."

"And the Vatican didn't give in?" Sarah joined the conversation definitively.

"The Vatican couldn't do anything. The Turk was in Italian custody," the barber explained while sipping a little of his tea. "But that's when we realized the attack could have been an inside job. That and other things we discovered later."

Rafael lifted his hand from Phelps's cup, permitting him to drink.

"And he killed them?" she asked.

The Russian looked uncomfortably at Rafael, a request for help the other understood.

"They were already dead before the call," Rafael finally said.

"How is that possible? Weren't they the price of exchange for the freedom of the Turk?"

A new, heavy silence.

"Let's say they served other purposes and let's not talk about it again," Rafael concluded peremptorily. He changed the subject. "Let's talk about now. What was your man doing in London?"

"Which man?" the other asked evasively.

"Grigori Nikolaievitch Nestov."

Ivanovsky squirmed in his chair, disguising his unease.

"I don't understand," he stammered.

"We're past that phase, Ivanovsky," Rafael scolded him without altering his tone.

He took his first sip of tea, showing confidence. Every gesture counted. He let the silence spread through the room as the hot liquid went down his throat.

"Grigori Nikolaievitch Nestov," Rafael repeated.

"He was a good man. And a good friend," Ivanovsky confessed at last, his eyes looking into space and his memory providing vivid images of the dead man. "Tell me, have you heard of Abu Rashid?"

"The name's not unfamiliar."

"Who's he?" Phelps asked, wrapped up in everything being said.

"Abu Rashid is a Muslim who lives in Jerusalem and sees the Virgin Mary."

"What?" Phelps was scandalized.

"It's true," Ivanovsky confirmed.

"Nonsense. I've never heard of such a thing," Phelps insisted.

"It's more common than you might think. Perhaps your friend from the Vatican can confirm it." The barber pointed an accusing finger at Rafael.

Rafael nodded.

Phelps and Sarah were shocked.

"It can't be."

"There are countless stories of similar things. But as fast as they appear, they disappear."

"What do you mean by that?" Phelps asked.

"Every time a case is identified, the subject disappears. We can go back more than three hundred years and the result is always the same," the barber said. "The same thing happened with this one."

"And what does Nestov have to do with Abu Rashid?" Rafael wanted to know.

"Nestov went to see Abu Rashid," the Russian barber explained, "in Jerusalem. We needed to confirm the veracity of the visions."

"And were they real?" Sarah and Phelps asked, avid with curiosity.

"We think so."

"You think so? You're not certain?" Sarah's professional side awakened. Wrap up the interview.

"We never saw each other after he went to Israel. We spoke on the phone. We know he met Abu Rashid and was disturbed by him."

"In what way?" Another question from Sarah.

Ivanovsky ignored her and continued as if he hadn't been interrupted.

"He spoke about the visions. About London. A woman in London."

Sarah swallowed saliva. She had to put her hands on the table to stop a slight trembling.

"What woman was that?" Rafael inquired. He didn't want to lose momentum.

"The name he gave was Sarah Monteiro," he revealed under pressure. It was an uncomfortable subject for the barber.

"And what did that woman have?" Rafael pursued.

"He said she was keeping a secret that would answer our questions."

Ivanovsky lowered his eyes, thinking about that moment.

They talked as if Sarah weren't there.

"And what are your questions?"

Ivanovsky turned around in his seat. "The main question is how did we get to this situation? Who were our enemies, and what part did they play in the whole disaster?"

"The answer is yourselves," Rafael answered provocatively. "You can't blame your enemies for your own faults."

"We had our faults, sure. Serious ones. More than anyone could imagine, but our enemies played the main role in the fall of our regime. And your pope was in it up to his eyeballs."

"Which one?"

"The pope at that time. He didn't care whether communism lasted as long as national socialism was avenged."

"Don't be ridiculous," Rafael protested. "Benedict the Sixteenth loved Hitler's policies like a rat loves laboratory experiments."

"I have my doubts."

"I have my doubts about this democracy you're living in today," Rafael answered.

"Don't we all. But, do you know what I say?" The question was rhetorical. He didn't wait for a reply. He answered his own question right away. "We've adopted the following phase of democracy. That of hidden totalitarianism. An illusory democracy that doesn't even exist. It just seems to."

"I don't question that. That's obviously the road you're taking. Don't forget I know no other regime than a totalitarian one."

"Ah, yes. How could I forget. The clergy is stuck in the Middle Ages. It suits you."

"Putin is no daisy, either."

"I have no comment. He's my president."

"Did Abu Rashid say anything else?"

It was better to avoid provocations. Let's not get off track.

"He said the temptation was great, but Nestov shouldn't go to London under any pretext. He would not return—"

"Alive." Sarah completed his sentence, astonished.

Ivanovsky shut his eyes.

"Rafael knows we're pragmatic men."

"Of course."

"Rationalizations. If we have a clue, we don't think twice. Besides, it wasn't really a threat, more a suggestion."

"What is certain is that Rashid was right. We don't know if it was coincidence or certainty."

Silence settled over the room as an homage to Nestov's soul and respect for the Muslim's prophetic gift.

"I don't believe the prophet was referring to the secret that marked the end of the communist regime," Rafael declared after a little.

"No?" The Russian was amazed.

"No."

"What are we talking about then?"

"Of the total rehabilitation of the old Soviet Union in relation to planning and executing the attempted assassination in 1981," the Italian recited.

"We know what we did and didn't do."

"But the world doesn't. Seventy percent of Catholics believe that you, the Bulgarians, Poles, and East Germans were responsible for the failed attempt. And the Italian Mitrokhin commission didn't help."

"That commission was a farce. Mitrokhin was a fraud," the barber grumbled.

"But it has a voice. The doubt will always persist."

"And the secret ends the doubts?"

"It ends them. But even with all the proof in the world, doubts will always exist."

"That's like everything."

"In any case, don't forget you gave orders to the Poles to do away with him."

"I don't know that."

"Naturally. Twenty-five frustrated attempts are reason enough for not knowing. Tell me something. Have you heard of a man named Nestor?"

Ivanovsky thought for a few moments.

"I don't believe I've ever known anyone by that name."

"He was a KGB agent," Rafael observed, half closing his eyes, waiting for a reply.

Ivanovsky shook his head no.

"I've never heard of him. I'll have to look in the personnel files."

Rafael took another sip of cold tea. "To summarize, Mitrokhin deceived them with a trick by giving a date you didn't know how to get out of. You know someone tried to kill the pope, which would have been a big favor for you if the attempt had come off, but they failed, and, worse than that, you got the blame. You don't have any idea who planned the attack of 'eighty-one, do you?" Rafael spoke too rapidly.

"We have some suspects."

"Who?"

"Personnel in the pay of the CIA, Italians, Muslims."

"Cold, cold, cold, my friend. They were all terrified, but they didn't have time."

"But our major suspect is someone inside the Vatican," Ivanovsky suggested.

"As simple as that." Rafael struck the table with the palm of his hand, sanctioning the Russian's answer.

"You should be the first to deny it," Ivanovsky argued.

"Then I deny it," Rafael said. "How do you come into the story now?"

"How do you come in?"

"By chance."

"Same with us."

"Who were you watching?" Rafael tried a different approach.

"We watch everyone."

Bad. The conversation was better, Sarah thought. It's one thing to confide actions and information from the past, another to describe the situation of the present.

"I'll ask you something else. Why did you kill the English couple and
CIA man in Amsterdam?"

To Sarah those words were like a punch in the stomach. Were they the
ones who killed her friends in cold blood? She couldn't believe it.

"We haven't killed anyone in Amsterdam recently," the Russian said.
"Why?

"They had a CD with interesting information, obtained and held by the
KGB until 'ninety-one and afterwards by your excellencies who inherited
the file."

"I don't know what you're talking about."

"Come on, barber. We were doing so well. . . . It's natural to have your
enemies and allies under constant surveillance. The Holy See does also.
Everyone does. What's curious is you've kept an organization like Opus
Dei under your watchful gaze. That's what isn't normal."

Sarah calmed her inner hurricane. But doubt remained. His saying
they didn't do it could be true or not.

Ivanovsky swallowed hard.

"We used the woman to demonstrate we were on top of things. We
gave her the disc with intelligence about what happened to the girls, but we
didn't kill the couple." He thought about whether to continue.

There was something that made him trust the Italian, and, really, his
instincts had never let him down. Ivanovskys had always had an innate talent for choosing the winning side in history.

"Their murder only shows one thing. . . ." He hesitated again.

"That you were being spied on or that whoever alerted you to the problem didn't speak to you alone."

"Don't make stuff up."

"I'm not," Rafael ventured firmly. He had already figured out the whole
web, or, at least, part of it. "Who put you on the trail of Opus Dei?"

"That information is confidential."

"Everything we've said is confidential."

The vacillating expression on the Russian's face made clear his inner conflict between duty and continuing. His confidence in Rafael gained ground.

"Let's say that someone alerted us to certain actions of that organization. Facts that turned out to be consistent and trustworthy," the barber explained. He got up to get an old bottle with clear liquid on a tray. He poured a little in the cup that had held the tea. The smell of alcohol filled the nasal passages of everyone present.

"Does anyone else want some?"

He held the mouth of the bottle over Phelps's cup, but Phelps put his hand up to decline. Rafael accepted and let him fill his cup. Sarah also declined the offer.

"Cheers," Rafael toasted, lifting his cup.

Ivanovsky joined him, lifting his cup with a thoughtful look.

"What was the interest of this someone?" Rafael asked.

The barber took a drink of vodka and took out a cigarette.

"Do you mind if I smoke?"

The question did not require an answer, since as he asked he was striking a match and lighting the cigarette. He leaned back, not far enough to fall, making himself comfortable. He had only to cross his legs and put his feet on the table to complete the scenario, but the narrow space of the room prevented those comforts. He crossed his arms with the cigarette held between the fingers of his right hand, letting the ashes fall on the table. Silence was the only reply.

"I'm going to tell you what I think happened," Rafael announced. "Someone sweet-talked you, which didn't take much, and put you on the trail of Opus Dei. It's not hard to figure out what they're doing. I bet that after a few days you got the general picture."

"And what's that?" It was the Russian's turn to be sarcastic. A little jab.

"That's what you don't understand. On the one hand you found a large-scale operation; on the other you couldn't find the thread to lead you to what's going on. Your friend, this *someone*, shed some light, very little, only what was necessary. I'll bet it was he who gave you the CD with instructions to give it back after you'd analyzed and processed it. So you ended up knowing everything had to do with the Pole. Or better, you ended up knowing what that *someone* wanted you to know."

"It's a nice guess," Ivanovsky interrupted with the same sarcasm.

"What else did you find out?" Rafael continued. "That the rich clergymen had ended up allying themselves with the CIA and were killing right and left."

The expression on Ivanovsky's face changed.

"Who told you that?" he asked with irritation.

"You know the fact that we have God on our side is a big advantage," Rafael finally answered, taking a sip of vodka. "It makes us omniscient."

"And how does this strike you?" Ivanovsky asked, like someone who doesn't like something.

"Are you asking me?"

"I am."

"Well, my guess seems plausible." A statement loaded with venom.

"Why has Opus Dei conspired with the CIA? What's the purpose?" the Russian demanded, interrupting him.

"What do you think?" Rafael answered with a question, testing the situation.

"Burning the file," Ivanovsky finally said.

"Burning the file?" Phelps stammered out. "What's that?"

"When someone eliminates loose ends," Rafael explained.

"Do you agree?" the barber asked Rafael. He was visibly interested.

"I won't say no. But why?"

"When they killed the pair in Amsterdam, that's what they wanted to make understood. Why is not easy to make out, but burning the file presupposes the elimination of elements that could undermine certain interests," he explained in a casual tone.

"Everything has to do with John Paul the Second. Isn't that what I said?" the man from the Vatican reminded them.

"Exactly," the barber confirmed.

"But John Paul the Second is dead."

"Of course he is," the other said thoughtfully. "Which takes us down other roads."

"What roads?" Rafael didn't drop his guard. Everything had to come out. Ivanovsky understood that. Confidence had been established, plainly.

"Opus Dei, as they call themselves, took care of the English couple as well as the CIA man, we believe mistakenly, a Spanish priest from Santiago de Compostela, and, presumably, Marcinkus in the United States."

"A priest from Santiago de Compostela? Are you certain?" Rafael interrupted.

"Yes. Though I didn't come across his name," Ivanovsky excused himself. "Why? Is there a problem?"

A black cloud crossed Rafael's face, but vanished soon.

"No, go on."

"We have already analyzed all the communications we had access to, surveillances, agents in the field, and we came up with two possibilities." He raised his finger. "Either they wanted to eliminate something based on a decision the Pole made during his life . . ."

"What?" Sarah and Phelps protested. Sarah believed the goodness emanating from Wojtyla was genuine and could not imagine ordering killings in his name to clean up anything.

"How dare you?" Phelps defended the deceased pope.

Ivanovsky ignored them and raised his other finger.

"Or Opus Dei has something rotten in its past it wants to hide. We've done an exhaustive investigation. We've done it for years and come to an interesting conclusion." He stopped speaking for several moments to increase the suspense. "There was a bishop in the Vatican, who's been mentioned, who was not what he seemed."

"No one is what he seems in any way. Especially in the Vatican," Rafael declared.

"This bishop got around quite smoothly. He used bankers, cardinals, priors, politicians, economists. He could do anything. Except pray. He was rarely seen at prayer, unless he had to say Mass. He gained the confidence of people. He was good friends with Paul the Sixth.

"The interesting fact we've discovered is that, in addition to being a member of a Masonic lodge, he was also a member of Opus Dei. We've uncovered this through facts found among his belongings. Opus Dei would never permit such a thing to be known. We also discovered an immense scheme of illegal financial manipulations done for this gentleman and his partners with the knowledge of certain members of the Vatican Curia, the Masonic lodge, and Opus Dei, although none of them knew that the others also knew about this. It was a deception carried out well by the bishop. His name was—"

"Paul Casimir Marcinkus," Rafael completed his words.

"Correct."

Him again, Sarah murmured to herself. *Always him.*

"Marcinkus," Phelps said with hate in his voice. "He never had any respect for the Church. An arrogant egomaniac."

"You knew him?" the Russian asked.

"I knew him. I was insulted and humiliated by that man."

"When was that?" Rafael wanted to know.

"When?" he responded with a question. He was nervous. "When? When they discovered all his dirty dealings."

"Do you mean you had knowledge of what we just said?"

"A little," he replied nervously.

"You're the first person I know who knew Marcinkus was Opus Dei."

"Well . . ." He hesitated. "I didn't . . ."

Suddenly Phelps raised his hand to his chest and looked like he was in pain.

"Are you all right?" Sarah asked, worried.

Phelps said nothing. He grabbed his chest with his hand and fell from his seat, striking his head on the floor.

"Vladimir," Ivanovsky shouted.

The Englishman twisted in pain.

Rafael placed his hand on his chest. "Do you need air?"

Phelps confirmed with a gesture. He was in agony.

"Vladimir," Ivanovsky shouted again. "Let's sit him up," the barber suggested.

"No. Let him be," Rafael ordered. "We shouldn't force him."

A tear rolled down Sarah's face. "What's wrong with him?"

No one answered. The wrinkled one came into the room.

"What's happening?"

"Get the car and call Mikhail. We have to take him to the hospital."

Vladimir left the room running.

A last grimace of pain, and Phelps lost consciousness. In spite of everything, calm descended on the room instantly.

Sarah looked at him collapsed, white, and turned her glance to Rafael.

"A heart attack," he said.

"That's right," the Russian agreed.

"Oh my God," Sarah exclaimed.

"We have to get him to a hospital as soon as possible," Rafael advised.

"We're already taking care of that," Ivanovsky said. "Let's go to the veterans' hospital."

Speaking Russian, he and Rafael separated a little from Sarah.

"He knows something we need to know," he whispered.

"It seems to me there is *someone* above all of us who knows much more," Rafael reflected.

"Who?"

"Your friend *someone*. I think I know who he is."

The other looked at him, frightened.

"Pray to God this one survives," Rafael said, turning around next to Sarah, who was on her knees over Phelps, pressing his inert hand.

60

The man sweated profusely. Perspiration stuck to his nude body. Pleasure required effort; with every lunge there was an answering moan. Sex is the mixing of bodies, in general two—but there is no limit to the human imagination—the exchange of fluids and sweat, saliva and one's desires. During the coupling almost nothing exists but the one and the other; the fire has to be put out.

"I really needed that," said the man.

"Me too. We've got to do it more often," the other suggested, grabbing a pack of cigarettes from on top of the table.

"It's dangerous," the first one cautioned. "Our uniforms could give us away."

"Don't be so hardheaded, Paul. I don't play when I'm on duty."

"We can't afford the luxury of being careless," Paul reaffirmed. He got up and sat on the edge of the bed. "Give me one."

His companion handed him the cigarette he'd already lit for himself and took another. He leaned against the bed board, almost sitting.

"They're not going to give up," Paul commented, exhaling smoke.

"Are you sure?"

"They already would have."

"That's not the impression I got when I contacted them," the other said.

The cigarette smoke created a haze in the poorly ventilated room, forming a shadowy atmosphere around the two men.

"It wasn't a good idea to call yourself the American," Paul grumbled.

"It's what popped into my head."

"You have to be careful. They might get suspicious."

"Let me worry about those things," the other said complacently. "After all, why do you want the Turk out? He's only going to create problems."

"This doesn't smell right to me. I heard the Pole was thinking about going to see him," he answered circumspectly.

"And what could happen? He doesn't know who he is," the other reiterated.

"The two of them together in the same room. It's not good."

"In the same cell, you mean," the other joked, getting a smile from Paul.

"I'd like to see the Pole in a cell. I have to find out his intentions. I think he's suspicious."

"It's just in your mind. He has no reason to distrust you," the other asserted.

"It must have been JC who carried out the plan. Hell. The Turk drew me in."

"JC has other plans."

"He only does what Licio tells him."

"Licio doesn't give any orders now."

They were silent for a few moments. The sweat had dried. They'd recovered their energy.

"Did you get rid of the car?" Paul asked.

"It won't be a problem for anyone now. It was sold up north. I'm going to have to buy another one."

"Buy it. A different brand. I don't like BMW."

"I was thinking of a Mercedes."

"Good idea. Buy a Mercedes," Paul agreed.

Paul finished his cigarette and continued looking at the ceiling, his hand behind his head. He didn't say anything for several minutes, just stared at the ceiling worn from the passage of years.

"I want you to find another one for me," he finally said.

The other looked at him disapprovingly.

"Another? It's dangerous, and it's a lot of work."

"Not if they're from far away. I don't want more from Rome or the Vatican. That was a mistake. I prefer one from Naples. They should be daring. Or even farther south. No more Romans," he demanded.

"Really, I don't ask them for their identifications ahead of time."

"And don't use the Avon trick again."

"What do you think I am?" the other protested, looking insulted. "I don't use the same trick twice."

"A pope's bodyguard should have no imagination," Paul kidded him.

"Take back what you said." The other got up. "Take back what you said."

"And if I don't?" Paul dared him.

The pope's bodyguard laughed.

61

Istanbul. Formerly Constantinople. The imperial city, cradle of civilization, frontier between Europe and Asia, point of separation or arrival for each of the continents, clash of ancestral cultures, land of European emperors and Arab sultans, Byzantines and Ottomans, the most prosperous city of Christianity for more than a thousand years.

They drove around the center for hours, this time more tightly crowded in the back where JC, Elizabeth, and Raul sat. In front was a Turkish driver with expert knowledge of the city, obviously, and the cripple, saturnine, cold, an observer alert to everything, inside and outside the car, in spite of the thousands found in this city, inhabitants, tourists, businesspeople.

They'd started with Beyoğlu, where they saw the Galata Tower, built in the sixth century. A couple of hours later they'd entered the route that ends at what is now an imperfect circle that covers the Bazar quarter, with the Süleymaniye Mosque marking the most distant point, the edifice built by Sinan over the Golden Horn in honor of Suleiman the Magnificent, where both are buried, though at opposite ends. The interior of the circle covers the Seraglio, as well, which includes the Topkapi Palace, the official residence of the sultans for four hundred years, and the Sultanahmet, that shelters within itself two other pearls, facing each other, the Blue Mosque and Hagia Sophia.

JC played the part of tourist guide, explaining the multicultural and historical points of each monument and place in that immense city.

"What's the purpose of this excursion?" Raul wanted to know, exhausted by such a tour shrouded by secrecy.

"I told you already. We're here to see a friend."

"And where is he?"

"He should be on his way to our meeting."

"What time is that set for?" the cripple asked.

"At eighteen hundred hours."

"See? Only a half hour from now."

"Where are we meeting him?" Raul asked again.

"You'll soon see," the old man replied evasively.

"Why Istanbul?" It was Elizabeth's turn to ask for answers.

"Why does someone move from England to a mountain in the Alentejo? How can you answer something like that? These are the imponderables of life. The tastes, desires. Some are able to fulfill them, others not."

"Do you always have an answer for everything?" Raul asked. He considered the ability both impressive and irritating.

"My dear captain, the day I don't, you can lower the flag to half-mast because I'll be dead."

"This friend we're going to visit. Is he like you?" Elizabeth asked.

She'd only looked at him twice, but she didn't have to do so again to know he didn't like her or her husband. The cripple in the front seat tolerated them only out of respect for the old man who gives him orders, thank God. As much as she tried, she couldn't imagine this old man, so frail and in precarious health, hurting a fly or leading such a vast organization with the purpose of . . . whatever their purpose was.

JC laughed at her question.

"No, men like me are dying out. I must be the last of a very underappreciated species. We're going to see a cardinal in the Church. A man much older than I."

We're going to see a cadaver? Elizabeth thought without saying it. It would be bad manners to insult the host.

"For some time I've wanted to ask you a question," Raul dared to say, looking him in the eye as if to ask permission.

He who is silent agrees, and JC was proof of this.

"Why did you accept the agreement last year?"

"In New York?"

Raul nodded yes.

"It served my interests," the old man answered.

Raul pulled up his undershirt and revealed a scar at the bottom of his stomach on the right side made by a deep incision. He arched his ribs a little so that another identical scar could be seen below his ribs. A sharp, cutting object had penetrated from one side to the other, leaving a scar that would last to the end of his days.

"Do you see what they did to me that day in the warehouse in New York? I don't see how that served your interests." He was angry, but JC didn't blink. Other people's pain didn't affect him.

"My dear captain. You can't criticize me for trying to get something back that was taken from me."

"I'm not criticizing. I simply don't believe it served your interests."

"What was the agreement?" Elizabeth asked.

She didn't know what they were talking about. Raul and Sarah had told her as little as possible about what happened the previous year to avoid a fight. Divorce was a real possibility, though. Sarah explained to her mother that her father wasn't at fault. He was swept up in a whirlwind of uncontrollable events, just like her. It was true.

"Would you prefer to tell her?" Raul challenged JC.

"I don't see any problem with that," the old man said, turning his gaze from the street to Elizabeth. "Your daughter had something in her possession that belonged to me."

"That's debatable," Raul grumbled.

"You asked me to tell her. You've got to let me tell my version," JC said without changing his calm tone.

"I'm only saying the ownership of those papers is relative. We know very well who they belong to."

"We do. They belonged to Albino Luciani until the date of his death, and afterwards to me."

Raul saw clearly he wouldn't change the old man's way of thinking no matter what arguments he used. He gave up and asked the old man to continue.

"Your daughter sent those documents to a journalist friend, and the agreement was a pact of mutual nonaggression, scrupulously complied with to the end."

"Why did you trust it?" Raul insisted.

"Because it didn't seem to me you'd sacrifice your lives for values or moral principles. You know as well as I it would've been a death sentence for everyone. Besides, I trust a maxim that I've always followed." He tapped the cripple on the shoulder, who looked ahead alertly. "Which is?"

"There are more tides than sailors." His dedicated assistant completed the statement.

JC looked at Raul and Elizabeth triumphantly. The brio of his personal pride began to sparkle.

"What do you mean by that?" Raul asked.

"Think back. The person who had custody of the documents was a lady, as I said, one of your compatriots," he added, indicating Elizabeth. "Called . . ." He tried to remember. He touched the cripple on the shoulder again. "What was her name?"

"Natalie. Natalie Golden."

"Natalie. Correct. Natalie . . . Golden."

"And what follows from there?" Raul was very curious, which, added to irritation, turned into impatience.

"From that follows the obvious question: what is a journalist's greatest ambition?"

Raul and Elizabeth exchanged looks. They knew perfectly well the aspirations of their only daughter, professionally. Make a difference. Tell a great story, the exclusive that will give them great prestige, although

Sarah was already heading down that road as the editor of international politics.

"You gave her an exclusive?" Elizabeth risked asking.

JC confirmed with a gesture.

"In exchange for the documents?" Raul couldn't control his nerves.

"It was a fair price," JC said. "Everything was done through intermediaries, obviously."

"How could she?" Raul asked, more to himself than the other passengers.

"The flesh is weak, my friend. In any case, the girl didn't use the story."

"Why?" Elizabeth asked, frightened.

"She was eliminated by the same people who tried to kill your daughter," he answered, with no attempt to beat around the bush.

"My God." Elizabeth, incredulous, put her face in her hands.

"How could that happen?" Raul stammered. He hadn't expected this, either.

"We're fighting a deadly force. Don't doubt it."

Raul released his breath, freeing a small part of the bitterness he felt at that moment.

Elizabeth crossed herself and closed her damp eyes. Neither of them knew Natalie personally. She was someone Sarah mentioned only professionally or personally in the emotional stories she told them from time to time on vacation, during a phone conversation, or in an e-mail. They were used to thinking of her as one of their daughter's best friends. Now all that had ended. Until this instant Elizabeth's fear had no face or personality. It seemed like something turbid, unhealthy, capable of everything and nothing, open to negotiating, to yielding, to hope. That had just been lost. They were in the middle of real danger, and any feeling of control was a complete illusion. Now the attention with which JC's assistant—since a lady doesn't call him "cripple"—watched everything and everyone made sense. The danger was out there at every corner, window, automobile, terrace. Everybody was suspicious, even innocent children. God have mercy on her daughter.

"Who guarantees that you aren't the one hunting my daughter?" Raul asked suspiciously.

"Think, my dear captain. Think," JC suggested, not at all offended.

Raul lowered his eyes. He'd let confusion overcome him. He had to be rational, logical, at times like this. "You have everything in your power again," Raul said.

JC confirmed with a gesture.

"You've got the bull by the horns," he said. "What's going to happen to us when this is all over?"

It was a pertinent question.

Elizabeth supported her husband's inquiry and shot a terrified look at the old man. He seemed to enjoy their worry. To be feared was an opportunity.

"Captain, listen to what I'm telling you. And the lady also. If I wanted to hurt you, I'd have done it already. If it were my intention to eliminate your daughter, she'd already be eliminated. I know what you're thinking. She fooled me once. Another reason to fear me. You can be certain that she won't do it twice. Not with me."

"It's time," the cripple observed, ignoring the conversation in the backseat.

The old man looked out the car window. They were passing the monumental Hagia Sophia, its six minarets outlined against the sky, constructed as a Byzantine temple, and in these times one of the most famous mosques in the world.

"Get to the place," he ordered.

The cripple whispered a kind of unintelligible litany to the driver, and he accelerated. It wasn't easy taking on Turkish traffic, especially in a city like Istanbul, when one has a schedule to keep. But these were shrewd men who were taking what seemed a tourist itinerary, but which actually corresponded to a radial perimeter that had nothing to do with security, but was meant to ensure it wouldn't take them more than ten minutes to get to the agreed upon location from any point. Everything was well planned.

The driver stopped the car on Sultanahmet Meydani. The cripple got out, opened the door first for JC, and waited for the other passengers to get out through the same door. Under normal conditions, Raul and Elizabeth would have admired the immense plaza situated between two great jewels of the Islamic world, Hagia Sophia, the great church transformed into a mosque in the fifteenth century, and the Blue Mosque, but not today.

"Wait," JC ordered as he gestured toward the cripple. The car continued to drive on with only the Turkish driver.

"What's going on?" Raul asked.

JC didn't answer, completely oblivious to the historical, cultural dimension that surrounded him, the cries of sellers of carpets and *simit*. His expression was serious.

Seconds later the cripple signaled for a *taksi*, among the many passing along the central street, and one stopped quickly. They got into a bright yellow vehicle.

The cripple gave the taxi driver instructions, and they took off.

For several minutes, no one disturbed the silence inside the taxi.

Raul was the first to do so.

"Why so much secrecy? Why did we change cars?" he whispered.

"Have you never heard that the careful man dies an old man, Captain?"

"The danger's that great?"

"They killed Natalie, Raul," Elizabeth mentioned. For her that was enough.

"It's not a question of danger, Captain, but of principles," JC clarified. "A man in my line of work can never drop his guard. Do it once, it may be all right, maybe nothing happens. Risk another time, one becomes negligent, and it's over. That won't happen to me. I accepted that many years ago. It's the secret of my success. Never, never leave a clue or loose ends."

Elizabeth trembled.

"You mean you have plans for us in the end?" Raul asked.

"Of course."

"We're loose ends, aren't we?"

"No, my dear captain. You're not loose ends. Nor am I going to explain the definition of loose ends. What I said about your daughter, I'll say to you, and you." He looked at Raul and Elizabeth. "If I wanted you dead, we wouldn't be having this conversation, or bringing you to see a friend." His expression was peremptory.

"Who is this friend?" Raul asked again.

"You'll soon find out," JC replied. "Enjoy the sights."

They didn't exchange another word until the end of the ride. Six minutes later, the cripple paid the fare with new Turkish lira and opened the door for the master and the couple.

The final destination wasn't far, nor could it be, since JC no longer had the stamina of former times and couldn't walk far. He limited himself to a few steps, at his own pace, always on flat terrain. Uphill was deadly.

They entered a secular building, rose-colored, with a group of black placards inscribed with gold letters at the entrance.

"What's this place?" Elizabeth asked.

"A *hamam*," JC answered, continuing ahead.

The cripple came last with his hand inside his jacket on his gun, alert as a falcon.

"What's a *haman*?" Elizabeth asked.

JC pointed at the plaques.

"It's in your language right here."

And in fact it was, a plaque, recently written with tourists in mind: REAL TURKISH BATH. 300 YEARS OLD.

"We are in the baths of Cağaloğlu, ordered built by Mehmet the First in the eighteenth century," JC explained.

They stopped at the entrance.

"In these baths the sections for men and women are separated. The entrance for women is on another street," JC said. "My assistant will stay here with you, and the captain and I will go in. Is that all right with you?"

The married couple agreed in part because there was nothing they could do. Of course Elizabeth wanted to go in, but she had to respect the cultural tradition different from her own. She couldn't help thinking that JC did this so that she would find out what was going on secondhand through her husband. In any case, someone would have to tell her everything.

The cripple approached JC and whispered something in his ear.

"I imagined so," the old man said in response. "Are you ready, Captain?"

Raul said nothing, but yes was understood.

The two men walked to the entrance, where JC let Raul go forward. The Portuguese sighed and continued walking into the unknown.

In the *camekan* they found the dressing rooms, small cubicles where several men changed their clothes, conversed, read newspapers, sipped tea. They were all Westerners, no Turks.

Raul stopped, expecting directions.

"Keep going," JC ordered.

They passed the next antechamber, the *soğukluk*, without stopping and stayed in the *hararet*. The steam was dense, and the heat immediately made them sweat.

"This isn't good for you," Raul warned with sweat running down his face. "Nor for me," he muttered.

"I imagined so," JC commented. "If it's not good for me, imagine for him."

Who? Raul thought.

Though the *hararet* was usually the most crowded part of the bath, there were few men that day. They made one out, stretched out on a table, being massaged expertly, but he didn't seem the least interested in secret conversation.

"That's enough for me," JC grumbled with his clothes soaked and breath panting. It was too much. "Sebastiani," he shouted.

He needed to wait only five seconds before the latter entered, an old man with a huge head of white hair dressed in a black suit, sitting in a wheelchair, pushed by a young cleric, his aide.

"JC."

"Sebastiani," he greeted him, suffocating, sweating, and tired. "What are we doing here?"

As incredible as it seemed, Sebastiani didn't seem affected by the temperature or the steam; his assistant, a young man about twenty years old, was dripping water from his face, stumbling as he walked, his vision clouded, and feeling as if he might faint at any moment.

"Ah, I'm getting used to it."

"What?"

"To hell," the other answered without thinking about it. "Isn't that where we're all going? That's what I think." He smiled sarcastically.

"I can't stand being here longer," JC said, holding on to Raul. "Let's get out of here."

The group passed into the *soğukluk*. JC and Raul needed a few minutes to recuperate. Sebastiani waited serenely without wiping the light sweat away that had broken out on his face. He won't have a problem surviving hell. The assistant thanked God that they had left the steam room, where they'd entered completely clothed, and sat down on the first bench he found, completely exhausted.

"Without question one should never go beyond the *camekan* in a Turkish bath. There's something to eat and drink there, and the steam doesn't kill you," JC declared.

"In hell you're not going to have to eat and drink," Sebastiani explained.

"Do you know someone who's been there and returned to tell about it?" JC asked.

"Don't question my beliefs," Sebastiani returned. "I don't impose my faith on anyone, but I don't allow it to be insulted, either."

JC respected his friend's warning. You have to divide in order to conquer sometimes.

"This is Captain Raul Brandão Monteiro. Portuguese military." JC made the introductions. "This is Sebastiano Corrado, cardinal of the Roman Catholic Church."

Raul inclined his head courteously. He had never met a cardinal.

"Cardinal without right of election. I'm ninety-four years old, you know. I'm a second-class cardinal. And you, Raul, a soldier without an army?"

"In fact, yes. I'm in the reserve." He smiled.

"You see? Our situations are similar," he observed.

"In the conclave of 1978, I was still a bishop. In the one of 2005, I was too old."

"It's because you didn't need to vote," JC declared.

"That's what I tell myself. There is room for only one pope at a time.

But I congratulate myself that the Pole lasted so many years, although it was bad for me."

"How are things in Fátima?" JC wanted to know.

"As always. It's strange to see people much younger than me, and all with atrophied minds."

"Look to your faith," JC admonished. "Don't offend that of others." He couldn't resist a gibe.

"Don't confuse faith with psychopathology," he answered with a guttural laugh no one else took up.

"What do you have for me?" JC pressured him.

The man opened his hand, palm upward. It was a silent message to his assistant, who placed a yellow envelope in it. Sebastiani gave it to JC.

"Is this it?"

"It is. Be careful." It was the first time his unpleasant face showed any suspicion. "The other one must be totally confused right now. He's discovered there's nothing there."

"Stupendous."

"What's going to happen now?"

JC took the envelope and looked seriously at everyone around.

"I've thrown out a lot of misinformation to make things very hard for everyone else," he said joyously. "Now the time has come for the famous JC to appear."

62

James Phelps hung on to the weak thread of life with all his strength, or, at least, that's how it seemed. He was shaken by intermittent jolts from the rusty van that rushed him to the veterans' hospital a few blocks from the barbershop.

They'd left through one of the closed doors in the passageway that opened onto another narrow hallway with a door to an underground parking garage at the end. The escape route in case an operation went wrong.

Rafael and Ivanovsky did the carrying with Sarah comforting Phelps. They put him in the middle seat of a 1980s Daihatsu with room for nine. Vladimir drove the "smoke bomb," as they lovingly called it for the excessive fumes that escaped through the exhaust pipe.

"Hang on," Rafael encouraged Phelps with his hands on his head.

Ivanovsky took the passenger seat to show Vladimir the way. A Russian mania for knowing more than others or thinking they did. Sarah was in the middle seat next to the sliding door. Phelps's feet were on her lap.

"Everything will be all right," she told him.

"Don't you believe in auto repair shops?" Rafael shouted so they could hear him over the turbulent engine. "The noise and fumes this car is emitting must be detectable from space," he added.

"This van's been retired a long time. It's the first time it's been used in fifteen years, or more," Ivanovsky also shouted. "You said you know who's behind all this?"

Sarah listened silently. Rafael knew who was behind the plot? Who?

Rafael gestured an affirmation. "I think so."

"Who?" Sarah and the Russian asked in unison.

"I can think of only one man capable of manipulating everything and everyone with such skill. JC. Do you know him?"

Of course, Sarah reflected. *Why didn't I think of that?*

"I've heard of him, but his existence has never been proved."

"He exists," Rafael confirmed, exchanging a long look with Sarah.

"Go down Ulitsa Varvarka," the barber ordered Vladimir.

They passed a packed Red Square, the Kremlin on the opposite side. Next to the walls was the mausoleum where the embalmed body of Lenin serves as a national and international tourist attraction, along with great men of the nation, a little to the back, Yuri Gagarin, Maxim Gorky, Brezhnev. The cathedral of Saint Basil with its onion dome cupolas, built by Ivan the Terrible, is in front of the Museum of History, separated by five hundred yards of Red Square.

It wasn't the first time Rafael had visited the city, but Sarah would've preferred another situation to enjoy the cultural, historical, and social attractions Moscow has to offer.

"Turn onto Ulitsa Varvarka."

"It's longer that way," Vladimir observed in Russian.

"Do what I tell you." Ivanovsky turned around to the back again. "What's the plan of this JC?"

"He has his own agenda," Rafael answered. "But this web is typical of him. He gives information to you, us, Opus Dei, a few clues to the Americans and English, and we all start moving, thinking we're the only ones."

"Where does this Spanish priest fit in?"

"I still don't know that. It doesn't mean everything's interconnected," Rafael said in a meditative way. Phelps let out a distant moan.

Sarah stroked his leg up to his thigh, with no untoward intentions, despite her uncomfortable attraction to men of the Church, albeit younger ones.

"You're going to be all right," she murmured.

"We have to find out what his plan is," Ivanovsky declared.

"Of course," Rafael agreed. *I know very well how to do that*, he thought. You can't share everything.

"Accelerate this piece of shit." Ivanovsky angrily turned to Vladimir. "The guy can't die on us. He has to tell us what he knows."

"It won't go any faster," Vladimir said as he floored the accelerator, unable to get past seventy.

Another moan from Phelps, this time more intense, almost louder than the engine noise of the Daihatsu.

"Stay calm. We're almost there," Rafael told him.

Sarah stroked his leg and thigh again, the right one, to be more precise, until something caught her attention, a rise, a projection about a centimeter in diameter running completely around his leg. Like a belt fastened to his thigh . . . very tightly.

What's this? she asked herself. At that precise moment Phelps opened his eyes and looked at her in a way he never had before. The thin, timorous old man completely lost consciousness.

A bang on the windshield snapped her out of the lethargy she'd sunk into. Phelps's eyes were closed. Perhaps it was her imagination, except the belt pressing into his thigh was real.

There was no time to think. A new bang made the Daihatsu roll toward the driver's side. Ivanovsky started to shout, along with Rafael, who grabbed the seat to avoid falling over Sarah, as he pressed down on Phelps with all his strength so that his dead weight wouldn't crush her.

"Damn," Rafael swore.

"What's going on?" Sarah cried.

Ivanovsky, leaning on the front panel, pulled two guns.

"They killed Vladimir," he warned. "Bastards."

Given the slow speed of the van, it stopped after a few yards and rolled over onto the side of the dead driver.

"What's going on?" Phelps's weak voice asked.

"Stay quiet. We're going to get you out of here," Rafael ordered, red from the effort of supporting him.

"Let's lower him slowly," Sarah suggested, drawing back to leave room. She noticed the glass in the sliding door was broken, and she was standing on the asphalt of the street.

Rafael put Phelps down carefully. He now had some control over his body, although he still had a hand on Phelps's chest. A few seconds later the Englishman was on the ground next to Sarah.

"What's happening?" he asked.

"We're being attacked," Sarah informed him, realizing for the first time the seriousness of the situation.

Rafael turned to Ivanovsky. "Give me one of those pieces."

The Russian hesitated, but finally tossed him one of the guns. He opened the door and looked around. Rafael broke the glass in the window that had been at the side before but now was the roof and stuck his head outside. This model had only one sliding door, on Sarah's side, now the floor of the van after it turned over. A shot pierced the frame a few inches from his face. The same happened to Ivanovsky. Both ducked back inside the van.

"Snipers," Rafael explained.

"That's right," the barber agreed.

"Russian mafia?" Phelps asked, still suffering.

"No," Ivanovsky contradicted him. "Americans. They can only be Americans. I can smell them," he lamented.

"Barnes," Sarah whispered.

"We have to do something," Rafael declared. The shots came from two places in front and behind the van.

He tried to get to the back where the window was intact. He watched for a long time.

"Give them a little taste, Ivanovsky."

"Why me?"

"Because you're there and I'm here. If you want, we can switch."

The two men looked at each other. Ivanovsky was in the front of the van, standing up, holding on to a seat, Rafael in back next to the rear window, Phelps and Sarah between them, also standing. The seats served as corners.

"Do you want to switch?" Rafael suggested again.

"No, I'll take care of it," the Russian growled, muttering some insult in Russian.

He held on to the seat and got up toward the door. From the back Rafael watched the buildings in his field of vision. He watched from one side of the glass with his body shielded by the thin metal of the back door.

Ivanovsky put his head out. A shot struck the van next to his head. He returned two shots over the building. Two shots back, closer, made holes in the metal. Another shot came from who knows where. Better not push his luck. He drew back inside the van.

"I've found him," Rafael said.

"Can you take him out?"

"It's done," he informed him.

A hole in the back window showed the deed. It had been the last shot the Russian heard before backing down.

"Why don't they shoot to kill?" the Russian asked.

"They must need one of us and can't risk it."

"What are we going to do?" Phelps asked.

"We stick our head out to see where the rest of them are, or wait for them to come looking for us," Rafael explained. "Either way . . ."

"We're screwed," the Russian admitted.

"I think we should take them on," Phelps declared, much recovered.

Sarah looked at him, amazed.

"Don't you have one of those for us?" Phelps asked, pointing to the gun.

"You know how to use this?"

"No, but I'll learn."

Ivanovsky thought for a minute and decided to take the gun off Vladimir's body, which was curled against the door, next to the floor.

You're not going to need it, my friend.

He gave it to Phelps carefully.

"The safety's on," he advised. "To take it off—"

Phelps took the gun knowledgeably, took the safety off, and shot Ivanovsky right in the middle of his head. He fell lifeless over Vladimir.

"I know how to remove an obstacle," he advised coldly.

Sarah gave a panicked cry, incredulous over what she'd seen.

Rafael aimed at Phelps, but Phelps grabbed Sarah and put the gun to her head.

"I'm not feeling well," he imitated himself, then immediately let out a sarcastic laugh that ended in a serious stare at Rafael. "Throw your gun out of the van."

"How can you do this?" Sarah said, feeling the hot barrel burning her scalp.

"Sarah knows very well what we're capable of doing to protect the good name of our Church." He turned to Rafael. "Throw the gun out. I'm not going to repeat myself."

Rafael broke the glass of the back window with one kick and threw the Glock to the asphalt, far off to the side of the van.

"You're a first-rate adversary, my friend," Phelps praised him. "You keep everything to yourself. But I've succeeded in getting you to give me everything I need."

"Do you think so?" Rafael asked daringly. "You're not as good an actor as you think."

"Don't underestimate me, my friend," the Englishman replied, if he was in fact an Englishman. "The heart attack was well rehearsed. I know how much you worried about me, and I appreciate it. I'd trust you in a similar occasion."

"I'm not talking about the heart attack. I applaud that performance in particular."

"What are you talking about then?" His curiosity was stimulated. A sarcastic smile stretched his thin lips.

"Your thigh that hurt you from time to time."

Sarah understood now the source of the pain.

"What about it?" Phelps's smile disappeared.

"Nothing would have happened if it had always been the same thigh. That's where you failed. Sometimes the right, sometimes the left. That means only one thing."

"A *cilice*, worn for penance." Sarah spoke. "That's what he had around his thigh. That's what occasionally caused him awful pain. The sharp barbs nailed into the flesh."

Phelps didn't like being mocked.

"In any case you've given me almost everything I need. I'll get my hands on the file you took from Sarah's house. With it, I'll make JC appear."

"If only it were that simple."

"What do you mean by that?" Phelps's good mood vanished in front of their eyes.

"You consider yourself a great manipulator, a first-rate actor, but you've been controlled the whole time."

Phelps applied more pressure with the gun against Sarah's head and pressed the trigger a little.

Sarah shut her eyes, terrified.

"Your bluff isn't convincing," Phelps finally said.

Three black vans with tinted windows stopped next to the overturned van. Several hooded men, armed with semiautomatics, surrounded the vehicle.

"Everything's okay," Phelps shouted.

Two men pulled Rafael outside, handcuffed him, and made him get into one of the vans. They did the same with Sarah.

A little later Phelps made his grand entrance.

There was another man inside the van. He wore dark glasses that matched his suit.

"Stuart."

"Phelps." He inclined his head with the necessary deference.

"What took you so long?"

"We had to wait where we wouldn't be noticed. You didn't exactly avoid the tourist sites."

"My beloved colonel, it looked like you were going to give me a real heart attack."

The two men laughed with pleasure.

"Let's get going," Stuart Garrison ordered. "We have a long trip ahead."

The vans pulled away, leaving the other van behind, the one with two corpses inside.

63

It was a night like others before and others that will come.

The innkeeper finished up the accounts from another day's work. It was normal not to have many guests this time of the year. It wasn't cold or hot enough. Business flourished in the middle of winter with the snow and the fascination it exerts over old and young alike, and in summer when green conquered the white, aided by the rise in temperature, encouraging sightseeing and religious tourism.

Today he had seven guests, among them two priests, a couple with a small boy, and two Benedictine sisters. All with full service for three days, with the grace of God. He expected some reservations for the weekend and so spent his days unworried.

Someone rang the bell at this hour of the night, some traveler in search of a room for the night. It happened. Despite closing the door of the inn as soon as the church chimed ten at night, he stayed on watch for the last-minute client or guest who had decided to enjoy the social life in the town.

He unlocked the door and opened it. Outside there were two men, an old man with a beard, sweating, another younger one who seemed more composed. He noticed some bruises on the old man's face that didn't inspire confidence. The young man carried a black briefcase like businessmen use to keep their documents.

"Hello."

"Good evening," the young man greeted him. "We'd like a room for the night."

It took him five seconds to forget the condition of the darker man, Arab perhaps, and remember that the inn was almost empty.

"Of course. Please come in."

He locked the door again and took them up to the second floor. The young man registered as Timothy Elton and paid in zlotys, leaving a generous tip.

Money is the universal language, whatever the currency. It's never too much, it slips through the fingers like water, and one can never hold on to it. It can be tamed, hypothetically, channeled here and there, but it has a propensity toward sudden flight. And it makes innkeepers everywhere forget the faces behind the hand that gives them the bills, although they may be beaten, sorrowful, sweating, dirty, tired, or proud.

"We don't wish to be disturbed," the young man emphasized, the only thing said during the process of registering.

"I understand," the innkeeper said, handing over the key to room 206, fastened to a shell.

The guests climbed the stairs. There was no elevator. A fundamental rule of inn-keeping was that the customer is always right. If his desire was not to be disturbed, he wouldn't be, except in the case of an emergency, which had never happened, thank God. There was a barrier of privacy that could never be crossed from the moment the guest shut himself inside the room. It was true that when one went to clean after checkout, or the daily tourist activity, one could learn something about the person in question, habits of hygiene, sex, or gastronomy. . . . In the thirty years of experience he had in the business, he'd acquired some psychic ability, nothing supernatural, based only on steady observation. He thought, for example, that cleaning room number 206 in the morning wouldn't take more than five minutes. There would be no trash in the wastebaskets, nor would the bathroom look used. The sheets on the bed would be untouched, as would the furniture. It'd look as if no one had occupied the room that night.

He'd had other guests like this in the past, whose traces were deliberately covered over or never left. In those situations one didn't ask intrusive questions of any kind; one took the money, signed the register, and forgot that a man named Timothy Elton accompanied by an old man had once stayed in the inn.

Behind the closed door with the number 206 fixed in the wood was a scene of one-sided nervousness. The younger man paced from one side to the other with his cell phone in hand with no call sent or even about to be made. Abu Rashid sat in a chair, distanced, free, watching the other's nervousness.

"I'm like the only responsible one," Tim said. "I can't get hold of my boss."

Sweat covered his face, an occupational hazard for men who work under specific instructions.

Abu Rashid closed his eyes and sighed. He withdrew from Tim's negative energy. He remained in that state many minutes, hours, concentrating on himself, peace, and good thoughts. He forgot there was someone else in the room, stopped hearing the frenetic pacing and complaints. He understood Tim's doubts, the dilemma, the disgust, solitude, sudden confusion. It was like having the umbilical cord cut while still inside the maternal womb.

When morning broke and entered the sinister hour of sepulchral silence, broken by cries and unknown sounds, Tim's steps were no longer heard in the room waiting for the call that hadn't come.

Abu Rashid felt a cold, cylindrical object pressed against his head. He knew what it was and didn't bother to open his eyes to see the menace.

"Who told you about the tomb?"

"You know as well as I do, Tim."

"Don't call me Tim," he shouted.

"What do you want me to call you? Timothy?"

Tim drew the gun away from Abu Rashid's head and scratched his head with the hand holding it. He took a deep breath and thought. He made sure the cell phone was closed. Everything was correct. Only the instructions were lacking.

"Who else knows about the tomb?"

"You, me, and whoever is giving you orders. Not even those directly involved know."

"But someone else has to know." Tim's voice stammered, confused. He was very tired, and Abu Rashid was not an easy prisoner. "The Americans? The Russians? With their secret satellites?"

"You know satellites, as advanced as they may be, cannot keep track of millions of people. They only keep watch on a small part of the globe. They only see one thing at a time. And while they're focused on one objective, they see nothing else. The idea that they can monitor everything and everybody every hour and minute is absurd. An attempt to frighten us. Only God can be in all places at all times, and so He helps us in all we want to do."

"Don't blaspheme," Tim cried, sitting on the edge of the bed. "This conversation about technology only proves that you know how things work." He pointed the gun at him.

"Why don't you try to kill me if that's your final judgment?"

Tim lowered both his eyes and the gun. He looked again at the cell phone on the bedspread.

"Don't worry. He'll call you," Abu Rashid assured him.

There was visible disturbance in Tim's face, a boy taken from his mother and father to be given orders and shown the path. Only orphan boys gathered into the bosom of the Catholic community could be initiated into the secret order of the Sanctifiers. Of those, very few were chosen to fill the sparse ranks of the elite group. Innumerable tests and discipline were necessary—thousands of hours of prayer to the Lord, theological, anthropological, sociological study, punishment of the flesh, several hours a day, religiously. A few blows of a whip striking the flesh and immediately the sharp pain vanquished evil thoughts, feelings, and other degeneracy.

Tim got up and took some white plastic cords out of the pocket of his jacket. He went over to the dreamy Abu Rashid and tied him to the chair to prevent him from getting away. That done, he opened the bathroom door and took off his jacket.

Abu Rashid opened his eyes.

"God is and always will be synonymous with love. Man is the one who has created sorrow and the dogma that suffering is the remedy for everything."

Tim ignored him and shut himself in the bathroom. The water ran in the tub and sink, strong streams to cover up the held-back moans. *Return me to the right road, Lord*, he murmured, bent over in the liberating pain. *Return me to Your Way.*

He turned off the faucets. Silence returned. Tim opened the door that separated the bathroom from the bedroom with his shirt on and buttoned. More self-possession was impossible, given the circumstances. He found Abu Rashid in the same position he'd left him. Eyes open, looking at him without blame . . . without the cords that had tied him. He looked closer. It couldn't be. He confirmed it. He squatted down to pick one up; it was cut. He took the gun he had left in his jacket on top of the bed. An irresponsible act, he recognized.

"Who cut the cords?"

"Our Lady," Abu Rashid answered.

The punch struck him full in his face.

"Who cut the cords?" Timothy repeated.

He opened the door of the room, gun in hand, and looked around. Everything was quiet. He did the same at the window. It was too dark to see anything.

"Our Lady," Abu Rashid said again.

Tim returned to the center of the room and sighed. *I'm going crazy.* He took in what had occurred and analyzed the cord again.

"Why didn't you run away or take the gun?" he finally asked.

"I don't need to," Abu Rashid declared, looking at him profoundly. "You still don't understand, Tim. I'm not your prisoner. I'm here of my free will. Sleep now. Tomorrow will be an important day."

64

A thin line separates patriotic duty from the temporary illusion of a comfortable life free of financial problems, as if money were the magic solution for earthly happiness. Even on a border as rigidly controlled as the Russian, greasing palms with dollars is sufficient stimulus. It's never been a question of honor or dignity, but of price.

As soon as they left Moscow, they went in civilian helicopters somewhere close to the border with Ukraine. From there they caught a plane that in a matter of seconds crossed the border, leaving the Russian authorities to deal with the dead agents. It would open a diplomatic conflict between America and Russia, but without proof the Westerners could deny any responsibility.

There were two stops on the long flight, but Rafael and Sarah couldn't calculate how long. They only knew they'd been traveling for hours. During the first stage they were blindfolded and forced to change planes. There the blindfolds were taken off, but even so there was nothing to orient them. They flew together in a compartment that was essentially a cell without windows. There was hardly space for the two seats where they sat tied with straps and chains above and below. You couldn't be claustrophobic and survive in such a narrow space. Even someone who'd never suffered previous symptoms would end up suffering, as happened to Sarah, who felt her nose and throat begin to close up. Being handcuffed didn't help. It didn't matter that they'd removed the blindfold. It wasn't really necessary since the walls around them were barely visible. Her respiratory panic increased when Rafael fell asleep. She felt alone, incapable of sleeping, consumed by her thoughts and speculations. In this case she had no control of the situation. Without any aces there was no way to negotiate. The only thing she could do was trust Rafael, who seemed to be sleeping the sleep of the innocents, completely carefree, as if he didn't expect an unforeseen torture session. Barnes was not going to forgive them, much less whoever was working for him.

How can he sleep? She couldn't get James Phelps out of her mind during the long flight. How was such deception possible? To gain their confidence, listen, suffer physically with them, only to gain some strange influence, whatever it was. A courteous man with an adorable frailty, who could be her father, until he looked at her with those cold eyes, repugnant, a taker of lives. There was a Portuguese proverb about he who sees faces, doesn't see hearts. There was no better way to illustrate the manipulative power of that Englishman. To think she'd been genuinely worried about his health. She couldn't help a certain negativity come over her, a loss of hope for humanity.

When she wasn't thinking these things, wondering about her fate, or fighting a panic attack, she watched Rafael sleeping deeply. No one would imagine he was in European airspace, a prisoner of the CIA in partnership with Opus Dei or whomever. She tried to touch his hand, even with her finger, but the strap was too tight.

Rafael didn't sleep for the whole trip, of course. When he wasn't sleeping, he talked to Sarah about superficial things.

"What's it like to be an editor of international politics?" he began asking.

"It's a lot of work, but the pay is good."

"I imagine so. I've read some of your stories. They're very good."

"Thanks. I've spent the whole year wondering why."

"Why what?"

"Why me? How did I get that position, almost as if I parachuted in?"

"What conclusion did you come to?"

"It could only be because JC put me there and gave me enough material to stay," Sarah argued. "I don't know why."

Rafael didn't indicate agreement or disagreement. He just kept chatting pleasantly, not a word about what was going on. Sarah assumed the reason was that there were other eyes and ears intent on what they said. They talked for several hours about various things until the second stop, probably for refueling. Outside they could hear noises of trucks and machinery checking what needed to be checked for the proper running of the airplane. They were not bothered at any time. It felt like they'd been forgotten.

An hour later the plane rolled down the runway and took off.

Sarah looked at Rafael for the umpteenth time. He'd fallen asleep again. She realized at that precise moment that he'd only talked about her. Absolutely nothing about himself . . . as was to be expected.

The door of the compartment opened, letting in a young blond man. His heavy fist landed in the middle of Rafael's sleeping face.

"Wake up," Herbert shouted with a serious expression.

Rafael opened his eyes, stunned. He had actually been sleeping.

"You've given us a lot of trouble," Herbert growled, loosening Sarah's straps.

"What I've done is make your work easier," Rafael declared. "If I'd wanted to give you trouble, I wouldn't be here right now."

"I know you're a brave man," Herbert accused him sarcastically, slapping him again on the same side. "That's for the men you made me lose."

"You must feel sorry for them," Rafael mocked.

Herbert knelt down to loosen the straps binding Sarah's legs and turned to lift her up.

"Now we're going to have a conversation," the captor said, forcing Sarah to get up. "I'm taking you to see the visitors."

"Give them a kiss for me," Rafael said before the door closed.

Let's stay at Sarah's side, since Rafael isn't going anywhere.

The plane was spacious. She hadn't noticed when they entered, considering she hadn't assimilated any of the unfolding events. Her mind was bombarded with images of the shot to Ivanovsky's head, the Russian eccentric who'd died in the service of his country, in an attack carried out by Chechen separatists, according to the newspaper headlines. Moscow would have to adopt more repressive measures against those terrorists who showed no respect for human lives.

Swivel seats were distributed through the cabin of what had to be a Boeing 7-something, outfitted with just about everything.

Sarah was pushed toward the front of the plane. Various agents were working throughout the plane, oblivious to her or Herbert. Computers, radar, flat screens reflecting graphs added to the crowded space. At the front was a closed door. Herbert opened it and pushed Sarah inside.

It was a small office for so many people. Sarah recognized only a few, Barnes, seated behind a desk, Staughton, Thompson, although she didn't know their names, and . . . Simon Lloyd.

"Simon," she shouted fervently.

She tried to reach him, but Herbert held her tightly. She evaluated his condition, and it didn't indicate good treatment. Bruises on his face, dried blood, and a swollen lower lip. Simon Lloyd had endured severe punishment, and she felt responsible, as if she'd done it herself.

"Oh, Simon."

He lifted his eyes as well as he could and bowed his head again, beaten.

There were more men in the small office, two seated, one in a wheelchair, who Sarah recognized as the man who was inside the black van they'd been put into in Moscow. Another two standing, and a woman. No sign of Phelps.

"He doesn't know anything. Why have you done this?" she protested emotionally.

"He doesn't, but you do. Take it as a warning," Barnes said seriously. He glanced at Herbert. "Go get the other one."

"With pleasure," replied Herbert, who was not given to taking orders. Things were going well. Opening the door, he encountered Phelps, and they looked at each other.

"Good work," Phelps praised him.

"You were magnificent."

"Have you told Marius?"

"He's waiting for us," Herbert told him.

"Perfect."

Herbert came close to his ear, so no one else would hear.

"You'll have to tell me how you did it. Everything turned out exactly as you said it would at our last meeting at the restaurant."

"Secrecy is the soul of business," Phelps replied without bothering to lower his voice.

They went their separate ways, Herbert in the direction of the cell where Rafael was, Phelps to make the narrow office even tighter.

Sarah felt a mixture of fear and nausea on seeing him. He shot her a sarcastic smile.

"How long before we land?" Barnes asked everyone and no one.

"An hour to Rome," the ever solicitous Staughton answered. "Excuse the question, but I recognize you from the Chelsea and Westminster Hospital. You were with the suspects and helped them." There was no reproach in his voice.

"Is that a question?" Phelps was impatient with interrogations.

"Quiet, Staughton," Littel interrupted. "Mr. Phelps was working as an infiltrator."

"You knew that?" Barnes wanted to understand, shaken.

"Obviously," Littel declared.

"My name is James William Phelps. I'm a bishop of the Roman Catholic Church and administrator of the Opus Dei prelature. Any other questions?"

"Who's the other man you communicated with?" Barnes asked.

"My number two. His purpose was to take care of everything while I was indisposed."

"Do you consider yourself a servant of the Church?"

Phelps turned his eyes to the source of the question . . . Sarah. She couldn't manage to keep quiet.

Phelps smiled. "The Church serves a purpose that I don't expect you to understand."

"It serves to kill?"

"To kill and create. It's much more than a house of prayer. The Church is the engine of the civilized world. The support for democracy."

Sarah threw him a look of incredulity.

"There are no free states without the Church. Every sacrifice is minor if we keep that in mind."

"Enough demagogy," Barnes ordered. "Let's get to what concerns us. Where are we?" His eyes never left Phelps. He was the one being asked for explanations. There were too many chiefs in the room.

"I infiltrated the heart of the enemy," the bishop said. "I was singled out as an assistant to a cardinal in the Holy See, who informed me about some lost papers of Albino Luciani and other paper that belonged to Wojtyla, in addition to a complete file on the steps that led to the May thirteenth, 1981, attempt on his life."

"Who are Albino Luciani and Wojtyla?" asked the diplomatic adjutant, Sebastian Ford, who'd joined the group.

"John Paul the First and John Paul the Second," Thompson whispered.

"As you can imagine, I never slept a night in peace after that," Phelps continued, repulsed by such gross ignorance. "In the pleasant conversation with my number two I learned the location of some documents. Others were within reach of the cardinal I serve, and my web of contacts got me the rest. I pulled strings to organize a competent, professional team and obtained your collaboration. It wasn't difficult given the favors your president and his family owe me."

"Have you managed to acquire all of them?" Littel asked.

"No," he admitted disagreeably. "But I know who has what's missing. I became an assistant for Father Rafael Santini, also known as Jack Payne, as you must know. He's a difficult man."

"Who's going to argue with that?" Barnes said.

"But no one is invincible."

At that precise moment the door opened to admit Rafael and Herbert. Those standing up moved to accommodate them.

"Speak of the devil . . ." Phelps said.

"The devil speaks," Rafael countered.

He got a smack on the head for that.

"Shut up. Speak when you're told to," Herbert warned. *One has to be courteous.*

"Go on. Who has what we need?" Barnes announced.

At that moment they heard over the intercom: "Gentlemen, this is the pilot here. We are descending into Rome. Landing in twenty minutes."

Phelps looked at Rafael, who looked back without blinking.

"Our friend here has the file."

"Him?" Barnes protested, pointing at Rafael.

"What's the matter, Barnes?" Littel asked.

"Good luck. I hope you have an alternative plan because he'll carry that information to the grave."

"What are you saying?" Now it was Phelps who didn't understand.

"My dear sir, this man is trained for the most dangerous missions. Unless you have some hold over him, the only thing torture will get from him is body parts and organs."

Phelps smiled. He understood the American's worry.

"Don't worry. He's going to tell us everything. We have the woman."

"What woman?" Sebastian Ford asked.

"Her." He pointed with irritation at Sarah Monteiro.

The room looked in silence at Phelps. *What did the woman have to do with Rafael?*

Phelps assumed the attitude of a teacher. *Was he the only one who noticed?*

"There are certain feelings between the two of them."

Sarah blushed.

Barnes looked at Rafael and Sarah, then at Littel.

"Do you believe it?"

"Phelps is the one who knows them," Littel answered with a shrug.

"And the rest of the documents?"

"My number two has discovered that the cardinal betrayed us. So they can only be in JC's hands."

"Then she's screwed." Barnes didn't mince words.

"Everything is as it needs to be. We know who has what. And I'm counting on your help to throw out some bait for JC," Phelps announced victoriously.

"What?"

"Ah . . . well. I want to talk to you about that," Littel said to Barnes, and got up. "We know you've worked with P2."

"P2?" Sebastian Ford asked again.

"JC's organization," Littel told him. "We need you to mount a plan to catch them."

"I can't do that," Barnes warned circumspectly.

"You have to," Littel argued. "It's an order."

Barnes snorted like a racehorse waiting to take off when the pistol fires.

"It's not like that. We have to separate things. We can't turn our back on some people only to benefit outside organizations. I understand your dilemma, Barnes, but we have no choice."

"I knew you weren't coming here just to be on my side."

Silence reigned in the room for a few moments, just enough not to last.

"At least we're in agreement," Phelps said with a mocking smile. "Anyone else have a question?"

"Why couldn't you sleep in peace?"

The glances turned toward Sarah, who had asked the question, then to Phelps.

"It's you who are going to be interrogated now, my dear," he answered uncomfortably.

"You don't want her to know that one of your members was behind the assassination attempt," Rafael interjected.

"Shut up," Phelps ordered.

Herbert smacked Rafael in the face again, harder this time.

"Who?" Sebastian Ford wanted to know.

"Paul Marcinkus," Rafael answered.

"Shut up, I said." Anger reddened Phelps's face.

"Marcinkus was P2," Barnes affirmed.

"And Opus Dei. They were the ones who recommended him to Paul the Sixth as IWR administrator."

"Don't say another word," Phelps yelled. "Get him out of here."

Herbert grabbed him and began to drag him out. It wasn't easy, even with Rafael handcuffed.

"You're protecting a murderer and a pedophile. That's what he doesn't want you to know."

Priscilla put her hand to her mouth, shocked. Littel and the others didn't seem surprised. Only Barnes's men showed no previous knowledge of this.

Phelps brought his hand to his mouth and sighed.

"Enough. This is going to be done the way we agreed. Is there any problem?" He spoke to Littel.

"Not on our part," he answered, looking at Barnes.

"Very well. Take those two to the cell. They'll be interrogated on the ground," Phelps commanded.

"Did you hear what he said?" Barnes demanded. "Staughton, Thompson, lend a hand." He looked at Rafael. "This time there's no accord to save you. I want to be the one who sends you from here to hell."

Rafael smiled provocatively.

"Where's the Muslim?" Phelps wanted to know.

"What Muslim?"

"Abu Rashid."

"We don't have him," Littel informed them. "He disappeared from Jerusalem days ago."

Phelps looked at him astonished.

"You don't have him?"

"No."

"The Russians don't have him. I heard the conversation they had with our friend here. He also seems to have never heard of him. I thought he could only be in your custody."

"He never has been," Littel asserted. "We have no idea where he could be."

"We'll have to resolve this," Phelps added.

"What about the journalist?" Garrison wanted to know.

"Kill him," Phelps said without thinking twice. "Let's go. Move."

Staughton and Thompson helped Herbert carry Sarah and Rafael.

She shot a last look at Simon Lloyd, who couldn't disguise the panic in his eyes.

"No one's going to kill anyone for now."

Everyone looked at Rafael.

"Oh, no?" Phelps mocked.

"No."

"And why not?"

You save your ace for the right moment.

65

Over the years the American archbishop had visited the papal office in the Apostolic Palace many times, most frequently during the era of his protector, Paul VI. One phone call was enough to find out the pope's schedule, and the gates opened immediately if there was an available time. He visited once during the short reign of Albino Luciani, on the evening of his death, to appeal to the pope not to accuse him of fraud and other more serious crimes. That visit was a complete failure. In the pontificate of Wojtyla, which had lasted twelve years so far, the visits could be counted on his two hands, decidedly fewer than a dozen. This was the first in the last five years.

The Pole was distracted, scrawling on a piece of paper, and hadn't invited him to sit down. Courtesy demanded he not do so on his own, especially in the office of the Supreme Pontiff, when he was right in front of him.

He stamped his signature on the lower part of the page printed with the papal seal, put down the gold pen, and looked, for the first time, at the American.

"Good evening, Nestor."

"Excuse me?" Marcinkus turned red with shame. Had he heard correctly?

"Nestor," the Pole repeated. "Isn't he your alter ego?"

"I don't understand, Your Holiness." The archbishop's uneasiness was obvious. He hadn't expected this reception.

"Don't play dumb." Wojtyla got right to the point. "I've known everything for a long time."

"All what, Your Holiness?"

"Well . . . let's go over the parts. I thought it was strange when I removed you from the IWR last year that you never came to ask for an explanation."

"The decision was yours to make, Your Holiness. I was in charge of the bank for eighteen years. It was normal that the time had come to leave," he responded naturally.

"All right, Nestor."

"Don't call me Nestor, Your Holiness."

"Paul and Nestor are the same person. A true chameleon, if you will." He looked at him gravely. "You tried to kill me."

"No, Holy Father," he contradicted him, but without much conviction.

"Sit down," he invited him. "Sit down and listen to a story."

Paul Marcinkus accepted Karol Wojtyla's request and sat down, while the pope got up and walked around the desk until he stopped behind the American, who felt threatened.

"About two years ago I received a mysterious phone call that led to an even more mysterious visit. Someone wished to discuss subjects of interest to me. Perhaps you've heard of this person. He calls himself JC. At the time I thought he might be comparing himself to Jesus Christ, but I don't think he had that grand pretension. I don't believe he has the same beliefs we do."

"I've never heard of him, Your Holiness," Marcinkus denied, without turning toward the Pole.

"No? Well, look, he knows you very well. He told me about your adventures in Masonry . . ."

"I can explain, Your Holiness." He turned to the pope, alarmed.

"You can? Belonging to a Masonic lodge results in direct excommunication without the right of explanations. Do you know anything about that, Nestor, 124, of the Loggia of Rome?"

Nestor . . . Paul hid his face in his hands.

"You can't believe just any person who appears so suddenly, Your Holiness. Many people wish us ill."

"You know something? You're right. That's exactly what I told your friend."

He raised his voice. "He's not my friend."

"And he was ready to prove what he'd said. Days later something was entrusted to me in a pretty packet that contained so many things that, even today, with the years that have passed, all of the ramifications and operations described have still not been analyzed."

Marcinkus sank into his chair.

"That was the reason for removing you from the IWR last year, which, I confess, I thought would be enough to see you go voluntarily. I was deceived. You didn't feel affected by these things. Therefore I'm going to summarize what came in the packet in one single statement. You're a criminal."

The American took his hands from his face and got up, stung by the insult.

"How dare you call me that!"

"I'm not the one calling you that, Paul. It's in the evidence. You can't contradict the facts." Wojtyla remained firm and certain.

"Evidence. Evidence. Don't throw evidence in my face," he spoke proudly. "I've given a lot to the Holy See. You've lost nothing." He disregarded completely the courtesy the pope deserves.

"Do I need to remind you how much your speculations at the Ambrosiano in the eighties cost us? Your absolution in 'eighty-four was less than peaceful and even less well explained."

Marcinkus stared at him with hate in his eyes.

"I knew that sooner or later you'd throw that in my face. I admitted the error when it happened."

"And why don't you admit it now?"

"The Holy Father is popular all over the world. The most popular pope in history. Who do you think makes that possible? Who finances your trips, the luxury in which you live?" he asked angrily.

"The faithful," Wojtyla replied.

"Don't make me laugh," Marcinkus joked with a sour smile. "It's thanks to people like me who wisely administer the goods of the Church over the centuries. The Holy Father wouldn't exist without me. I'm the true pope of all this. And if you intend to prosecute me, something can always happen," he threatened.

The pope walked around the desk and picked up the piece of paper with the seal. He sighed deeply.

"Effective immediately, the archbishop is removed from all the functions that occupy the Holy See. He will return to his archdiocese, from which he will not return again."

"You can't do that to me," he shouted.

Wojtyla ignored his tone.

"You'll be taken by helicopter directly to the Fiumicino airport, where you'll continue on a flight that will take you to the United States."

"You're playing with fire."

"The press will be told of your voluntary retirement because of fatigue and homesickness. It's my wish that this case be closed immediately without scandal. The proof will be deposited in the Secret Archives of the Vatican without more investigation. If this decision doesn't please you, I'll be happy to hand you over to the Italian authorities, who are eager to charge you. The choice is yours," Wojtyla concluded peremptorily, turning his back.

Marcinkus let himself sink in the chair. Tears of rage welled up in his eyes and ran down his face. He sat there for several minutes, breathing in the oppressive silence. He had come to Rome in 1950 and had never left. Living in the United States was unthinkable, like a prison sentence. He decided to get up and walk toward the office door. He opened it and remained without moving, defeated, old.

Karol Wojtyla looked out at the plaza, hidden by the white curtains.

"Ten o'clock tonight at the heliport. Don't be late."

66

Istanbul had as much movement at night as during the day. Life swirled through the streets and alleys, allied to the nocturnal mysteries that fill this enigmatic city.

The group led by the old man with the cane, whose handle formed the gold head of a lion, mingled with the thousands of tourists who crammed the tourist spots. An old man with a married couple and another man—they could easily pass for close family members, if it was in their interest to create that image.

They passed through the Hippodrome, whose obelisks still survived, although the amphitheater that seated a hundred thousand people had to be imagined. They went into Hagia Sophia, the cathedral converted into a mosque and then into a museum, where emperors and sultans were once crowned. It served Greeks and Ottomans, survived Constantinople, and remained a symbol of the city and Turkey. They dined at Cati in Beyoğlu, at a table next to a window with views of the Bosporus. They began with *corbasi*, yogurt soup, with vegetables; then, as the main course, had *hunkar beğendili köfte*, meatballs with eggplant puree, mixed with cheese, and a variety of kebabs.

Raul and Elizabeth had many questions, but didn't ask any. They were astonished at the way JC delighted over the food he was serving.

"Turkish Palace cooking," he said. "Delicious."

The couple scarcely tasted the food. They picked at it more out of courtesy and sympathy than hunger, even though they hadn't eaten well for days.

The cripple maintained his cool pose. He ate, but not like a savage. He was always the same. Polite, silent, he ate to survive, no other reason, and looked around from time to time to assure himself of the old man's safety. That was his only preoccupation; everything else was secondary.

"What time is our meeting?" the old man asked him.

"He'll call us as soon as he arrives."

"Tell him to come here."

"All right."

The cripple got up and left with his cell phone in his hand. A private call away from the chaos of the restaurant.

"Who's coming?" Elizabeth asked.

"Another friend?" Raul added.

"An ally . . . I hope," he replied, not paying attention, bringing a meatball to his mouth. "Hmm . . . delicious."

"How can you live like this?" Elizabeth asked, scandalized.

"How do you mean, my dear?"

"Like this." She didn't know how to explain it. "Walking a tightrope."

"Don't be fooled, Mrs. Monteiro. Politicians are the ones who live on a tightrope. Presidents, prime ministers, senators, representatives walk a tightrope. They know that living at the will of the electorate is thankless. No matter what they do the public is never grateful. That's why they sell themselves to corporations and lobbies. In short, they take care of their future. People like you also walk a tightrope. I don't."

"Do you call this a life of peace and quiet?" Raul put in.

"What more could you desire? Dining at the finest restaurant in Istanbul after a guided tour. Tomorrow, who knows, Amsterdam, Bangkok."

"Don't be funny," Raul exclaimed.

JC drank a little *vişne suyu*, cherry juice, to moisten his words. "My life was very quiet until last year. Your friend is the one who stirred things up. Don't forget it."

"I know that perfectly well. That's another story."

"In any case this year reminded me of my adventurous youth. I'm old. I've been old a long time. My appearance doesn't deceive. I was retired in my villa, making decisions over telephone, with a glass of whiskey in hand, reading the *Corriere* and *La Repubblica*, to keep up with the stupidities they publish. For the first time in fifteen years, I feel alive. For someone whose active military, political, and clandestine life began in the Second World War and continued to the end of the Cold War, to be physically inactive is frustrating. Now I'm in the field again, and no price can be put on that."

He's human, after all, the Monteiros thought.

"As I see it, this is all a game for you," Raul commented.

"In a way. A game with grave consequences for whoever loses."

"Things aren't black or white, isn't that so?" Elizabeth asked, more depressed every minute. Time was passing, and she urgently needed news about her daughter.

"Things are black and white, but not for the common person," he said, taking a little more puree.

"This pope has secrets, too?" Raul inquired.

"Who doesn't?" He wiped his mouth with the cloth napkin. "As your Messiah said, *he who is without sin* . . . Not even the saints that the Holy Mother Church canonizes are without stains. No one passes through life without sin . . . even if only in thought. It's not evil. It's intrinsic to being human."

"That scares me," Elizabeth confessed.

"There's a Brazilian writer, whose name I don't remember, who said something about this. If we could look through the doors of our neighbors, no one would shake hands with anyone. That's more or less so."

"Nelson Rodrigues," Raul added.

"That's right," JC confirmed, remembering the name of the author.

"Do you have any news of my daughter?" Raul asked a question that hadn't crossed Elizabeth's lips for a long time.

"Not yet."

"Is that really true? You're not trying to avoid telling us bad news in any way?" Her worry as a mother loosened her tongue.

"Look me in the eye." He waited for her to do it. "Do you believe I'd have any problem telling you that the worst has happened to your daughter, if that were the case? After all that you've heard?"

Elizabeth lowered her eyes. Bad news travels fast; good news at a snail's pace.

"It doesn't matter to you?"

"It does," he answered without emotion. "You need to know that the negotiations I'm about to begin can affect her fate . . . for better or worse."

"Please, don't let them hurt her," Elizabeth implored.

JC sipped a little more *vişne suyu* and expressed no sign of commitment. Elizabeth tried to speak reason to her motherly heart, but it was useless. JC wouldn't let anything affect his plans. In the end nothing would go beyond business with human lives at stake.

The cripple returned to the table with a tall, impeccably dressed man. He was barely middle-aged, and his muscular body indicated hours a day in the gym, his tan regular hours in a tanning salon. He was a man who cultivated his body, and therefore his health.

"What's the hurry?" he asked impolitely. He hadn't come of his own free will. Some customers looked over at the table.

"Please, sit down," JC invited him, cheerful and serene. Attitude was important.

The man wanted to show his indignation a little more, but the old man's look made him think twice. He sat down in the cripple's chair.

"I'm all ears," he said rudely.

"Ah, you Americans . . . always so arrogant," JC sighed.

The man got up immediately.

"I didn't come here to be insulted. Are you listening to me?"

A firm hand on his shoulder obliged him to sit. The cripple didn't like this kind of behavior in front of the old man.

"Calm down, Oliver."

"How do you know my name?" he asked, surprised.

"I know a lot about you, my friend. Oliver Cromwell Delaney, born in 1966, Dover, Delaware, father of two lovely daughters—"

"Who are you? What do you want from me?" His nervousness was apparent. Things get complicated when strangers start mentioning your daughters. He took out his cell phone.

"I'm going to call my security—"

"You're not going to call anyone," the cripple warned, grabbing the phone from his hand. "Stay in your chair and be quiet."

"Excuse my faithful assistant's bad manners," JC excused him sardonically.

Raul and Elizabeth looked on, intimidated.

"Where was I? Oh, father of two beautiful twin daughters, Joanne and Kathleen, eleven years old. Consul in Istanbul. I could enumerate your biography in detail, but we don't have time."

"What do you want?"

"I need you to put me in contact urgently with George. I could do it through my own channels, but it'd take time to authenticate the call."

"Who's George?"

"Your superior."

"I don't have any superior named George."

"No?" JC asked with a sarcastic smile on his lips.

Oliver looked thoughtful. "I'm not . . . Ah . . . You're talking about George . . ."

"The same."

67

With every step the body weighed more. The sweat that a short time ago was only scattered drops on their faces had become streams that dripped off their chins onto the floor. The two men dragged the mound of inert flesh, bent over in the shared effort.

"Do they think we're pack mules?" Staughton protested.

"Apparently," Thompson said. Talking only wasted energy necessary for carrying out the task.

"Do you think he opened his mouth?"

"No. If he had, we'd be carrying a corpse."

"Barnes kicked the shit out of him," Staughton said.

"True. He gave it to him good. Old-school."

He was alluding to the fact they hadn't used the most modern methods of extracting information. Electric shock was still idolized within this community. Sleep deprivation was extremely efficient, when you had time, which was not the case here. A battery of drugs and injections might or might not work, depending on the mental and physical condition of the individual. None of these techniques had been used on Rafael. They'd thrown unexpected punches or slapped him and kicked him down below, which is what had left him in the sorry condition we witness here. Barnes, Herbert, and Phelps himself hadn't had to ask or stand on ceremony to use

Rafael as a punching bag. There was a close relationship between the degree of pain a person could support and death. It was the fine line that marked the difference between good and bad work. So we see the two men from the agency carrying Rafael's inert but still living body. It only meant he hadn't said anything to his interrogators, or, if he had, it wasn't satisfactory. Still, there was time to drag that information out by the same method, or others.

Thus the discouraged faces of Barnes, Herbert, Phelps, and the others, spread around the Center of Operations for the agency in Rome.

"The guy is tough," Littel said, seated, smoking a cigar, where he'd been during the whole interrogation. He hadn't stained his expensive suit or carefully manicured hands. That was work for others. They didn't pay him to get dirty.

"He's a son of a bitch," Barnes contradicted him. He turned to Phelps with a critical expression. "I told you you wouldn't get anything out of him."

"Calm down, Dr. Barnes. In five minutes bring the woman in. You'll see how we find things out," he declared confidently.

"I hope so," Littel said. "Today is the last round of the U.S. Open, and I don't want to miss it."

"I missed Wimbledon, and I'm here," Barnes answered.

"You hate tennis," Littel argued back.

There were more people in the room than usual, maintaining a sepulchral silence, the better to ignore what was to come. We refer to Wally Johnson, always at Littel's side as his bodyguard, Colonel Stuart Garrison, whose efficiency stood out in the capture of the fugitives, Priscilla Thomason, the devoted secretary. She'd asked permission to leave during the interrogation, but couldn't avoid seeing the victim's condition when he left the room, aided by Staughton and Thompson, not to say dragged, carried, transported. Sebastian Ford rounded out the group, upset because a drop of blood had stained the collar of his shirt. He hadn't even been close to the gang pounding the man as if there were no tomorrow. He tried to clean it with a handkerchief monogrammed with the initials SF, but the blood became an untamed smear.

"Hell," he complained, a little more loudly than he wanted.

All of them looked disapprovingly at him with his handkerchief wet with saliva rubbing the white collar.

"I'll be right back," Sebastian Ford stammered, leaving the room.

"Politicians," Phelps remarked scornfully as soon as Ford left.

"I know from experience he'd let the woman die if he thought she could reveal the location of the Muslim and the file," Barnes said worriedly.

"Well then, let them all die," they heard a voice suggest from the door.

"Marius. My good Marius," Phelps greeted the white-haired man with an embrace.

"James. Things have not gone as well as we would wish," Marius Ferris alerted him.

"They could be worse."

Marius Ferris looked around the room. "Gentlemen, good afternoon to you all."

Barnes remembered him from other operations.

"Where's your lord?"

"The Lord is in heaven," Ferris answered a little arrogantly.

"No one is what he appears," Barnes finally said. Nothing surprised him after so many years of service to the republic.

"He hasn't talked, Marius," Phelps informed him.

"I knew it. Sebastiani has betrayed us, also," he said, closing his fists in anger. "Do they have family we could use to put pressure on them?"

"Nothing. The journalist has a mother who knows nothing. We didn't get anywhere pressuring him on that. If he knew something, he'd have confessed it with the beating we gave him. The parents of the woman have disappeared," Littel declared. "They haven't been seen anywhere."

Phelps put his hand on Marius Ferris's shoulder.

"This is the work of the old man."

"I think so, too," he confirmed. "It's the old fox. We should have known he'd make a move."

"That means he's been helping them from the beginning," Phelps reflected.

"He must have thrown more wood on the fire, without doubt."

"Herbert, go get the woman."

"With pleasure," the sadistic aide answered.

"Let's get this over with," James Phelps decided.

68

Rafael was thrown into the cell against the bare wall, followed by a dry "Welcome to Rome" from Thompson.

Sarah cried out when she saw him in that condition.

"Oh, my God. Rafael," she cried.

But he didn't answer. He looked unconscious, but was probably in too much pain to say anything.

Simon watched Sarah's distress, unable to do anything. Rafael had endured more blows than he had. He hoped he wouldn't see Sarah come back in the same way.

The cell had four concrete walls and a concrete floor, without windows, mattresses, or toilet . . . nothing. Sarah put Rafael's head on her lap and stroked it tenderly.

"Good God, what've they done to you," she whispered, stroking his hair and face.

"They're not playing games," Simon said.

"They're barbarians." She looked at Rafael sadly. She'd never seen him like this. "I see they didn't leave you in peace, either," she said to Simon, without stopping the caresses.

"They left me for a time. The editor told me not to leave the house for any reason."

"Roger?"

"Yes. I knew I should've gone somewhere else. When they threw me in the door, I felt like my heart would jump out of my mouth."

"What did they want from you?"

"To know about the file and someone named Abu Rashid."

"Who's this Abu Rashid?" Sarah wondered. She'd already heard the name in Moscow.

"I have no idea. But do you think they believed me?"

Simon looked at Sarah sadly, as if he had something to say and didn't dare say it.

"What's the matter?" she asked.

"Do you think . . ." He didn't like to raise the subject. "Do you think they'll do the same with you?"

Sarah hadn't thought of that before. She'd only worried about Simon and Rafael, never about herself, ignoring that at any moment the door might open to take her for interrogation.

"Let's not think about that," she said, hiding the fear she felt. "Besides, I know no more than you." That didn't entirely make sense, since the fact that Simon knew nothing hadn't prevented them from leaving bruises all over his body.

Through the irony of fate, which likes to manifest itself at appropriate times, the lock on the door came to life.

Sarah surrendered to panic. Her time had come, her hour to endure the harshness of a group of impatient men who'd do anything to achieve their objective.

The door opened to admit a man dressed in an impeccable suit, at first glance. He bent over Rafael.

"What have they done to you, friend?" he said sadly.

"Who are you?" Sarah asked.

"That's not important. You've never seen me here. Understand?"

He stuck his hand inside a briefcase, took out a Beretta with a silencer, and left it next to Rafael.

"This is the most I can do," he said. "Good-bye."

Sarah and Simon didn't understand what was happening. Who was this man? Why was he leaving them a gun? For a woman it's natural to look at an unknown man with X-ray vision, and she did.

"Later," the man said farewell.

Suddenly Rafael's hand grabbed the man's arm.

"John Cody," he whispered weakly.

The said John Cody leaned over Rafael.

"My friend. I can't delay."

"I need a favor." Rafael's voice seemed to come from a deep well.

"Yes, if I can do it."

"You only have to . . . to . . . to call a number. . . ." He pulled him down closer and spoke into his ear. "He should be confused. Tell him . . . Tell him . . ." It was an effort to talk. "Tell him not to do anything until he receives new instructions."

The man sighed as if something was tiring his mind, a difficult weight to support.

"My friend, you have to be strong. Wait it out. This'll be resolved." He gripped his hand strongly. "They've killed your uncle."

He got up without taking his eyes from Rafael.

"I've got to go."

A tear could be seen running down Rafael's face.

The friend left, closing the door behind him. You could see the blood-stain on the neck of his shirt.

69

I want explanations," Barnes demanded.

"I do, too," Phelps warned. "We can't leave here without them. The woman has to talk."

"I'm not talking about her. I'm talking about you and your men."

"I've already given all the explanations I have to give," he said peremptorily.

"One more." Barnes looked at Littel. "The Spanish are giving us grief because of the priest who was shot to death in the cathedral of Santiago de Compostela."

Phelps smiled and exchanged a conspiratorial look with Marius Ferris.

"What makes you think we have something to do with that?"

"Do you want to go down that road?" Barnes hated many things, but high on the list, along with lying and betrayal, was omission. The simple fact of wanting to make him look like an idiot. With the years he'd spent in the business . . . they ought to show him more respect when they encountered him.

"To where?" Phelps's sarcasm was obvious.

"Your assistant, your number two, as you call him, is not very good at covering his tracks," Barnes declared.

"And why should he cover them, if you don't mind my asking?"

"Mr. Marius Ferris landed at the airport in Santiago de Compostela from Madrid on the morning of the day Father Clemente was killed. And, big coincidence"—Barnes raised his voice and hands theatrically—"your helper arrived in Vigo the same day." Barnes got up, leaned on the table with his arms, and shot a firm, hard look at him. "Do you mind telling me about it?"

"Would somebody mind turning on the air conditioner?" Littel asked. "We're getting fried in here."

In fact, they were all sweating, heat combined with suspicion.

"Very well," Phelps conceded. "There were signs the file on the Turk was in Don Clemente's hands. Herbert searched his rooms, and Marius took care of things personally."

"And they killed him because . . ."

"They didn't leave evidence. It was decided from the beginning it'd be that way, without witnesses. We've complied."

"You should've informed us."

"Aren't you the ones who always know everything?" Marius Ferris said sarcastically.

"Why did you think they'd be in his possession?" Littel asked. "From what we know, Rafael took the Turk's file from the woman's house."

"Don Clemente had several meetings with Rafael in the last year. Two in Santiago, one in Rome, and another in London."

"They knew each other?" Barnes wanted to know.

"More than that . . . they were relatives," Phelps informed him.

"Don Clemente was Rafael's uncle," Marius Ferris added.

"You killed his uncle?" Littel asked.

"And we're going to kill the nephew," Phelps affirmed with the sarcastic smile of a mischievous child.

"Does he know?" Barnes asked.

"It's not very likely."

"We shouldn't waste time. We have to eliminate him as soon as possible," a worried Barnes stated.

Sebastian Ford came into the room again, suffocating. Sweat ran down his face. His armpits soaked his shirt. He'd taken off his jacket and loosened his tie a little—a politician giving the impression of working.

"What kept you so long? Where've you been?" Littel asked.

"Uh . . . I was trying to get the spot out, but it won't go away," the other replied.

"I'll buy you another one, then," Littel replied.

"And burn that one," Barnes ordered. "I don't want any evidence." He turned toward Phelps, the helmsman. "What made you follow the uncle and nephew?"

"Once more owing to the confidence of the cardinal I serve . . ." He interrupted himself with the expression of someone who'd just realized the truth suddenly.

"You served," Barnes completed the thought with a scornful expression. "Who told you what you wanted to hear . . ."

Phelps's expression changed completely. His cheeks turned red, and the color spread over the rest of his face.

"What's the matter?" Marius Ferris asked.

The door opened again to let in Staughton, Thompson, and Herbert, who seemed to be tolerating one another. In Herbert's claws Sarah was white as chalk, in a state of suppressed panic. They followed the looks fixed on the blushing Phelps and realized instantly something was not right. The anger flowing from the priest could be felt for miles. Barnes repressed a certain personal satisfaction. He hated people who thought they were so superior they were beyond ordinary people.

"It looks like you're the one who ended up being manipulated," Barnes concluded.

"Don't be ridiculous," Phelps shouted.

"What's going on?" Herbert wanted to know. When he'd left, everything was fine.

"Don't raise your voice with me," Barnes ordered firmly. "I'm likely to forget we're associates and finish this up completely." He waited for his words to sink into Phelps's mind. "We found out here that the cardinal he serves or served has betrayed us. What he told him in secret has turned out to be false. He happened to see the uncle talking to his nephew, perhaps giving him something, to convince him he had everything under control. Everything was under control, but by them, not you . . . or us."

"They're in a cell. The woman's here under our control," Phelps argued, thwarted.

"But they still have everything we wanted. And where are the ringleaders? JC, the cardinal, and their team? Running everything from their box seats, drinking champagne and eating caviar."

They all listened to Barnes in silence. Phelps, with his eyes closed, looked like he wanted to deny the arguments, but his rationality prevented him.

Barnes was right. He'd been deceived, but there was a remedy. He approached Sarah and grabbed her by the hair without pity. Sarah twisted and screamed.

"No. No."

They sat her violently in an empty chair.

"Where's Abu Rashid?"

"I don't know," Sarah answered, frightened.

A strong slap jolted her face to the side.

"Where's the file on the Turk?"

"I don't know."

The tears from the first slap flew out with the second, still harder, from the other side.

"Where's JC?" The questions followed faster.

Sarah didn't reply, but the slaps didn't stop, shaking her whole head inside.

"We're going to drag everything you know out of you," Phelps cried, leaning over her and brutally pulling her hair.

"I want the whole truth. If not, your parents are going to suffer."

Broken down in silent tears, Sarah looked at him. She didn't give voice to the sorrow filling her, driving her to shout, to moan, to give up. Mentioning her parents was cruel, hard. Could it be they'd caught them? Would that mean they'd also caught JC? Or was it all a lie to make her tell everything . . . but what? She knew nothing.

Another angry slap. James Phelps was beside himself. His flinty eyes sparked out uncontrollable fury. A thread of blood trailed from her mouth.

Phelps's arm reached back again to gain force for another brutal slap, but was prevented by a strong hand, heavy as a blackjack, that grabbed and stopped it.

"Calm down, Phelps," Barnes recommended. "We want her alive. Stop now."

"She's going to tell everything," Phelps said with a maniacal look.

"Everything she knows . . . which might be nothing," Barnes said.

The American circled Sarah, intimidating her. He knew she feared him because in the past she'd seen what he was capable of doing.

"Sarah Monteiro, born April eighth, 1976, journalist, Portuguese, resident of London, daughter of a Portuguese father and English mother." Barnes's tone was calm but electrifying, psychic. There was a door he had to open, her ultimate defense, that which guarded everything. "She had an abortion in 2007 as a consequence of which she almost died."

Barnes was silent for a few moments and then put his lips close to her ear.

"Look carefully at the people in this room." He stepped back, grasped her hard by the head and chin, and shouted, "Don't leave anyone out."

Sarah had no choice. Stuart Garrison in his wheelchair, a deathly stare, cold, as if he were in a theater watching a boring film. Priscilla Thomason, a notepad in her hand, closed, watching her with consternation and pain, because of Littel and his will or lack of will. Littel remained seated, with his legs crossed, reading some reports that had little to do with this case. His lack of interest in Sarah was obvious. He was there to serve the wishes of the president of the United States of America . . . or not. Wally Johnson, in his army uniform with the braids of a lieutenant colonel fixed to the shoulders, reminded her of a sentinel guarding the fort, firm, alert, prepared to destroy any threat. Sebastian Ford, whom Sarah recognized as the man who'd entered the cell to see Rafael. Rafael's man on Barnes's team. Barnes had no idea. Ford watched her with compassion, a politician with feelings. Here votes didn't count, there was no campaign, nothing to win. Herbert, the faithful aide, seemingly everything men of power needed to do their dirty work, and also the clean work. Staughton, the man of data more than field operations. Thompson distanced from her. Habit creates defenses, the mind adapts and rejects the idea that what the person is doing is wrong. He always acted in the best interest of the American nation. Last of all, the old man with white hair who seemed out of place. He was Marius Ferris, the frail parish priest who knew New York. He couldn't be part of that dark gang of wrongdoers. Or could he? A joking smile on his part answered Sarah's doubts.

Barnes's hands squeezed her face, causing an anguished feeling.

"We are the only people in the world who know you're *still* alive."

A shiver ran down Sarah's spine.

Barnes took his gun from the holster and pressed the cold barrel against her forehead.

"Do yourself a favor and spit out all you know."

Sarah took a breath anxiously. Her tears flowed copiously; a thread of blood ran from her lips and mouth. They could beat her to death. She had nothing to say.

The tension was broken by the polyphonic sound of the "Star-Spangled Banner" making almost all those present straighten their shoulders. The sound came from a cell phone clamoring for the attention of its owner, Harvey Littel.

"That's illegal," a stern-faced Barnes objected. He left Sarah and sat at the desk, leaving his gun to the side.

"Every American should have that music on his cell phone," Littel asserted before answering it.

The assistant subdirector listened to the caller.

"Just a moment." He lowered the phone and looked at those in the room seriously. "Leave," he ordered.

In spite of the generality implied in the order, they all knew that the instruction applied only to the lower-level employees, Colonel Garrison, Priscilla, Wally Johnson, Sebastian Ford, Staughton, and Thompson. But no one moved.

"Ask your men to wait outside," Littel told Phelps.

The Englishman only needed to frown, and Herbert and Marius Ferris followed in the steps of the others.

"And the woman?" Phelps asked.

"Let her stay," Littel declared. "It'll be another secret to carry to the grave."

Sarah preferred to leave for a change of air instead of staying with these men.

Littel set the cell phone on speaker.

"You can forward me the call."

Barnes was filled with curiosity, as was Phelps. Who could it be?

In less than five seconds they heard the twanging voice of the Texan.

"Harvey?"

Sarah, in the midst of confusion and pain, thought she'd heard that voice somewhere. But she could have been mistaken.

"Yes, Mr. President."

Barnes stood up straight as a pole. The president for the second time in a short while.

"Is Barnes there with you?"

"He is . . . I am, Mr. President," he answered nervously, sitting down in the chair at the desk.

"Great. Great. Listen carefully. Effective immediately, I want the agency out of the operation."

Phelps turned red upon hearing the words. He must not have heard right. Sarah felt the same for other reasons.

Littel got up suspiciously.

"Mr. President, could you repeat that?"

"I want the agency out of the operation immediately. Take your briefcases, turn out the lights, and close the door."

"You can't do something like that," Phelps returned.

"Who's speaking?" asked the most powerful man in the world on the other end of the line.

"Jim Phelps, Mr. President," Littel told him.

"Ah, yes. Jim." The president indicated he knew Phelps.

"What is this, sir? We have an agreement," the Englishman reminded him.

"Our agreement required a series of conditions you haven't fulfilled."

"What do you mean by that? It's not over yet. I'm about to comply." Irritation rose more and more in his voice.

"It's over, Jim. I want all those implicated out of this and the prisoners freed. I assure you this is best for you."

"You don't even know what's best for yourself," Phelps replied. The explosion had to happen. His world was crashing down around him. A decision like this deprived him of something he was just starting to enjoy. "You can't agree to something and then quit in the middle."

"The agreement was to tie up all the loose ends. You had my complete support, and for that reason you're in Rome with my men. You painted an easy scenario, and the conclusion we've come to is that your enemy has all the evidence, and I'm asking you to terminate everything. If not . . ."

"What?" Phelps was possessed.

"What you've heard. JC has contacted me. He has everything. He was specific in saying he wants everything stopped or you're going to suffer a disaster."

Phelps was in anguish. Defeated by the old fox who'd anticipated every one of his steps. He'd dangled the carrot in front of him and manipulated him at his will.

"Everything stays the same. No one leaves hurt," George added. "Accept it and go along with it, Jim."

If we looked closely, we'd see a tear welling up in Phelps's eye. Accept, conform, lose. All this work for nothing. No, this couldn't happen. They had an agreement. Damn JC.

"What about the tomb?" Phelps wanted to know.

"Everything stays as it is," the president repeated.

"And the woman, the agent of the Vatican . . ."

"Release them immediately. Now, I've got other things to do. I've given my orders. I count on you to carry them out, Littel."

"Of course, Mr. President."

"You, too, Barnes."

"Of course," Barnes answered, tripping over his words.

The call was over. Sarah was incredulous. She didn't know whether to feel relieved or suspicious. Be that as it may, a huge about-face had happened at the right moment.

"Bastard," Phelps cursed, defeated.

"Everything calculated," Barnes analyzed. "You've heard the orders. Let's close this screwed-up case."

"No," Phelps stammered.

"No? You heard the same thing I did. I'm not going to contradict a direct order of the president," Barnes warned with certainty.

"Before turning in the arms we should kill the prisoners."

"I'd love to. Especially that bastard Rafael. But the orders are explicit," Barnes reminded him.

"Let's say they were already dead."

"Tell me something, Jim." Littel spoke. "Suppose we do what you say. Will the transfer continue online?"

"My word is good. Five million in cash, when and where you want it," Phelps guaranteed him.

"Transfer? What transfer?" Barnes asked.

Sarah felt a shiver in her guts.

"Ten million," Littel said.

Phelps looked Harvey Littel in the eye with a serious, pragmatic expression.

"Ten million it is."

"Littel, what the hell are you saying? The president was very clea—"

Before completing the sentence, Barnes lay on the floor with a bullet in his forehead. Littel looked at the body coldly, the gun with a silencer in his hand, which Barnes had forgotten on the desk. Phelps smiled diabolically, and Sarah wept for Natalie, Greg, Clemente, Rafael, Simon, her father, her mother . . . and Barnes. He wasn't on her side, but he hadn't sold out.

"Go get the other two," Littel ordered, looking at Sarah with a Machiavellian expression, a simple way of saying *you're next* without opening his mouth. He wiped down the gun with a silk handkerchief and put it in the hand of Barnes, who stared ahead, devoid of life. What a hell of a way to die.

70

Tim had slept like a baby. It was a long time since he'd felt such a profound spiritual peace. The phantoms that all his life had tortured his dreams and, night after night, transformed them into nightmares had disappeared, blown by the wind far away from him. A peaceful, friendly night, impregnated with the scent of spring, between warm and cold, nature in her eternal search for the perfect balance. A perfect night he'd never imagined could exist.

For the first time in his life he woke up sleepy, dazzled by the sunlight coming in the open window of the room in the inn, and forgot the prayers to the Creator of all things, an unpardonable fault in the eyes of the clerical tutors who molded his character in his early years. The first thought of the day should be of the Creator, God, as should be the last, and all other thoughts during the day. Nothing else existed but God, and he should think of Him all the time. So it was said and is said in the monastery where he was brought up and lived since infancy to the sound of carnivorous whips tearing his skin and that of others.

He faced the strong morning sun and sat on the edge of the bed.

"You slept well," he heard a voice say. Abu Rashid, seated in the chair where Tim had seen him for the last time before falling asleep.

"Yes."

"It wasn't a question," Abu Rashid sweetly contradicted him. "I know you slept well."

Tim closed his eyes and took a deep breath. The weight he felt on himself the day before had disappeared. He felt light, rejuvenated, fresh.

"This is the true peace," Abu Rashid affirmed. "It has nothing to do with orders, sacrifice, suffering. What you feel now is communion with God. A perfect harmony with nature, with the universe."

"Was it the Virgin who told you that?"

"Any wise person comes to that conclusion."

Tim looked around, inspecting the room, used to the intense light now. The white, strong sun embracing the world with energy. For a moment, not seeing the black briefcase, he felt a weight in his stomach.

"It's under the bed," Abu Rashid told him. "I don't want you to miss anything."

Tim squatted down and grabbed the briefcase. The key code and lock didn't look tampered with.

"Didn't you want to see what was inside?" he asked curiously.

"I know what's in there," the Muslim confirmed. "I don't have to see it."

"Or maybe your visionary powers couldn't decipher the code?" he said in a challenging way.

"I like to see you calmer, Tim. You seem different." Abu Rashid deliberately ignored the provocation.

"I feel strange," Tim confessed. "As if I were the father of a large family I needed to support with a lot of sacrifice, I alone, and suddenly they don't need me, and I can live my own life. A life I didn't know I had."

Tim looked, amazed, at the old Muslim. He'd never opened up to anyone, much less a stranger. He'd learned to hold all his frustrations and confusions within himself, since that was one of the teachings of the monastery. He'd summarized his whole existence in one statement to a man he'd wanted to kill the day before.

"What's in the case?" Tim finally asked.

"The fact I don't know shows my honesty. After all, the code is your birth date. I could've looked in it anytime I wanted."

They both smiled calmly. Abu Rashid was not a fake, and, taking that into consideration, Tim should have shot him. He hadn't received instructions at the appointed time. When that happened the Sanctifier was supposed to make the most appropriate decision to safeguard the Church. But that didn't bother Tim today. Life was giving him another chance, and he was going to take advantage of it. The dark time that he'd spent in the arms of the elite who swept their problems under the carpet was over.

"I'm going to take you back to your house," he decided.

"That's not necessary. I know the way."

"It's fair that I take you. I was the one who snatched you from your normal life."

"No, Tim. I said it yesterday, and I'll say it again. You never took me away from anything. I'm here of my own free will. This isn't over yet."

Tim got up, startled. "Yes, it's over. I don't want to keep doing this."

"That's a wise decision, but first you have to answer the phone."

"What—"

The cell phone on the table started to ring at that precise moment. With an instinctive move, decisively, Tim grabbed it, brought it to his ear, and listened.

"Who's there?" he asked suspiciously.

The caller identified himself, explained the situation, and gave the message. That must have been what happened, but only Tim could confirm it.

"Listen, Sebastian, I'm going to take the man home," Tim told him. "He has a special gift, but I'm not going to sentence him." He looked at Abu Rashid, who smiled at him. It was possible for a man to change overnight.

The person speaking on the other end said a few more words that Tim listened to attentively.

"Affirmative. I'll wait for him to tell him my decision," he stated categorically. "He knows where I am," he added. He frowned. "Has something happened to him?"

Sebastian presented his version of the facts, retouched, politically correct, or, on the contrary, he mentioned only Rafael's momentary inability to talk with Tim by phone.

"When will he be able to? Any idea?"

Another evasive, conciliatory reply from Sebastian Ford. *I can't tell you, but I hope soon.* Something like that.

"Do me the favor of telling him I'm going to take the man to Jerusalem and return to the agreed-upon place. I'll stay there eight days. If he doesn't show up, give him my greetings and best wishes." There was a new happiness in Tim's voice, a valid reason to live. Life was beautiful, finally.

The caller hung up, and Tim did the same.

"It's clear," he declared. "I'm going to take a shower and we'll go. You must miss your house," Tim said.

"My house is always in my heart. I can't miss something that's always with me. My house is the universe," the Muslim said with shining eyes. "Today is the first day of the rest of your life."

Even the shower felt different. It washed away the poverty of his spirit and opened his soul to new dimensions. A succession of images flowed through his mind, reviving feelings he thought didn't exist or had been extinguished. Loneliness was not a way of life but an aberration that darkened his being and ennobled inner demons. The water washed, carried away, poured, expelled, cleaned, and refreshed. That was its nature, the amplitude of its being. He thought of love, the family he didn't have but could begin to have. A multitude of opportunities passed through his mind.

Tim didn't know how long he'd let the water run, since he'd lost track of the seconds, the gallons of water, the bath accessories. Renewed, he smiled when he realized he'd showered with the door open, something he'd have condemned before.

"Ready to return—" Tim interrupted himself.

There was no one in the room. The door was closed with the lock set, the window closed from inside. Abu Rashid had disappeared into thin air. Tim couldn't help feeling a mixture of sadness and happiness. A smile passed over his lips, a tear came to his eye.

On top of the bed a gilded object, small, cylindrical, shining . . . A bullet.

71

"Jesus Christ, what's happened here?" Staughton asked, surprised to see the corpse of his director stretched out on the floor with a vacant stare, dead. A tear ran down his face, a suppressed sorrow, genuine, unforeseen. "How could this happen?"

The rest of Barnes's team and those of Littel and Phelps returned to the interrogation room astonished. Phelps was absent. He'd gone to find the prisoners. They all looked at Barnes's lifeless body.

"We've received a call from the Oval Office," Littel explained.

"From the Oval Office?" Sebastian Ford asked.

"Exactly," Littel affirmed. He approached Sarah and used his own silk handkerchief as a gag. "The president in person ordered us to finish everything and leave no survivors." He looked at Sarah warningly.

Thompson and Staughton were in shock. They couldn't believe their eyes. Barnes was immortal, invincible.

"Barnes was angry with the president's decision." His voice trembled with emotion. He spoke in a low voice, almost a whisper. "He even got rude. He said things had to be carried out to the end. It gave a bad impression. The president raised his voice and said the final word was his, and if Barnes didn't know his place, he'd have to be better informed." He was silent for a few seconds, letting his words sink in. "As soon as the president was off the phone, he put the gun to his head and fired."

"My God," Staughton exclaimed.

"And now?" Thompson asked in a restrained voice. In spite of being accustomed to death, when it happened to your own, in your own house, unexpectedly, you suffered like anyone else.

"We're going to obey the president's orders. Eliminate the prisoners and lock the door," Littel declared, condescending to the general feeling in the room.

Staughton and Thompson were the most upset, understandably, since they'd worked daily with Barnes for many years. The man had an intimidating voice, could act impulsively, eat like a savage, swear constantly, flip over the table if things weren't going his way, but he was fair, a friend in his way, a companion, cautious. He never risked the life of an agent.

How was it possible that Geoffrey Barnes, a career man with an enviable record, used to working under pressure, could have ended his life in such . . . such . . . a cowardly way? In spite of everything, Barnes was balanced. For Staughton and Thompson this ending was like a mathematical operation, adding two and two, the result of which was five or three.

"Nobody expected it. It was too much for anyone," Littel argued. "Staughton, Thompson, go home. Take a few days to get over it. We'll finish the operation."

"No," Staughton dissented. "We want to stay with the chief." He didn't take his eyes off the cadaver.

"Staughton," Littel shouted. He had to get in front of him and shake him to make the traumatized Staughton look at him. "Staughton. Today Barnes will be on a plane going home."

"I want to go with him."

"Me too," Thompson declared.

"Very well." He turned to the lieutenant colonel. "Wally, go with these two good men. Take them around Rome."

"To Saint Peter's?" Wally Johnson suggested.

"To Saint Peter's," Littel agreed. "Excellent idea. Pray a little, refresh their ideas, and at the end of the day put them on the same plane with their boss. It's a promise."

Littel gave Staughton a friendly slap on the shoulder and turned his back. Wally Johnson helped him toward the door. Thompson followed. Their last look before leaving the room was at Geoffrey Barnes, their unhappy director.

Three went out, another three came in, Phelps with the remaining prisoners, Rafael and Simon, who had an expression deeper than panic. Fear of death. Rafael could now support himself on his feet, although a little shakily. A swollen eye impeded his full vision. They were forced to sit on chairs next to Sarah.

"Take that body out of here," Littel ordered no one in particular.

Since the only helpers worthy of the name in the room were Priscilla and Herbert, there was no doubt to whom the task fell. Herbert approached Barnes, took him by the feet, and dragged him toward the door.

"That's not the most dignified way to treat the body of a director of the CIA," Colonel Garrison warned. "There is protocol—"

"That can't be observed at the moment," Littel interrupted.

"If you want, I can take him by the arms," Herbert malevolently challenged.

Stuart Garrison shot him a look of hate. Under other circumstances that boy would eat those words one by one.

Herbert continued the operation, dragging the corpse in stages. Immediately sweat began to run down his face. Barnes was very heavy.

"Now us." Littel turned toward Simon, Rafael, and Sarah.

Phelps faced them euphorically. These three deaths were going to be expensive, but at least the loose ends had been tied up for three out of four. JC alone was missing, the astute old man. One only had to find the right time.

Sarah and Simon closed their eyes, anticipating the worst.

"Herbert," Littel called. "Do the honors."

Herbert promptly left off what he was doing. Barnes wasn't going anywhere, after all. He drew his gun from the holster.

"With pleasure."

"Do you want to say anything?" Littel asked with a sarcastic smile.

The silence spoke for itself. Simon didn't dare open his mouth, Sarah was gagged. Even though she didn't want to be silent, she had to be.

"Courage is stupidity in this case," Phelps said. "I have a question, if you don't mind." He was speaking to Rafael. "Who did you speak with in the apostolic apartments that morning in the Vatican?"

Rafael smiled bleakly. "No one."

"You won't answer?" Phelps was furious.

"I am answering. No one. We were only there to arouse your curiosity. I knew that would draw you in more. You think you fooled us all, even the pope. It was completely the opposite." His smile changed to a loud laugh.

Littel gestured with his head that Herbert was authorized to summarily execute the prisoners. Soon they'd only be names that passed from earth without leaving their marks on history. Rafael Santini, Sarah Monteiro, Simon Lloyd, forgotten by the world, would cease to count or even figure in the death statistics.

Herbert removed the safety on the gun, provided with a silencer, but Phelps grabbed it from his hand, infuriated, and pointed it at Rafael.

A shot.

Two shots. Whispered.

Before they understood anything, we see Herbert grab his chest and fall. The same for Phelps, who was already dead before he fell. A thin stream of blood ran from a hole in the middle of his head. He died without knowing how.

Rafael got up before any reaction. Priscilla screamed in panic. Sarah and Simon opened their eyes to see this hellish scene. Three corpses on the floor, Colonel Garrison trying to draw his gun, Marius Ferris shocked, completely astonished, Rafael behind Littel, his gun pressed into the assistant subdirector's head.

"Do you want to say anything?" he asked close to Littel's ear.

"Don't do anything stupid," Marius Ferris said.

"More than you've done would be impossible." He pressed the barrel harder against Littel's head. "Be calm," Rafael advised him. "Look what you've done."

"Me? I need to warn you it's a serious crime to interfere with an agent of the federal government."

"I'm not going to interfere. I'm going to kill you," Rafael warned, grinding his teeth.

"Let's be reasonable," Garrison argued. "Surely we can come to an agreement without wasting more lives."

"Are you concerned about your own, Colonel?" It was a rhetorical question. "I don't remember seeing you concerned about lives in Moscow," he added bitterly.

Garrison lowered his head.

Rafael looked at Sarah.

"Take off that gag."

Sebastian Ford obeyed the order, shook out the silk handkerchief, and let it fall on the floor. Littel turned red. Sarah breathed in desperately, like someone had just pulled her from underwater.

"Barnes didn't commit suicide." She pointed at Littel. "He's the one who killed him."

Priscilla looked at her, frightened. Garrison lifted up his head in fury.

"How could you?" An accusing finger from the colonel.

"Ten million dollars," Sarah clarified. "That was motive enough."

"Right. Are you going to take the word of a criminal?" Littel countered with a superior attitude in spite of his precarious situation.

Rafael pushed him forward so hard that he fell on the floor next to the bodies of Phelps and Herbert.

"Look at the patriot." Stuart Garrison pointed his gun at Littel.

"What do you think you're doing?" Littel shouted. "Kill him," he ordered.

The colonel shifted his aim to Rafael, who kept his gun on Littel.

"Don't even think about it," Sebastian Ford said, pointing a gun in turn at Stuart Garrison's head.

"Drop the gun, Sebastian," Littel ordered.

"Until we verify what happened here, there will be no more deaths. I'm starting an investigation, and if you're guilty, Harvey . . . God and the president have mercy on your soul."

"The president gave precise orders to kill the prisoners," Littel shouted.

"And did he give orders to kill Barnes in cold blood?" Sebastian argued in the same tone. He turned to Rafael. "Get out of here. Disappear."

"You can't do that, Sebastian," Littel alleged.

"This smelled wrong to me from the start, Harvey. Let them go now."

Marius Ferris raised his hands to his chest and fell on the floor. A sharp pain ran through his coronary arteries, his heart put to the test by extreme emotion.

Rafael bent over him and murmured in his ear.

"God doesn't sleep. The dead are going to take care of you now. Live many years with them. We'll see you in the beyond."

He escorted Sarah and Simon out of the Center of Operations.

In the room Priscilla cried like a child, Marius had fainted from the pain of the heart attack, Sebastian Ford remained with the gun pointed at the head of the hesitant colonel.

"Give me the gun, Colonel," Sebastian ordered. Littel stayed crouched on the floor, looking into space, desperate, frustrated.

Sebastian Ford took the cell phone and made a call.

"Sebastian Ford, code 1330. I want a rescue team in the Center of Operations in Rome, ASAP." He looked at Littel. "There are agents dead and arrested."

He disconnected, and straightened the neck of his shirt.

It was over.

72

THE CONFESSION
December 27, 1983

Twenty minutes could be a long time.

In the narrow cell four people pressed together, only one talking, the rest listening.

Two years, seven months, and fourteen days he'd spent in judicial confinement for having carried out an unsuccessful attempt on the pope's life.

The Supreme Pontiff sat on a small chair brought in especially for him. His secretary and the guard entrusted with preventing any possible menace against His Holiness waited standing up, although the latter had to pretend not to hear what was being said.

Not for a moment had the Turk left his position as a penitent, his hands touching the white tunic.

"Was it so simple, my son?" asked the Holy Father, to whom the gift of omnipotence hadn't been granted.

"It was."

"A simple phone call and a meeting?"

The other said nothing. His silence was agreement. Besides he was the one who had told the story.

"And his name?"

"I don't know."

"You didn't ask?"

"No. He paid half in our first and only meeting. You don't question men like that."

"Where was that meeting?"

"In Athens."

"When?"

"In March."

They let the silence settle around them. He had to think more deeply about what had been said.

The Holy Father placed a benevolent hand on the head of his beloved, unsuccessful executioner. A sincere caress filled with positive energy and love from someone who knew there was nothing to forgive.

"In regard to the date and time," the Supreme Pontiff returned. "Was that decided by you?"

"No. I didn't decide anything. I received orders with the precise date and time."

"How much ahead of time?"

"Eight days. Time enough to prepare myself. I arrived in Milan on the seventh of May and Rome, the tenth of May."

The pope and his secretary exchanged glances, hiding the unease caused by that answer.

"Did you act alone?"

"As far as I know, yes," the Turk responded, bowing his head.

"I believe you, my son."

"Was there a plan for escape?" Only the Holy Father formulated the questions.

The young man raised his head, letting his shame show.

"There was," he confessed, bowing his head again. He didn't continue.

The pope had to force his reply by lifting the Turk's head so that he would look him in the eye. There was no room for pardons or vengeance. What's done was done.

"To flee under cover of the confusion . . . stupid, I know now."

"How were they going to pay you the rest of the money?"

"It depended. If I survived, fifteen days later in a place to be determined. It would be in cash. If I was caught, it would be given to my family."

"Had you foreseen that possibility?"

"Never," the Turk alleged. "After all, I fired six times. Even today I don't know how you can be here talking to me."

"No bullet can kill unless it's the will of God."

"I am completely aware of that. I know exactly where I pointed the gun."

In spite of the kind attitude of the Polish pope, he clearly wanted to bring together all the facts of the case. Someone in the heart of his own clerical family wished him ill. Once he knew that, his disgust was incredible. It was as if they shared the same blood, since a man of the Church lived among his clerical brothers more than his family members. They were only a far-off memory of Wadowice on Ulica Koscielna.

He knew that the simple fact of being chosen by the Holy Spirit—and one hundred and ten cardinals—to direct the destinies of the Church had earned him many enemies. According to his mental arithmetic, at least half of the ninety-seven who voted for him. It was known that after a certain time, the factions in which the conclave was divided would have to reach a gentlemen's agreement to permit the choice of only one of all those eligible. Besides those forty-eight cardinals and half of those who simply didn't like him as a person, there were also assistants, secretaries, subsecretaries, priests, bishops, archbishops, monsignors, simple employees without a diploma in theology. Any one of them might be behind all this, but he could only manage to call one to mind.

"Does the name Nestor mean anything to you?" the Holy Father asked.

The young Turk searched his memory for the name.

"That name means nothing to me," he finally said.

"Could it have been the name of the man who hired you?"

"It could."

"Did he seem Eastern European? A Soviet?"

"Soviet? No way. American or English," the young man replied.

Wojtyla got up suddenly, leaving the Turk on his knees.

"Holy Father, I'm worried about what they could do to my family." He grasped the white tunic begging for mercy. "Protect them. Please. I'm desperate."

The Pole looked him up and down, thoughtfully.

"Someone has threatened you, my son?"

"Me, no. But they've threatened my family. If I open my mouth, they're going to pay."

The pope assumed a serious expression. One had to adopt measures very carefully. The pieces fit together very easily. He needed no guarantee to feel that the young man's admissions were the truth, without inventions, knowing he could even be sacrificing his family.

"Get up and listen carefully," he ordered decisively. "From today on, your family will be mine, and mine, yours. I'll protect them with all my power."

Tears ran down the young Turk's submissive face.

"But remember. Never tell this to anyone. Make up a new version each day. Say whatever comes into your head. One thing in the morning, and another, completely different, in the afternoon."

The young man looked at the pope in surprise. The pope understood his confusion.

"We're going to save your family and mine . . . ours. The best for yours and mine is that no one know the truth. The truth could kill the Church, my family, and, consequently, yours . . . ours."

The young Turk's legs doubled under him, and he fell on the floor weeping copiously.

The pope stroked the Turk's head and started for the door. He looked at him one last time.

"I came here to see my executioner, and I leave with a friend in my heart."

Twenty minutes can be a long time.

73

Amen.

—*The last word of John Paul II before his death,* April 2, 2005

Eight days have passed, though they seemed like months. Sarah has wandered through the small city of Wadowice, fifty kilometers from Krakow, in the venerable land of Poland. She's passed by number seven on Ulica Koscielna and visited the house where the young Karol Wojtyla was born and raised. The place where Wojtyla's life began, which led to his becoming the most beloved pope in history, it must be confessed, filled her with emotion. One thing was certain, sooner or later, one day he would be Saint John Paul. Keeping in mind all that Sarah had come to know in this last week, it was just that it be so. If a saint worthy of the name exists, he was it. A man who helped his executioner from the beginning without judgment, censure, or reprobation, who gave himself to God without anything and without anything departed to Him. Humble, benevolent, placid, serene, the highest example for millions of the faithful. What was important was to believe in God the Father, Omnipotent, Creator of all that was, is, and will be to eternity.

The car came down Ulica Wisniowa and entered Gimnazjalna. Rafael drove. He didn't wear cassock or suit, just jeans and a sweater, since this was spring, the mild season of the year.

"Do you miss much?" Sarah asked.

"No," he answered without taking his eyes off the road.

Sarah remembered a few days ago when Rafael drove her to Rome for the reunion with her parents. The meeting was in the Piazza Navona, full of people in mid-afternoon. Elizabeth covered her with kisses and embraces, as did Raul. They radiated health and looked tan.

"Were you at the beach while I was gone?" Sarah asked jokingly.

"Istanbul has this effect on people," JC interjected, sending a shiver down Sarah's spine; she had not expected to see him.

"JC," she stammered.

Rafael looked him over from top to bottom, evaluating him. He looked older than a year ago. Time had passed and worn him down. The cripple looked at Rafael out of the corner of his eye, anger present but controlled, as it had to be. He couldn't help but think about the disability in his leg and who was responsible for it, there in front of him, with a few dark bruises on his face, nothing to leave a scar, while his walking . . .

JC watched Sarah with a cool stare. He enjoyed it. He knew they all feared him except for Rafael, from whom he'd just turned his eyes away.

"You've conducted yourself well," he praised him.

"I tried," Rafael replied.

There were no thanks or appreciations.

"What's going to happen to Harvey Littel?" Sarah timidly asked.

"He's going to be promoted to secretary of defense."

"What? You're joking." Sarah was shocked.

JC showed her the front page of *The New York Times* where she could read the headline: "Harvey Littel to Run Defense." Sarah read it but couldn't believe it. How could that be possible? A small headline at the bottom of the page caught her attention: "Ford Accused of Pedophilia." Sebastian Ford, Rafael's man on Barnes's and Littel's team. He who risked his life to save Rafael and, as a consequence, her and Simon.

"I don't understand," Sarah protested. "How could this happen?"

She looked at Rafael, who didn't look surprised.

"Littel belongs to the system. He knows a lot. Now they've put him in a position out of the CIA, but where he's going to have all his movements watched by the CIA . . . and public opinion. They're keeping the dog, but on a shorter leash," JC explained.

"And you? Have you seen what's happening to your friend?" Sarah spoke angrily.

"Littel's revenge. In politics there's no room for honest men," Rafael said. "But don't worry. The Vatican's going to need his services as a mediator with the United States."

So, at first blush, nothing seemed bad. Rafael was not the type to turn his back on friends, that was certain, especially those who hadn't turned their backs on him in his hour of need.

"What happened finally? What was it Phelps wanted?" Sarah changed the subject. She needed explanations.

"Phelps wanted what many people do. To get rid of anything that could be harmful to the image of his organization. No one could know that Marcinkus was Opus Dei."

"And P2," Sarah added.

"Yes, but that didn't matter to him. He was afraid that someone would find out that a man like that, who presided over the operations of the IWR for such a long time, could be linked to the organization. It would be a step away from discovering that Marcinkus had made an attempt on the pope's life, and, worst of all, was recommended for that position by Opus Dei's own founder José María Escrivá."

"Oh, my God."

"But you also had your own agenda," Rafael accused him.

"I'm sorry about your uncle," JC said.

"You're not sorry about him."

"I like direct people." He turned to Sarah. "There's a box in the post office at Kings Cross that this key unlocks." He showed her a small key and placed it in her hand. "Inside you'll find a pile of documents and copies I collected over my lifetime."

Sarah couldn't believe what she was hearing. JC trusted her.

"Soon you'll receive instructions about what to do with them," he said.

"Don't do what you did with the Turk's file," he criticized. He looked at Rafael. "Help her with anything she needs."

The priest said neither yes nor no.

The old man took a yellow envelope out of his jacket that Raul recognized as the one that Cardinal Sebastiani had handed him in Istanbul.

"Add this to the spoils."

"What is it?" Sarah asked curiously.

"A letter that should have been delivered to Wojtyla but never was."

"Can I read it?"

"Please," JC permitted her.

Sarah opened the envelope and took out a paper worn through the passage of years. It was once white, the date above, 11/04/1981.

"Sebastiani didn't want to believe the letter. He hid it as if this action would put off the warning until much later. That same day, the Pole was shot, and Sebastiani knew it was true."

To my very esteemed Holy Father:

I take the liberty to address myself to Your Excellency with the deepest humility.

I know you will consecrate your pontificate to the Virgin Mary, since you feel the same love for Her as I do.

I wrote to many predecessors of the Holy Father in the same respectful terms that I write in these lines. . . . The Virgin has always sent me, and sends me, many different revelations all my simple life.

In one of my recent visions, the person of the Holy Father was mentioned:

"Tell him that no bullet will kill unless it is His will. Men love to make others suffer, they don't respect the values of goodness and love, but that is not reason enough not to forgive. Unconditional love implies unconditional forgiveness. The two go hand in hand like brothers."

You will be remembered every day in my prayers to the Merciful Lord and the Lady of the Rosary.

Respectfully,
Lúcia de Jesus dos Santos

"That's incredible," Sarah declared ecstatically.

JC turned his back accompanied by the cripple. Everything had been predicted.

"Where are you going?" Sarah asked him.

The old man turned to her.

"I'm going where we all have to go. Stay out of trouble."

"Thank you for my job at the newspaper."

JC looked from her to Rafael.

"I'm not the one to thank. If it were up to me, you'd have been dead in London or New York a year ago."

He flashed a sarcastic smile and continued toward the rest of his life. They would never see him again.

Sarah considered his words now inside the car on the streets of Wadowice. Rafael followed a secondary road that led to the outskirts.

"Why did you get the job for me at the newspaper?" she asked.

Rafael drove in silence.

"Don't I deserve an answer?" she pressured him, slightly insulted.

"I didn't get you any job."

"Are you lying, Father Rafael?" she reproved him ironically.

"Why did someone have to find you a job?" Rafael continued, confused. "Did it ever cross your mind you got the position on your own merits?"

Sarah had never seen things in this light. On the other hand, he could be trying to mislead her for some other reason. Let him have his way.

They entered a very steep dirt road.

"Where are we going? Cross-country?" Sarah protested.

"Only a few more miles."

They continued in silence for a few minutes, not a contemplative silence appropriate to the situation, but an oppressive, awkward silence.

"How could the pope pardon someone who wished him such ill?" Sarah asked.

"He was a noble soul."

"I think he would have liked to read the letter," Sarah added, mentioning the letter she had read in the Piazza Navona and carried with her.

"He always knew that the bullet was special. Divinely turned aside inside his body."

"A holy bullet."

"A holy bullet."

"I'm sorry about your uncle Clemente," Sarah finally said. She should have said it much earlier but hadn't been able.

"Thanks."

"Were you very close?"

"He was my only living relative," he admitted.

They arrived at an enormous gate with two wings, fixed in a high wall that surrounded an enormous property. It was open, so Rafael drove in without stopping. The road continued for a few more miles.

Where the hell are we going? Sarah wondered, tired of so much mystery.

Silence descended again. Rafael and Sarah were only comfortable with each other when the situation involved revolvers, shots, bombs, chases, and torture. A ride in the car through the fields on a sunny day was too complicated for both of them to deal with.

"I hope you'll look upon me as a family member," Sarah suggested sincerely.

Rafael looked at her and stopped the car.

"Thanks, I already do."

They exchanged looks, and for moments nothing else existed. Only she and he inside the car.

A knock on the window woke them from their romantic trance.

"We've arrived," Rafael told her.

He opened the door and left the car, while Sarah closed her eyes in frustration before getting out.

"Tim," Rafael greeted him.

"How are you, Rafael?"

"I got here at the last moment, but I got here."

Sarah joined them. They were in an open space surrounded by trees. On one side there was a kind of well.

"This is Sarah, a . . . close friend."

"How do you do?" He shook her hand. "Tim Baynard."

Sarah looked at him. He was a calm, happy man. He carried a black briefcase he gave to Rafael.

"Safe and sound."

Tim went over to the well that turned out to be stairs going underground. The panel that covered it was half open. It wouldn't have been easy for Tim to lift it alone.

"Let's go," he said, going down rapidly ahead of them.

Sarah couldn't figure out precisely how long they descended, but she was surprised to see electric lights illuminating the way, very different from Moscow.

"This is private property?" Rafael asked.

"Yes, bought by the Vatican," Tim answered eagerly.

"Do you know what you're going to do with your life now?" Rafael changed the subject.

"No. Time will tell. Whatever comes, I hope it'll be for the best."

"That's a good philosophy," Rafael agreed.

They entered something that seemed to be a crypt, confirmed as such by a tomb in the center of the wide space.

It was new, granite, with letters engraved in gold.

Krystian Janusz Wladyslaw.

II-IV-MMV.

"What does that mean?" Sarah asked, confused.

"Thirty-three days after his interment in the tomb of the popes in the Vatican, Karol Józef Wojtyla was brought here secretly in accordance with his wishes. Here he'll rest for eternity under this name. If someday someone enters here mistakenly, he won't know to whom it refers."

Sarah got down on her knees on the floor next to the tomb holding the body of the most beloved pope of all times. She let tears of emotion fall.

"There's now nothing to keep me here," Tim said to Rafael. "Keep this as a memory."

He left a gilded object, small, cylindrical, bright in his hand . . . a bullet.

"Good-bye."

"Good-bye."

Alone. Rafael approached Sarah and gave her his hand to help her up.

They remained for a moment holding hands, keeping watch on Karol Wojtyla's tomb.

"And now?" Sarah asked emotionally.

Rafael looked at her, and, afterward, at the tomb.

"This isn't over yet."